Bleak House

The gardens of Lowfield Hall are overgrown now and weeds push their way up through the gravel of the drive. One of the drawing-room windows, broken by a village boy, has been boarded up, and wisteria, killed by summer drought, hangs above the front door like an old dried net.

It has become a bleak house, fit nesting place for the birds.

Before Eunice came, before Eunice left and left desolation behind her, Lowfield Hall was not like this. It was as well kept as its distant neighbors, as comfortable, as warm, as elegant, and, seemingly, as much a sanctuary as they. Its inhabitants were safe and happy, and destined to lead long secure lives.

But on an April day they invited Eunice in.

A JUDGEMENT IN STONE

Ruth Rendell

BANTAM BOOKS
TORONTO · NEW YORK · LONDON

All of the characters in this book
are fictitious, and any resemblance
to actual persons, living or dead,
is purely coincidental.

This low-priced Bantam Book
has been completely reset in a type face
designed for easy reading, and was printed
from new plates. It contains the complete
text of the original hard-cover edition.
NOT ONE WORD HAS BEEN OMITTED.

A JUDGEMENT IN STONE
*A Bantam Book / published by arrangement with
Doubleday & Company, Inc.*

PRINTING HISTORY
Doubleday edition published February 1978
Detective Book Club edition published December 1977
G. K. Hall & Company edition published June 1978
Bantam edition / January 1979
2nd printing .... February 1981

*Bantam Books are published by Bantam Books, Inc. Its trade-
mark, consisting of the words "Bantam Books" and the por-
trayal of a bantam, is Registered in U.S. Patent and Trademark
Office and in other countries. Marca Registrada. Bantam
Books, Inc., 666 Fifth Avenue, New York, New York 10103.*

PRINTED IN THE UNITED STATES OF AMERICA

11 10 9 8 7 6 5 4 3 2

For Gerald Austin, with love

1

Eunice Parchman killed the Coverdale family because she could not read or write.

There was no real motive and no premeditation. No money was gained and no security. As a result of her crime, Eunice Parchman's disability was made known not to a mere family or a handful of villagers but to the whole country. She accomplished by it nothing but disaster for herself, and all along, somewhere in her strange mind, she knew she would accomplish nothing. And yet, although her companion and partner was mad, Eunice was not. She had the awful practical sanity of the atavistic ape disguised as twentieth-century woman.

Literacy is one of the cornerstones of civilization. To be illiterate is to be deformed. And the derision that was once directed at the physical freak may, perhaps more justly, descend upon the illiterate. If he or she can live a cautious life among the uneducated, all may be well, for in the country of the purblind the eyeless is not rejected. It was unfortunate for Eunice Parchman, and for them, that the people who employed her and in whose home she lived for ten months were peculiarly literate. Had they been a family of philistines, they might be alive today and Eunice free in her mysterious dark freedom of sensation and instinct and blank absence of the printed word.

They belonged to the upper middle class and they lived a conventional upper-middle-class life in a country house. George Coverdale had a philosophy degree, but since the age of thirty he had been managing director of his late father's company, Tin Box Coverdale, at Stantwich in Suffolk. With his wife and his three children, Peter, Paula, and Melinda, he had occupied a large 1930-ish house on the outskirts of Stantwich until his wife died of cancer when Melinda was twelve.

Two years later, at the wedding of Paula to Brian Caswall, George met Jacqueline Mont. She also had been married before, had divorced her husband for desertion, was then thirty-seven, and had been left with one son. George and Jacqueline fell in love more or less at first sight and were married three months later. George bought a manor house ten miles from Stantwich and went to live there with his bride, with Melinda, and with Giles Mont, Peter Coverdale having at that time been married for three years.

When Eunice Parchman was engaged as their housekeeper George was fifty-seven and Jacqueline forty-two. They took an active part in the social life of the neighborhood, and in an unobtrusive way had slipped into playing the parts of the squire and his lady. Their marriage was idyllic and Jacqueline was popular with her stepchildren, Peter, a lecturer in political economy at a northern university, Paula, now herself a mother and living in London, and Melinda, who, at twenty, was reading English at the University of Norfolk at Galwich. Her own son, Giles, aged seventeen, was still at school.

Four members of this family—George, Jacqueline, and Melinda Coverdale and Giles Mont—died in the space of fifteen minutes on February 14, St. Valentine's Day. Eunice Parchman and the prosaically named Joan Smith shot them down on a Sunday evening while they were watching opera on television. Two weeks later Eunice was arrested for the crime —because she could not read.

But there was more to it than that.

2

The gardens of Lowfield Hall are overgrown now and weeds push their way up through the gravel of the drive. One of the drawing-room windows, broken by a village boy, has been boarded up, and wisteria, killed by summer drought, hangs above the front door like an old dried net. Bare ruined choirs where late the sweet birds sang.

It has become a bleak house, fit nesting place for the birds that Dickens named Hope, Joy, Youth, Peace, Rest, Life, Dust, Ashes, Waste, Want, Ruin, Despair, Madness, Death, Cunning, Folly, Words, Wigs, Rags, Sheepskin, Plunder, Precedent, Jargon, Gammon, and Spinach.

Before Eunice came, before Eunice left and left desolation behind her, Lowfield Hall was not like this. It was as well kept as its distant neighbors, as comfortable, as warm, as elegant, and, seemingly, as much a sanctuary as they. Its inhabitants were safe and happy, and destined surely to lead long secure lives.

But on an April day they invited Eunice in.

A little blustery wind was blowing the daffodils in the orchard, waves on a golden sea. The clouds parted and closed again, so that at one moment it was winter in the garden and at the next an uneasy summer. And in those somber intervals it might have been snow, not the blossom of the blackthorn, that whitened the hedge.

Winter stopped at the windows. The sun brought in

flashes of summer to match the pleasant warmth, and it was warm enough for Jacqueline Coverdale to sit down to breakfast in a short-sleeved dress.

She was holding a letter in her hand, in her left hand on which she wore her platinum wedding ring and the diamond cluster George had given her on their engagement.

"I'm not looking forward to this at all," she said.

"More coffee, please, darling," said George. He loved watching her do things for him, as long as she didn't have to do too much. He loved just looking at her, so pretty, his Jacqueline, fair, slender, a Lizzie Siddal matured. Six years of marriage, and he hadn't got used to the wonder of it, the miracle that he had found her. "Sorry," he said. "You're not looking forward to it? Well, we didn't get any other replies. Women aren't exactly queueing up to work for us."

She shook her head, a quick pretty gesture. Her hair was very blond, short and sleek. "We could try again. I know you'll say I'm silly, George, but I had a sort of absurd hope that we'd get—well, someone like ourselves. At any rate, a reasonably educated person who was willing to take on domestic service for the sake of a nice home."

"A lady, as they used to say."

Jacqueline smiled in rather a shamefaced way. "Eva Baalham would write a better letter than this one. E. Parchman! What a way for a woman to sign her name!"

"It was correct usage for the Victorians."

"Maybe, but we're not Victorians. Oh dear, I wish we were. Imagine a smart parlormaid waiting on us now, and a cook busy in the kitchen." And Giles, she thought but didn't say aloud, obliged to be well-mannered and not to read at table. Had he heard any of this? Wasn't he the least bit interested? "No income tax," she said, "and no horrible new houses all over the countryside."

"And no electricity either," said George, touching the radiator behind him, "or constant hot water, and perhaps Paula dying in childbirth."

"I know." Jacqueline returned to her original tack.

"But that letter, darling, and her bleak manner when she phoned. I just know she's going to be a vulgar lumpish creature who'll break the china and sweep the dust under the mats."

"You can't know that, and it's hardly fair judging her by one letter. You want a housekeeper, not a secretary. Go and see her. You've fixed this interview, Paula's expecting you, and you'll only regret it if you let the chance go by. If she makes a bad impression on you, just tell her no, and then we'll think about trying again."

The grandfather clock in the hall struck the first quarter after eight. George got up. "Come along now, Giles, I believe that clock's a few minutes slow." He kissed his wife. Very slowly Giles closed his copy of the Bhagavad Gita which had been propped against the marmalade pot, and with a kind of concentrated lethargy extended himself to his full, emaciated, bony height. Muttering under his breath something that might have been Greek or, for all she knew, Sanskrit, he let his mother kiss his spotty cheek.

"Give my love to Paula," said George, and off they went in the white Mercedes, George to Tin Box Coverdale, Giles to the Magnus Wythen Foundation School. Silence settled upon them in the car after George, who tried, who was determined to keep on trying, had remarked that it was a very windy day. Giles said, "Mmm." As always, he resumed his reading. George thought, Please let this woman be all right, because I can't let Jackie keep on trying to run that enormous place, it's not fair. We shall have to move into a bungalow or something, and I don't want that, God forbid, so please let this E. Parchman be all right.

There are six bedrooms in Lowfield Hall, a drawing room, a dining room, a morning room, three bathrooms, a kitchen, and what are known as usual offices. In this case, the usual offices were the back kitchen and the gun room. On that April morning the house wasn't exactly dirty but it wasn't clean either. There was a bluish film on all the thirty-three windows, and the film was decorated with fingerprints and finger smears. Eva Baalham's, and probably, even after two months, those of the last and most lamentable of all the *au pairs*. Jacqueline had worked it out once and estimated that six thousand square feet of carpet covered the floors. This, however, was fairly clean. Old Eva loved plying the vacuum cleaner while chatting about her relations. She used a duster too, up to eye level. It was just unfortunate that her eyes happened to be about four feet nine from the ground.

Jacqueline put the breakfast things in the dishwasher, the milk and butter in the fridge. The fridge hadn't been defrosted for six weeks. Had the oven *ever* been cleaned? She went upstairs. It was awful, she ought to be ashamed of herself, she knew that, but her hand came away gray with dust from the banisters. The little bathroom, the one they called the children's bathroom, was in a hideous mess, Giles's latest acne remedy, a kind of green paste, caked all over the basin. She hadn't made the beds. Hastily she pulled the pink sheet, the blankets, the silk counterpane up over the six-foot-wide mattress she shared with George. Giles's bed could stay the way it was. She doubted if he would notice anyway. Wouldn't notice if the sheets all turned purple and there was a warming pan in it instead of an electric blanket.

Attention to her own appearance she didn't skimp. She often thought it was a pity she wasn't as house-proud as she was Jacqueline-proud, but that was the way it was, that was the way *she* was. Bath, hair, hands, nails, warmer dress, sheer tights, the new dark green shoes, face painted to look *au naturel*. She put on the mink George had given her for Christmas. Now down to the orchard to pick an armful of daffodils for Paula. At any rate, she kept the garden nice, not a weed to be seen, and there wouldn't be, not even in the height of summer.

Waves on a golden sea. Snowdrops nestling under the whiter hedge. Twice already, this dry spring, she had mown the lawns, and they were plushy green. An open-air lady I am, thought Jacqueline, the wind on her face, the thin sharp scents of spring flowers delighting her. I could stand here for hours, looking at the river, the poplars in the water meadows, the Greeving Hills with all those cloud shadows racing, racing . . . But she had to see this woman, this E. Parchman. Time to go. If only she turns out to like housework as much as I like gardening.

She went back into the house. Was it her imagination, or did the kitchen really not smell at all nice? Out through the gun room, which was in its usual mess, lock the door, leave Lowfield Hall to accumulate more dust, grow that much more frowsty.

Jacqueline put the daffodils on the back seat of the Ford and set off to drive the seventy miles to London.

George Coverdale was an exceptionally handsome man, classic-featured, as trim of figure as when he had rowed for his university in 1939. Of his three children, only one had inherited his looks, and Paula Caswall was not that one. A sweet expression and gentle eyes saved her from plainness, but pregnancy was not becoming to her, and she was in the eighth month of her second pregnancy. She had a vigorous mischievous little boy to look after, a fairly big house in Kensington to run, she was huge and tired and her ankles were swollen. Also she was frightened. Patrick's birth had been a painful nightmare, and she looked forward to this coming delivery with dread. She would have preferred to see no one and have no one see her. But she realized that her house was the obvious venue for an interview with this London-based prospective housekeeper, and being endowed with the gracious manners of the Coverdales, she welcomed her stepmother affectionately, enthused over the daffodils, and complimented Jacqueline on her dress. They had lunch, and Paula listened with sympathy to Jacqueline's doubts and forebodings about what would ensue at two o'clock.

However, she was determined to take no part in this interview. Patrick had gone for his afternoon sleep, and when the doorbell rang at two minutes to two Paula did no more than show the woman in the

navy-blue raincoat into the living room. She left her
to Jacqueline and went upstairs to lie down. But in
those few seconds she spent with Eunice Parchman
she felt a violent antipathy to her. Eunice affected her
in that moment as she so often affected others. It was
as if a coldness, almost an icy breath, emanated from
her. Wherever she was, she brought a chill into the
warm air. Later Paula was to remember this first impression and, in an agony of guilt, reproach herself
for not warning her father, for not telling him of a
wild premonition that was to prove justified. She did
nothing. She went to her bedroom and fell into a
heavy troubled sleep.

Jacqueline's reaction was very different. From having been violently opposed to engaging this woman,
till then unseen, she did a complete about-face within
two minutes. Two factors decided her, or her principal weaknesses decided for her. These were her
vanity and her snobbishness.

She rose as the woman came into the room and
held out her hand.

"Good afternoon. You're very punctual."

"Good afternoon, madam."

Except by assistants in the few remaining old-fashioned shops in Stantwich, Jacqueline hadn't been addressed as "madam" for many years. She was delighted. She smiled.

"Is it Miss Parchman or Mrs.?"

"Miss Parchman. Eunice Parchman."

"Won't you sit down?"

No repulsive chill or, as Melinda would have put it,
"vibes" affected Jacqueline. She was the last of the
family to feel it, perhaps because she didn't want
to, because almost from that first moment she was
determined to take Eunice Parchman on, and then,
during the months that followed, to keep her. She saw
a placid-looking creature with a rather too small head,
pale firm features, permed brown hair mixed with
gray, small steady blue eyes, a massive body that
seemed to go neither out nor in, large shapely hands,
very clean with short nails, large shapely legs in

heavy brown nylon, large feet in somewhat distorted black court shoes. As soon as Eunice Parchman had sat down she undid the top button of her raincoat to disclose the polo neck of a lighter blue ribbed jumper. Calmly she sat there, looking down at her hands folded in her lap.

Without admitting it even to herself, Jacqueline Coverdale liked handsome men and plain women. She got on well with Melinda but not so well as she got on with the less attractive Paula and Peter's *jolie laide* wife, Audrey. She suffered from what might be called a Gwendolen complex, for, like Wilde's Miss Fairfax, she preferred a woman to be "fully forty-two and more than usually plain for her age." Eunice Parchman was at least as old as herself, very likely older, though it was hard to tell, and there was no doubt about her plainness. If she had belonged to her own class, Jacqueline would have wondered why she didn't wear makeup, undergo a diet, have that tabby-cat hair tinted. But in a servant, all was as it should be.

In the face of this respectful silence, confronted by this, to her, entirely prepossessing appearance, Jacqueline forgot the questions she had intended to ask. And instead of examining the candidate, instead of attempting to find out if this woman were suitable to work in her house, if she would suit the Coverdales, she began persuading Eunice Parchman that they would suit her.

"It's a big house, but there are only three of us except when my stepdaughter comes home for the weekend. There's a cleaner three days a week, and of course I should do all the cooking myself."

"I can cook, madam," said Eunice.

"It wouldn't be necessary, really. There's a dishwasher and a deep freeze. My husband and I do all the shopping." Jacqueline was impressed by this woman's toneless voice that, though uneducated, had no trace of a cockney accent. "We do entertain quite a lot," she said almost fearfully.

Eunice moved her feet, bringing them close together. She nodded slowly. "I'm used to that. I'm a hard worker."

At this point Jacqueline should have asked why Eunice was leaving her present situation, or at least something about her present situation. For all she knew, there might not have been one. She didn't ask. She was bemused by those "madams," excited by the contrast between this woman and Eva Baalham, this woman and the last pert-to-pretty *au pair*. It was all so different from what she had expected.

Eagerly she said, "When could you start?"

Eunice's blank face registered a faint surprise, as well it might.

"You'll want a reference," she said.

"Oh yes," said Jacqueline, reminded. "Of *course*."

A white card was produced from Eunice's large black handbag. On it was written in the same handwriting as the letter that had so dismayed Jacqueline in the first place: Mrs. Chichester, 24 Willow Vale, London, S.W. 18, and a phone number. The address was the one which had headed Eunice's letter.

"That's Wimbledon, isn't it?"

Again Eunice nodded. No doubt she was gladdened by this erroneous assumption. They discussed wages, when she would start, how she would travel to Stantwich. Subject, of course, Jacqueline said hastily, to the reference being satisfactory.

"I'm sure we shall get on marvelously."

At last Eunice smiled. Her eyes remained cold and still, but her mouth moved. It was certainly a smile. "Mrs. Chichester said, could you phone her tonight before nine? She's an old lady and she goes to bed early."

This show of tender regard for an employer's wishes and foibles could only be pleasing.

"You may be sure I shall," said Jacqueline.

It was only twenty past two and the interview was over.

Eunice said, "Thank you, madam. I can see myself out," thus indicating, or so it seemed to Jacqueline, that she knew her place. She walked steadily from the room without looking back.

If Jacqueline had had a better knowledge of Greater London she would have realized that Eunice Parchman had already told her a lie, or at least acquiesced in a misapprehension. For the postal district of Wimbledon is S.W. 19, not S.W. 18, which designates a much less affluent area in the borough of Wandsworth. But she didn't realize and she didn't check, and when she entered Lowfield Hall at six, five minutes after George had got home, she didn't even show him the white card.

"I'm sure she'll be ideal, darling," she enthused, "really the kind of old-fashioned servant we thought was an extinct breed. I can't tell you how quiet and respectful she was, not a bit pushing. I'm only afraid she may be too humble. But I *know* she's going to be a hard worker."

George put his arm around his wife and kissed her. He said nothing about her *volte-face*, uttered no "I told you so's." He was accustomed to Jacqueline's prejudices, succeeded often by wild enthusiasm, and he loved her for her impulsiveness, which in his eyes made her seem young and sweet and feminine. What he said was, "I don't care how humble she is or how pushing, as long as she takes some of the load of work off your hands."

Before she made the phone call Jacqueline, who had an active imagination, had formed a picture in her mind of the kind of household in which Eunice Parchman worked and the kind of woman who employed her. Willow Vale, she thought, would be a quiet tree-lined road near Wimbledon Common, number 24 large, Victorian; Mrs. Chichester an elderly gentlewoman with rigid notions of behavior, demanding but just, autocratic, whose servant was leaving her because she wouldn't, or couldn't afford to, pay her adequate wages in these inflationary times.

At eight o'clock she dialed the number. Eunice Parchman answered the phone herself by giving the code correctly, followed by the four digits slowly and precisely enunciated. Again calling Jacqueline "madam," she asked her to hold the line while she fetched Mrs. Chichester. And Jacqueline imagined her crossing a somber overfurnished hall, entering a large and rather chilly drawing room where an old lady sat listening to classical music or reading the "In Memoriam" column in a quality newspaper. There, on the threshold, she would pause and say in her deferential way:

"Mrs. Coverdale on the phone for you, madam."

The facts were otherwise.

The telephone in question was attached to the wall on the first landing of a rooming house in Earlsfield, at the top of a flight of stairs. Eunice Parchman had been waiting patiently by it since five in case, when it rang, some other tenant should get to it first. Mrs. Chichester was a machine-tool operator in her fifties called Annie Cole who sometimes performed small services of this kind in exchange for Eunice agreeing not to tell the post office how, for a year after her mother's death, she had continued to draw that lady's pension. Annie had written the letter and the words on the card, and it was from her furnished room, number 6, 24 Willow Vale, S.W. 18, that Eunice now fetched her to the phone. Annie Cole said:

"I'm really very upset to be losing Miss Parchman, Mrs. Coverdale. She's managed everything so wonderfully for me for seven years. She's a marvelous worker, an excellent cook, and so house-proud! Really, if she has a fault, it's that she's too conscientious."

Even Jacqueline felt that this was laying it on a bit thick. And the voice was peculiarly sprightly—Annie Cole couldn't get rid of Eunice fast enough—with an edge to it the reverse of refined. She had the sense to ask why this paragon was leaving.

"Because I'm leaving myself." The reply came without hesitation. "I'm joining my son in New Zealand. The cost of living is getting impossible here, isn't it? Miss Parchman could come with me, I should welcome the idea, but she's rather conservative. She prefers to stay here. I should like to think of her settling in a nice family like yours."

Jacqueline was satisfied.

"Did you confirm it with Miss Parchman?" asked George.

"Oh, darling, I forgot. I'll have to write to her."

"Or phone back."

Why not phone back, Jacqueline? Dial that number again now. A young man returning to his room next to Annie Cole's, setting his foot now on the last step of that flight of stairs, will lift the receiver. And when you ask for Miss Parchman he will tell you he has never heard of her. Mrs. Chichester, then? There is no Mrs. Chichester, only a Mr. Chichester, who is the land-lord, in whose name the phone number is but who himself lives in Croydon. Pick up the phone now, Jacqueline . . .

"I think it's better to confirm it in writing."

"Just as you like, darling."

The moment passed, the chance was lost. George did pick up the phone, but it was to call Paula, for the report on her health he had received from his wife had disquieted him. While he was talking to her, Jac-queline wrote her letter.

And the other people whom chance and destiny and their own agency were to bring together for destruction on February 14? Joan Smith was preach-ing on a cottage doorstep. Melinda Coverdale, in her room in Galwich, was struggling to make sense out of *Sir Gawain and the Green Knight*. Giles Mont was reciting mantras as an aid to meditation.

But already they were gathered together. In that moment when Jacqueline declined to make a phone call, an invisible thread lassoed each of them, bound them one to another, related them more closely than blood.

3

George and Jacqueline were discreet people and they didn't broadcast their coming good fortune. But Jacqueline did mention it to her friend Lady Royston, who mentioned it to Mrs. Cairne when the eternal subject of getting someone to keep the place clean came up. The news seeped through along the ramifications of Higgses, Meadowses, Baalhams, and Newsteads, and in the Blue Boar it succeeded as the major topic of conversation the latest excesses of Joan Smith.

Eva Baalham hastened, in her oblique way, to let Jacqueline know that she knew. "You going to give her telly?"

"Give whom—er—television?" said Jacqueline, flushing.

"Her as is coming from London. Because if you are I can as like get you a set cheap from my cousin Meadows as has the electric shop in Gosbury. Fell off the back of a lorry, I reckon, but ask no questions and you'll get no lies."

"Thank you so much," said Jacqueline, more than a little annoyed. "As a matter of fact, we're buying a color set for ourselves and Miss Parchman will be having our old one."

"Parchman," said Eva, sitting on a windowpane before giving it a wipe with her apron. "Would that be a London name, I wonder?"

"I really don't know, Mrs. Baalham. When you've finished whatever you're doing to that window,

14

perhaps you'd be good enough to come upstairs with me and we'll start getting her room ready."

"I reckon," said Eva in her broad East Anglian whine. She never called Jacqueline "madam," it wouldn't have crossed her mind. In her eyes, the only difference between herself and the Coverdales was one of money. In other respects she was their superior since they were newcomers, and not even gentry but in trade, while her yeomen ancestors had lived in Greeving for five hundred years. Nor did she envy them their money. She had quite enough of her own and she preferred her council house to Lowfield Hall, great big barn of a place, must cost a packet keeping that warm. She didn't like Jacqueline, who was mutton dressed as lamb and who gave herself some mighty airs for the wife of the owner of a tin-can factory. All that will-you-be-so-good and thank-you-so-much nonsense. Wonder how she'll get on with this Parchman? Wonder how I will? Still, I reckon I can always leave. There's Mrs. Jameson-Kerr begging me to come on her bended knees and she'll pay sixty pence an hour.

"God help her legs," said Eva, mounting the stairs.

At the top of the house a warren of poky attics had long since been converted into two large bedrooms and a bathroom. From their windows could be seen one of the finest pastoral views in East Anglia. Constable, of course, had painted it, sitting on the banks of the river Beal, and as was sometimes his way he had shifted a few church towers the better to suit his composition. It was lovely enough with the church towers in their proper places, a wide serene view of meadows and little woods in all the delicious varied greens of early May.

"Have her bed in here, will she?" said Eva, ambling into the bigger and sunnier of the bedrooms.

"No, she won't." Jacqueline could see that Eva was preparing to line herself up as secretary, as it were, of the downtrodden domestic servants' union. "I want that room for when my husband's grandchildren come to stay."

"You'll have to make her comfortable if you want her to stop." Eva opened a window. "Lovely day. Going to be a hot summer. The Lord is on our side, as my cousin as has the farm always says. There's young Giles going off in your car without so much as by your leave, I reckon."

Jacqueline was furious. She thought Eva ought to call Giles Mr. Mont, or at least "your son." But she was glad to see Giles, who was on half-term, leave his voluntary incarceration at last to get some fresh air.

"If you'd be so kind, Mrs. Baalham, we might start moving the furniture."

Giles drove down the avenue between the horse-chestnut trees and out into Greeving Lane. The lane is an unclassified road, just wide enough for two cars to pass if they go very slowly. Blackthorn had given place to hawthorn, and the hedges were creamy with its sugary scented blossom. A limpid blue sky, pale green wheat growing, a cuckoo calling—in May he sings all day—an exultation of birds caroling their territorial claims from every tree.

Pretending that none of it was there, refusing, in spite of his creed, to be one of the oneness of it, Giles drove over the river bridge. He intended to get as little fresh air as was compatible with going out of doors. He loathed the country. It bored him. There was nothing to do. When you told people that they were shocked, presumably because they didn't realize that no one in his senses could spend more than a maximum of an hour a day looking at the stars, walking in the fields, or sitting on riverbanks. Besides, it was nearly always cold or muddy. He disliked shooting things or fishing things out of streams or riding horses or following the hunt. George, who had tried to encourage him in these pursuits, had perhaps at last understood the impossibility of the task. Giles never, but *never*, went for a country walk. When he was compelled to walk to Lowfield Hall from the point where the school bus stopped, about half a mile, he kept his eyes on the ground. He had tried shutting them, but he had bumped into a tree.

London he loved. Looking back, he thought he had been happy in London. He had wanted to go to a boarding school in a big city, but his mother hadn't let him because some psychologist had said he was disturbed and needed the secure background of family life. Being disturbed didn't bother him, and he rather fostered the air he had of the absentminded, scatty, preoccupied young intellectual. He was intellectual all right, very much so. Last year he had got so many O Levels that there had been a piece about him in a national newspaper, he was certain of a place at Oxford, and he knew as much Latin, and possibly more Greek, than the man who professed to teach him these subjects at the Magnus Wythen.

He had no friends at school, and he despised the village boys, who were interested only in motorcycles, pornography, and the Blue Boar. Ian and Christopher Cairne and others of their like had been designated his friends by parental edict, but he hardly ever saw them, as they were away at their public schools. Neither the village boys nor those at school ever attempted to beat him up. He was over six feet and still growing. His face was horrible with acne, and the day after he washed it his hair was again wet with grease.

Now he was on his way to Sudbury to buy a packet of orange dye. He was going to dye all his jeans and T-shirts orange in pursuance of his religion, which was, roughly, Buddhism. When he had saved up enough money he meant to go to India on a bus and, with the exception of Melinda, never see any of them again. Well, maybe his mother. But not his father or stuffy old George or self-righteous Peter or this bunch of peasants. That is, if he didn't become a Catholic instead. He had just finished reading *Brideshead Revisited* and had begun to wonder whether being a Catholic at Oxford and burning incense on one's staircase might not be better than India. But he'd dye the jeans and T-shirts just in case.

At Meadows' garage in Greeving he stopped for petrol.

"When's the lady from London coming, then?" said Jim Meadows.

"Mm?" said Giles.

Jim wanted to know so that he could tell them in the pub that night. He tried again. Giles thought about it reluctantly. "Is today Wednesday?"

" 'Course it is." Jim added, because he fancied himself as a wit, "All day."

"They said Saturday," said Giles at last. "I think."

It might be and it might not, thought Jim. You never knew with him. Needed his head seeing to, that one. It was a wonder she let him out alone at the wheel of a good car like that. "Melinda'll be home to get a look at her, I reckon."

"Mm," said Giles. He drove off, rejecting the green stamps.

Melinda would be home. He didn't know whether this was pleasing or disquieting. On the surface, his relationship with her was casual and even distant, but in Giles's heart, where he often saw himself as a Poe or Byron, it simmered as incestuous passion. This had come into being, or been pushed into being, by Giles six months before. Until then Melinda had merely been a kind of quasi-sister. He knew, of course, that since she was not his sister or even his half-sister there was nothing at all to stop their falling in love with each other and eventually marrying. Apart from the three years' age difference, which would be of no importance later on, there could be no possible objection on anyone's part. Mother would even like it and old George would come round. But this was not what Giles wanted or what he saw in his fantasies. In them Melinda and he were a Byron and an Augusta Leigh who confessed their mutual passion while walking in Wuthering Heights weather on the Greeving Hills, a pastime which nothing would have induced Giles to undertake in reality. There was little of reality in any of this. In his fantasies Melinda even looked different, paler, thinner, rather phthisic, very much of another world. Confronting each other, breathless in the windswept darkness, they spoke of how their love must remain forever secret, never of course to be consummated. And though they married other people, their passion endured and was whispered of as something profound and indefinable.

He bought the dye, two packets of it called Nasturtium Flame. He also bought a poster of a Pre-Raphaelite girl with a pale green face and red hair, hanging over a balcony. The girl was presumably craning out of her window to moon after a lost or faithless lover, but from her attitude and the nauseous pallor of her skin, she looked more as if, while staying in a hotel in an Italian holiday resort, she had eaten too much pasta and was going to be sick. Giles bought her because she looked the way Melinda would look in the terminal stages of tuberculosis.

He returned to the car to find a parking ticket on the windscreen. He never used the car park. It would have meant walking a hundred yards. When he got home Eva had gone and so had his mother, who had left a note on the kitchen table for him. The note began "Darling," and ended "love from Mother" and the middle was full of needless information about the cold lunch left for him in the fridge and how she had to go to some Women's Institute meeting. It mystified him. He knew where his lunch would be, and he would never have dreamed of leaving a note for anyone. Like all true eccentrics, he thought other people very odd.

Presently he fetched all his clothes downstairs and put them with the dye and some water in the two large pans his mother used for jam making. While they were boiling, he sat at the kitchen table eating chicken salad and reading the memoirs of a mystic who had lived in a Poona ashram for thirty years without speaking a word.

On the Friday afternoon Melinda Coverdale came home. The train brought her from Galwich to Stantwich, and the bus to a place called Gallows Corner two miles from Lowfield Hall. There she alighted and waited for a lift. At this hour there was always someone passing on his or her way home to Greeving, so Melinda hoisted herself up onto Mrs. Cotleigh's garden wall and sat in the sun.

She was wearing overlong jeans rolled up to the

knees, very scuffed red cowboy boots, an Indian cotton shirt, and a yellow motoring hat, vintage 1920. But for all that, there was no prettier sight to be seen on a sunny garden wall between Stantwich and King's Lynn. Melinda was the child who had inherited George's looks. She had his straight nose and high brow, his shapely sensitive mouth, and his bright blue eyes. And her dead mother's mane of golden hair, the color of Mrs. Cotleigh's wallflowers.

An energy that never seemed to flag, except where Middle English verse was concerned, kept her constantly on the move. She lugged her horse's nosebag holdall up onto the wall beside her, pulled out a string of beads, tried it on, made a face at the textbooks which hope rather than experience had persuaded her to bring, then flung the bag down on the grass and jumped after it. Cross-legged on the bank while the useless bus passed in the opposite direction, then to pick poppies, the wild red poppies, weeds of Suffolk, that abound on this corner where once the gibbet stood.

Five minutes later the chicken farm van came along, and Geoff Baalham, who was second cousin to Eva, called, "Hi, Melinda! Can I drop you?"

She jumped in, hat, bag, and poppies. "I must have been there half an hour," said Melinda, who had been there ten minutes.

"I like your hat."

"Do you really, Geoff? You are *sweet*. I got it in the Oxfam shop." Melinda knew everyone in the village and called everyone, even ancient gaffers and gammers, by their Christian names. She drove tractors and picked fruit and watched calvings. In the presence of her father, she spoke more or less politely to Jameson-Kerrs, Archers, Cairnes, and Sir Robert Royston, but she disapproved of them as reactionary. Once, when the foxhounds had met on Greeving Green, she had gone up there waving an anti-bloodsports banner. In her early teens she had gone fishing with the village boys and with them watched the hares come out at dusk. In her late teens she had danced with them at Cattingham "hops" and kissed them behind the village hall. She was as gossipy as their mothers and as involved.

"What's been going on in merry old Greeving in my absence? Tell all." She hadn't been home for three weeks. "I know, Mrs. Archer's eloped with Mr. Smith."

Geoff Baalham grinned widely. "Poor old sod. I reckon he's got his hands full with his own missus. Wait a minute, let's see. Susan Meadows, Higgs that was, had her baby. It's a girl and they're calling it Lalage."

"You don't *mean* it!"

"Thought that'd shake you. Your ma's got herself on the parish council, though I reckon you know about that, and—wait for it—your dad's bought color telly."

"I talked to him on the phone last night. He never said."

"No, well, only got it today. I had it all from my auntie Eva an hour back." The people of Greeving are careless about the correct terms for relations. One's stepmother is as much one's ma or mum as one's natural mother, and a female second cousin, if old enough, is necessarily auntie. "They're giving the old one to the lady help that's coming from London."

"Oh, God, how mean! Daddy's such a ghastly fascist. Don't you think that's the most undemocratic fascist thing you've ever heard, Geoff?"

"It's the way of the world, Melinda, love. Always has been and always will be. You oughtn't to go calling your dad names. I'd turn you over and tan your backside for you if I was him."

"Geoff Baalham! To hear you, no one'd think you're only a year older than me."

"Just you remember I'm a married man now, and that teaches you the meaning of responsibility. Here we are, Lowfield Hall, *madame*, and I'll take my leave of you. Oh, and you can tell your ma I'll be sending them eggs up with Auntie Eva first thing Monday morning."

"Will do. Thanks tremendously for the lift, Geoff. You are *sweet*."

"Cheerio then, Melinda."

Off went Geoff to the chicken farm and Barbara

Carter, whom he had married in January, but thinking what a nice pretty girl Melinda Coverdale was—that hat, my God!—and thinking too of walking with her years before by the river Beal and of innocent kisses exchanged to the rushing music of the mill.

Melinda swung up the long drive, under the chestnuts hung with their cream and bronze candles, around the house, and in by the gun-room door. Giles was sitting at the kitchen table reading the last chapter of the Poona book.

"Hi, Step."

"Hallo," said Giles. He no longer used the nickname that once had served for each to address to the other. It was incongruous with his Byronic fantasies, though these always crumbled when Melinda appeared in the flesh. She had quite a lot of well-distributed flesh, and red cheeks, and an aggressive healthiness. Also she bounced. Giles sighed, scratched his spots, and thought of being in India with a begging bowl.

"How did you get red ink on your jeans?"

"I didn't. I've dyed them, but the dye didn't take."

"Mad," said Melinda. She sailed off, searched for her father and stepmother, found them on the top floor putting finishing touches to Miss Parchman's room. "Hallo, my darlings." Each got a kiss, but George got his first. "Daddy, you've got a suntan. If I'd known you were coming home so early I'd have phoned T.B.C. from the station. Geoff Baalham gave me a lift and he said his auntie Eva'll bring the eggs first thing on Monday and you're giving our new housekeeper the old telly. I said I never heard anything so fascist in all my life. Next thing, you'll be saying she's got to eat on her own in the kitchen."

George and Jacqueline looked at each other.

"Well, of course."

"How awful! No wonder the revolution's coming. *A bas les aristos.* D'you like my hat, Jackie? I bought it in the Oxfam shop. Fifty p. God, I'm *starving*. We haven't got anyone awful coming tonight, have we? No curs or cairns or roisterers?"

"Now, Melinda, I think that's enough." The words were admonitory but the tone was tender. George was incapable of being really cross with his favorite child. "We're tolerant of your friends and you must be tolerant of ours. As a matter of fact, the Roystons are dining with us."

Melinda groaned. Quickly she hugged her father before he could expostulate. "I shall go and phone Stephen or Charles or someone and *make* him take me out. But I tell you what, Jackie, I'll be back in time to help you clear up. Just think, you'll never have to do it again after tomorrow when Parchment Face comes."

"Melinda . . ." George began.

"She has got rather a parchment look to her face," said Jacqueline, and she couldn't help laughing.

So Melinda went to the cinema in Colchester with Stephen Crutchley, the doctor's son. The Roystons came to dine at Lowfield Hall, and Jacqueline said: Wait till tomorrow. Don't you envy me, Jessica? But what will she be like? And will she really come up to these glowing expectations? It was George who wondered. Please God, let her be the treasure Jackie thinks she is. *Schadenfreude* made Sir Robert and Lady Royston secretly hope she wouldn't be, but cut on the same lines as their Anneliese, their Birgit, and that best-forgotten Spanish couple.

Time will show. Wait till tomorrow.

4

The Coverdales had speculated about Eunice Parchman's work potential and her attitude, respectful or otherwise, toward themselves. They had allotted her a private bathroom and a television set, some comfortable chairs and a well-sprung bed rather as one sees that a workhorse has a good stable and manger. They wanted her to be content because if she were contented she would stay. But they never considered her as a person at all. Not for them as they got up on Saturday, May 9, E-Day indeed, any thoughts as to what her past had been, whether she were nervous about coming, whether she were visited by the same hopes and fears that affected them. At that stage Eunice was little more than a machine to them, and the satisfactory working of that machine depended on its being suitably oiled and its having no objection to stairs.

But Eunice was a person. Eunice, as Melinda might have put it, was for real.

She was the strangest person they were ever likely to meet. And had they known what her past contained, they would have fled from her or barred their doors against her as against the plague. Not to mention her future, now inextricably bound up with theirs.

Her past lay in the house she was now preparing to leave. An old terraced house, one of a long row in Rainbow Street, Tooting, with its front door opening directly onto the pavement. She had been born in that house forty-seven years before, the only child of a Southern Railway guard and his wife.

From the first her existence was a narrow one. She seemed one of those people who are destined to spend their lives in the restricted encompassment of a few streets. Her school was almost next door, Rainbow Street Infants, and those members of her family she visited lived within a stone's throw. Destiny was temporarily disturbed by the coming of the Second World War. Along with thousands of other London schoolchildren, she was sent away to the country before she had learned to read. But her parents, though dull, unaware, molelike people, were upset by reports that her foster mother neglected her, and fetched her back to them, to the bombs and the war-torn city.

After that Eunice attended school only sporadically.

To this school or that school she went for weeks or sometimes months at a time, but in each new class she entered, the other pupils were all far ahead of her. They had passed her by, and no teacher ever took the trouble to discover the fundamental gap in her acquirements, still less to remedy it. Bewildered, bored, apathetic, she sat at the back of the classroom, staring at the incomprehensible on page or blackboard. Or she stayed away, a stratagem always connived at by her mother. Therefore, by the time she came to leave school, a month before her fourteenth birthday, she could sign her name, read "The cat sat on the mat" and "Jim likes ham but Jack likes jam," and that was about all. School had taught her one thing—to conceal, by many subterfuges and contrivances, that she could not read or write.

She went to work in a sweetshop, also in Rainbow Street, where she learned to tell a Mars bar from a Crunchie by the color of its wrapping. When she was seventeen, the illness which had threatened her mother for years began to cripple her. It was multiple sclerosis, though it was some time before the Parchmans' doctor understood this. Mrs. Parchman, at fifty, was confined to a wheelchair, and Eunice gave up her job to look after her and run the house. Her days now began to be spent in a narrow twilight world, for illiteracy is a kind of blindness. The Coverdales, had they been told of it, would not have believed such a world could exist. Why didn't she educate herself? they would have asked. Why didn't she go to evening classes, get a job, employ someone to look after her mother, join a club, meet people? Why, indeed? Between the Coverdales and the Parchmans a great gulf is fixed. George himself often said so, without fully considering what it implied. A young girl to him was always some version of Paula or Melinda, cherished, admired, educated, loved, brought up to see herself as one of the top ten percent. Not so Eunice Parchman. A big rawboned plain girl with truculent sullen eyes, she had never heard a piece of music except for the hymns and the extracts from Gilbert and Sullivan her father whistled while he shaved. She had never seen any picture of note but *The Laughing Cavalier* and the *Mona Lisa* in the school hall, and she was so steeped in ignorance that, had you asked her who Napoleon was and where was Denmark, she would have stared in uncomprehending blankness.

There were things Eunice could do. She had considerable manual dexterity. She could clean expertly and shop and cook and sew and push her mother up to the common in her wheelchair. Was it so surprising that, being able to do these things, she should prefer the safety and peace of doing them and them alone? Was it odd to find her taking satisfaction in gossiping with her middle-aged neighbors and avoiding the company of their children who could read and write and who had jobs and talked of things beyond her comprehension? She had her pleasures, eating the chocolate she loved and which made her grow stout, ironing, cleaning silver and brass, augmenting the family income by knitting for her neighbors. By the time she was thirty she had never been into a public house, visited a theater, entered any restaurant more grand than a teashop, left the country, had a boyfriend, worn makeup, or been to a hairdresser. She had twice been to the cinema with Mrs. Samson next door and had seen the Queen's wedding and coronation on Mrs. Samson's television set. Between the ages of seven and twelve she four times traveled in a long-distance train. That was the history of her youth.

Virtue might naturally be the concomitant of such sheltering. She had few opportunities to do bad things, but she found them or made them.

"If there's one thing I've taught Eunice," her mother used to say, "it's to tell right from wrong." It was a gabbled cliché, as automatic as the quacking of a duck but less meaningful. The Parchmans were not given to thinking before they spoke, or indeed to thinking much at all.

All that jerked Eunice out of her apathy were her compulsions. Suddenly an urge would come over her to drop everything and walk. Or turn out a room. Or

take a dress to pieces and sew it up again with minor alterations. These urges she always obeyed. But-
toned up tightly into her shabby coat, a scarf tied
around her still-beautiful thick brown hair, she would
walk and walk for miles, sometimes across the river
bridges and up into the West End. These walks were
her education. She saw things one is not taught in
school even if one can read. And instincts, not controlled or repressed by reading, instructed her as to
what these sights meant or implied. In the West End
she saw prostitutes, in the park people making love,
on the commons homosexuals, waiting furtively in the
shadows to solicit likely passersby. One night she
saw a man who lived in Rainbow Street pick up a boy
and take him behind a bush. Eunice had never heard
the word "blackmail." She didn't know that demanding money with menaces is a popular pastime punish-
able by the law. But neither, probably, had Cain
heard the word "murder" before he struck his brother
down. There are age-old desires in man which man
needs no instruction to practice. Very likely Eunice
thought she was doing something original. She waited
until the boy had gone and then she told her neighbor
she would tell his wife unless he gave her ten shillings a week not to do so. Horribly frightened, he
agreed and gave her ten shillings a week for years.

Her father had been religious in his youth. He
named her after a New Testament character, and
sometimes, facetiously, would refer to this fact, pro-
noucing her name in the Greek way.

"What have you got for my tea tonight, Eu-nicey,
mother of Timothy?"

It riled Eunice. It rankled. Did she vaguely ponder
on the likelihood that she would never be the mother
of anyone? The thoughts of the illiterate are registered
in pictures and in very simple words. Eunice's vo-
cabulary was small. She spoke in clichés and catch
phrases picked up from her mother, her aunt down
the road, Mrs. Samson. When her cousin married, did
she feel envy? Was there bitterness as well as greed
in her heart when she began extracting a further
ten shillings a week from a married woman who was

having an affair with a salesman? She expressed to
no one her views on life or the emotions.

Mrs. Parchman died when Eunice was thirty-sev-
en, and her widower immediately took over as resident invalid. Perhaps he thought Eunice's services
too good to waste. His kidneys had always been weak,
and now he cultivated his asthma, taking to his bed.

"I don't know where I'd be without you, Eu-nicey,
mother of Timothy."

Alive today, probably, and living in Tooting.

Eunice's urges pressed her to walk, one day to get
on a coach and have a day in Brighton, another to
take all the furniture out of the living room and paint
the walls pink. Her father went into hospital for the
odd fortnight.

"Mainly to give you a break, Miss Parchman," said
the doctor. "He could go at any time, he could last
for years."

But he showed no signs of going. Eunice bought
him nice bits of fish and made him steak-and-kidney
pudding. She kept up his bedroom fire and brought
him hot water to shave in while he whistled "The King
of Love My Shepherd Is" and "I Am the Lord High
Executioner." One bright morning in spring he sat
up in bed, pink-cheeked and strong, and said in the
clear voice of one whose lungs are perfectly sound:

"You can wrap me up warm and put me in Mum's
chair and take me up on the common, Eu-nicey,
mother of Timothy."

Eunice made no reply. She took one of the pillows
from behind her father's head and pushed it hard
down on his face. He struggled and thrashed about
for a while, but not for long. His lungs, after all, were
not quite sound. Eunice had no phone. She walked
up the street and brought the doctor back with her.
He asked no questions and signed the death certificate at once.

Now for freedom.

She was forty and she didn't know what to do
with freedom when she had it. Get over that ridicu-

lous business of not being able to read and write, George Coverdale would have said. Learn a useful trade. Take in lodgers. Get some sort of social life going. Eunice did none of these things. She remained in the house in Rainbow Street, for which the rent was scarcely now more than nominal, she had her blackmail income, swollen now to two pounds a week. As if those twenty-three years had never been, those best years of all her youth passed as in the twinkling of an eye, she went back to the sweetshop and worked there three days a week.

On one of her walks she saw Annie Cole go into a post office in Merton with a pension book in her hand. Eunice knew a pension book when she saw one. She had been shown by her father how to sign his as his agent. And she knew Annie Cole by sight too, having observed her leaving the crematorium just before Mr. Parchman's funeral party had arrived. It was Annie Cole's mother who had died, and now here was Annie Cole collecting her pension and telling the counter clerk how poor Mother had rallied that day. The advantage of being illiterate is that one achieves an excellent visual memory and almost total recall.

Annie thereby became Eunice's victim and amanuensis, paying her a third of that pension and doing needful jobs for her. She also, because she bore no malice, seeing Eunice's conduct as only natural in a catch-as-catch-can world, became the nearest Eunice ever had to a friend until she met Joan Smith. But it was time now to kill Mother off finally, she was getting scared, only Eunice as beneficiary wouldn't let her. She determined to be rid of Eunice, and it was she who, having flattered her blackmailer to the top of her bent on her housewifely skills, produced as if casually the Coverdales' advertisement.

"You could get thirty-five pounds a week and all found. I've always said you were wasted in that shop."

Eunice munched her Cadbury's filled block. "I don't know," she said, a favorite response.

"That place of yours is falling down. They're always talking about pulling that row down. It'd be no loss, I'm sure." Annie scrutinized *The Times*, which she had picked at random out of a litter bin. "It sounds ever so nice. Why not write to them and just see? You don't have to go there if you don't fancy it."

"You can write if you want," said Eunice.

Like all her close acquaintances, Annie suspected Eunice was illiterate or semiliterate, but no one could ever be quite sure. Eunice sometimes seemed to read magazines and she could sign things. There are many people, after all, who never read or write, although they can. So Annie wrote the letter to Jacqueline, and when the time came for the interview it was Annie who primed Eunice.

"Be sure to call her 'madam,' Eun, and don't speak till you're spoken to. Mother was in service when she was a girl and she knew all about it. I can give you a good many of mother's tips." Poor Annie. She had been devoted to her mother, and the pension-book fraud had been perpetrated as much as a way of keeping her mother alive and with her as for gain. "You can have a lend of Mother's court shoes too. They'll be about your size."

It worked. Before Eunice could think much about it, she was engaged as the Coverdales' housekeeper, and if it was at twenty-five rather than thirty-five pounds a week, either seemed a fortune to her. And yet, why was she so easily persuaded, she who was as bound to her burrow and her warren as any wild animal?

Not for change, not for pastures new, not for adventure, pecuniary advantage, or even the chance of showing off the one thing she could do well. Largely, she took the job to avoid responsibility.

While her father was alive, though things had been bad in many respects, they had been good in one. He took responsibility for the rent and the rates and the services bills, for filling in forms and reading what had to be read. Eunice took the rates around to the council offices in cash, paid the gas and electricity bills in the same way. But she couldn't hire television or buy it on the H.P. There would have been forms to fill in. Letters and circulars came. She couldn't read them.

Lowfield Hall would solve all that and, as far as she could see, receive her and care for her in the only way she was interested in, forever.

The house was rendered up to an amazed and delighted landlord, and Mrs. Samson saw to the selling of the furniture. Eunice watched the valuing of her household goods, the indifference on the man's face, with an inscrutable expression. She packed everything she possessed into two suitcases, borrowed from Mrs. Samson. In her navy skirt, hand-knitted navy jumper, and raincoat, she made, characteristically, her farewells to that kind neighbor, that near-mother who had been present when her own mother gave her birth.

"Well, I'm off," said Eunice.

Mrs. Samson kissed her cheek, but she didn't ask Eunice to write to her, for she was the only living person who really knew.

At Liverpool Street Station Eunice regarded trains —trains proper, not tubes—for the first time in nearly forty years. But how to find which one to take? On the departure board, white on black, were meaningless hieroglyphs.

She hated asking questions, but she had to.

"Which platform for Stantwich?"

"It's up on the board, lady."

And again, to someone else: "Which platform for Stantwich?"

"It's up on the board. Thirteen. Can't you read?"

No, she couldn't, but she didn't dare say so. Still, at last she was on the train, and it must be the right one, for by now eleven people had told her so. Out into the country the train took her, and back into the past. She was a little girl again, going with her school to Taunton and safety, and her whole future was before her. Now, as then, the stations passed, nameless and unknown.

But she would know Stantwich when she got there, for the train and her future went no further.

5

She was bound to fail. She had no training and no experience. People like the Coverdales were far removed from any people she had ever known, and she was not accommodating or adaptable. She had never been to a party, let alone given one, never run any house but the one in Rainbow Street. There was no tradition of service in her family and no one she knew had ever had a servant, not even a charwoman. It was on the cards that she would fail abysmally.

She succeeded beyond her own stolid hopes and Jacqueline's dreams.

Of course, Jacqueline didn't really want a housekeeper at all. She didn't want an organizer and manager but an obedient maid of all work. And Eunice was accustomed to obedience and hard work. She was what the Coverdales required, apparently without personality or awareness of her rights or that curiosity that leads an employee to pry, quiet and respectable, not paranoid except in one particular, lacking any desire to put herself on the same social level as they. Aesthetic appreciation for her was directed to only one end—domestic objects. To Eunice a refrigerator was beautiful, while a flower was just a flower, the fabric of a curtain lovely, whereas a bird or a wild animal at best "pretty." She was unable to differentiate, as far as its aesthetic value was concerned, between a *famille rose* vase and a Teflon-lined frying pan. Both were "nice" and each would receive from her the same care and attention.

These were the reasons for her success. From the first she made a good impression. Having eaten the last of the Bounty bar she had bought herself at Liverpool Street, she alighted from the train, no longer nervous now that there was nothing to be deciphered. She could read "Way Out"; that wasn't a problem. Jacqueline hadn't told her how she would know George, but George knew her from his wife's not very kind description. Melinda was with him, which had floored Eunice, who was looking for a man on his own.

"Pleased to meet you," she said, shaking hands, not smiling or studying them, but observing the big white car.

George gave her the front seat. "You'll get a better view of our beautiful countryside that way, Miss Parchman."

The girl chattered nineteen to the dozen all the way, occasionally shooting questions at Eunice. D'you like the country, Miss Parchman? Have you ever been up in the Fens? Aren't you too hot in that coat? I hope you like stuffed vine leaves. My stepmother's doing them for tonight. Eunice answered bemusedly with a plain yes or no. She didn't know whether you ate stuffed vine leaves or looked at them or sat on them. But she responded with quiet politeness, sometimes giving her small tight smile.

George liked this respectful discretion. He liked the way she sat with her knees together and her hands folded in her lap. He even liked her clothes which, to a more detached observer, would have looked like standard issue to prison wardresses. Neither he nor Melinda was aware of anything chilly or repulsive about her.

"Go the long way round through Greeving, Daddy, so that Miss Parchman can see the village."

It was thus that Eunice was given a view of her future accomplice's home before she saw that of her victims. Greeving Post Office and Village Store, Prop. N. Smith. She didn't, however, see Joan Smith, who was our delivering Epiphany People literature. But she wouldn't have taken much notice of her if she had been there. People didn't interest her. Nor did the countryside and one of the prettiest villages in Suffolk. Greeving was just old buildings to her, thatch and plaster and a lot of trees that must keep out the light. But she did wonder how you managed when you wanted a nice bit of fish or suddenly had a fancy, as she often did, for a pound box of chocolates.

Lowfield Hall. To Eunice it might have been Buckingham Palace. She didn't know ordinary people lived in houses like this, which were for the Queen or some film star. In the hall, for the first time, all five of them were together. Jacqueline, who dressed up for any occasion, who got into emerald velvet trousers and red silk shirt and Gucci scarf to greet her new servant, was there waiting. And even Giles was there. Passing through at that particular moment, looking vaguely for his Hindi primer, he had been collared by his mother and persuaded to remain for an introduction.

"Good evening, Miss Parchman. Did you have a good journey? This is my son Giles."

Giles nodded absently and escaped upstairs without a backward glance. Eunice hardly noticed him. She was looking at the house and its contents. It was almost too much for her. She was like the Queen of Sheba when she saw King Solomon—there was no more spirit in her. But none of her wonderment showed in her face or her demeanor. She stood on the thick carpet, among the antiques, the bowls of flowers, looking first at the grandfather clock, then at herself reflected in a huge mirror with gilded twirls around the edge of it. She stood half-stunned. The Coverdales took her air for poise, the silent self-sufficient containment of the good servant.

"I'll take you to your room," said Jacqueline. "There won't be anything for you to do tonight. We'll go upstairs and someone will bring your bags up later."

A large and pleasant room met Eunice's eyes. It was carpeted in olive-drab Wilton, papered in a pale yellow with a white vertical stripe. There were two darker yellow easy chairs, a cretonne-covered settee, a bed with a spread of the same material, and a long built-in cupboard. The windows afforded a splendid view, *the* view, which was better seen from here than from any other room in the house.

"I hope you find everything to your liking."

An empty bookcase (destined to remain so), a bowl of white lilac on a coffee table, two lamps with burnt-orange shades, two framed Constable reproductions, *Willy Lott's Cottage, The Leaping Horse.* The bathroom had light green fittings, and olive-green towels hung on a heated rail.

"Your dinner will be ready for you in the kitchen in half an hour. It's the door at the end of the passage behind the stairs. And now I expect you'd like to be left alone for a while. Oh, here's my son with your bags."

Giles had been caught by George and coaxed into bringing up the two cases. He dumped them on the floor and went away. Eunice disregarded him, as she had largely disregarded his mother. She was staring at the one object in those two rooms which really interested her, the television set. This was what she had always wanted but been unable to buy or hire. As the door closed behind Jacqueline, she approached the set, looked at it, and then, like someone resolved upon using a dangerous piece of equipment that may explode or send a shock up one's arm, but knowing still that it must be used, it must be attempted, she pounced on it and switched it on.

On the screen appeared a man with a gun. He was threatening a woman who cowered behind a chair. There was a shot and the woman fled screaming down a corridor. Thus it happened that the first program Eunice ever saw on her own television dealt with violence and with firearms. Did it, and its many successors stimulate her own latent violence and trigger off waves of aggression? Did fictional drama take root in the mind of the illiterate so that it at last bore terrible fruit?

Perhaps. But if television spurred her on to kill the Coverdales, it certainly played no part in directing her to smother her father. At the time of his death the only programs she had seen on it were a royal wedding and a coronation.

However, though she was to become addicted to the set, shutting herself up with it, drawing her curtains against the summer evenings, that first time she watched it for only ten minutes. She ate her dinner cautiously, for it was like nothing she had ever eaten before, was taken over the house by Jacqueline, instructed in her duties. From the very beginning she enjoyed herself. A few little mistakes were only natural. Annie Cole had taught her how to lay a table, so she did that all right, but on that first morning she made tea instead of coffee. Eunice had never made coffee in her life except the instant kind. She didn't ask how. She very seldom asked questions. Jacqueline assumed she was used to a percolator—Eunice didn't disillusion her—while they used a filter, so she demonstrated the filter. Eunice watched. It was never necessary for her to watch any operation of this kind more than once for her to be able to perform it herself.

"I see, madam," she said.

Jacqueline did the cooking. Jacqueline or George did the shopping. In those early days, while Jacqueline was out, Eunice examined every object in Lowfield Hall at her leisure. The house had been dirty, by her standards. It brought her intense pleasure to subject it to a spring cleaning. Oh, the lovely carpets, the hangings, the cushions, the rosewood and walnut and oak, the glass and silver and china! But best of all was the kitchen with pine walls and cupboards, a double steel sink, a washing machine, a dryer, a dishwasher. It wasn't enough for her to dust the porcelain in the drawing room. It must be washed.

"You really need not do that, Miss Parchman."

"I like doing it," said Eunice.

Fear of breakages rather than altruism had prompted Jacqueline to protest. But Eunice never broke anything, nor did she fail to replace everything on the exact spot from where she had taken it. Her visual memory imprinted neat permanent photographs in some department of her brain.

The only things in Lowfield Hall which didn't interest her and which she didn't handle or study were the contents of the morning-room desk, the books, the letters from George in Jacqueline's dressing table. Those things and, at this stage, the two shotguns.

Her employers were overwhelmed.

"She's perfect," said Jacqueline, who, parceling up George's shirts for the laundry, had had them taken out of her hands by Eunice, laundered exquisitely by Eunice between defrosting the fridge and changing the bed linen. "D'you know what she said, darling? She just looked at me in that meek way she has and said, 'Give me those. I like a bit of ironing.'"

Meek? Eunice Parchman?

"She's certainly very efficient," said George. "And I like to see you looking so happy and relaxed."

"Well, I don't have a thing to do. Apart from her once putting the green sheets on our bed and once simply ignoring a note I left her, I haven't had a fault to find. It seems absurd calling those things faults after old Eva and that dreadful Ingrid."

"How does she get on with Eva?"

"Ignores her, I think. I wish I had the nerve. D'you know, Miss Parchman can sew too. I was trying to turn up the hem of my green skirt, and she took it and did it perfectly."

"We've been very lucky," said George.

So the month of May passed. The spring flowers died away and the trees sprang into leaf. Pheasants came into the fields to eat the green corn, and the nightingale sang in the orchard. But not for Eunice. Hares, alert and quivering, cropped under the hedges, and the moon rose slowly behind the Greeving Hills, red and strange like another sun. But not for Eunice. She drew the curtains, put on the lamps and then the television. Her evenings were hers to do as she liked with. This was what she liked. She knitted. But gradually, as the serial or the sporting event or the cops-and-robbers film began to grip her, the knitting fell into her lap and she leaned forward, enthralled by an innocent childlike excitement.

She was happy. If she had been capable of analyzing her thoughts and feelings and of questioning her motives, she would have said that this vicarious living was better than any life she had known. But had she been capable of that, it is unlikely she would have been content with so specious a way of spending her leisure. Her addiction gives rise to a question. "Wouldn't some social service have immensely benefitted society—and saved the lives of the Coverdales —had it recognized Eunice Parchman's harmless craving? Give her a room, a pension, and a television set and leave her to worship and to stare for the rest of her life? No social service came into contact with her until it was far too late. No psychiatrist had ever seen her. Such a one would only have discovered the root cause of her neurosis if she had allowed him to discover her illiteracy. And she had been expert at concealing it since the time when she might have been expected to overcome it. Her father, who could read perfectly well, who in his youth had read the Bible from beginning to end, was her principal ally in helping her hide her deficiency. He, who should have encouraged her to learn, instead conspired with her in the far more irksome complexities not learning entailed.

When a neighbor, dropping in with a newspaper, had handed it to Eunice, "I'll have that," he had been used to say, and looking at the small print, "Don't strain her young eyes." It came to be accepted in her narrow circle that Eunice had poor sight, this solution generally being the one seized upon by the uneducated literate to account for illiteracy.

"Can't read it? You mean you can't *see?*"

When she was a child she had never wanted to read. As she grew older she wanted to learn, but who could teach her? Acquiring a teacher, or even trying to acquire one, would mean other people finding out. She had begun to shun other people, all of whom seemed to her bent on ferreting out her secret. After a time, this shunning, this isolating herself, became automatic, though the root cause of her mis-anthropy was half-forgotten.

Things could not hurt her, the furniture, the orna-ments, the television. She embraced them, they aroused in her the nearest she ever got to warm emo-tion, while to the Coverdales she gave the cold shoul-der. Not that they received more of her stoniness than anyone else had done. She behaved to them as she had always behaved to everyone.

George was the first to notice it. Of all the Cover-dales, he was by far the most sensitive, and therefore the first to see a flaw in all this excellence.

6

They sat in church on Sunday morning and Mr. Archer began to preach his sermon. For his text he took "Well done, thou good and faithful servant. Thou hast been faithful over a few things; I will make thee ruler over many things." Jacqueline smiled at George and touched his arm, and he smiled back, well-satis-fied.

On the following day he remembered those ex-changed smiles and thought he had been fatuous, perhaps overcomplacent.

"Paula's gone into hospital," Jacqueline said when he came home. "It's really rather awful the way they fix a day for your baby to be born these days. Just take you in and give you an injection and hey presto!"

"Instant infants," said George. "Has Brian phoned?"

"Not since two."

"I'll just give him a ring."

They were dining, as they often did when alone, in the morning room. Eunice came in to lay the table. George dialed, but there was no reply. A second after he put the phone down, it rang. After answering Paula's husband in monosyllables, after a final "Call me back soon," he walked over to Jacqueline and took her hand.

"There's some complication. They haven't decided yet, but she's very exhausted and it'll probably mean an emergency cesarean."

"Darling, I'm so sorry, what a worry!" She didn't tell him not to worry, and he was glad of it. "Why don't you phone Dr. Crutchley? He might reassure you."

"I'll do that."

Eunice left the room. George appreciated her tactful silence. He phoned the doctor, who said he couldn't comment on a case he knew nothing about, and reassured George only to the extent of telling him that, generally speaking, women didn't die in childbirth anymore.

They ate their dinner. That is, Giles ate his dinner, Jacqueline picked at hers, and George left his almost untouched. Giles made one small concession to the seriousness of the occasion and the anxiety of the others. He stopped reading and stared instead into space. Afterward, when the suspense was over, Jacqueline said laughingly to her husband that such a gesture from Giles was comparable to a pep talk and a bottle of brandy from anyone else.

The suspense didn't last long. Brian called back twice, and half an hour after that was on the line to say a seven-pound boy had been delivered by cesarean operation and Paula was well.

Eunice was clearing the table. She must have heard it all, George's "Thank God!" Jacqueline's "That's wonderful, darling. I'm so happy for you," Giles's "Good," before he took himself off upstairs. She must have heard relief and seen delight. Without the slightest reaction, she left the room and closed the door.

Jacqueline put her arms around George and held

him. He didn't think about Eunice then. It was only as he was going to bed, and heard faintly above him the hum of her television, that he began to think her behavior strangely cold. Not once had she expressed her concern during the anxious time, or her satisfaction for him when the danger was past. Consciously he hadn't waited for her to do so. At the time he hadn't expected a "I'm so glad to hear your daughter's all right, sir," but now he wondered at the omission. It troubled him. Lack of care for a fellow woman, lack of concern for the people in whose home one lived, were unnatural in any woman. Well done, thou good and faithful servant . . . But that had not been well done.

Not for the world would George have spoken of his unease to Jacqueline, who was so happy and contented with her employee. Besides, he wouldn't have wanted a loquacious servant, making the family's affairs her affairs and being familiar. He resolved to banish it from his mind.

And this he did quite successfully until the christening of the new baby, which took place a month later.

Patrick had been christened at Greeving, Mr. Archer was a friend of the Coverdales, and a country christening in summer is pleasanter than one in town. Paula and Brian and their two children arrived at Lowfield on a Saturday at the end of June and stayed till the Sunday. They had quite a large party on the Saturday afternoon. Brian's parents and his sister were there, the Roystons, the Jameson-Kerrs, an aunt of Jacqueline's from Bury and some cousins of George's from Newmarket. And the arrangements for eating and drinking, carried out by Eunice under Jacqueline's directions, were perfect. The house had never looked so nice, the champagne glasses been so well-polished. Jacqueline didn't know they possessed so many white linen table napkins, had never seen them all together before and all so freshly starched. In the past she had sometimes been reduced to using paper ones.

Before they left for the church Melinda came into the drawing room to show Eunice the baby. He was to be called Giles, and Giles Mont, aghast at the idea now, had been roped in to be godfather before he realized what was happening. She carried him in in the long embroidered christening robe that she herself, her brother and sister, and indeed George himself, had once worn. He was a fine-looking baby, large and red and lusty. On the table, beside the cake, was the Coverdales' christening book, a volume of listed names of those who had worn the robe, when and where they had been baptized and so on. It was open, ready for this latest entry.

"Isn't he *sweet*, Miss Parchman?"

Eunice stood chill and stiff. George felt a coldness come from her as if the sun had gone in. She didn't smile or bend over the baby or make as if to touch his coverings. She looked at him. It wasn't a look of enthusiasm such as George had seen her give to the silver spoons when she laid them out on the saucers. Having looked at him, she said:

"I must get on. I've things to see to."

Not one word did he or Jacqueline receive from her during the course of the afternoon, when she was in and out with trays, as to the attractiveness of the child, their luck in having such a fine day, or the happiness of the young parents. Cold, he thought, unnaturally cold. Or was she just painfully shy?

Eunice was not shy. Nor had she turned from the baby because she was afraid of the book. Not directly. She was simply uninterested in the baby. But it would be true to say that she was uninterested in babies because there are books in the world.

The printed word was horrible to her, a personal threat to her. Keep away from it, avoid it, and from all those who will show it to her. The habit of shunning it was ingrained in her; it was no longer conscious. All the springs of warmth and outgoing affection and human enthusiasm had been dried up long ago by it. Isolating herself was natural now, and she was not aware that it had begun by isolating herself from print and books and handwriting.

Illiteracy had dried up her sympathy and atrophied her imagination. That, along with what psychologists call *affect*, the ability to care about the feelings of others, had no place in her makeup.

General Gordon, in attempting to raise the morale of the besieged inhabitants of Khartoum, told them that when God was handing out fear to the people of the world, at last He came to him. But by that time God had no more fear to give, so Gordon was created without fear. This elegant parable may be paraphrased for Eunice. When God came to her, He had no more imagination or affect to give.

The Coverdales were interferers. They interfered with the best intentions, those of making other people happy. If it were not such an awful thing to say of anyone (to quote one of Giles Mont's favorite authors), one could say that they meant well. They were afraid of being selfish, for they had never understood what Giles knew instinctively, that selfishness is not living as one wishes to live, it is asking others to live as one wishes to live.

"I'm worried about old Parchment Face," said Melinda. "Don't you think she has a terrible life?"

"I don't know," said Giles. Melinda was paying one of her rare visits to his room, sitting in fact on his bed, and this both made him happy and threw him into a panic. "I haven't noticed."

"Oh, you—you never notice anything. But I can tell you she does. She's never once been out, not all the time she's been here. All she does is watch television. Listen, it's on now." She paused dramatically and turned her eyes up to the ceiling. Giles went on with what he had been doing when she first came in, pinning things up on the cork tiles with which he had covered half one of the walls. "She must be terribly lonely," said Melinda. "She must miss her friends." She grabbed Giles by the arm and swung him around. "Don't you *care?*"

Her touch gave him a shock and he blushed. "Leave her alone. She's all right."

"She's not. She can't be."

"Some people like being alone." He looked vaguely around his room, at the heap of orange clothes, the muddle of books and dictionaries, the stacks of half-finished essays on subjects not in the Magnus Wythen curriculum. He loved it. It was better than anywhere else except possibly the London Library, where he had once been taken by a scholarly relative. But they won't let you rent a room in the London Library, or Giles would have been at the top of their housing list. "I like being alone," he said.

"If that's a hint to me to go . . ."

"No, no, it isn't," he said hastily, and resolving to declare himself, began in a hoarse trilling voice, "Melinda . . ."

"What? Where did you get that awful poster? Is she supposed to have a green face?"

Giles sighed. The moment had passed. "Read my Quote of the Month."

It was written in green ink on a piece of paper pinned to the cork wall. Melinda read it aloud. " 'Why should the generations overlap one another at all? Why cannot we be buried as eggs in neat little cells with ten or twenty thousand pounds each wrapped around us in Bank of England notes, and wake up, as the Sphex wasp does, to find that its papa and mama have not only left ample provision at its elbow but have been eaten by sparrows some weeks before?' "

"Good, isn't it? Samuel Butler."

"You can't have that on the wall, Step. If Daddy or Jackie saw it, it'd absolutely freak them out. Anyway, I thought you were supposed to be doing classics."

"I may not do anything," said Giles. "I may go to India. I don't suppose," greatly daring, "you'd want to come too?"

Melinda made a face. "I bet you don't go. You know you won't. You're just trying to get off a subject that might involve you. I was going to ask you to come down with me and confront Daddy and make him do something about her. But I bet you'll say you won't."

Giles pushed his fingers through his hair. He would have liked to please her. She was the only person in the world he cared much about pleasing. But there were limits. Not even for her would he defy his principles and flout his nature. "No," he said, and gloomily, almost sorrowfully, contorting his face in a kind of hopelessness, "No, I won't do that."

"Mad," said Melinda, and bounced out.

Her father and Jacqueline were in the garden, in the midsummer dusk, surveying what Jacqueline had done that day. There was a heavy sweet scent from the first flowers on the tobacco plants.

"I've been thinking, my darlings. We ought to do something about poor old Parchment Face, take her out, give her an interest."

Her stepmother gave her a cool smile. In some respects Jacqueline could fill the wasp role her son had meted out to her. "Not everyone is such an extrovert as you, you know."

"And I think we've had enough of that Parchment Face business, Melinda," said George. "You're no longer the naughtiest girl in the sixth."

"Now you're evading the issue."

"No, we're not. Jackie and I have been discussing that very thing. We're quite aware *Miss* Parchman hasn't been out, but she may not know where to go, and it's difficult without a car."

"Then lend her a car! We've got two."

"That's what we're going to do. The chances are she's too shy to ask. I see her as a very shy woman."

"Repressed by a ruling class," said Melinda.

It was Jacqueline who made the offer.

"I can't drive," said Eunice. She didn't mind saying this. There were only two things she minded admitting she couldn't do. Hardly anyone in her circle had been able to drive, and in Rainbow Street it had been looked on as a rather bizarre accomplishment for a woman. "I never learned."

"What a pity! I was going to say you could borrow my car. I really don't know how you'll get around without transport."

"I can go on the bus." Eunice vaguely supposed a

red double decker trundled around the lanes with the frequency of the 88 in Tooting.

"That's just what you can't do. The nearest bus stop's two miles away, and there are only three buses a day."

Just as George had detected a flaw in his housekeeper, so now Eunice sensed a small cloud threatening her peaceful life. This was the first time any Coverdale had shown signs of wanting to change it. She waited uneasily for the next move, and she didn't have to wait long.

Progenitor of Coverdales, George was the arch-interferer of them all. Employees were hauled into his office at T.B.C. and advised about their marriages, their mortgages, and the higher education of their children. Meadows, Higgs, and Carter matrons were accustomed to his entering their cottages and being told to get the dry-rot people in, or why not grow a few vegetables on that piece of ground? Ever such a nice man was Mr. Coverdale, but you don't want to take no notice of what he says. Different in my gran's time. The squire *was* the squire then, but them old days are gone, thank God. George went on interfering—for the good of others.

He bearded the lion in its den. The lion looked very tame and was occupied in womanly fashion, ironing one of his dress shirts.

"Yes, sir?" Her tabby-cat hair was neatly combed, and she wore a blue-and-white-checked cotton dress.

All his life George had been looked after by women, but none of them had ever attempted the formidable task of washing, starching, and ironing a "boiled" shirt. George, if he ever thought about it at all, supposed that there was a special mystique attached to these operations, and that they could only be performed in a laundry by a clever machine. He smiled approvingly.

"Ah, I can see I'm interrupting an expert at a very skilled task. You're making a fine job of that, Miss Parchman."

"I like ironing," said Eunice.

"I'm glad to hear it, but I don't suppose you like

being confined at Lowfield Hall all the time, do you? That's what I've come to talk about. My wife tells me you've never found time in your busy life to learn to drive a car. Am I right?"

"Yes," said Eunice.

"I see. Well, we shall have to remedy that. What would you say to driving lessons? I shall be happy to foot the bill. You're doing well by us and we'd like to do something for you in return."

"I couldn't learn to drive," said Eunice, who had been thinking hard. The favorite excuse came out. "My sight wouldn't be up to it."

"You don't wear glasses."

"I should do. I'm waiting for my new pair."

In-depth questioning elicited that Eunice should have glasses, had been in need of new ones when she came to Greeving, had "let it slide," couldn't, even with glasses, read a number plate or a road sign. She must have her eyes tested forthwith, said George, he would see to it himself and drive her into Stant-wich.

"I feel rather ashamed of myself," he said to Jac-queline. "All the time the poor woman was as blind as a bat. I don't mind telling you now we know the reason for it, but I was beginning to find that reserve of hers quite off-putting."

Alarm showed in her eyes. "Oh, George, you mustn't say that! Having her has made such a dif-ference to my life."

"I'm not saying a thing, darling. I quite understand she's very shortsighted and was much too diffident to say so."

"The working classes are absurd about things like that," said Jacqueline, who would have suffered ag-onies struggling with contact lenses, would have bumped into walls rather than wear glasses. They both felt immensely satisfied with George's discov-ery, and it occurred to neither of them that a pur-blind woman could hardly have cleaned the win-dows to a diamond brilliance or watched the television for three hours every evening.

7

At forty-seven, Eunice had better sight than Giles Mont at seventeen. Sitting beside George in the car, she wondered what to do if he insisted on coming into the optician's with her. She was unable to concoct any excuse to avoid this happening, and her experience was inadequate to teach her that middle-aged conservative landowners do not generally accompany their middle-aged female servants into what is virtually a doctor's surgery. A sullen puzzled resentment simmered within her. The last man who sought to make her life insupportable had got a pillow over his face for his pains.

A slight fillip came to her spirits at the sight, at last, of shops, those familiar and wonderful treasure houses that had seemed left behind forever. They got an even greater lift when George showed no sign of accompanying her into the optician's. He left her with a promise to be back in half an hour and the instruction to have any bill sent to him.

Once the car had gone, Eunice walked around the corner, where she had noticed a confectioner's. She bought two Kit-Kats, a Mars bar, and a bag of marshmallows, and then she went into a teashop. There she had a cup of tea, a currant bun, and a chocolate éclair, which made a nice change from cassoulets and vine leaves and all those made-up dishes she got at Lowfield Hall. The picture of respectability was Eunice on that Saturday morning, sitting upright at her table in her navy-blue Crimplene suit, nylon stockings, Annie Cole's mother's court shoes, an "invisible" net on her hair. No one would have supposed her mind was racing on lines of deception— deception that comes so easily to those who can read and write and have IQs of 120. But at last a plan was formed. She crossed the road to Boots' and bought two pairs of sunglasses, not dark ones but faintly tinted, one pair with a crystal-blue frame, the other of mock tortoiseshell. Into her handbag with them, not to be produced for a week.

The Coverdales seemed surprised they would be ready so quickly. She was taken to Stantwich the second time by Jacqueline, who luckily didn't go with her into the optician's because of the impossibility of parking on a double yellow line. It was bad enough having to pay the fines incurred by Giles. Eunice bought more chocolate and consumed more cake. She showed the glasses to Jacqueline and went so far as to put the crystal-blue pair on. In them she felt a fool. Must she wear them all the time now, she who could see the feathers on a sparrow's wing in the orchard a hundred feet away? And would they expect her to *read?*

Nobody really lives in the present. But Eunice did so more than most people. For her, five minutes' delay in dinner now was more important than a great sorrow ten years gone, and to the future she had never given much thought. But now, with the glasses in her possession, occasionally even on her nose, she became very aware of the printed word which surrounded her and to which, at some future time, she might be expected to react.

Lowfield Hall was full of books. It seemed to Eunice that there were as many books here as in Tooting Public Library, where once, and once only, she had been to return an overdue novel of Mrs. Samson's. As small flattish boxes, she saw them, packed with mystery and threat. One entire wall of the morning room was filled with bookshelves, in the drawing room great glass-fronted bookcases stood on either side of the fireplace, and more shelves filled the twin alcoves. There were books on bedside tables, magazines and newspapers in racks. And they read books all the time. It seemed to her that they must read to provoke her, for no one, not even schoolteachers, could read that much for pleasure. Giles was never without a book in his hand. He even brought his reading matter into her kitchen and sat absorbed in it, his elbows on the table. Jacqueline read every novel of note, and she and George re-read their way through Victorian novels, their close-ness emphasized by their often reading some work of Dickens or Thackeray or George Eliot at the same time, so as later to discuss a character or a scene to-gether. Incongruously, it was the student of English literature who read the least, but even so Melinda was often to be found in the garden or lying on the morning-room floor with one of Mr. Sweet's gram-mars before her. This was not from inclination but because of a menace from her tutor—"If we're going to make the grade we shall have to come to grips with those Anglo-Saxon pronouns before next term, shan't we?" But how was Eunice to know that?

She had been happy, but the glasses had de-stroyed her happiness. She had been content with the house and the lovely things in the house, and the Coverdales had hardly existed for her, so little no-tice had she taken of them. Now she could hardly wait for them to go away on that summer holiday they were always talking about and planning for.

But before they went, and they were not going until the beginning of August, before their depar-ture set her free to expand, to explore, and to meet Joan Smith, three unpleasant things happened.

The first was nothing in itself. It was what it led up to that bothered Eunice. She dropped one of Geoff Baalham's eggs on the kitchen floor. Jacqueline, who was there, said only, "Oh dear, what a mess!" and Eunice had cleaned it up in a flash. But on the following morning she went up to turn out Giles's bedroom, always a formidable task, and for the first time she allowed herself to look at his cork wall. Why? She could hardly have answered that herself, but perhaps it was because she was now equipped to read, made vulnerable, as it were, to reading, and because she had now become aware of the oppressive number of books in the house. There was a message on the wall beside that nasty poster. "Why" it began. She could read that word without much difficulty when it was printed. "One" she could also read, and "eggs." Giles evidently meant it for her and was reproaching her for breaking that egg. She didn't care for his reproaches, but suppose he broke his silence —he never spoke to her—to ask her why. Why hadn't she obeyed his "why" message? He might tell his stepfather, and Eunice was on tenterhooks whenever George looked at her unbespectacled face.

At last the message was taken down, but only to be replaced by another. Eunice was almost paralyzed by it, and for a week she did no more in Giles's room than pull up the bedclothes and open the window. She was as frightened of those pieces of paper as another woman would have been had Giles kept a snake in his room.

But not so frightened as she was of Jacqueline's note. This was left on the kitchen table one morning while Eunice was at the top of the house making her own bed. When she came downstairs, Jacqueline had driven off to London to see Paula, to have her hair cut, and to buy clothes for her holiday.

Jacqueline had left notes for her before, and had wondered why the otherwise obedient Miss Parchman never obeyed the behests in them. All, however, was explained by her poor sight. But now Eunice had her glasses. Not that she was wearing them. They were upstairs, stuffed into the bottom of her knitting bag. She stared at the note, which meant as much to her as a note in Greek would have meant to Jacqueline—precisely as much, for Jacqueline could recognize an alpha, an omega, and a pi just as Eunice knew some capital letters and the odd monosyllabic word. But connecting those words, deciphering longer ones, making anything of it, that was beyond her. In London she would have had Annie Cole to help her. Here she had no one but Giles, who wandered through the kitchen to cadge a lift to Stantwich, to

moon about the shops and spend the afternoon in a
dark cinema. He didn't so much as glance at her,
and she would rather do anything than ask help
from him.

It wasn't one of Eva Baalham's days. Could she
lose the note? Inventiveness was not among her gifts.
It had taken all her puny powers to convince George
that the optician's bill hadn't come because she had
already paid it, liked to be independent, didn't want
to be "beholden."

And then Melinda came in.

Eunice had forgotten she was in the house, she
couldn't get used to these bits of kids starting their
summer holidays in June. Melinda danced in at midday, pretty healthy buxom Melinda in too-tight
jeans and a Mickey Mouse T-shirt, yellow hair in
Dutch-girl pigtails, her feet bare. The sun was shining, a wind was blowing, the whole kitchen was
radiated with fluttering dancing sunbeams, and Melinda was off to the seaside with two boys and
another girl in an orange-and-purple-painted van. She
picked up the note and read it aloud. "What's this?
'Please would you be awfully kind and if you have
the time press my yellow silk, the one with the
pleated skirt. I want to wear it tonight. It's in my
wardrobe somewhere up on the right. Thank you so
much, J.C.' It must be for you, Miss Parchman. D'you
think you could do my red skirt at the same time?
Would you?"

"Oh yes, it's no trouble," said the much-relieved
Eunice with quite a broad smile for her.

"You are *sweet*," said Melinda.

August came in with a heat wave, and Mr. Meadows, the farmer whose land adjoined George's, began
cutting his wheat. The new combine harvester
dropped bales of straw shaped like slices of Swiss
roll. Melinda picked fruit, along with the village wom-
en, in the cherry orchards, Giles put up a new Quote
of the Month, again from Samuel Butler, Jacqueline
weeded the garden and found a thorn-apple, poisonous
but beautiful and bearing a single white trumpet

flower among the zinnias. And at last it was time to go away, August 7.

"I won't forget to send you a card," said Melinda, recalling as she did from time to time that it was her duty to cheer old Parchment Face up.

"You'll find any numbers and addresses you may want in the directory by the phone." This from Jacqueline, while George said, "You can always send us a telegram in case of emergency."

Useless, all of it, had they but known it.

Eunice saw them off from the front door, wearing the crystal-blue glasses to allay admonition. A soft haze lay over Greeving at this early hour, a haze thickened by smoke, for Mr. Meadows was burning the stubble off his fields. Eunice didn't linger to appreciate the great purple dahlias, drenched with dew, or listen to the cuckoo's last calls before his departure. She went quickly indoors to possess what she had looked forward to.

Her purpose didn't include neglecting the house, and she went through her usual Friday routine, but with certain additional tasks. She stripped the beds, threw away the flower arrangements—more or less dead, anyway, nasty messy things, dropping petals everywhere—and hid, as best she could, every book, magazine, and newspaper. She would have liked to cover the bookcases with sheets, but only madness goes that far, and Eunice was not mad.

Then she cooked herself a dinner. The Coverdales would have called it lunch because it was eaten at one o'clock. They were not to know how dreadfully their housekeeper had missed a good solid hot meal eaten in the middle of the day. Eunice fried (fried, not grilled) a big steak from the deep freeze, fried potatoes too, while the runner beans, the carrots, and the parsnips were boiling. Apple pudding and custard to follow, biscuits and cheese and strong black tea. She washed the dishes, dried them, and put them away. It was a relief not to be obliged to use that dishwasher. She never had liked the idea of dirty plates with gravy or crumbs all over them hanging about in there all day, even though the door was shut and you couldn't see them.

Mrs. Samson used to say that a woman's work is never done. Not even the most house-proud could have found more work to be done in Lowfield Hall that day. Tomorrow she would think about taking down the morning-room curtains, but not today, not now. Now for a thoroughgoing indulgence in, an orgy of, television.

August 7 was to be recorded as the hottest day of the year. The temperature rose to seventy-eight, eighty, until by half-past two it touched eighty-five. In Greeving, jam-making housewives left their kitchens and took the sun on back doorsteps; the weir on the river Beal became a swimming pool for little Higgses and Baalhams; farm dogs hung out their tongues; Mrs. Cairne forgot discretion and lay on her front lawn in a bikini; Joan Smith propped her shop door open with a box of dog biscuits and fanned herself with a fly swat. Eunice went upstairs, drew her curtains, and settled down in deep contentment with her knitting in front of the screen. All she needed to make her happiness perfect was a bar of chocolate, but she had long ago eaten up all those she had bought in Stantwich.

Sports first. People swimming and people racing around stadiums. Then a serial about much the same sort of characters as those Eunice had known in Rainbow Street. A children's program, the news, the weather forecast. She never cared much for the news, and anyone could see and feel what the weather was and was going to be. She went downstairs and fetched herself jam sandwiches and a block of chocolate ice cream. At eight o'clock her favorite program of the entire week was due to begin, a series about policemen in Los Angeles. It is hard to say why Eunice loved it so much. Certainly she confounded those analysts of escape channels who say that an audience must identify. Eunice couldn't identify with the young police lieutenant or his twenty-year-old blond girlfriend or with the gangsters, tycoons, film stars, call girls, gamblers, and drunks who abounded in each adventure. Perhaps it was the clipped harsh repartee she liked, the inevitable car chase and the indispensable shooting. It had irked her exceedingly to miss an episode as she had often done in the past, the Coverdales seeming deliberately to single out Friday as their entertaining night.

There was no one to disturb her this time. She laid down her knitting the better to concentrate. It was going to be a good story tonight, she could tell that from the opening sequence, a corpse in the first two minutes and a car chase in the first five. The gunman's car crashed, half-mounting a lamppost. The car door opened, the gunman leaped out, across the street, firing his gun, dodging a policeman's bullets, into the shelter of a porch, pulling a frightened girl in front of him as his shield, again taking aim. . . . Suddenly the sound faded and the picture began to dwindle, to shrink, as it was sucked into a spot in the center of the screen like black water draining into a hole. The spot shone like a star, a tiny point of light that burned brightly and went out.

Eunice switched it off, switched it on again. Nothing happened. She moved knobs on the front of it and even those knobs on the back they said you should never touch. Nothing happened. She opened the plug and checked that the wires were all where they ought to be. She took out the fuse and replaced it with one from her bedlamp.

The screen remained blank, or rather, had become merely a mirror, reflecting her own dismayed face and the hot red sunset burning through a chink between the closed curtains.

8

It never occurred to her to use the color set in the
morning room. She knew it was usable, but it was
theirs. A curious feature of Eunice Parchman's
character was that, although she did not stop at murder or blackmail, she never in her life stole anything
or even borrowed anything without its owner's con-
sent. Objects, like spheres of life, were appointed,
predestined, to certain people. Eunice no more cared
to see the order of things disturbed than George did.

For a while she hoped that the set would right itself, start up as spontaneously as it had failed. But
each time she switched it on it remained blank and
silent. Of course she knew that when things went
wrong you sent for the man to put them right. In
Tooting you went round to the ironmonger's or the
electric people. But here? With only a phone and an
indecipherable list of names and numbers, a useless incomprehensible directory?

Saturday, Sunday, Monday. The milkman called
and Geoff Baalham with the eggs. Ask them and have
them tell her to look such and such a number up in
the phone book? She was cruelly bored and frus-
trated. There were no nieghbors to pass the time of
day with, no busy street to watch, no buses or tea-
shops. She took down the curtains, washed and ironed
them, washed paintwork, shampooed the carpets,
anything to pass the slow, heavy, lumbering time.

It was Eva Baalham, arriving on Wednesday, who
discovered what had happened, simply as a result of

56

asking Eunice if she had watched the big fight on the previous evening. And Eva only asked that for something to say, talking to Miss Parchman being a sticky business at the best of times.

"Broke down?" said Eva. "I reckon you'll have to have that seen to, then. My cousin Meadows that keeps the electric shop in Sudbury, he'd do that for you. I tell you what, I'll leave doing the old bits of silver till Friday and give him a ring."

A long dialogue ensued with someone called Rodge in which Eva inquired after Doris and Mum and "the boy" and "the girl" (young married people, these last, with children of their own) and finally got a promise of assistance.

"He says he'll pop in when he knocks off."

"Hope he doesn't have to take it away," said Eunice.

"Never know with the old sets, do you? You'll have to have a look at the paper instead."

Literacy is in our veins like blood. It enters every other phrase. It is next to impossible to hold a real conversation, as against an interchange of instructions and acquiescences, in which reference to the printed word is not made or in which the implications of something read do not occur.

Rodge Meadows came, and he did have to take the set away.

"Could be a couple of days, could be a week. Give me a ring if you don't hear nothing from Auntie Eva. I'm in the book."

Two days later, in the solitude and silence and boredom of Lowfield Hall, a compulsion came over Eunice. Without any idea of where to go or why she was going, she found herself changing the blue-and-white-check dress for the Crimplene suit, and then making her first unescorted assay into the outside world. She closed all the windows, bolted the front door, locked the door of the gun room, and started off down the drive. It was August 14. If the television set hadn't broken down she would never have gone. Sooner or later one of her own urges or the efforts of the Coverdales would have got her out of that house, but she would have gone in the evening or on a Sunday afternoon when Greeving Post Office and Village Store, Prop. N. Smith, would have been closed. If, if if . . . If she had been able to read, the television might still have held charms for her, but she would have looked the engineer's number up in the phone book on Saturday morning, and by Tuesday or Wednesday she would have had that set back. On Saturday the fifteenth, Rodge did, in fact, return it, but by then it was too late and the damage was done.

She didn't know where she was going. Even then, it was touch and go whether she went to Greeving at all, for she took the first turn off the lane, and two miles and three quarters of an hour later she was in Cocklefield St. Jude. Not much more than a hamlet is Cocklefield St. Jude, with an enormous church but no shop. Eunice came to a crossroads. The signpost was useless to her but she wasn't afraid of getting lost. God tempers the wind to the shorn lamb, and as compensation perhaps for her singular misfortune she had been endowed with a sense of direction and a "nose" for where she was, almost as good as an animal's. Accordingly, she took the narrowest exit from the cross, which led her down a sequestered defile, a lane no more than eight feet wide and overhung with the dark late-summer foliage of ash and oak, and where one car could not pass another without drawing deep into the hedge.

Eunice had never been in such a place in her life. A cow with a face like a great white ghost stuck its head over the hedge and lowed at her. In a sunny patch, where there was a gap in the trees, a cock pheasant with clattering feathers lolloped across in front of her, all gilded chestnut and fiery green. She marched on, head up, alarmed but resolute, knowing she was going the right way.

And so, at last, to Greeving. Into the heart of the village itself, for the lane came out opposite the Blue Boar. She turned right, and having passed the terrace of cottages inhabited by various Higgses and

Newsteads and Carters, the small Georgian mansion of Mrs. Cairne, and the discreet, soberly decorated neonless petrol station kept by Jim Meadows, she found herself on the triangle of turf outside the village store.

The shop was double-fronted, being a conversion of the ground floor of a largish, very old cottage, whose front gable was half-timbered and whose roof was badly in need of rethatching. Behind it was a garden which sloped down to the banks of the Beal that, at this point, curved out of the meadows to run under Greeving Bridge. Greeving Village store is now efficiently run by Mr. and Mrs. Mann, but at that time the two large windows held a dusty display of cereal packets, canned fruit, and baskets of not very fresh-looking tomatoes and cabbages. Eunice approached one of these windows and looked inside. The shop was empty. It was often empty, for the Smiths charged high prices while necessarily stocking only a small selection of goods. Greeving residents with cars preferred the supermarkets of Stantwich and Colchester, availing themselves only of the post-office facilities of their village store.

Eunice went in. On the left the shop was arranged for self-service with wire baskets provided. On the right was a typical sub-post-office counter and grille with, beside it, a display of sweets and cigarettes. At one time there had been a bell which rang each time the door was opened, but this had gone wrong and the Smiths had never had it mended. Therefore, no one heard her enter. Eunice examined the shelves with interest, noting the presence of various commodities she well knew from shopping expeditions in South London. But she couldn't read? Yet who does *read* the name of a product or its manufacturer's name on a packet or tin? One goes by the color and the shape and the picture as much if one is professor of etymology as an illiterate.

It was a month since she had tasted a sweet. Now she thought the most desirable thing in the world would be to have a box of chocolates. So she walked up to the counter on the left of the grille and, having waited in vain for a few seconds, she coughed. Her cough resulted in a door at the back of the shop opening and in the appearance of a woman some few years older than herself.

Joan Smith was at this time fifty, thin as a starved bird, with matchstick bones and chicken skin. Her hair was the same color as Jacqueline Coverdale's, each aiming, of course, at attaining Melinda's natural fine gold by artificial means. Jacqueline was more successful because she had more money to spend. Joan Smith's coiffure, wiry, stiff, glittering, had the look of one of the yellow metal pot scourers displayed for sale on her shelves. Her face was haphazardly painted, her hands red, rough, and untended. In her shrill voice, cockney overlaid with refinement, not unlike Annie Cole's, she asked Eunice what she could do for her.

For the first time the two women looked at each other, small blue eyes meeting sharp gray ones.

"Pound box of Black Magic, please," said Eunice.

How many thousands of pairs of people, brought together into a partnership for passion, for pain, for profit, or for disaster, have commenced their relationship with words as mundane as these?

Joan produced the chocolates. She always had a sprightly manner, coy, girlish, arch. Impossible for her simply to hand an object to anyone and take the money. First must come elaborate flourishes, a smile, a little hop that almost lifted her feet out of her Minnie Mouse shoes, her head roguishly on one side. Even toward her religion she kept up a familiar jolly attitude. The Lord was her friend, brutal to the unregenerate, but matey and intimate with the chosen, the kind of pal you might take to the pictures and have a bit of giggle with afterward over a nice cuppa.

"Eighty-five p.," said Joan, "if you *please.*" She rang it up on the till, eyeing Eunice with a little whimsical smile. "And how are they all enjoying their holiday, or haven't you heard?"

Eunice was amazed. She didn't know, and was never really to know, that very little can be kept secret in an English village. Not only did everyone in

Greeving know where the Coverdales had gone, when they had gone, when they were coming back, and roughly what their trip cost, but they were already aware that she herself had paid her first visit to the village that afternoon. Nellie Higgs and Jim Meadows had spotted her, the grapevine was at work, and her appearance and the motive for her walk would be discussed and speculated about in the Blue Boar that night. But to Eunice, that Joan Smith should recognize her and know where she worked was little short of magical divination. It awoke in her a kind of wondering admiration. It laid the foundation of her dependence on Joan and her belief, generally speaking, in the rightness of everything Joan said.

But all she said then was, "I haven't heard."

"Well, early days yet. Lovely to get away for three weeks, isn't it? Change'd be a fine thing. Ever such a nice family, aren't they? Mr. Coverdale is what I call a real gentleman of the old school, and she's a real lady. Never think she was forty-eight, would you?" Thus Joan added six years to poor Jacqueline's age from no motive but pure malice. In fact, she heartily disliked the Coverdales because they never patronized her shop, and George had been known to criticize the running of the post office. But she had no intention of admitting these feelings to Eunice until she saw how the land lay. "You're lucky to work for them, but they're lucky to have you, from all I've heard."

"I don't know," said Eunice.

"Oh, you're being modest, I can see that. A little bird told me the Hall'd never looked so spick-and-span. Makes a change, I daresay, after old Eva giving it a lick and a promise all these years. Don't you get a bit lonesome, though?"

"I've got the TV," said Eunice, beginning to expand, "and there's always a job wants doing."

"You're right. I know I'm run off my feet with this place, it's all go. Not a churchgoer, are you? No, I'd have spotted you if you'd been to St. Mary's with the family."

"I'm not religious. Never seemed to have the time."

"Ah, you don't know what you miss," said proselytizing Joan, wagging a forefinger. "But it's never too late, remember. The patience of the Lord is infinite and the bridegroom is ever ready to welcome you to His feast. Lovely weather He's sending us, isn't it, especially for those as don't have to sweat their guts out slaving for others."

"I'll be getting back now," said Eunice.

"Pity Norm's got the van or I could run you back." Joan came to the door with Eunice and turned the notice to *Closed*. "Got your chocs? That's right. Now, don't forget, if ever you're at a loose end, I'm always here. Don't be afraid of putting me out. I've always got a cup of tea and a cheery word for a friend."

"I won't," said Eunice ambiguously.

Joan waved merrily after her. Across the bridge went Eunice, and along the white lane to Lowfield Hall. She took the box of chocolates out of the paper bag, threw the bag over a hedge, and munched an orange cream. She wasn't displeased to have had a chat. Joan Smith was just the sort of person she got on best with, though the hint of getting her to church smacked a little of interference in her life. But she had noted something exceptionally soothing about their talk. The printed word or anything associated with it hadn't remotely come up.

But Eunice, with her television set returned and as good as new, wouldn't have considered seeking Joan Smith out if Joan Smith had not first come to her.

This birdlike, bright-haired, and bright-spirited little body was as devoured with curiosity about her fellowmen as Eunice was indifferent to them. She also suffered from a particular form of paranoia. She projected her feelings onto the Lord. A devout woman must not be uncharitable, so she seldom indulged her dislike of people by straight malicious gossip. It was not she who found fault with them and hated them, but God; not she but God on whom they had inflicted imaginary injuries. "Vengeance is mine, saith the Lord: I will repay." Joan Smith was merely his humble and energetic instrument.

She had long wanted to know more about the in-

terior of Lowfield Hall and the lives of its occupants
—more, that is, than she could gain by occasionally
steaming open their post. Now was her chance. She
had met Eunice, their initial chat had been entirely
satisfactory, and here was a postcard come from
Crete, from Melinda Coverdale, and addressed to
Miss E. Parchman. Joan kept it back from the regular
postwoman's bag and on the Monday she took it up
to the Hall herself.

Eunice was surprised and not a little put out to see
her. She recoiled from the postcard as from an insect
with a sting and muttered her usual defense:

"I can't see that without my glasses."

"I'll read it to you, shall I, if I won't be intruding?
'This is a super place. Temperature in the upper
80's. We have been to the Palace of Knossos where
Theseus killed the Minotaur. See you soon. Melinda.'
How lovely. Who's this Theseus, I wonder? Must have
missed that in the paper. There's always a terrible lot
of fighting and killing in those places, isn't there?
What a lovely kitchen! And you keep it like a new
pin. Eat your dinner off the floor, couldn't you?"

Relieved and gratified, Eunice came out of herself
enough to say, "I was just going to put the kettle on."

"Oh no, thank you, I couldn't stop. I've left Norm all
alone. Fancy her writing 'Melinda' like that. I will
say for her, she's no snob, though there are sides to
her life distressing to the Lord in His handmaiden."
Joan uttered this last in a brisk and practical way, as
if God had given her His opinion while dropping in
for a natter. She peered through the open door into
the passage. "Spacious, isn't it? Could I just have a
peep in the drawing room?"

"If you want," said Eunice. "I've no objection."

"Oh, they wouldn't mind. We're all friends in this
village. And speaking as one who has been a sinner
herself, I wouldn't set myself above those who haven't
found the strait gate. No, you'll never hear me say,
'Thank God I am not as other men are, even as this
publican.' Beautiful furnishings, aren't they, and in the
best of taste?"

The upshot of all this was that Joan was taken on a

tour of Lowfield Hall. Eunice, somewhat overawed by all this educated talk, wanted to show off what *she* could do, and Joan gratified her by frequent exclamations of delight. They went rather further than they should have done, Eunice opening Jacqueline's wardrobe to display her evening gowns. In Giles's room, Joan stared at the cork wall.

"Eccentric," she said.

"He's just a bit of a boy," said Eunice.

"Terrible, those spots he has, quite a disfigurement. His father's in a home for alcoholics, as of course you know." Eunice didn't, any more than anyone else did, including Jeffrey Mont. "He divorced her, and Mr. Coverdale was the corespondent, though his wife had only been dead six months. I don't sit in judgment, but I can read my Bible. 'Whosoever shall marry a divorced woman, committeth adultery.' What's he got that a bit of paper stuck up there for?"

"That's always there," said Eunice. Was she at last to discover what Giles's message to her said?

She was.

In a shrill, amazed, and outraged tone, Joan read aloud:

"'Warburg's friend said to Warburg, of his wife who was ill, "If it should please God to take one or other of us, I shall go and live in Paris.'"

This quotation from Samuel Butler had no possible application to anything in Giles's life, but he liked it and each time he read it it made him laugh.

"Blasphemous," said Joan. "I suppose it's something he's got to learn for school. Pity these teachers don't have more thought for a person's soul."

So it was something he had to learn for school. By now Eunice felt quite warmly toward Joan Smith, sent by some kindly power to enlighten her and set her mind at rest.

"You won't say no to that cup of tea now, will you?" she said when, the carpet, bathroom, and television set having been admired (though not, according to Joan, good enough for a superior housekeeper like yourself, more a companion really), they were once more in the kitchen.

"I shouldn't, not with Norm all on his own-io, but if you twist my arm."

Joan Smith stayed for a further hour, during which time she told Eunice a number of lies about the Coverdales' private life, and attempted unsuccessfully to elicit from her hostess details of hers. Eunice was only a little more forthcoming than she had been at their first meeting. She wasn't going to tell this woman, helpful as she had been, all about Mum and Dad and Rainbow Street and the sweetshop, not she. Nor was she prepared to go with Joan to some prayer meeting in Colchester on the following Sunday. What, swap her Sunday-evening spy serial for hymn singing with a lot of cranks?

Joan didn't take offense.

"Well, I'll say thanks for the magical mystery tour and your generous hospitality. And now I must be on my way or Norm'll think I've met with an accident."

She laughed merrily at this prospect of her husband's anxiety and drove off in the van, calling "Cheeri-bye" all the way down the drive.

9

The relationship between Eunice Parchman and Joan Smith was never of a lesbian nature. They bore no resemblance to the Papin sisters, who, while cook and housemaid to a mother and daughter in Le Mans, murdered their employers in 1933. Eunice had nothing in common with them except that she also was female and a servant. She was an almost sexless being, without normal or abnormal desires, whose vague rest-

lessness over the Eu-nicey-mother-of-Timothy business had long ago been allayed. As for Joan Smith,
she had exhausted her sexual capacities. It is probable
that, like Queen Victoria in the anecdote, Eunice,
for all her adventurous wanderings, did not know
what lesbianism was. Joan Smith certainly knew, had
very likely experimented with it, as she had experimented with most things.

For the first sixteen years of her life Joan Smith,
or Skinner as she then was, led an existence which
any psychologist would have seen as promising to result in a well-adjusted, worthy, and responsible member of society. She was not beaten or neglected or
deserted. On the contrary, she was loved, cherished,
and encouraged. Her father was an insurance salesman, quite prosperous. The family lived in a house
which they owned in the better part of Kilburn, the
parents were happily married, and Joan had three
brothers older than herself who were all fond of and
kind to their little sister. Mr. and Mrs. Skinner had
longed for a daughter and been ecstatic when they
got one. Because she was seldom left to her own de-
vices but talked to and played with almost from
birth, she learned to read when she was four, went
happily off to school before she was five, and by the
age of ten showed promise of being cleverer than any
of her brothers. She passed the Scholarship and went
to the high school, where she later gained her School
Certificate, with the fairly unusual distinction, her results were so good, of an exemption from Matricula-
tion.

The war was on and Joan, like Eunice Parchman,
had gone away from London with her school. But to
foster parents as kind and considerate as her own.
For no apparent reason, suddenly and out of the blue,
she walked into the local police station in Wiltshire,
where she accused her foster father of raping and
beating her, and she showed bruises to support this
charge. Joan was found not to be a virgin. The foster
father was charged with rape but acquitted because
of his sound and perfectly honest alibi. Joan was

taken home by her parents, who naturally believed there had been a miscarriage of justice. But she only stayed a week before decamping to join the author of her injuries, a baker's roundsman in Salisbury. He was a married man, but he left his wife and Joan stayed with him for five years. When he went to prison for defaulting on the maintenance payments to his wife and two children, she left him and returned to London. But not to her parents, whose letters she had steadfastly refused to answer.

Another couple of years went by, during which Joan worked as a barmaid, but she was dismissed for helping herself from the till, and she drifted into a kind of suburban prostitution. She and another girl shared a couple of rooms in Shepherds Bush, where they entertained an artisan clientele who paid them unbelievably low rates for their services. From this life, when she was thirty, Joan was rescued by Norman Smith.

A weak and innocent creature, he met Joan when she was to a hairdresser's in Harlesden for a tint and perm. One side of this establishment was for the ladies, the other a barbershop, but there was much coming and going on the part of the assistants, and Norman often stopped for a chat with Joan while she was under the dryer. She was almost the first woman he had looked at, certainly the first he had asked out. But she was so kind and sweet and friendly, he didn't feel at all intimidated. He fell violently in love with her and asked her to marry him the second time he found himself alone with her. Joan accepted with alacrity.

Norman had no idea how she had earned her living, believing her story that she had taken in typing and occasionally been a free-lance secretary. They lived with his mother. After a year or two of furious daily quarrels with old Mrs. Smith, Joan found the best way of keeping her quiet was to encourage her hitherto controlled fondness for the bottle. Gradually she got Mrs. Smith to the stage of spending her savings on half a bottle of whiskey a day.

"It would kill Norman if he found out," said Joan.

"Don't you tell him, Joanie."

"You'd better see you're in bed then when he comes home. That poor man idolizes you, he puts you on a pedestal. It'd break his heart to know you were boozing all day, and under his roof too."

So old Mrs. Smith, with Joan's encouragement, became a self-appointed invalid. For most of each day she was in bed with her whiskey, and Joan helped matters along by crushing into the sugar in her tea three or four of the tranquilizers the doctor had prescribed for her own "nerves." With her mother-in-law more or less comatose, Joan returned by day to the old life and the flat in Shepherds Bush. She made very little money at it, and her sexual encounters had become distasteful to her. A remarkable fact about Joan was that, though she had had sexual relations with hundreds of men as well as with her own husband, she had never made love for pleasure or had a "conventional" illicit affair except with the baker's roundsman. It is hard to know why she continued as a prostitute. Out of perversity perhaps, or as a way of defying Norman's extreme working-class respectability.

If so, it was a secret way, for he never found her out. It was she eventually who boldly and ostentatiously confessed it all to him.

And that came about as the result of her conversion. Since she was fourteen—and she was now nearly forty—she had never given a thought to religion. But all that was necessary to turn her into a raving Bible-thumper was a call at her front door by a man representing a sect called the Epiphany People.

"Not today, thanks," said Joan, but having nothing better to do that afternoon, she glanced through the magazine, or tract, he had left on the doorstep. By one of those coincidences that are always happening, she found herself on the following day actually passing the Epiphany People's temple. Of course it wasn't really a coincidence. She had passed it a hundred times before but had never previously noticed what it was. A prayer meeting was beginning. Out of curiosity Joan went in—and was saved.

The Epiphany People were a sect founded in California in the 1920's by a retired undertaker called Elroy Camps. Epiphany, of course, is January 6, the day on which the Magi are traditionally supposed to have arrived in Bethlehem to bear witness to the birth of Christ and to bring him gifts. Elroy Camps and his followers saw themselves as "Wise Men" to whom a special revelation had been granted: that is, they and only they had witnessed the divine manifestation, and hence only they and a select band of the chosen would find salvation. Indeed, Elroy Camps believed himself to be a reincarnation of one of the Magi and was known in the sect as Balthasar.

A strict morality was adhered to, members of the sect must attend the temple, pay a minimum of a hundred proselytizing house calls a year, and hold to the belief that within a very short time there would be a second Epiphany in which they, the new wise men, would be chosen and the rest of the world cast into outer darkness. Their meetings were vociferous and dramatic, but merry too with tea and cakes and film shows. New members were called upon to confess their sins in public, after which the rest of the brethren would burst into spontaneous comment and end by singing hyms. Most of these had been written by Balthasar himself.

The following is an example:

As the Wise Men came riding in days long gone by,
So we ride to Jesus with hearts held up high;
Bearing our sins as they bore him presents,
That shall be washed white in his holy essence.

At first it seems a mystery why all this should have made an appeal to Joan. But she had always loved drama, especially drama of a nature shocking to other people. She heard a woman confess her sins, loudly proclaiming such petty errors as bilking London Transport, fraudulent practice with regard to her housekeeping money, and visits to a theater. How much better than that could she do! She was forty, and even she could see that, with her faded fair hair and fine pale skin, she hadn't worn well. What next? A grim obscure domesticity in Harlesden with old Mrs. Smith, or the glorious publicity the Epiphany People could give her. Besides, it might all be true. Very soon she was to believe entirely in its truth.

She made the confession of the year. It all came out. The congregation were stunned by the revelation of Joan's excesses, but she had been promised forgiveness and she got it, as much as the woman who had traveled on the tube without a ticket got it.

Joan, the faithless wife, opened her heart to a stunned and disillusioned Norman. Joan, the evangelist, went from house to house in Harlesden and Wood Lane and Shepherds Bush, not only distributing tracts but recounting to her listeners how, until the Lord called her, she had been a "harlot" and a scarlet woman.

"I was arrayed in purple and scarlet color," said Joan on the doorstep. "I had a golden cup in my hand full of the abominations and filthiness of my fornication. I was the hold of every unclean spirit and a cage of every unclean and hateful bird."

It wasn't long before some wit was making snide cracks while in the barber's chair about unclean and hateful birds. In vain did Norman ask his wife to stop it. He had suffered enough in learning of her former mode of life without this. The street buzzed with it and the boys called after him as he went to work.

But how do you reproach a woman who has reformed, who counters every reproof with a total agreement? "I know that, Norm, I know I was steeped in lowness and filth. I sinned against you and the Lord. I was a lost soul, plunged in the abominations of iniquity."

"I just wish you wouldn't tell everyone," said Norman.

"Balthasar said there is no private atonement."

Then old Mrs. Smith died. Joan was never at home and she was left all day in a cold and filthy house.

She got out of bed, fell, and lay on the floor for seven hours in only a thin nightgown. That night, not long after Norman had found her, she died in hospital. Cause of death: hypothermia. In other words, she had died of exposure. Again the street buzzed, and it was not only schoolboys who called after Norman.

His mother had left him the house and a thousand pounds. Norman was one of those people—and they are legion—whose ambition is to keep a country pub or shop. He had never lived in the country or run a grocer's, but that was what he wanted. He underwent training with the Post Office, and at about the same time as the Coverdales bought Lowfield Hall, he and Joan found themselves proprietors of Greeving Village Store. Greeving, because the only other Epiphany Temple in the country was in Nunchester.

The Smiths ran the store with disastrous inefficiency. Sometimes it opened at nine, sometimes at eleven. The post office was, of course, open during its prescribed hours, but Joan (for all her virtuous protestations to Eunice) left Norman in sole charge for hours and he couldn't leave his cubbyhole behind the grille to serve other customers. Those who had been regulars drifted away. The rest, compelled through carelessness to allegiance, grumbled ferociously. Joan investigated the mails. It was her duty, she said, to find out the sinners who surrounded her. She steamed open envelopes and reglued them. Norman watched in misery and despair, longing for the courage to hit her and hoping against all odds and his own nature that he would one day find it.

They had no children and now Joan was passing through what she called an "early change." Considering she was fifty, it might have been thought that her menopause was neither early nor late, but right on time.

"Norm and I always longed for kiddies," she was in the habit of saying, "but they never came. The Lord knew best, no doubt, and it's not for us to question His ways."

No doubt He did. One wonders what Joan Smith

would have done with children if she had had them.
Eaten them, perhaps.

10

For a long time George Coverdale had suspected one
of the Smiths of tampering with his post. Only a week
before he went on holiday an envelope containing a
letter from his son Peter showed a glue smear under
the flap, and a parcel from the book club to which
Jacqueline subscribed had obviously been opened
and retied with string. But he hesitated to take action without positive proof.

He hadn't set foot in the shop or used the post office since the day, some three years before, when, in
front of an interested audience of farm laborers'
wives, Joan had gaily reproached him for living with
a divorced woman and exhorted him to abandon his
sinful life and come to God. After that he had
posted his letters in Stantwich and given Joan no
more than a stiff nod when he met her in the village.
He would have been appalled had he known she had
been in his bedroom, fingered his clothes, and toured
his house.

But when he and his family returned from holiday
there was no sign that Eunice had defected from her
established ways.

"I don't believe she's been out of the house, darling," said Jacqueline.

"Yes, she has." Village gossip always reached them
by way of Melinda. "Geoff told me. He got it from
Mrs. Higgs, the Mrs. Higgs who rides the bike, she's

his grandma's sister-in-law. She saw her out for a walk in Greeving."

"Good," said George. "If she's happy pottering about the village, I won't press her about the driving lessons. But if you should get it via the bush telegraph that she's got hankerings to learn, perhaps you'll let me know."

Late summer, early autumn, and the vegetation seemed to become too much for man and nature itself to control. The flowers grew too tall and too straggly, the hedges overbrimmed with leaves, with berries and tendrils of the bryony, and the wild clematis, the Old Man's Beard, cast over all its filmy fluffy cloak. Melinda went blackberrying, Jacqueline made bramble jelly. Eunice had never before seen jam being made. As far as she had known, if it didn't exactly descend like manna from heaven, at least it was only available in jars from a shop. Giles picked no blackberries, nor did he attend the Harvest Festival at St. Mary's. On the cork wall he pinned a text of his own, a line that might have been written for him: *Some say life is the thing, but I prefer reading,* and he went on struggling through the Upanishads.

Pheasant shooting began. Eunice saw George go into the gun room, take the shotguns down from the wall and, leaving the door to the kitchen open, clean and load them. She watched with interest but in innocence, having no idea of their being of future use to her.

George cleaned and loaded both guns, but not because he had any hope of Giles accompanying him on the shoot. He had bought the second gun for his stepson, just as he had bought the fishing tackle and the fat white horse, now eating its head off down in the meadow. Three autumns of apathy and then downright opposition on Giles's part had taught George to abandon hope of making him a sportsman. So the second gun was lent to Francis Jameson-Kerr, stockbroker son of the brigadier.

Pheasants were plentiful, and from the kitchen window, then from the kitchen garden where she went to cut a cabbage, Eunice watched the three of them bag four brace and a hen bird. A brace for the Jameson-Kerrs, a brace each for Peter and Paula, the remaining birds for Lowfield Hall. Eunice wondered how long the bloodied bundles of feathers were to be hung in the back kitchen before she had the pleasure of tasting this hitherto unknown flesh. But she wasn't going to ask, not she. A week later Jacqueline roasted them, and as Eunice tucked into the thick slice of breast on her plate, three little round pellets of shot rolled out into the gravy.

The shopping was always done by Jacqueline, or a list phoned by Jacqueline to a Stantwich store and the goods later collected by George. It was a chronic source of anxiety to Eunice that one day she might be called on to phone that list, and one Tuesday in late September this happened.

The phone rang at eight in the morning. It was Lady Royston to say that she had fallen, thought she had broken her arm, and could Jacqueline drive her to hospital in Colchester? Sir Robert had taken one car, her son the other, and then, having taken it into her head to begin picking the apple crop at the early hour of seven-thirty, she had climbed the ladder and slipped on a broken rung.

The Coverdales were still at breakfast. "Poor darling Jessica," said Jacqueline, "she sounded in such pain. I'll get over there straight away. The shopping list's ready, George, so Miss Parchman can phone it through when the shop opens, and then perhaps you'll be an angel and pick it up?"

George and Giles finished their breakfast in a silence broken only by George's remarking, in the interest of being a good stepfather, that such a brilliant start to the day could only indicate rain later. Giles, who was thinking about an advertisement he had seen in *Time Out* asking for a tenth passenger in a minibus to Poona, said "Could it?" and he didn't know anything about meterology. Eunice came in to clear the table.

"My wife's had to go out on an errand of mercy,"

said George, made pompous by Eunice's forbidding presence, "so perhaps you'll be good enough to get on to this number and order what's on the list."

"Yes, sir," said Eunice automatically.

"Ready in five minutes, Giles? Give it till after nine-thirty, will you, Miss Parchman? These shops don't keep the early hours they did in our young days."

Eunice stared at the list. She could read the phone number and that was about all. By now George had disappeared to get the Mercedes out. Giles was upstairs. Melinda was spending the last week of her holiday with a friend in Lowestoft. The beginning of a panic stirring, Eunice thought of asking Giles to read the list to her—one reading would be enough for her memory—on the grounds that her glasses were somewhere up at the top of the house. But the excuse was too feeble as she had an hour in which to fetch those glasses herself, and now, anyway, Giles was crossing the hall in his vague sleepwalking way, leaving the house, slamming the front door behind him. In despair, she sat down in the kitchen among the dirty dishes.

All her efforts went into rousing some spark out of that atrophied organ, her imagination. By now an inventive woman would have found ways of combating the problem. She would have said she had broken her reading glasses (and trodden on them to prove it) or feigned illness or fabricated a summons to London to the bedside of a sick relative. Eunice could only think of actually taking the list to the Stantwich store and handing the list to the manager. But how to get there? She knew there was a bus, but not where it stopped, only that the stop was two miles distant; not when it ran or where precisely it went or even where the shop was. Presently habit compelled her to stack the dishes in the washer, wipe clean the surface, go upstairs to make the beds and gaze sullenly at Giles's Quote of the Month, which would have had a peculiarly ironical application to herself had she been able to understand it. Nine-fifteen. Eva Baalham didn't come on Tuesdays, the milkman had already been. Not that Eunice would have dared expose herself by asking for enlightenment from these people. She would have to tell Jacqueline that she had forgotten to phone, and if Jacqueline came back in time to do it herself . . . She glanced up again at the cork wall, and then into her mind came a clear picture of having stood just here with Joan Smith.

Joan Smith.

No very lucid plan had formed. Eunice was just as anxious for Joan Smith not to know her secret as for Eva or the milkman or Jacqueline not to know it. But Joan too had a grocer's shop, and once the list was in her hands, there might be a way. She put her best hand-knitted cardigan on over her pink cotton frock and set off for Greeving.

"Long time no see," said Joan, sparkling. "You are a stranger! This is Norman, my better half. Norm, this is Miss Parchman from the Hall I was telling you about."

"Pleased to meet you," said Norman Smith from behind his grille. Enclosed by bars, he had the look of some gloomy ruminant animal, a goat or llama perhaps, which has too long been in captivity to recall its freedom but still frets dully within its cage. His face was wedge-shaped, white and bony, his hair sandy gray. As if he were sustaining the cud-chewing image, he munched spearmint all day long. This was because Joan said he had bad breath.

"Now, to what do we owe the pleasure of your visit?" said Joan. "Don't tell me Mrs. Coverdale's going to patronize our humble abode at last. That *would* be a red-letter day."

"I've got this list." Looking vaguely about her at the shelves, Eunice thrust the list at Joan.

"Let me see. We *have* got the plain flour and the oats, that I do know. But, my goodness, kidney beans and basil leaves and garlic!" The bad shopkeeper's excuse came to Joan's aid. "We're waiting for them to come in," she said. "But, I tell you what, you read it out and I'll check what we do have."

"No, you read it. I'll check."

"There's me being tactless again! Ought to remember your eye trouble, didn't I? Here goes, then."

Eunice, checking and finding only two items available, knew that she was saved, for Joan read the list out in a clear slow voice. It was enough. She bought the flour and the oats, which would have to be hidden, would have to be paid for out of her own money, but what did that matter? A warm feeling for Joan, who had saved her again, welled in Eunice. Dimly she remembered feeling something like this long ago, ages ago, for her mother, before Mrs. Parchman became ill and dependent. Yes, she would have the cup of tea Joan was offering, and take the weight off her feet for ten minutes.

"You'll just have to phone that Stantwich place," said Joan, who thought she saw it all, that Eunice had come to the village store off her own bat. "Use our phone, go on. Here's your list. Got your glasses?"

Eunice had. The ones with the tortoiseshell frames. While Joan bustled about with the teacups, she made her call, almost dizzy with happiness. Appearing to read aloud what she in fact remembered brought her a pleasure comparable to, but greater than, the pride of a traveler who has one idiomatic French phrase and chances to bring it out successfully at the right time without evoking from his listener a single question. Seldom did it happen to her to *prove* she could read. And, putting the phone down, she felt toward Joan the way we do feel toward those in whose hearing we have demonstrated our prowess in the field where we least possess it—warm, prideful, superior yet modest, ready to be expansive. She praised the "lovely old room," ignoring its untidy near-squalor, and she was moved so far as to compliment Joan on her hair, her floral dress, and the quality of her chocolate biscuits.

"Fancy them expecting you to hump all that lot back," said Joan, who knew they hadn't. "Well, they say he's a hard man, reaping where he has not sown and gathering where he has not stored. I'll run you home, shall I?"

"I'd be putting you out."

"Not at all. My pleasure." Joan marched Eunice through the shop, ignoring her husband, who was peering disconsolately inside a sack as into a nosebag. The old green van started after some heavy manipulation with the choke and kicks at the accelerator. "Home, James, and don't spare the horses!"

The van coughed its way up the lane. Joan took Eunice to the front door of Lowfield Hall. "Now, one good turn deserves another, and I've got a little book here I want you to read." She produced a tract entitled *God Wants You for a Wise Man*. "And you'll pop along to our next meeting with me, won't you? Sunday night. I won't call for you, but you be in the lane at half-five and I'll pick you up. Okay?"

"All right," said Eunice.

"Oh, you'll love it. We don't have a prayer book like those church people, just singing and love and uttering what comes into our hearts. And then there's tea and a chat with the brethren. God wants us to be joyful, my dear, when we have given our all to Him. But for those who deny Him there shall be weeping and gnashing of teeth. Did you knit your cardigan yourself? I think it's smashing. Don't forget your flour and your oats."

Well content, Joan drove back to Norman and the store. It might seem that she had nothing to gain from friendship with Eunice Parchman, but in fact she was badly in need of a satellite in the village. Norman had become a cipher, not much more than a shell of a man, since his wife's revelations of what his early married life had truly been. They hardly spoke these days, and Joan had given up pretending to her acquaintances that they were an ideal couple. Indeed, she told everyone that Norman was her cross, though one that it was her duty as his wife to bear, but that he had turned his back on God and so could be no companion for such as she. God was displeased with him. Therefore she, as His handmaid, must concur in that displeasure. These pronouncements, made publicly along with others implying that Joan had the infallibility of God's personal assistant, had put off such Higgses, Baalhams, and Newsteads as might have become her friends. People said good morning to her but otherwise ostracized her. They thought she was mad, as she probably was even then.

She saw Eunice as malleable and green. And also, to do her justice, as a lost sheep who might be brought to the Colchester fold. It would be a triumph for her, and pleasant, to have a faithful admiring attendant to introduce to the Epiphany People and be seen by unregenerate Greeving as her special pal.

Eunice, flushed with success, turned out the morning room, and was actually washing down its ivory-painted walls when Jacqueline came back.

"Heavens, what a rush! Poor Lady Royston's got a multiple fracture of her left arm. Spring cleaning in September? You're an indefatigable worker, Miss Parchman. I hardly like to ask if you saw to my shopping list."

"Oh yes, madam. Mr. Coverdale will pick it up at five."

"That's marvelous. And now I'm going to have an enormous sherry before my lunch. Why don't you have a break and join me?"

But this Eunice refused. Apart from a rare glass of wine at a relative's wedding or funeral, she had never tasted alcohol. This was one of the few things she had in common with Joan Smith, who, though fond enough of a gin or a Guinness in her Shepherds Bush days, had eschewed liquor on signing the Epiphany pledge. *God Wants You for a Wise Man* necessarily remained unread, but Eunice went to the meeting, where no one expected her to read anything. She enjoyed the ride in Joan's van, the singing and the tea, and by the time they were back in Greeving a date had been made for her to have supper with the Smiths on Wednesday, and they were Joan and Eunice to each other. They were friends. In the sterile existence of Eunice Parchman, Mrs. Samson and Annie Cole had a successor.

Melinda went back to college, George shot more pheasants, Jacqueline planted bulbs and trimmed the shrubs and cheered up Lady Royston, Giles learned gloomily that the tenth place in the bus to Poona had been filled. Leaves turned from dark green to bleached gold, the apples were all gathered and the cob nuts ripened. The cuckoo had long gone, and now the swallows and the flycatchers departed for the south.

On Greeving Green the hunt met and rode down the lane to kill two hours later in Marleigh Wood.

"Good morning, Master," said George at his gate to Sir Robert Royston—George, who would call him Bob at any other time.

And "Good morning, sir," said Bob in his pink coat and hard hat.

October, with its false summer, its warm sadness, mists and mellow fruitfulness and sunshine turning to gold the haze that lingered over the river Beal.

11

Melinda would have learned that when Eunice went out, as she now frequently did, it was to visit Joan Smith, and that when she set off in the dusk on Sunday evenings the Smiths' van was waiting for her at the end of the drive. But Melinda was back at college and had returned to her father's house only once in the month since her departure. And on that one occasion she had been very quiet and preoccupied for her, not going out but playing records or sitting silent and deep in thought. For Melinda had fallen in love.

So although every inhabitant of Greeving who was not an infant or senile followed with close interest the Parchman-Smith alliance, the Coverdales knew nothing about it. Often they didn't know that Eunice wasn't in the house, so unobtrusive was she when there. Nor did they know that when they went out Joan Smith came in and passed many a pleasant evening with Eunice, drinking tea and watching television on the top floor. Giles, of course, was invariably in. But they took care not to speak on the stairs, the thick carpet muffled the sound of an extra set of footsteps, and they passed unseen and unheard by him into Eunice's bedroom, where the incessant drone of the television masked the murmur of their voices.

And yet that friendship would have foundered in its earliest days had Eunice had her way. The warmth she felt for Joan when her delight over the deciphering of the shopping list subsided, and she began to look on Joan, as she had always looked on most people, as someone to be used. Not to be blackmailed for money this time, but rather to be placed in her power as Annie Cole had been, so that she could always be relied on as an interpreter and trusted not to divulge her secret if she discovered it.

It looked as if Eva Baalham had delivered Joan into her hands.

Eva was disgruntled these days because, although she now had more rewarding employment with Mrs. Jameson-Kerr, her working hours at Lowfield Hall had been reduced to one morning a week. And this demotion she blamed on Eunice, who did with ease all the jobs she used to groan over and, if the truth were admitted, did them a lot better. As soon as she thought she saw a way of needling Eunice, she set about doing so.

"I reckon you're very pally with that Mrs. Smith then."

"I don't know," said Eunice.

"Always in and out of each other's places. That's what I call very pally. My cousin Meadows that's got the garage, he saw you out in her van last week. Maybe there's things about her you don't know."

"What?" said Eunice, breaking her rule.

"Like what she was before she came here. A street woman, she was, no better than a common prostitute." Eva wasn't going to destroy the esoteric quality of this by saying it was generally known. "Used to go with men, and her husband never knew a thing, poor devil."

That night Eunice was invited to the Smiths' for supper. They ate what she liked and never got at Lowfield Hall, eggs and bacon and sausages and chips. Afterward she had a chocolate bar from the shop. Norman sat silent at the table, then departed for the Blue Boar, where, out of pity, some Higgs or Newstead would play darts with him. Bumper cups of tea were served. Joan leaned confidingly across the table and began to preach the gospel according to Mrs. Smith. Having finished the last square of her fudge wafer, Eunice seized her opportunity.

She interrupted Joan in her louder, more commanding voice. "I've heard something about you."

"Something nice, I hope," said Joan brightly.

"Don't know about nice. That you used to go with men for money, that's what I heard."

A kind of holy ecstasy radiated Joan's raddled face. She banged her flat bosom with her fist. "Oh, I was a sinner!" she declaimed. "I was scarlet with sin and steeped in the foulest mire. I went about the city as an harlot, but God called me and, lo, I heard Him! I shall never forget the day I confessed my sins before the multitude of the brethren and opened my heart to my husband. With true humility, dear, I have laid bare my soul to all who would hear, so that the people may know even the blackest shall be saved. Have another cup, do."

Amazement transfixed Eunice. No potential blackmail victim had ever behaved like this. Her respect for Joan became almost boundless and, floored, she held out her cup meekly.

Did Joan guess? Perhaps. She was a clever woman and a very experienced one. If it were so, the hoisting of Eunice with her own petard must have brought her enormous amusement without in the least alienating her. After all, she expected people to be sinners. She wasn't a Wise Man for nothing.

The yellow leaves were falling, oak and ash and elm, and the redder foliage of the dogwood. What flowers remained had been blackened by the first hard frost, and fungus grew under hedges and on fallen trees, the oyster mushroom and the amethyst agaric. Rethatching began on James Newstead's cottage, his garden filled with the golden straw from a whole wheatfield.

George in dinner jacket and Jacqueline in a red silk gown embroidered with gold went to Covent Garden to see *The Clemency of Titus* and spent the night at Paula's. The Quote of the Month was from Mallarmé: *The flesh is sad, alas, and I have read all the books.* But Giles, far from having read all the books, was deep in Poe. If, as seemed likely, he was never going to make it to India, he might ask Melinda to share a flat with him when they had completed their educations. A Gothic-mansion flat was what he had in mind, in West Kensington, say, a kind of diminutive House of Usher with floors of ebon blackness and feeble gleams of encrimsoned light making their way through the trellised panes.

But Melinda, unknown to him, was in love. Jonathan Dexter was his name, and he was reading modern languages. George Coverdale had often wondered, though never spoken his thoughts aloud even to Jacqueline, whether his younger daughter was as innocent as her mother had been at her age. But he doubted it, and was resigned to her having followed the current trend of permissiveness. He would, in fact, have been surprised and pleased had he known Melinda was still a virgin, though anxious if he had guessed how near she was to changing that irrevocable condition.

Now that the ice was, as it were, broken, Eunice often went out walking. As she had roved London, so she roved the villages, marching from Cocklefield to Marleigh, Marleigh to Cattingham, through the leaf-strewn lanes and, as St. Luke's little summer gave place to the deep of autumn, daring the still-dry footpaths that crossed the fields and skirted the woods. She walked purposelessly, not pausing to look, through breaks in the trees, at the long blue vistas of wooded slopes and gentle valleys, hardly noticing the countryside at all. Here it was the same for her as it had been in London. She walked to satisfy some craving for freedom and to use up that energy housework could not exhaust.

She and Joan Smith never communicated by phone. Joan would arrive in the van when she was sure Lowfield Hall was empty but for Eunice. Whatever friend she visited, Jacqueline must pass through Greeving, and she seldom passed without being observed by Joan from the village store. And then Joan would drive up to the Hall, make her way in through the gun room without knocking, and within two minutes Eunice had the kettle on.

"Her life's just one round of amusement. Sherry-partying with that Mrs. Cairne she is this morning. One can just imagine what goes on in the mind of God when He looks down on that sort of thing. The wicked shall flourish like the green bay tree, but in the morning they were not, nay, they were not to be found. I've got four calls to make in Cocklefield this morning, dear, so I won't stop a minute." By calls Joan didn't mean store or postal deliveries, but proselytizing visits. As usual, she was armed with a stack of tracts, including a new one got up to look like a comic and artfully entitled *Follow My Star*.

So fervid an Epiphany Person was she that often when Eunice called, during her walks, at the store only Norman was found to be in charge. And then, from behind the bars of his cage, he shook his head lugubriously.

"She's off out somewhere."

But sometimes Eunice called in time to be taken with Joan on her rounds, and from the passenger seat in the van she watched her friend preaching on cottage doorsteps.

"I wonder if you have time to spare today to glance at a little book I've brought . . ."

Or around the council estates that clung to the

fringe of each village, red-brick boxes screened from the ancient settlement by a barrier of conifers. Occasionally a naive householder asked Joan in, and then she was gone some time. But more often the door was shut in her face and she would return to the van, radiant with the glow of martyrdom.

"I admire the way you take it," said Eunice. "I'd give them as good as I got."

"The Lord requires humility of His servants, Eun. Remember, there are some who will be carried by the angels into Abraham's bosom and some who will be tormented by the flame. Don't let me forget to stop at Meadows', we're nearly out of petrol."

They presented a strange sight, those two, to the indignant watcher as she dropped *Follow My Star* into her dustbin. Joan so spindly with bones like those of a starved child pictured in a charity appeal, her religion having done nothing to conquer her ingrained habit, almost unconscious now, of getting herself up in whore's garb: short skirt, black "glass" stockings, down-at-heel patent shoes, great shiny handbag, and fleecy white jacket with big shoulders. Her hair was like an inverted bird's nest, if birds ever built with golden wire, and on her pinched little face the makeup was rose and blue and scarlet.

Eunice might have been chosen as the perfect foil to her. She had added to her wardrobe since coming to Lowfield Hall only such garments as she had knitted herself, and on those chilly autumn days she wore a round woolly cap and a scarf of dark gray-blue. In her thick maroon-colored coat, she towered above Joan, and the contrast was best seen when they walked side by side, Joan teetering and taking small rapid steps, Eunice Junoesque with her erect carriage and steady stride.

In her heart, each thought the other looked a fool, but this did not alienate them. Friendship often prospers best when one party is sure she has an ascendency over the other. Without letting on, Eunice thought Joan brilliantly clever, to be relied on for help whenever she might be confronted by reading matter, but mutton dressed as silly young lamb all the same, a hopeless housewife and a slattern. Without letting on, Joan saw Eunice as eminently respectable, a possible bodyguard too if Norman should ever attempt to carry out his feeble threat of beating her up, but why dress like a policewoman?

Joan made Eunice presents of chocolate each time she came to the shop. Eunice had knitted Joan a pair of gloves in her favorite salmon pink and was thinking of beginning on a jumper.

All Saints', November 1, was Jacqueline's forty-third birthday. George gave her a sheepskin jacket, Giles a record of Mozart concert arias. Melinda sent a card with a scrawled promise of "something nice when I get around to coming home." The parcel, containing a new novel, which arrived from Peter and Audrey, had obviously been opened and resealed. George marched off to Greeving Post Office and Village Store and complained to Norman Smith. But what to say in answer to Norman's defense that the book on arrival was half out of its wrappings and that his wife had repacked it herself for safety's sake? George could only nod and say he wouldn't take it further—for the present.

That week he went for his annual checkup to Dr. Crutchley and was told his blood pressure was up, nothing to worry about but you'd better go on these tablets. George wasn't a nervous man or one who easily panicked, but he decided he had better make his will, a proceeding he had been procrastinating about for years. It was this will which has given rise to the litigation that still continues, that keeps Lowfield Hall ownerless and deserted, that has soured the lives of Peter Coverdale and Paula Caswall and keeps the tragedy fresh in their minds. But it was carefully drawn up, with all forethought. Who then could have foreseen what would happen on St. Valentine's Day? What lawyer, however circumspect, could have imagined a massacre at peaceful Lowfield Hall?

A copy of the will was shown to Jacqueline when she got home from a meeting of the parish council.

" 'To my beloved wife, Jacqueline Louise Coverdale,' "

she read aloud, " 'the whole of my property known as Lowfield Hall, Greeving, in the county of Suffolk, unencumbered, and to be hers and her heirs' and successors' in perpetuity.' Oh, darling, 'beloved wife'! I'm glad you put that."

"What else?" said George.

"But shouldn't it just be for my life? I've got all the money Daddy left me, and what I got for my house, and there'd be your life assurance."

"Yes, and that's why I've willed all my investments to the girls and Peter. But I want you to have the house, you love it so. Besides, I hate those pettifogging arrangements where the widow only gets a life interest. She's a nonpaying tenant to a bunch of people who can't wait for her to die."

"Your children wouldn't be like that."

"I don't think they would, Jackie, but the will stands. If you predecease me, I've directed that the Hall is to be sold after my death and the proceeds divided between my heirs."

Jacqueline looked up at him. "I hope I do."

"Hope you do what, darling?"

"Die first. That's what I mind about your being older than me, that you're almost certain to die first. I might be a widow for years, I can't bear the thought of it, I can't imagine a single day without you."

George kissed her. "Let's *not* talk of wills and graves and epitaphs," he said, so they talked about the parish-council meeting instead, and fund-raising for the new village hall, and Jacqueline forgot the hope she had expressed.

It was not destined to be gratified, though she was to be a widow for only fifteen minutes.

12

The Epiphany Temple in Nunchester is on North
Hill just above the cattle market. Therefore it is not
necessary when driving there from Greeving to pass
through the town, and Joan Smith could make the
journey in twenty minutes. Eunice enjoyed the Sunday-night meetings. Hymn sheets were provided, but
as anyone knows who has tried to give the impression
that he has the Church of England morning service
off by heart (actually to use the Prayer Book being
to betray unpardonable ignorance), it is quite easy to
mouth what other people are mouthing and muffle
one's lack of knowledge in folded hands brought to
the lips. Besides, Eunice had only to hear a hymn
once to know it forever, and soon, in her strong con-
tralto, she was singing with the best of them:

Gold is the color of our Lord above,
And frankincense the perfume of His love;
Myrrh is the ointment which, with might and
   main,
He pours down from heaven to heal us of our pain.

Elroy Camps was no Herbert or Keble.
After the hymns and some spontaneous confessing
—almost as good as television, this bit—the brethren
had tea and biscuits and watched films about black or
brown Epiphany People struggling on in remote
places (*in partibus infidelium,* as it were) or delivering the Epistle of Balthasar to famine-stricken persons

too weak to resist. Also there was friendly gossip, mostly about worldly people who hadn't seen the light, but uttered in a pious way and shoving the onus of censure and blame off onto God. Certainly the brethren honored the precept of "Come unto me, all ye that labor and are heavy laden, and I will give you rest."

On the whole, they were and are a jolly lot. They sing and laugh and enter with gusto into their own confessions and those of new converts. They talk of God as if He were a trendy headmaster who likes the senior boys to call Him by His Christian name. Their hymns are not unlike pop songs and their tracts are lively with comic strips. The idea of the elect being Wise Men who follow a star is not a bad one. The Camps cult would probably have been latched onto by young people of the Jesus-freak kind but for its two insuperable drawbacks distasteful to anyone under forty—and to most people over forty, come to that. One is its total embargo on sexual activity, whether the parties are married or not; the other its emphasis on vengeance against the infidel, which means any non-Epiphany Person, a vengeance that is not necessarily left to God but may be carried out by the chosen as His instruments. In practice, of course, the brethren do not go about beating up their heretical neighbors, but the general impression is that if they do they will be praised rather than censured. After all, if God is their headmaster, they are all prefects.

Eunice absorbed little of this doctrine, which, in any case was implicit rather than proclaimed. She enjoyed the social life, almost the first she had ever known. The brethren were her contemporaries or her seniors; no one questioned her or attempted to interfere unpleasantly with her life or manipulated her into corners where she would be expected to read. They were friendly and cajoling and liberal with tea and biscuits and fruit cake because, of course, they saw her as a future convert. But Eunice was determined never to convert, and for her usual reason for not doing something. She wouldn't have minded the confessing because she would have confessed nothing beyond the usual run of evil thoughts and ambitions, but once she had taken that step she would be obliged to make the duty calls. And she knew only too well from her visits with Joan what that entailed. Reading. Drawing the attention of the visited to points in *Follow My Star*, picking appropriate bits out of the Bible, arguing with frequent reference to the printed word.

"I'll think about it," she said in her ponderous way when Joan pressed her. "It's a big step."

"A step toward Bethlehem which you would never regret. The Son of Man cometh like a thief in the night, but the foolish virgin has let her lamp go out. Remember that, Eun."

This exchange took place one raw damp afternoon when Eunice had walked down to the village store for a cup of tea, a chat, and to collect her week's supply of chocolate bars, which had again become an indispensable part of her diet. As they came out of the shop together, Jacqueline also came out of Mrs. Cairne's house, where she had been on some Women's Institute matter. They didn't notice her, but she saw them, and although Joan came only as far as the triangle of turf, it was obvious that what was taking place was no ordinary farewell of shopkeeper to customer. Joan was laughing in her shrill way, and while doing so she stuck out her hand and gave Eunice one of those playful pushes on the arm women of her kind do give to women friends in the course of making a joking reproof. Then Eunice walked off in the direction of the Hall, turning twice to wave to Joan, who waved back quite frenziedly.

Jacqueline started her car and caught Eunice up just beyond the bridge.

"I didn't know you were friendly with Mrs. Smith," she said when Eunice, somewhat reluctantly, had got in beside her.

"I see a bit of her," said Eunice.

There seemed no answer to make to this. Jacqueline felt she couldn't very well dictate to her housekeeper as to whom she chose for her friends. Not in these days. It wasn't Eunice's afternoon off, but they had all forgotten about those prescribed afternoons and evenings off since their holiday. She went out when she chose. After all, why not? It wasn't as if she neglected her duties at Lowfield Hall; far from it. But Jacqueline, who until now had had no fault to find with her housekeeper, who had been aghast when George, five months before, voiced faint qualms, was suddenly made uncomfortable. Eunice sat beside her, eating chocolates. She didn't eat them noisily or messily, but wasn't it odd that she should be eating them at all, munching silently and not offering the bag? Nothing would have induced Jacqueline to eat a chocolate under any circumstances, but still . . . And hobnobbing with Mrs. Smith as if they were fast friends? Some awareness that George, if told of it, would concur rather too emphatically in her own view stopped her mentioning it to him.

Instead, with her own particular brand of feminine perverseness, she praised Eunice to the skies that evening, pointing out how beautifully all the silver was polished.

In Galwich, Melinda Coverdale, wise or foolish, had surrendered her virginity to Jonathan Dexter. It happened after they had shared a bottle of wine in his room and Melinda had missed the last bus. Of course, the wine and the bus were not accidental happenings. Both had been inwardly speculating about them all the evening, but they were handy excuses for Melinda next day. She hardly needed consolation, though, for she was very happy, seeing Jonathan every day and spending most nights in his room. Sweet's Anglo-Saxon and Baugh on the history of the English language weren't so much as glanced at for a fortnight, and as for Goethe, Jonathan had found his Elective Affinities elsewhere.

At Lowfield Hall Jacqueline had made four Christmas puddings, one of which would be sent to the Caswalls, who couldn't face the upheaval of bringing two infants to Greeving for the holiday. She wondered what to buy for George, but George had everything—and so had she. Eunice watched her ice the

Christmas cake, and Jacqueline waited for her to make some remark, reminiscing or sentimental, when the plaster Santa Claus, the robins, and the holly leaves were fixed to the frosting, but Eunice said merely that she hoped the cake would be large enough, and she only said that when asked for her opinion.

Disillusionment over India had killed Oriental religion for Giles. It would never, anyway, have fitted with his plans for himself and Melinda. He saw them sharing their flat, devout Catholics both, but going through agonies to maintain their chaste and continent condition. Perhaps he would become a priest, and if Melinda were to enter a convent they might—say twice a year—have special dispensations to meet and, soberly garbed, have tea together in some humble café, not daring to touch hands. Or like Lancelot and Guinevere, but without the preceding pleasures, encounter each other across a cathedral nave, gaze long and long, then part without a word. Even to him, this fantasy seemed somewhat extreme. Before becoming a priest he must become a Catholic, and he was looking around Stantwich for someone to give him instruction. Latin and Greek would now have their uses, so Virgil and Sophocles received more attention. He put that line from Chesterton up on the wall, the bit about the twitch upon the thread, and he was reading Newman.

Winter had stripped bare the woods and the hedges, and screaming gulls followed Mr. Meadows' plough. The magical light of Suffolk became wan and opalescent, and the sky, as the earth turned its farthest from the sun, almost green with a streaking of long butter-colored clouds. Blood is nipped and ways be foul and nightly sings the staring owl. From cottage chimneys the smoke of log fires rose in long gray plumes.

"What are you doing for our Lord's nativity?" said Joan in the tone of someone asking a friend to a birthday party.

"Pardon?" said Eunice.

"Christmas."

"Stopping at the Hall. They've got folks coming."

"It does seem a shame you having to spend the Lord's birthday among a bunch of sinners. There's nothing to choose between the lot of them. Mrs. Higgs that rides the bike, she told Norm that Giles is consorting with Catholic priests. God doesn't want you contaminated by the likes of that, dear."

"He's only a bit of a boy," said Eunice.

"You can't say that about his adulterous stepfather. Coming in here and accusing Norm of tampering with his post! Oh, how far will the infidel go in his persecution of the elect! Why don't you come to us? We'll be very quiet, of course, but I think I can guarantee you a goodly reflection and the company of loving friends."

Eunice said she would. They were drinking tea at the time in Joan's squalid parlor, and the third loving friend, in the shape of Norman Smith, came in looking for his dinner. Instead of fetching it, Joan went off into a repetition of her confession, which the slightest mention of others who had offended in a similar, or assumed by her to be similar, way was likely to evoke.

"You've led a pure life, Eun, so you can't know what mine has been, delivering up my body, the temple of the Lord, to the riffraff of Shepherds Bush. Submitting myself unheeding to the filth of their demands, every kind of disgusting desire which I wouldn't name to a single lady, agreed to for the sake of the hard cash that my husband couldn't adequately provide."

Courage came at last to Norman. He had had two whiskeys in the Blue Boar. He advanced on Joan and hit her in the face. She was a very small woman, and she fell off her chair, making glugging noises.

Eunice rose ponderously to her feet. She went up to Norman and took him by the throat. She held the chicken skin of his throat as she might hold a hank of wool, and she laid her other hand hard on his shoulder.

"You leave her alone."

"I've got to listen to that, have I?"

"If you don't want me shaking the life out of you."
Eunice suited the action to the threat. It was for her a
wholly delightful experience and one which she
vaguely wondered she hadn't indulged in before. Norman cringed and shuddered as she shook him; his eyes
popped and his mouth fell open.

Joan's trust in her as a bodyguard had been justified.

She sat up and said dramatically, "With God's help,
you have saved my life!"

"Load of rubbish," said Norman. He broke free and
stood rubbing his throat. "You make me sick, the pair
of you. Couple of old witches."

Joan crawled back into her chair to examine her
injuries, a ladder in one of her stockings and what
would develop into a mild black eye. Norman hadn't
really hurt her. He was too feeble and, basically,
too frightened of her to do that. Nor had she struck
her head when she fell. But something happened
to her as the result of that weak blow and that fall.
Psychological perhaps, rather than physical—and connected also with the glandular changes of the menopause? Whatever it was, Joan was altered. It was
gradual, of course, it hardly showed itself on that evening except in a brighter glitter in her eyes and shriller
note to her voice. But that evening was the beginning
of it. She had reached the edge of a pit in which was
nothing short of raving madness, and she teetered
there on the brink until, two months later, whipped-up
fanaticism toppled her over.

13

"We'll go in the front way," said Eunice, back from the Epiphany meeting. She sensed that Joan would be unwelcome at the Hall, though Joan had never told her so, had, on the contrary, at the time of her first visit said that the Coverdales would not object to her exploring their house because "we're all friends in this village." She had never heard from George or Jacqueline a hint of their suspicions as to their post, but, somehow, by means of her peculiar and often unreliable intuition, she knew. Just as she was aware that, had she brought home with her Mrs. Higgs of bicycle fame or Mrs. Jim Meadows, these ladies would have been graciously received by any Coverdale who chanced to see them.

Joan didn't mean to stop long, having only come to have her measurements taken for some secret plan of Eunice's to do with a Christmas present. They were already on the top flight when Giles's bedroom door opened and he came out.

"Looks as if he was backward to me," said Joan in Eunice's room. She flounced out of her white coat. "Bit retarded, if you know what I mean."

"He won't say a word," said Eunice.

But there she was wrong.

Giles wouldn't have said a word if he hadn't been asked. That wasn't his way. He had gone downstairs to fetch his Greek dictionary, which he thought he had left in the morning room. There he found his mother alone, watching a concert of chamber music on the television. George had gone out for half an hour to discuss with the brigadier how to counter a proposal to build four new houses on a piece of land near the river bridge.

Jacqueline looked up and smiled. "Oh, darling," she said, "it's you."

"Mm," said Giles, groping under a pile of Sunday papers for his Liddell and Scott.

"I thought I heard someone on the stairs, but I imagined it was Miss Parchman coming in."

Occasionally it flashed across Giles's brain that he ought, say once a day, to utter a whole sentence rather than a monosyllable to his mother. He was quite fond of her really. So he forced himself. He stood up, spiky-haired, spotty, myopic, the mad young professor weighted down by a learned tome.

"You did," he said in his vague abstracted way, "with that old woman from the shop."

"What old woman? What on earth do you mean, Giles?"

Giles didn't know the names of anyone in the village. He never went there if he could help it. "The lunatic woman with the yellow hair," he said.

"*Mrs. Smith?*"

Giles nodded and wandered off toward the door, his dictionary already open, muttering something that sounded to Jacqueline like "anathema, anathema." Her patience with him snapped. Briefly she forgot what he had said, or the significance of it.

"Oh, Giles darling, you must *not* call people lunatics. Giles, wait a minute, *please*. Couldn't you possibly stop down here with us sometimes in the evenings? I mean, you can't have that much homework, and you know you can do it with your eyes shut. You're turning into a hermit, you'll get like that man who sat on top of a pillar!"

He nodded again. The admonition, the request, the flattery, passed over him unheard. He considered very seriously, rubbing one of his spots.

At last he said, "St. Simeon Stylites," and walked slowly out, leaving the door open.

Exasperated, Jacqueline slammed it. For a while,

her concert being over, she sat thinking how much she loved her son, how proud she was of his scholastic attainments, how ambitious for him—and how much happier she would have been had he been more like George's children. And then, because it was useless trying to do anything about Giles, who would surely one day become normal and nice, she returned to what he had said. Joan Smith. But before she could dwell much on it, George came in.

"Well, I think we shall put a spoke in their wheel. Either this place is scheduled as an Area of Natural Beauty or else it isn't. If it comes to a public inquiry, we shall all have to get together and brief counsel. You say the parish council are very much opposed?"

"Yes," said Jacqueline. "George, Mrs. Smith from the store is upstairs. She came in with Miss Parchman."

"I thought I saw the Smiths' van in the lane. How very unfortunate."

"Darling, I don't want her here. I know it sounds silly, but it makes me feel quite ill to think of her being here. She goes about telling people Jeffrey divorced me and named you, and that he's a dipsomaniac and all sorts of things. And I *know* she opened the last letter I had from Audrey."

"It doesn't sound silly at all. The woman's a menace. Did you say anything?"

"I didn't see her. Giles did."

George opened the door. He did so at the precise moment Eunice and Joan were creeping down the stairs in the dark. He put on the light, walked along the passage, and confronted them.

"Good evening, Mrs. Smith."

Eunice was abashed, but not Joan. "Oh, hallo, Mr. Coverdale. Long time no see. Bitterly cold, isn't it? But you can't expect anything else at this time of year."

George opened the front door for her and held it wide. "Good night," he said shortly.

"Cheeri-bye!" Joan scuttled off, giggling, a schoolgirl who has been caught out of bounds.

Thoughtfully, he closed the door. When he turned around, Eunice had disappeared. But in the morning, before breakfast, he went to her in the kitchen. This time she wasn't doing miracles with his dress shirt. She was making toast. He had thought of her as shy, and had blamed all her oddities on her shyness, but now he was aware, as he had been once six months before, of the disagreeable atmosphere that prevailed wherever she was. She turned around to look at him the way an ill-tempered cow had once looked at him when he went too close to its calf. She didn't say good morning, she didn't say a word, for she knew why he had come. A violent dislike of her seized him, and he wanted the kitchen back in its disordered state, the saucepans still not washed from the night before, an *au pair* muddling through.

"I'm afraid I've got something rather unpleasant to say, Miss Parchman, so I'll make it as brief as possible. My wife and I don't wish to interfere in your personal life, you are at liberty to make what friends you choose. But you must understand we cannot have Mrs. Smith in this house."

He was pompous, poor George. But who wouldn't have been, in the circumstances?

"She doesn't do any harm," said Eunice, and something stopped her calling him "sir." She was never again to call George "sir" or Jacqueline "madam."

"I must be the best judge of that. You have a right to know the grounds of my objection to her. I don't think one can seriously say a person does no harm when she is known to spread malicious slanders and —well, to abuse her husband's position as postmaster. That's all. I can't, of course, prevent your visiting Mrs. Smith in her own home. That is another matter. But I will not have her here."

Eunice asked no questions, offered no defense. She shrugged her massive shoulders, turned away, and pulled out the grill pan on which three slices of toast were burned black.

George didn't wait. But as he left the kitchen he was sure he heard her say, "Now look what you've made me do!"

He talked about it in the car to Giles, because Giles was there and his mind was full of it and, anyway, he was always racking his mind for something to say to the boy.

"You know, I've been very loath to admit it, but there's something definitely unpleasant about that woman. Perhaps I shouldn't be saying this to you, but you're grown up, you must be aware of it, feel it. I don't quite know the word I want to describe her."

"Repellent," said Giles.

"That's exactly it!" George was so delighted not only to have been supplied with this adjective but also because it had been supplied, quite forthcomingly, by Giles, that he took his eyes off the road and had to swerve sharply to avoid hitting Mr. Meadows' ancient Labrador, which was ambling along in the middle of the lane. "Look where you're going, you daft old thing," he called after it in a kind of affectionate relief. "Repellent, that's the word. Yes, she sends shivers up my spine. But what's to be done, Giles, old boy? Put up with it, I suppose?"

"Mm."

"I daresay it's just made me a bit nervous. I'm very likely exaggerating. She's taken an enormous burden of work off your mother's shoulders."

Giles said, "Mm," again, opened his case, and began muttering bits out of Ovid. Disappointed, but well aware that there was to be no repetition of that inspired contribution to this very one-sided discussion, George sighed and gave up. But a very nasty thought had struck him. If Eunice had been able to drive, if she had been driving this car five minutes before, he was intuitively certain she wouldn't have swerved to avoid the dog, or if it had been a child, to avoid that either.

Jacqueline left a note in the kitchen to say she would be out all day. She didn't want to see Eunice, who was upstairs doing the "children's" bathroom. It was a pity, she now thought, that Giles had told her about seeing Joan Smith, and an even greater one that she had been so impulsive as to tell George. Eunice might leave, or threaten to leave. Jacqueline drove off through the village to the Jameson-Kerrs' house, and when she saw the smeary windows, the dust lying everywhere, and her friend's rough red hands, she told herself that she must keep her servant at any cost and that the occasional presence of Joan Smith was a small price to pay.

Joan saw the car go by and put on her fleecy coat.

"Off to the Hall, I suppose?" said Norman. "I wonder you don't live up there with Miss Frankenstein."

Though she had once done so, Joan no longer unloaded her biblical claptrap onto her husband. He was the only person she knew who escaped it. "Don't you say a word against her! If it wasn't for her I might be dead."

Munching gum, Norman peered into one of his sacks. "Stupid fuss to make about a little tap."

"If it wasn't for her," shouted Joan with a flash of wit, "you wouldn't be looking at mailbags, you'd be sewing them."

She jumped into the van and roared up over the bridge. Eunice was in the kitchen, loading the washing machine with sheets and shirts and table linen.

"I saw her go off in her car, so I thought I'd pop up. Did you get into a row last night?"

"Don't know about a row." Eunice closed the lid of the machine and put the kettle on. "He says you're not to come here."

Joan's reaction was loud and violent. "I knew it! I could see it coming a mile off. It's not the first time the servants of God have been persecuted, Eun, and it won't be the last." She swept out a spindly arm, narrowly missing the milk jug. "Look what you do for them! Isn't the laborer in the vineyard worthy of his hire? He'd have to pay you twice what you're getting if you didn't have that poky room up there, but he doesn't think of that. He's no more than a landlord, and since when's a landlord got a right to interfere with a person's friends?" Her voice rose to a tremulous shriek. "Even his own daughter goes about saying he's a fascist. Even his kinsmen stand afar from him. Woe to him whom the Lord despiseth!"

Unmoved by any of this, Eunice stared stolidly at

the boiling kettle. No surge of love for Joan rose in her, no impulse of loyalty affected her. She was untouched by any of that passion which heats one when one's basic rights are threatened. She simply felt, as she had been feeling ever since the night before, that her life was being interfered with. At last she said, in her heavy level way:

"I don't mean to take any notice."

Joan let out a shrill laugh. She was enormously pleased. She bubbled with excitement. "That's right, dear, that's my Eun. You make him knuckle under. You show him it's not everyone that goeth when he says go and cometh when he says come."

"I'll make the tea," said Eunice. "Have a look at that note she's left, will you? I've left my glasses upstairs."

14

During term Melinda had only twice been home, but now that term had come to an end. Jonathan was going to Cornwall with his parents until after the New Year, and she had been invited to go with them, but it would have taken more than being in love to keep Melinda from Lowfield Hall at Christmas. With promises to phone every day, to write often, they parted and Melinda got on the train for Stantwich.

Again it was Geoff Baalham who picked her up at Gallows Corner. No great coincidence this, as Geoff was always returning from his egg-delivery round at about this time. But on December 18 it was dark at five, the windows of the van were closed and the heater on, and Melinda wore an embroidered afghan coat and a big fur hat. Only the boots were the same.

"Hi, Melinda. You *are* a stranger. Don't tell me it's your studies been keeping you up in Galwich."

"What else?"

"A new boyfriend, or that's what I heard."

"You just can't keep anything to yourself in this place, can you? Now, tell me what's new."

"Barbara's expecting. There'll be another little Baalham come July. Can you see me as a dad, Melinda?"

"You'll be marvelous. I'm so glad, Geoff. Mind you give my love to Barbara."

"Of course I will," said Geoff. "Now, what else? My auntie Nellie had a nasty fall off her bike and she's laid up with a bad foot. Did you hear about your dad throwing Mrs. Smith out of the house?"

"You don't mean it!"

"It's a fact. He caught her sneaking down the stairs with your lady help and he told her not to come there again, and then he threw her out. She's got bruises all down her side, or so I heard."

"He's a terrible fascist, isn't he? But that's *awful.*"

"Don't know about awful, not when you think what she says about your ma and opens their letters, according to what I hear. Well, here's where I leave you, and tell your ma I'll drop the eggs in first thing Monday."

Geoff drove home to Barbara and the chickens, thinking what a nice girl Melinda was—that crazy fur hat!—and that the boyfriend was a lucky guy.

"You didn't really throw Mrs. Smith out and bruise her all down her side, did you?" said Melinda, bursting into the morning room, where George, the carpet covered with a sheet, was cleaning his guns because it was too cold in the gun room.

"That's a nice way to greet your father when you haven't seen him for a month." George got up and gave her a kiss. "You're looking well. How's the boyfriend? Now, what's all this about me assaulting Mrs. Smith?"

"Geoff Baalham said you had."

"Ridiculous nonsense. I never touched the woman. I didn't even speak to her beyond saying good night. You ought to know village gossip by this time, Melinda."

Melinda threw her hat onto a chair. "But you did say she mustn't come here again, Daddy?"

"Certainly I did."

"Oh, poor Miss Parchman! It's awfully feudal interfering with her friendships. We were so worried because she didn't know anyone or go anywhere, and now she's got a friend you won't have her in the house. It's a *shame*."

"Melinda . . ." George began.

"I shall be very nice to her. I'm going to be very kind and caring. I can't bear to think of her not having a single friend."

"It's her married friend I object to," said George wickedly, and he laughed when Melinda flounced out.

So that evening Melinda began on a disaster course that was to lead directly to her death and that of her father, her stepmother, and her stepbrother. She embarked on it because she was in love. It is not so much true that all the world loves a lover as that a lover loves all the world. Melinda was moved by her love to bestow love and happiness, but it was tragic for her that Eunice Parchman was her object.

After dinner she jumped up from the table and, to Jacqueline's astonishment, helped Eunice to clear. It was to Eunice's astonishment too, and to her dismay. She wanted to get the dishes done in time to watch her Los Angeles cop serial at eight, and now here was this great tomboy bouncing about and mixing gravied plates up with water glasses. She wasn't going to speak, not she, and perhaps the girl would take the hint and go away.

A kind of delicacy, an awareness of the tasteful thing, underlay Melinda's extrovert ways, and she sensed that it would be disloyal to her father to mention the events of the previous Sunday. So she began on a different tack. She could hardly have chosen a worse subject, but for one.

"Your first name's Eunice, isn't it, Miss Parchman?"

"Yes," said Eunice.

"It's a biblical name, but of course you know that. But I think it's Greek really. Eu-nicey or maybe Eu-nikey. I'll have to ask Giles. I didn't do Greek at school."

A dish was banged violently into the machine. Melinda, herself a habitual dish-banger, took no notice. She sat on the table.

"I'll look it up. The Epistle to Timothy, I think. Of course it is! Eu-nicey, mother of Timothy."

"You're sitting on my tea towel," said Eunice.

"Oh, sorry. I'll have to check, but I think it says something about thy mother Eunice and thy grandmother Lois. I don't suppose your mother's name is Lois, is it?"

"Edith."

"Now, that must be Anglo-Saxon. Names are fascinating, aren't they? I love mine. I think my parents had very good taste calling us Peter and Paula and Melinda. Peter's coming next week, you'll like him. If you'd had a son, would you have called him Timothy?"

"I don't know," said Eunice, wondering why she was being subjected to this persecution. Had George Coverdale put her up to it? Or was it just done to mock? If not, why did that great tomboy keep smiling and laughing? She wiped all the surfaces viciously and drained the sink.

"What's your favorite name, then?" said her inquisitor.

Eunice had never thought about it. The only names she knew were those of her relatives, her few acquaintances, and those she had heard spoken on television. From this last, in desperation she selected, recalling her hero whose latest adventure she would miss if she didn't get a move on.

"Steve," she said and, hanging up her tea towel, marched out of the kitchen. It had been an intellectual effort which left her quite exhausted.

Melinda was not dissatisfied. Poor old Parchman was obviously sulking over the Joan Smith business, but she would get over that. The ice had been broken, and Melinda hoped confidently for a rapport to have grown up between them before the end of her holiday.

"Eu-nee-kay," said Giles when she asked him, and, "There was this man, you see, who got drunk at a party, and he was staggering home at about three in the morning when he landed up in the entrance to a block of flats. Well, he looked at all the names by the bells, and there was one called S. T. Paul. So he rang that bell, and when the guy came down, all cross and sleepy in his pajamas, the man said, 'Tell me, did you ever get any replies to your letters?'" He let out a great bellow of laughter at his own joke, then abruptly became doleful. Maybe he shouldn't tell jokes like that with his conversion in view.

"You're crazy, Step," said Melinda. She didn't appreciate, was never to appreciate, that she was the only person to whom her stepbrother ever uttered more than one isolated sentence. Her mind was on Eunice, whom she sought out, armed with the Bible, next day with a dictionary of proper names. She lent her magazines, took her the evening paper George brought home, and obligingly ran upstairs to fetch her glasses when Eunice said, as she always did, that she hadn't got them with her.

Eunice was harassed almost beyond bearing. It was bad enough that Melinda and Giles were about the house all day so that Joan Smith couldn't come to see her. But now Melinda was always in her kitchen or following her about "like a dog," as she told Joan. And she was perpetually on tenterhooks, what with those books and papers constantly being thrust under her nose—which she didn't tell Joan.

"Of course you know what all that amounts to, don't you, Eun? They're ashamed of their wicked behavior, and they've put that girl up to soft-soaping you."

"I don't know," said Eunice. "She gets on my nerves."

Her nerves were playing her up, as she put it to

herself, in a way they had never done before. But she was powerless to deal with Melinda, that warm unsnubbable girl. And once or twice, while Melinda was haranguing her about names or the Bible or Christmas or family histories, she wondered what would happen if she were to pick up one of those long kitchen knives and use it. Not, of course, Eunice being Eunice, what the Coverdales would do or what would become of her, but just the immediate consequence—that tongue silenced, blood spreading over and staining that white neck.

On the twenty-third Peter and Audrey Coverdale arrived.

Peter was a tall pleasant-looking man who favored his mother rather than his father. He was thirty-one. He and his wife were childless, from choice probably, for Audrey was a career woman, chief librarian at the university, where he had a post as lecturer in political economy. Audrey was particularly fond of Jacqueline. She was a well-dressed elegant bluestocking, four years older than her husband, which made her only seven years Jacqueline's junior. Before training as a librarian she had been at the Royal Academy of Music, which Jacqueline had attended before her first marriage. The two women read the same kind of books, shared a passionate love of Mozartian and pre-Mozartian opera, loved fashion and talking about clothes. They corresponded regularly, Audrey's letters being among those examined by Joan Smith.

They hadn't been in the house more than ten minutes when Melinda insisted on taking them to the kitchen and introducing them to Eunice.

"She's a member of this household. It's awfully fascist to treat her like a bit of kitchen equipment."

Eunice shook hands.

"Will you be going away for Christmas, Miss Parchman?" said Audrey, who prided herself, as Jacqueline did, on having a fund of small talk suitable for persons in every rank of life.

"No," said Eunice.

"What a shame! Not for us, of course. Your loss will be our gain. But one does like to be with one's family at Christmas."

Eunice turned her back and got the teacups out.

"Where did you get that awful woman?" Audrey said to Jacqueline later. "My dear, she's creepy. She's not human."

Jacqueline flushed as if she personally had been insulted. "You're as bad as George. I don't want to make a friend of my servant, I want her the way she is, marvelously efficient and unobtrusive. I can tell you, she really knows her job."

"So do boa constrictors," said Audrey.

And thus they came to Christmas.

George and Melinda brought holly in to decorate Lowfield Hall, and from the drawing-room chandelier hung a bunch of mistletoe, the gift of Mr. Meadows, in whose oaks it grew. More than a hundred cards came for the Coverdales, and these were suspended on strings in a cunning arrangement fixed up by Melinda. Giles received only two personal cards, one from his father and one from an uncle, and these, in his opinion, were so hideous that he declined to put them up on his cork wall where the Quote of the Month was: *To love oneself is the beginning of a lifelong romance.* Melinda made paper chains, bright red and emerald and shocking blue and chrome yellow, exactly the kind of chains she had made every year for fifteen years. Jacqueline took much the same view of them as her son did of his cards, but not for the world would she have said so.

On the day itself the drawing room was grandly festive. The men wore suits, the women floor-length gowns. Jacqueline was in cream velvet, Melinda in a 1920's creation, rather draggled dark blue crepe de chine embroidered with beads, which she had bought in the Oxfam shop. They opened their presents, strewing the carpet with colored paper and glitter. While Jacqueline unwrapped the gold bracelet that was George's gift, and Giles looked with something nearing enthusiasm on an unabridged Gibbon in six volumes, Melinda opened the parcel from her father.

It was a tape recorder.

15

Everyone was drinking champagne, even Giles. He had been prevailed upon by his mother to come downstairs and was morosely resigned to staying downstairs all day. And it would be worse tomorrow, when they would be having a party. In this view Melinda concurred—all those cairns and curs and roisterers—and she sat on the floor next to him, telling him how wonderful Jonathan was. Giles didn't much mind this. Byron, after all, was never perturbed by the existence of Colonel Leigh, and Christmas would be bearable if such conclaves with Melinda became the rule. He fancied that the others had noticed their closeness and were overawed by the mystery of it.

Far from noticing anything about her son except that he was there for once, Jacqueline was thinking about the one absent member of the household.

"I really do feel," she said, "that we ought to ask Miss Parchman to sit down to lunch with us."

A spontaneous groan from all but Belinda.

"A female Banquo," said Audrey, and her husband remarked that Christmas was supposed to be for merrymaking.

"And for peace and good will," said George. "I don't find the woman personally congenial, as you all know, but Christmas is Christmas and it's not pleasant to think of her eating her lunch out there on her own."

"Darling, I'm so glad you agree with me. I'll go and ask her, and then I'll lay another place."

But Eunice was not to be found. She had tidied the kitchen, prepared the vegetables, and gone off to the village store. There in the parlor, undecorated by holly or paper garlands, she and Joan and a gloomy sullen Norman ate roast chicken, frozen peas, and canned potatoes, followed by a Christmas pudding from the shop. Eunice enjoyed her meal, though she would have liked sausages as well. Joan had cooked some sausages but had forgotten to serve them, and Norman, made suspicious by a peculiar smell, found them moldering in the grill pan a week later. They drank water, and afterward strong tea. Norman had got some beer in, but this Joan had deposited in the bin just before the dustmen called. She was in raptures over the salmon-pink jumper Eunice had knitted for her, rushed away to put it on, and preened about in it, striking grotesque model-girl attitudes in front of the finger-marked mirror. Eunice received an enormous box of chocolates and a fruit cake from stock.

"You'll come back tomorrow, won't you, dear?" said Joan.

And so it happened that Eunice also spent Boxing Day with the Smiths, leaving Jacqueline to cope with food and drink for the thirty guests who came that evening. And the effect on Jacqueline was curious, twofold. It was as if she were back in the old days, when the entire burden of the household work had been on her shoulders, and in Eunice's absence she appreciated her almost more than when she was there. This was what it would be like permanently if Eunice were to leave. And yet for the first time she saw her housekeeper as George and Audrey and Peter saw her, as uncouth and boorish, a woman who came and went as she pleased and who saw the Coverdales as so dependent on her that she held them in the hollow of her hand.

The New Year passed, and Peter and Audrey went home. They had asked Melinda to go back with them for the last week of her holiday, but Melinda had refused. She was a very worried girl. Each day that passed made her more anxious. She lost her sparkle, moped about the house, and said no to all the invitations she got from her village friends. George and Jacqueline thought she was missing Jonathan, and tactfully they asked no questions.

For this Melinda was deeply thankful. If what she feared was true—and it must be true now—they would have to know sometime. Perhaps it might be possible to get through this, or out of this, without George ever suspecting. Children understand their parents as little as parents understand their children. Melinda had had a happy childhood and a sympathetic devoted father, but her way of thinking was infected by the attitude of her friends to their parents. Parents were bigoted, prudish, moralistic. Therefore hers must be, and no personal experience triumphed over this conviction. She guessed she was George's favorite child. All the worse. He would be the more bitterly disappointed and disillusioned if he knew, and his idealistic love for her would turn to disgust. She imagined his face, stern and yet incredulous, if he were even to suspect such a thing of his youngest child, his little girl. Poor Melinda. She would have been flabbergasted had she known that George had long supposed her relationship with Jonathan to be a fully sexual one, regretted it, but accepted it philosophically as long as he could believe there was love and trust between them.

Every day, of course, she had been having long phone conversations with Jonathan—George was to be faced with a daunting bill—but so far she hadn't breathed a word. Now, however, on January 4, she knew she must tell him. This wasn't as bad as telling her father would be, but bad enough. Her experience of this kind of revelation had been culled from novel and magazine reading and from old wives' gossip in the village. When you told the man, he stopped caring for you, he dropped you, didn't want to know, or at best shouldered his responsibility while implying it was all your fault. But she had to tell him. She couldn't go on carrying this frightening secret another day on her own, especially as, that morning, she had been violently sick on waking.

She waited until George had gone to work and Jacqueline and Giles to Colchester in the second car, Jacqueline supposing that while she was shopping her son would be visiting a friend—a friend at last!—though, in fact, he was to receive his first instruction from Father Madigan. Eunice was upstairs making beds. There were three telephones at Lowfield Hall, one in the morning room, an extension in the hall, and another extension by Jacqueline's bed. Melinda chose the morning-room phone, but while she was getting enough courage together to make her call, it rang. Jonathan.

"Hold on a minute, Jon," she said. "I want to close the door."

It was at that precise moment, while Jonathan was holding the line and had briefly laid down the receiver to light a cigarette, while Melinda was closing the morning-room door, that Eunice lifted the receiver on Jacqueline's bedroom extension. She wasn't spying. She was too uninterested in Melinda and too repelled by her attentions deliberately to eavesdrop. She picked up the receiver because you cannot properly dust a telephone without doing so. But as soon as she heard Melinda's first words she was aware that it would be prudent to listen.

"Oh, Jon, something awful! I'll come straight out with it, though I'm scared stiff to tell you. I'm pregnant. I know I am. I was sick this morning and I'm nearly two weeks overdue. It'll be frightful if Daddy or Jackie find out, Daddy would be so let down, he'd hate me, and what am I going to *do?*"

She was nearly crying. Choked by tears that would soon spill over, she waited for the stunned silence. Jonathan said quite calmly, "Well, you've got two alternatives, Mel."

"Have I? You tell me. I can't think of anything but just running away and dying!"

"Don't be so wet, lovely. You can have an abortion if you really want . . ."

"Then they'd be sure to know. If I couldn't get it on

the National Health and I had to have money or they wanted to know my next of kin or . . ."

By now Melinda was hysterical. Like almost all women in her particular situation, she was in a blind unreasoning panic, fighting against the bars of the trap that was her own body. Eunice screwed up her nose. She couldn't stand that, lot of fuss and nonsense. And perhaps it was something else as well, some unconscious sting of envy or bitterness, that made her lay the receiver down. Lay it down, not replace it. It would be unwise to do that until after their conversation was over. She moved away to dust the dressing table, and thus she missed the rest.

"I don't like the idea of abortion," said Jonathan. "Do get yourself together, Mel, and calm down. Listen, I want to marry you, anyway. Only I thought we ought to wait till we've got our degrees and jobs and whatever. But it doesn't matter. Let's get married as soon as we can."

"Oh, Jon, I do love you! Could we? I'd have to tell them, even though we're both over eighteen, but, Jon . . ."

"But nothing. We'll get married and have our baby and it'll be great. You come up to Galwich tomorrow instead of next week and I'll hitch back and you can stay with me and we'll make plans. Okay?"

It was very much okay with Melinda, who, having wept with despair, was now bubbling with joy. She would go to Jonathan next day and tell George she'd been staying with a friend in Lowestoft. It was awful lying to him, but all in a good cause, better that than let him know, wait till they'd published the banns or got the license. And so on. She wasn't sick on January 5. Before she had packed her case, she knew her fears had been groundless, the symptoms having resulted from anxiety and their cessation from relief. But she went just the same, and had a taxi from the station to Jonathan's flat, she was so impatient to tell him she wasn't going to have a baby after all.

Being in possession of someone else's secret reminded Eunice of the days of blackmailing the homosexual and, of course, Annie Cole. It was a piece of information which Joan Smith would have delighted to hear, Joan who rather resented the way Eunice never told her anything about the private lives of the Coverdales. She wasn't going to tell her this either. A secret shared is no longer a secret, especially when it has been imparted to someone like Joan Smith, who would whisper it to what customers she still retained, in no time. No, Eunice was going to keep this locked in her boardlike bosom, for you never knew when it might come in useful.

So, on the following night, when she climbed into the van that was waiting for her in Greeving Lane, she gave nothing away.

"I noticed the Coverdale girl went back to her college yesterday," said Joan. "Bit early, wasn't it? All set for a week of unbridled cohabitation with that boyfriend she's got, I daresay. She'll come to a bad end. Mr. Coverdale's just the sort of hard man to cast his own flesh and blood out of the house if he thought they'd been committing fornication."

"I don't know," said Eunice.

Twelfth Night, January 6, Epiphany, the greatest day in the calendar for the disciples of Elroy Camps. The meeting was sensational—two really uninhibited confessions, one of them rivaling Joan's own, an extempore prayer shrieked by Joan at the top of her voice, five hymns.

> Follow the star!
> Follow the star!
> The Wise Men turn not back.
> Across the desert, hills, or foam,
> The star will lead them to their home,
> White or brown or black!

They ate seed cake and drank tea. Joan became more and more excited until, eventually, she had a kind of seizure. She fell on the floor, uttering prophecies as the spirit moved her, and waving her arms and legs about. Two of the women had to take her into a side room and calm her down, though on the whole the Epiphany People were rather gratified than dismayed by this performance.

Only Mrs. Elder Barnstaple, a sensible woman who came to the meetings for her husband's sake, seemed disquieted. But she supposed Joan was "putting it on." Not one of that company guessed at the truth, that Joan Smith was daily growing more and more demented and her hold on reality becoming increasingly tenuous. She was like a weak swimmer whose grasp of a slippery rock has never been firm. Now her fingers were sliding helplessly down its surface, and currents of madness were drawing her into the whirlpool.

She hardly spoke as she drove the van home, but from time to time she let out little bursts of giggles like the chucklings of something unhuman that haunted those long pitch-dark lanes.

16

Bleak midwinter, and the frosty wind made moan. Eva Baalham said that the evenings were drawing out, and this was true, but not that one would notice. The first snow fell in Greeving, a dusting of snow that thawed and froze again.

On the cork wall, from St. Augustine: *Too late loved I Thee, O Thou Beauty so ancient and so new, too late came I to love Thee!* For Giles the road to Rome was not entirely satisfactory, as Father Madigan, accustomed until recently to Tipperary peasants, expected from him their ignorance and their blind faith. He didn't seem to understand that Giles knew

more Greek and Latin than he and had got through
Aquinas before he was sixteen. In Galwich Melinda
was blissfully happy with Jonathan. They were still
going to get married, but not until she had taken her
degree in fifteen months' time. To this end, because
she would need a good job, she was working quite
hard, between making love and making plans, at her
Chaucer and her Gower.

The cold pale sun pursued a low arc across a cold
pale sky, aquamarine and clear, or appeared as a pud-
dle of light in a high gray field of cloud.

January 19 was Eunice's forty-eighth birthday. She
noted its occurrence but she told no one, not even
Joan. It was years since anyone had sent her a card
or given her a present on that day.

She was alone in the house. At eleven the phone
rang. Eunice didn't like answering the phone, she
wasn't used to it and it alarmed her. After wondering
whether it might not be better to ignore it, she
picked up the receiver reluctantly and said hallo.

The call was from George. Tin Box Coverdale had
recently changed their public-relations consultants,
and a director of the new company was coming to
lunch, to be followed by a tour of the factory. George
had prepared a short history of the firm which had
been established by his grandfather—and had left his
notes at home.

He had a cold and his voice was thick and hoarse.
"The papers I want you to find are in the writing
desk in the morning room, Miss Parchman. I'm not
sure where, but the sheets are clipped together and
headed in block capitals: 'Coverdale Enterprises from
1895 to the Present Day.' "

Eunice said nothing.

"Now, I'd appreciate it if you'd hunt them out."
George let out an explosive sneeze. "I beg your pardon. Where was I? Oh yes. A driver from here is
already on his way, and I want you to put the papers
into a large envelope and give them to him when he
comes."

"All right," said Eunice hopelessly.

"I'll hold the line. Have a look now, will you? And come back and tell me when you've found them."

The desk was full of papers, many of them clipped together and all headed with something or other. Eunice hesitated, then replaced the receiver without speaking to George again. Immediately the phone rang. She didn't answer it. She went upstairs and hid in her own room. The phone rang four more times, and then the doorbell. Eunice didn't answer that either. Although she wasn't celebrating her birthday, it did strike her that it was very disagreeable having this happen today of all days. A person's birthday ought to be nice and peaceful, not upset by this kind of thing.

George couldn't understand what had happened. The driver came back empty-handed, the consultant left without the Coverdale history. George made a sixth call and at last got hold of his wife, who had been in Nunchester having her hair tinted. No, Miss Parchman wasn't ill and had just gone out for a walk. The first thing he did when he got home was find the papers on the very top of the pile in the writing desk.

"What happened, Miss Parchman? It was of vital importance to me to have those papers."

"I couldn't find them," said Eunice, laying the dinner table, not looking at him.

"But they were on the top. I can't understand how you could miss them. My driver wasted an hour coming over here. And surely, even if you couldn't find them, you could have come back and told me."

"They cut us off."

George knew that was a lie. "I rang back four times."

"It never rang," said Eunice, and she turned on him her small face, which now seemed to have increased in size, to have swollen with resentment. Hours of brooding had filled her with gall, and now she used to him the tone her father had so often heard in the last weeks of his life. "I don't know anything about any of it." For her, she was quite voluble. "It's no good asking me, because I don't know." The blood crept up her throat and broke in a dark flush across her face. She turned her back on him.

George walked out of the room, impotent in the face of this refusal to take responsibility, to apologize or even discuss it. His head was thick with his cold and felt as if stuffed with wet wool. Jacqueline was making up her face in front of her dressing-table mirror.

"She's not a secretary, darling," she said, echoing the words he had used to her when she had hesitated about engaging Eunice. "You mustn't expect too much of her."

"Too much! Is it too much to ask someone to find four clearly labeled sheets of paper and hand them over to a driver? Besides, it isn't that which I mind so much. I never really knew what dumb insolence meant before, it was just a phrase. I know now. She doesn't give the number or our name when she answers the phone. If a pig could say hallo it would sound just like Miss Parchman."

Jacqueline laughed, smudging her mascara.

"And to put the phone down on me! Why didn't she answer when I called back? Of course the phone rang, it's just nonsense to say it didn't. And she was positively rude to me when I spoke to her about it."

"I've noticed she doesn't like doing things which are—well, outside what she thinks of as her province. It's always the same. If I leave her a note, she'll do what it asks, but a bit truculently, I always think, and she doesn't like making phone calls or answering the phone." She spoke quite blithely, as if laughing off "men's nonsense," humoring and soothing him because his cold was now worse than hers.

George hesitated, put his hand on her shoulder. "It's no good, Jackie, she'll have to go."

"Oh no, George!" Jacqueline spun around on her stool. "I can't do without her. You can't ask that of me just because she let you down over those papers."

"It isn't just that. It's her insolence and the way she looks at us. Have you noticed she never calls us by our names? And she's dropped that 'sir' and 'madam.' Not that I care about that, I'm not a snob," said

George, who did and was, "but I can't put up with bad manners and lying."

"George, please give her one more chance. What would I do without her? I can't face the thought of it."

"There are other servants."

"Yes, old Eva and *au pairs*," said Jacqueline bitterly. "I had some idea what it would be like at our Christmas party. I didn't enjoy it, if you did. I was doing the food all day and running around all night. I don't think I spoke to anyone except to ask if they wanted another drink."

"And for that I have to put up with a servant who would have been a credit to the staff at Auschwitz?"

"One more chance, George, *please*."

He capitulated. Jacqueline could always win him over. Could he pay too high a price, he asked himself, to see his beloved wife happy and relaxed and beautiful? Could he pay too much for peace and domestic comfort and a well-run elegant home? Was there anything he wouldn't part with for that?

Except my life, he might have answered, except my life.

He intended to react by taking a firm line with Eunice; in accordance with his calling, to manage and direct her. He wasn't a weak man or a coward, and he had never approved the maxim that it is better to ignore unpleasantness and pretend that it does not exist. She must be admonished when she returned his smile and his "good morning" with a scowl and a grunt, or he would have a quiet talk with her and elicit from her what the trouble was and how they had failed.

He admonished her only once, and then jocularly. "Can't you manage a smile when I speak to you, Miss Parchman? I don't know what I've done to deserve that grim look."

Beseechingly, Jacqueline's eyes met his. Eunice took no notice, apart from slightly lifting her shoulders. After that he said no more. He knew what would happen if he tried a tête-à-tête with her. "There's nothing

wrong. It's no use talking about it because there's
nothing." But he realized, if Jacqueline did not, that
they were conciliating Eunice Parchman, allowing her
to manage and direct them. For Jacqueline's sake and
to his own self-disgust, he found himself smiling fa-
tuously at his housekeeper whenever they encountered each other, asking her if her room was warm
enough, if she had enough free time, and once if she
would *mind* staying in on a certain evening when
they had guests for dinner. His warmth was met by
not a shred of reciprocation.

February came in with a snowstorm.
Only in pictures and on television had Eunice seen
real country snow before, as against the slush which
clogged the gutters of Tooting. It had never occurred
to her that snow was something that could bother
people or change their lives. On the morning of Monday, February 1, George was up before she was and,
with an unwilling sleepy Giles, clearing in the long
drive two channels for the wheels of the Mercedes.
The first light had brought Mr. Meadows out with his
snowplough into the lane. A shovel and boots and
sacks were put into the car's boot, and George and
Giles set off for Stantwich with the air of arctic ex-
plorers.
Against a livid sky the great flakes whirled, and the
landscape was blanketed but for the dark demarca-
tions of hedges and the isolated blot of a skeleton tree.
No going out for Jacqueline that day or the next or the
next. She phoned to cancel her appointment with the
hairdresser, her lunch with Paula, the evening engage-
ments. Eva Baalham didn't bother to phone and say
she wasn't coming. She just didn't come. You took
that sort of thing for granted in East Anglia in February.
So Jacqueline was imprisoned with Eunice Parchman. Just as she was afraid to use her car, so were her
neighbors who might have used theirs afraid to call
on her. Once she would have seen the coming of the
snow as a possible topic of conversation between herself and Eunice, but now she knew better than to try.

Eunice accepted the snow as she accepted rain and wind and sunshine. She swept the paving outside the gun-room door and the front steps without comment. Silently she went about her work. When Jacqueline, unable to repress herself, exclaimed with relief at the sound of George's car successfully returned through the thickening drifts, she reacted no more than if this had been a normal day of ordinary weather.

And Jacqueline began to see George's point of view. Being snowbound with Eunice was more than disconcerting. It was oppressive, almost sinister. She marched doggedly through the rooms with her duster and her polishing cloths. Once, when Jacqueline was seated at the desk writing to Audrey, the half-filled sheet of paper was lifted silently from under her nose while a duster was wiped slowly across the surface of inlaid leather and rosewood. It was as if, Jacqueline said later to her husband, she were a deaf patient in a home for the handicapped and Eunice a ward maid. And even when the work was done and Eunice departed upstairs to watch afternoon serials, she felt that it was not the snow alone which pressed a ponderous weight on the upper regions of Lowfield Hall. She found herself treading carefully, closing doors discreetly, sometimes just standing in the strange white light that is uniquely the reflection thrown back from snow, gleaming, marmoreal, and cold.

She was not to know, never dreamed, that Eunice was far more afraid of her than she was intimidated by Eunice; that the incident of the Coverdale history papers had made her retreat totally into her shell, for if she were to speak or allow them to speak to her, that archenemy of hers, the printed word, would rise up and assail her. Reading in an armchair pulled close to a radiator, reading to please Eunice and keep clear of her, Jacqueline never guessed that she could have done nothing to please Eunice less or arouse her more to hatred.

Every evening that week she needed twice her usual allowance of sherry to relax her before dinner.

"Is it worth it?" said George.

"I talked to Mary Cairne on the phone today. She said she'd put up with positive abuse, let alone dumb insolence, to have a servant like Miss P."

George kissed his wife but couldn't resist a dig. "Let her try it, then. It's nice to know Miss P.'ll have somewhere to go when I sack her."

But he didn't sack her, and on the Thursday—Thursday, February 4—something happened to distract them from their discontentment with their housekeeper.

17

Things were getting too much for Norman Smith. He also was snowbound with a fellow being who was uncongenial to him, only the fellow being was his wife.

Norman had often in the past told Joan she was mad, but in much the same way as Melinda Coverdale told Giles Mont he was mad. He didn't intend to imply she was insane. But now he was sure she literally was mad. They still shared a bed. They belonged in that category of married people who share a bed without thinking about it, who would have shared a bed even if they were not on speaking terms. But often now Norman woke in the night to find Joan absent, and then he heard her in some other part of the house laughing to herself, laughing maniacally, or singing snatches of Epiphany hymns or reciting prophecies in a shrill uneven voice. She had ceased altogether to clean the house or dust the goods in the shop or sweep the shop floor. And each morning she bedizened herself in bits of bizarre clothing saved from her Shepherds Bush days, her face painted like a clown's.

She ought to see a doctor. Norman knew quite well that she was in need of treatment for her mind. A psychiatrist was the sort of doctor she ought to see, but how to get her to one? How to go about it? Dr. Crutchley held surgery twice a week in Greeving in a couple of rooms in a converted cottage. Norman knew Joan wouldn't go of her own volition, and he couldn't imagine going *for* her. What, sit in that waiting room among coughing and snuffling Meadowses and Baalhams and Eleighs, and then explain to a tired and harassed doctor that his wife sang in the night and bawled bits from the Bible at his customers and wore knee socks and short skirts like a young girl?

Besides, the worst manifestation of her madness he couldn't confess to anyone.

Lately she seemed to think she had a right, godlike or as God's censor, to investigate any of the mail that passed through Greeving Post Office. He couldn't keep the mail sacks from her. He tried locking them up in the outside lavatory, but she broke the lock with a hammer. And now she was an expert at steaming open envelopes. He winced and trembled when he heard her telling Mrs. Higgs that God had punished Alan and Pat Newstead by killing their only grandchild, information Joan had culled out of a letter from the distraught father. And when she imparted to Mr. Meadows of the garage that George Coverdale was in debt to his wine merchant, he waited till the shop was empty and then he struck her in the face. Joan only screamed at him. God would have vengeance on him, God would make him a leper and an outcast who dared not show his face in the haunts of men.

This was one of her prophecies which was to prove only too true.

On Friday, February 5, when the thaw had begun and the lane between Greeving and Lowfield Hall could be negotiated without a struggle, George Coverdale walked into the village store at nine in the morning. That is, he walked in after he had banged peremptorily on the front door and fetched Norman, who was still at breakfast, out to open up.

"You're early, Mr. Coverdale," said Norman nervously. It was seldom that George had set foot on that threshold, and Norman knew his coming boded ill.

"In my opinion, nine is not early. It's the time I usually reach my place of business, and if I shan't do so this morning it's because the matter I have to discuss with you is too serious to postpone."

"Oh yes?" Norman might have stood up to George, but he quailed when Joan, her yellow hair in curlers, her skin-and-bone body wrapped in a dirty red dressing gown, appeared in the doorway.

George took an envelope from his briefcase. "This letter has been opened and resealed," he said, and he paused. It was horrible to him to think of Joan Smith spreading about the village that his wine merchant was threatening him with proceedings. And it was made all the more horrible by the fact that the letter was the result of a computer mistake. George, having paid his bill in early December when it was due, and argued the whole thing out with the retailer by phone and obtained a fulsome apology for his error. But he scorned to defend himself to these people. "There are smears of glue on the flap," he said, "and inside I found a hair which I venture to suggest comes from the head of your wife."

"I don't know anything about it," Norman muttered. He had unwittingly used Eunice Parchman's phrasing, and this inflamed George.

"Perhaps the postmaster at Stantwich will. I intend to write to him today. I shall lay the whole matter before him, not forgetting previous occasions when I have had cause for suspicion, and I shall demand an official inquiry."

"I can't stop you."

"Very true. I merely felt it was just to tell you what I mean to do so that you have warning in advance. Good morning."

All this time Joan had said nothing. But now, as

George moved toward the door, distastefully eyeing the dusty packets of cornflakes and baskets of shrunken moldy vegetables, she darted forward like a spider or a crab homing on its prey. She stood between George and the door, against the door, her sticklike arms spread against the glass, the red wool sleeves falling back from flesh where the subcutaneous tissue had wasted away. She lifted her head and screamed at him:

"Generation of vipers! Whoremonger! Adulterous beast! Woe to the ungodly and the fornicators!"

"Let me pass, Mrs. Smith," said George levelly. Not for nothing had he seen service under fire in the Western Desert.

"What shall be done unto thee, thou false tongue? Sharp arrows of the mighty with coals of juniper." Joan waved her fist in his face. "God will punish the rich man who taketh away the livelihood of the poor. God will destroy him in his high places." Her face was suffused with blood, her eyes white with the pupils cast up.

"Will you get your wife out of my way, Mr. Smith!" said George, enraged.

Norman shrugged. He was afraid of her and powerless.

"Then I will. And if you care to sue me for assault, you're welcome."

He pushed Joan and got the door open. Outside in the car, Giles, the least involved of people, was actually watching with interest. Joan, only temporarily worsted, ran after George and seized his coat, shouting gibberish, her dressing gown flapping in the icy wind. And by now Mrs. Cairne had appeared at her window, Mr. Meadows by his petrol pumps. George had never been so embarrassed in his life; he was shaking with distaste and repulsion. The whole scene was revolting to him. If he had witnessed it in the street, an angry man, a half-dressed woman clinging to his coat, shouting abuse at him, he would have turned the other way, vanished as fast as possible. And here he was, one of the protagonists.

"Be quiet, take your hands off me," he found himself shouting back at her. "This is outrageous!"

And then at last Norman Smith did come out and get hold of his wife and manhandle her back into the shop. Afterward, Meadows of the garage said he slapped her, but George didn't wait to see. With what shreds of dignity remained to him, he got into the car and drove off. For once he was glad of Giles's detachment. The boy was smiling distantly. "Lunatic," he said before lapsing back into his own mysterious thoughts.

The incident upset George for the day. But he wrote his letter to the Stantwich postmaster without mentioning the scene of the morning or even that he had particular grounds for suspecting the Smiths.

"Let's hope we're going to have a quiet weekend," he said to Jacqueline. "What with battling to work through all this snow every day and then this fracas this morning, I feel I've had enough. We're not going anywhere, are we, or having anyone in?"

"Just to the Archers' tomorrow afternoon, darling."

"Tea with the rector," said George, "is just the kind of somniferous non-event I can do with at present."

Melinda was not expected home, and Giles didn't count. It was rather like having a harmless resident ghost, Jacqueline sometimes thought sadly. It stalked the place, but it didn't bother you or damage things, and on the whole it kept quietly to the confines of the haunted room. She wondered from whose writings he had taken the Quote of the Month: *I hope never again to commit a mortal sin, nor even a venial one, if I can help it.*

It was the last quotation Giles was ever to pin to his cork wall, and perhaps it was appropriate that the lines he had chosen, from Charles VII of France, were said to be their author's dying words.

But, as it happened, Melinda did come home. Since January 5 she hadn't been back to Lowfield Hall, and her conscience was troubling her. Of course she would go home for the thirteenth, for that was George's birthday, but it seemed awful to stay away for five weeks. Also there was the matter of the tape recorder. George's present was her most prized possession, and because of it she was the envy of her college friends. Melinda didn't like to say no to people who asked to borrow it, but when someone took it to a folk concert and afterward left it all night in an unlocked car, she thought the time had come to remove it from harm's way.

Without having told anyone she was coming, she arrived in Stantwich as the dull red sun was setting, and at Gallows Corner after dark. She was just a little too late for Geoff Baalham, who had passed that way ten minutes before, and it was Mrs. Jameson-Kerr who picked her up and told her George and Jacqueline had gone to tea at the rectory.

Melinda went into the house through the gun room and immediately upstairs to find Giles. But Giles also was out. He had taken the Ford and, after a session with Father Madigan, gone to a cinema. The house was warm, spotless, exquisitely tidy and silent. Silent, that is, but for the muted tumult throbbing through the first-floor ceilings from Eunice Parchman's television. Melinda put the tape recorder on her chest of drawers. She changed into a robe she had made herself out of an Indian bedspread, put a shawl over her shoulders and a string of limpet shells around her neck, and well pleased with the result, went down to the morning room. There she found a stack of new magazines which she took into the kitchen. Ten minutes later Eunice, coming down to remove from the deep freeze a chicken casserole for the Coverdales' supper, found her seated at the table with a magazine open in front of her.

Melinda got up courteously. "Hallo, Miss Parchman. How are you? Would you like a cup of tea? I've just made it."

"I don't mind," said Eunice, the nearest she ever got to a gracious acceptance of any offer. She frowned. "They're not expecting you."

"I do live here, it's my home," was what Melinda might have said, but she was not a prickly or defensive girl. Besides, here was an opportunity to go on being nice to Miss Parchman, whom she had neglected along with her family since the New Year. So she smiled and said she had made her decision on the spur of the moment, and did Miss Parchman take milk and sugar?

Eunice nodded. The magazine on the table intimidated her as much as a spider might have intimidated another woman. She hoped Melinda would concentrate on it and shut up while she drank her tea, which she rather regretted accepting. But it was evident that Melinda intended to concentrate on it only with her participation. She turned the pages, keeping up a running commentary, looking up from time to time with a smile for Eunice and even passing her the magazine for her to look at a picture.

"I don't like those mid-calf-length skirts, do you? Oh, look at the way that girl has done her eyes! It must take hours, I shouldn't have the patience. All those forties fashions are coming back. Did they really dress like that when you were young? Did you wear bright red lipstick and stockings? I've never possessed a pair of stockings."

Eunice, who still wore them and who had never possessed a pair of tights, said she wasn't much for dress. Lot of nonsense, she said.

"Oh, I think it's fun." Melinda turned the page. "Here's a questionnaire. *Twenty Questions to Test If You're Really in Love*. I must do it, though I know I am. Now, let's see. Have you got a pencil or a pen or something?"

A firm shake of the head from Eunice.

"I've got a pen in my bag." This battered holdall, literally a carpetbag made out of Turkey rug, Melinda had dumped in the gun room. Eunice, watching her fetch it, hoped she would take bag, pen, and magazine elsewhere, but Melinda returned to her place at the table. "Now, 'Question 1: Would you rather be with him than . . .?' Oh, I can see the answers at the bottom, that's no good. I'll tell you what, you ask me the questions and tick whether I get three marks or two or one or none at all. Okay?"

"I haven't got my glasses," said Eunice.

"Yes, you have. They're in your pocket."

And they were. The tortoiseshell ones, the pair the Coverdales knew as her reading glasses, were sticking out of the right-hand pocket of her overall. Eunice didn't put them on. She did nothing, for she didn't know what to do. She couldn't say she was too busy —busy with what?—and nearly half a pint of hot tea remained in the mug Melinda had given her.

"Here." Melinda passed her the magazine. "Please do. It'll be fun."

Eunice took it in both hands and stumbled from memory through that first line Melinda had read. " 'Would you rather be with him than . . . ?' " She stopped.

Melinda reached across and picked the glasses out of her pocket. Eunice was cornered. A flush darkened her face to a deep wine color. She looked up at the girl, and her underlip trembled.

"What is it?" There was a let-out here if only Eunice had known it. For, instantly, Melinda jumped to a conclusion. Miss Parchman had reacted rather like this before, when asked what name she would have given her son if she had had one. Obviously there was something in her past that was still painful, and she, very tactlessly, had again touched the scar of that ancient disappointed love. Poor Miss Parchman, who had once loved someone and was now an old maid. "I didn't mean to upset you," she said gently. "I'm sorry if I said something to hurt you."

Eunice didn't answer. She didn't know what on earth the girl was talking about. But Melinda took her silence as a sign of unhappiness, and she was seized by a need to do something to make things all right again, to distract Eunice's mind. "I really am sorry. Let's do the quiz on the opposite page, shall we? It's all about how good a housewife one is. You do it for me and see how hopeless I am, and then I'll do it for you. I bet you get top marks." Melinda held up the glasses for Eunice to take them.

And now Eunice should have made capital out of Melinda's misapprehension. Nothing more would have been needed but for her to say yes, Melinda had upset her, and to have walked with dignity out of the room. Such conduct would have won for her the dismayed sympathy of all the Coverdales and have supplied George with his answer. What was the root cause of Miss Parchman's sullenness and depression? A womanly sorrow, a lost love. But Eunice had never been able to manipulate people because she didn't understand people or the assumptions they made and the conclusions they drew. She understood only that she was on the brink of having her disability discovered, and because of the awful crushing domination of that disability, she thought she was nearer to that brink than she actually was. She thought Melinda already guessed, and that was why, having mockingly said she was sorry, she was trying to test her out to confirm her assumption.

The glasses, held between Melinda's finger and thumb, hovered between the two women. Eunice made no move to take them. She was trying to think. What to do, how to get out of it, what desperate measure she could seize on. Puzzled, Melinda let her hand fall, and as she did so she looked through them from a short distance and saw that they were of plain glass. Her eyes went to Eunice's flushed face, her blank stare, and pieces of the puzzle, hitherto inexplicable— the way she never read a book, looked at a paper, left a note, got a letter—fell into place.

"Miss Parchman?" she said quietly, "are you dyslexic?"

Vaguely, Eunice thought this must be the name of some eye disease. "Pardon?" she said in swelling hope.

"I'm sorry. I mean you *can't* read, can you? You can't read or write."

18

The silence endured for a full minute.

Melinda too had blushed. But although she was aware enough to have guessed at last, her sensitivity didn't extend to understanding how appalling that discovery was for Eunice. She was only twenty.

"Why didn't you tell us?" she said as Eunice got up. "We'd have understood. Lots of people are dyslexic, thousands of people actually. I did some work on a study of it in my last year at school. Miss Parchman, shall I teach you to read? I'm sure I could. It'd be fun. I could begin in the Easter holidays."

Eunice took the two mugs and set them on the draining board. She stood still with her back to Melinda. She poured the remains of her tea down the sink. Then she turned around slowly and, with no outward sign that her heart was drumming fast and heavily, fixed Melinda with her apparently emotionless implacable stare.

"If you tell anyone I'm what you said, that word, I'll tell your dad you've been going with that boy and you're going to have a baby."

She spoke so levelly and calmly that at first Melinda hardly understood. She had led a sheltered life, and no one had ever really threatened her before.

"*What* did you say?"

"You heard. You tell them, and I'll tell them about you." Abuse wasn't Eunice's forte, but she managed. "Dirty little tart, that's what you are. Dirty interfering little bitch."

Melinda went white. She got up and walked out of the kitchen, stumbling over her long skirt. Out in the hall her legs almost gave way, she was shaking so much, and she sat down in the chair by the grandfather clock. She sat there with her fists pressed to her cheeks till the clock chimed six and the kitchen door opened. A wave of sickness hit her at the thought of even seeing Eunice Parchman again, and she fled into the drawing room, where she fell onto the sofa and burst into tears.

It was there that George found her a few minutes later.

"My darling, what is it? What on earth's happened? You mustn't cry like this." He lifted her and hugged her in his arms. There had been a quarrel, he thought, with that boy, and that was why she had come home to an empty comfortless house. "Tell Daddy." He forgot she was twenty. "Tell me all about it and you'll feel better."

Jacqueline said nothing but "I'll leave you two alone." George never interfered between her and Giles, and she never interposed her voice between him and his children.

"No, Jackie, you're not to go." Melinda sat up and scrubbed at her eyes. "Oh, I am a *fool!* I'll tell you both, but it's so awful."

"As long as you're not ill or hurt," said George, "it isn't awful."

"Oh, God." Melinda swallowed, took a deep breath. "I'm so glad you've come back!"

"Melinda, please tell us what's the matter."

"I thought I was going to have a baby but I'm not," said Melinda in a rush. "I've been sleeping with Jon since November. I know you'll be cross, I know you'll be disappointed, but I do love him and he loves me and it's all right, really it is, and I'm not going to have a baby."

"Is that all?" said George.

His daughter stared at him. "Aren't you mad with me? Aren't you shocked?"

"I'm not even surprised, Melinda. For heaven's sake,

d'you think me that much of a fuddy-duddy? D'you think I haven't noticed that things have changed since I was young? I won't say I don't regret it, I won't say I wouldn't rather you hadn't, and I shouldn't like you to be promiscuous. But I'm not in the least shocked."

"You are *sweet*." She threw her arms around his neck.

"And now perhaps you'll tell us," said George, disengaging himself, "why you were crying? I presume you're not sorry you aren't pregnant?"

Melinda managed a watery smile. "It was that woman—Miss Parchman. It's unbelievable, Daddy, but it's true. She found out. She must have overheard me talking on the phone to Jon at Christmas, and when I—well, found out something about her, she said she'd tell you. She threatened me. Just now. She said she'd tell you I was pregnant."

"*She did what?*"

"I said it was unbelievable."

"Melinda, of course I believe you. The woman actually blackmailed you?"

"If that's blackmail, yes."

"What were her exact words?"

Melinda told him. "And she called me a tart. It was awful."

Silent until now, Jacqueline spoke. "She must leave, of course. Now. At once."

"Darling, I'm afraid she must. I know what it means to you, having her, but . . ."

"It doesn't mean a thing. I never heard anything so odious and revolting in my life. To dare to threaten Melinda! She must be told at once. You'll have to do it, George, I couldn't trust myself."

He gave her a glance that was passionate in his appreciation of her loyalty. And then, "What did you find out about her, Melinda?"

Fatal question. It was a pity George hadn't waited to ask it until after he had dismissed Eunice. For his daughter's answer moved him as the substance of that answer had never moved her, and he was softened by pity.

Eunice believed that her threat had succeeded, and a pride in her achievement went a long way toward conquering distress. That great tomboy had looked really upset. She wouldn't give Eunice away, for, as Joan had said, her father would turn her out of the house. The television on for a variety show, she had watched for a quarter of an hour, knitting away, when there came a knock on her door. Melinda. They always came to you after the first shock was over to beg you not to tell. And even though you promised, they kept wanting reassurance. It had been that way with the married woman and Annie Cole. Eunice opened the door.

George walked in. "You can guess why I've come, Miss Parchman. My daughter naturally told me what passed between you. I cannot have a person who threatens a member of my family in my household, so you will, of course, leave as soon as possible."

It was a tremendous shock to Eunice, who said nothing. The program had been interrupted for the commercials, and the one currently showing consisted mainly of printed words, a list of East Anglican stores. George said, "We'll have that off, if you don't mind. It can hardly be of interest to *you*."

Eunice understood. He knew. She who was without sensitivity in all other respects had an acute delicate awareness in this one. And he, watching her, understood too. Her flush and the distortion of her face told him he had gone too far under gross provocation. He had committed that most uncouth of sins, mocked the hunchback's hump.

"You haven't a contract," he said quickly, "so I could ask you to leave at once, but all things considered, we'll say a week. That will give you opportunity to look around for other employment. But in the meantime you will please keep to this room and leave the housework to my wife and Mrs. Baalham. I am prepared to give you a reference as to your efficiency, but I could give no assurance to your personal integrity." He went out and closed the door.

It would be hard to imagine Eunice Parchman in tears, and she didn't cry now. Alone in a place where she might have indulged her feelings, she gave no sign of having any. She neither shook nor sighed nor was sick. She turned on the television and watched it, though slumped a little more heavily than usual in her armchair.

Her illiteracy had been known to three people, but to none of them had it come as a sudden and shocking revelation. Her parents had never thought it important. Gradually Mrs. Samson had come to know it and to accept it as she accepted that another child in Rainbow Street was a mongol, but it wasn't the kind of thing you talked about, certainly not to Eunice herself. No one had ever talked to her about it; no whole group of people had ever, all at once, become aware of it. In the days that followed, when she was more or less confined to her room, she thought not at all about where she should go or what she should do, what employment she could find or where she could live. She took very little thought for the morrow, for Mrs. Samson or Annie Cole would take her in if she turned up on their doorsteps with her cases, but she thought exhaustively about the Coverdales' discovery, which she believed must now be spread all over Greeving. It stopped her going out. It stopped her from going to the village store, and once, when Jacqueline was out and Joan called, she didn't respond to Joan's screeched greeting but stayed in hiding upstairs.

It seemed to her that the Coverdales must spend all their time discussing her disability and laughing about it with their friends. She was partly wrong and partly right, for George and Jacqueline were prevented from doing the latter by honorable feelings and also because it would have made them look very foolish not to have realized before that their housekeeper couldn't read. They told people they had dismissed her for insolence. But to each other they did talk quite a lot about it, and even laughed in a wondering way, and longed for next Monday, and shut themselves up in the drawing room when Eunice crept down for her meals.

Unmoved by any feelings of loyalty or duty to her friend, Eunice thought the best thing would be to avoid Joan and escape from Greeving without ever seeing her again. Things were bad enough without Joan's sympathy and solicitude and tedious questions, for by now Joan also must know. Joan, in fact, did know. Or, that is, she knew of Eunice's dismissal, for the Mrs. Higgs who was distinguished by *not* riding a bike had told her about it on Tuesday. She waited for Eunice to come, she did her best to get into Lowfield Hall, and when she couldn't, she took the only course open to her—even Joan was afraid to telephone—and sent a message.

That year St. Valentine's Day fell on a Sunday, so valentines needs must arrive on the Saturday. None came for the Coverdales, but one did arrive at Lowfield Hall among the birthday cards for George. It was addressed to Eunice, and Jacqueline handed it to her with a quiet "This is for you, Miss Parchman."

Both women flushed, both knew Eunice couldn't read it. She took it upstairs and looked in bewilderment at the gaudy picture of two cherubs twining a garland of pink roses around a blue heart. There were bits of writing all over it. Eunice threw it away.

George became fifty-eight on February 13, and cards came for him from his wife and all his children. *All my love, darling, your Jackie. Many happy returns and love, Paula, Brian, Patrick, and little Giles. Love from Audrey and Peter. Lots of love, Melinda—see you Saturday afternoon.* Even Giles had sent a card, inappropriately (or very appropriately) a reproduction of Masaccio's *Expulsion from Paradise.* He didn't go so far as to provide a present, though George got a watch, to replace his twenty-five-year-old one, from Jacqueline, and a record token and a book token from his married son and daughter respectively. That night they were going to dine *en famille* at the Angel at Cattingham.

George drove to Stantwich and picked Melinda up at the station. She presented him with a rather awful scarf that looked as if it had come from the Oxfam

shop, though it hadn't, and George thanked her lav-
ishly.

"Time I forgot all this nonsense at my advanced
age," he said, "but none of you will let me."

"Well," said Melinda, who had actually been giving
a little time to studying one of her set plays, "who's
born the day that I forget to send to Antony shall die
a beggar."

"My God, the child's been doing some work for a
change!"

As they entered the house she looked inquiringly at
her father, and George understood. "Upstairs," he
said with a jerk of his head.

Melinda smiled. "Have you put her under house ar-
rest?"

"In a way. She goes on Monday morning."

They dressed up to go out, Jacqueline in the cream
velvet, Melinda in her spangled blue, and they were
an impressive sight as they walked into the hotel dining room. A handsome family, even Giles, who was
at any rate tall and thin, not looking at all bad in his
one suit and with his spots rather quiescent at the
moment.

Afterward the waiters and the other diners were
to wish they had taken more notice of this happy
family, this doomed family. They wished they had
known, and then they would have listened to the
Coverdales' lighthearted conversation and paid more
attention to Jacqueline's appearance, the evidences of
Giles's superlative intellect, Melinda's charm, George's
distinguished presence. They didn't know, so they
had to confess ignorance when the newspaper reporters questioned them, or—and this happened more often—invent all kinds of prognostications and doleful
premonitions which they were convinced they had
been aware of at the time. The police also questioned
some of them, and their ignorance was proved by
none of them recalling a discussion between the Coverdales that would have been of relevance in solving
the case sooner than it was solved.

This conversation was on the subject of a television

program to take place on the following night, a film of a Glyndebourne production of *Don Giovanni*, due to last from seven until after ten.

"Do you have to get back tomorrow night, Melinda?" asked George. "It seems a pity for you to miss this, it's supposed to be the television event of the year. I could drive you to Stantwich first thing on Monday."

"I haven't got a lecture on Monday. Nothing till a tutorial at two."

"What he really means, Melinda," said her stepmother, laughing, "is that he wants some moral support in the car when he drives the Parchman to the station."

"Not at all. I shall have Giles."

Jacqueline and Melinda laughed. Giles looked up seriously from his duck and green peas. Something moved him. His conversion? The fact that it was George's birthday? Whatever it was, he was inspired for once to say the perfect thing.

"I will never desert Mr. Micawber."

"Thank you, Giles," said George quietly. There was an odd little silence in which, without speaking or glancing at each other, Giles and his stepfather approached a closeness never before attained. Given time, they might have become friends. No time was to be given them. George cleared his throat and said, "Seriously, Melinda, why not stay for the film?"

It wasn't the prospect of missing work which made Melinda hesitate, but of missing Jonathan. They had been together every day and almost every night for weeks now. She would miss him painfully tonight. Must she now contemplate another night without him? It seemed selfish to refuse. She loved her father. How wonderful he and Jacqueline had been last week over that hateful business, how loyal and unwavering! And not a word of reproach for her, not even a warning to be careful. But Jonathan . . .

She had come to a parting of the ways. Ahead of her the road forked. One path led to life and happiness, marriage, children, the other was a dead end, a cul-de-sac. No Through Road. She hesitated. She chose.

"I'll stay," she said.

From the village store Joan Smith watched the Mercedes pass through the village. Five minutes later she was at the Hall, inside the Hall, for she had skipped in her new, thoroughly insane way through the gun room to surprise Eunice as she sat devouring egg and chips and lemon cheesecake at the kitchen table.

"Oh, Eun, you must be brokenhearted. The base ingratitude after what you've done for them. And for a little thing like that!"

Eunice was not pleased to see her. The "little thing" must surely be her inability to read. Her appetite gone, she glowered and waited for the worst. Eventually it was not the worst but the best that came, but she had to wait for that.

"All packed, are you, dear? No doubt you've got plans of your own. Anyone with your skills won't have far to look for a brilliant situation, but I want you to know you're welcome to make your home with us. While Joanie has a spare bed and a roof over her head, you're welcome. Though the Lord only knows how long it'll be spared to use while the wicked man rageth." Joan panted from her efforts, said breathlessly yet coyly, "Did you get anything by the post today?"

Hard color came into Eunice's cheeks. "Why?"

"Oh, she's blushing! Did you think you'd got an admirer in the village, Eun? Well, you have, dear. Me. Why ever didn't you read my message on the back? I knew they'd be out, I said I'd pop up."

Eunice had supposed Melinda had sent the mocking valentine. But this wasn't the source of her overwhelming tremendous relief. Joan didn't know, it hadn't reached Joan. Relief threw her back, quite wan and weak, in her chair. She approached love for Joan in that moment, and she couldn't have done enough for her. Recovered and almost ebullient, she made tea, cudgeled her poor imagination to invent details of her dismissal to satisfy Joan, denounced the Coverdales with bitterness, promised Joan her attendance on the following night, her last night, at the temple in Colchester.

"Our last time together, Eun. And I was counting on your company when Elder Barnstaple and Mrs. come to us for supper on Wednesday. But God isn't mocked, dear. You'll rise again in all your glory when he's in the pit, when they're reaping the punishment of their iniquity. Oh yes, when they're heaped with retribution."

Taking very little notice of all this, of Joan's ravings and prancings, Eunice nevertheless ministered to her like the Martha she was, pouring tea and slicing cheesecake and promising no end of things, like coming back to see Joan at her first opportunity, and writing to her (of all things!) and swearing, in very un-Eunice-like fashion, undying friendship.

Joan seemed to have an instinct about when it was safe to remain and when to go, but this time, so vehement were they and with so much to talk about, that the van had only just turned out of the drive when the Mercedes came up it. Eunice tramped off to bed.

"Back to the grind on Monday," said Jacqueline, leaving a satiny stripe in the dust where she had run her finger across the surface of her dressing table. "I feel as if I've had nine months' holiday. Ah, well, all good things come to an end."

"And all bad ones," said George.

"Don't worry. I'm just as glad as you to see the back of her. Had a nice day, darling?"

"I have had a lovely day. But all my days are lovely with you."

She got up, smiling at him, and he took her in his arms.

19

In church on Sunday morning, their last morning, the Coverdales murmured that they had done those things which they ought not to have done, and left undone those things which they ought to have done. They uttered this in a reverent and quite sincere way, but they did not really think about what they were saying. Mr. Archer preached a sermon about how one ought to be kind to old people, to one's elderly relatives, which had no bearing on anything in the Coverdales' lives, though plenty on the lives of Eunice Parchman and Joan Smith. After church they had sherry at the Jameson-Kerrs', and lunch was late, not on the table till three.

The weather was non-weather, windless, damp, the sky overcast, but already the first signs of spring had appeared. Early spring is not green but red, as each twig in the hedges takes on a crimson sheen from the rising vitalizing sap. In the garden of Lowfield Hall the snowdrops were coming out, first flowers of spring, last flowers the Coverdales would ever see.

Melinda had phoned Jonathan before she went to church, speaking to him for the last time. For the last time Giles saw the Elevation of the Mass. Although he was not yet received into the Church, kind Father Madigan had heard his confession and shriven him, and Giles was perhaps in a state of grace. For the last time George and Jacqueline had a Sunday-afternoon doze in the morning room, and at five George

moved the television set into the drawing room, plug-
ging in the aerial to the socket between the front
windows.

When she woke up Jacqueline read the article on
Don Giovanni in the *Radio Times,* and then she went
into the kitchen to make tea. Eunice passed through
the kitchen at twenty-five past five in her dark red
coat and woolly hat and scarf. The two women pre-
tended not to have seen each other, and Eunice left
the house by way of the gun room, closing the door
quietly behind her. Melinda fetched her tape recorder
and, putting her head around the door of Giles's
sanctum, told him she meant to record the opera.

"I suppose you won't even come down for it," she
said.

"I don't know."

"I wish you would. I'd like you to."

"All right," said Giles.

The dark winter's day had slipped, without any
apparent sunset, into dark winter's night. There was
no wind, no rain, no stars. It was as if the moon had
died, for it had not been seen for many nights. All
around isolated Lowfield Hall the undulating fields,
the deserted threading lanes, and the small crowding
woods were enclosed by impenetrable blackness.
Not quite impenetrable, for, from the Stantwich road,
the traveler would be able to make out the Hall as a
brilliant spot of light. How far this little candle throws
his beams! So shines a good deed in a naughty world.

Joan and Eunice reached the Epiphany Temple at
five to six, and Joan behaved peaceably, perhaps
with an ominous quietness, during the hymn singing
and the confessing. Afterward, while they were eating
seed cake and Joan was recounting details of her sinful past to a new member, Mrs. Barnstaple came up
to her and said rather stiffly that she and the Elder
would be unable to visit the Smiths on Wednesday
evening. Now, the Barnstaples lived in Nunchester,
and efficient as the grapevine was, it didn't extend to
Nunchester. Mrs. Barnstaple had taken her decision
because, although she knew Joan was a good Epiph-

any Person whom the Lord had pardoned, she couldn't (as she told her husband) stomach listening to any more of that stuff about goings-on in Shepherds Bush while she was eating. But Joan took her refusal as reaction to the news of the inquiry set in train by George Coverdale, and she jumped up, giving a loud scream.

"Woe to the wicked man who spreadeth slanders in the ears of the innocent!" Joan didn't necessarily quote from the Bible. Just as often she ranted in biblical language what she thought ought to have been in the Bible. "The Lord shall smite him in his loins and in his hip and his thigh. Praised be the Lord who chooseth His handmaid to be His weapon and His right hand!"

Her body was charged with a frenetic energy. She screeched, and spittle sprayed from her mouth. For a few seconds the brethren enjoyed it, but they were not mad, only misguided fanatics, and when Joan's eyes rolled and she began tugging at her hair, actually pulling some of it out, Mrs. Barnstaple tried to get hold of her. Joan gave her a great push, and that lady fell backward into the arms of her husband. Eunice was appealed to, but Eunice didn't want to do anything to antagonize Joan, who was now in control of the whole assembly, raving incomprehensible words and throwing herself backward and forward in a frenzy.

Then, as suddenly as she had begun, she stopped. It was mediumistic, the change that came over her. At one moment she seemed possessed by an enraged spirit, the next she had fallen spent and silent into a chair. In a small voice she said to Eunice, "We'll be on our way when you're ready, Eun."

They left the temple at twenty past seven, Joan driving like a cautious learner.

Grouped a suitable twenty feet away from the television set, George and Jacqueline sat together on the sofa, Melinda on the floor at her father's feet, Giles hunched in an armchair. The tape recorder was on. Having fidgeted with it during the overture, moving it about and watching it anxiously, Melinda grew less and less aware of its presence as the opera proceeded. She was all set to identify with every female character. She was Anna, she would be Elvira and, when the time came, Zerlina too. She leaned her head against George's arm of the sofa, for George, in her eyes, had become the Commendatore, fighting a duel and getting himself killed for his daughter's honor, though she didn't quite see her Jonathan as the Don.

Elegant Jacqueline, in green velvet trousers and gold silk shirt, penciled a critical note or two on the margin of the *Radio Times.* Under her breath she whispered, following Ottavio, "Find husband and father in me!" and she darted a soft look at George. But George, being a man, a handsome and sexually successful man, couldn't help identifying with the Don. He didn't want a catalog of women, he only wanted his Jacqueline, and yet . . .

"I will cut out his heart!" sang Elvira, and they laughed appreciatively, all but Giles. He was only there for Melinda's sake, and the age of reason and manners had never held much appeal for him. He alone heard a footstep on the gravel of the drive at twenty to eight while Scene Two and the Catalog Song were ending, for he alone was not concentrating on the music. But of course he did nothing about it. That wasn't his way.

Looking indignant, Jacqueline added a line to her notes as Scene Three opened. The time approached five minutes to eight. As Giovanni sang, *"O, guarda, guarda* [Look, look]!" the Smiths' van entered the drive of Lowfield Hall and crept, with only side lights on, almost to the front door. But the Coverdales did not look, or hear any extraneous sound. Even Giles heard nothing this time.

Joan's driving had become erratic, and her jerky zigzagging from slow lane to fast was a frightening experience even for phlegmatic Eunice.

"You'd better calm down if you don't want us both killed."

The admonitions of those who seldom remonstrate

are more effective than the commands of naggers.
But Joan was in no state to adopt the happy mean. It
was neck or nothing for her, and she crawled along
the lane to Greeving.

"Come in for a bit," said Eunice.

"That'd be Daniel into the lion's den," said Joan
with a shriek of laughter.

"You come in. Why shouldn't you? A cup of tea'd
calm you down."

"I like your spirit, Eun. Why shouldn't I? They
can't kill me, can they?"

Joan kangaroo-hopped the van in too high a gear
up the drive. It was Eunice, the nondriver, who
grabbed the gear lever and stamped on the clutch so
that they could approach more quietly. The van was
left standing on the broad gravel space, a little way
from the streak of light that fell from between the
drawing-room curtains.

"They're looking at the TV," said Eunice.

She put the kettle on while Joan lingered in the
gun room.

"Poor little birds," she said. "It doesn't seem right.
What have they done to him?"

"What have *I* done?" said Eunice.

"Too right." Joan took one of the guns down and
leveled it playfully at Eunice. "Bang, bang, you're
dead! Did you ever play cowboys when you were a
kid, Eun?"

"I don't know. Come on, tea's ready." In spite of her
defiant words, she was nervous that Joan's hysterical
voice would penetrate to the drawing room and be
heard above the music. They mounted the first flight
of stairs, Eunice carrying the tray, but they never
reached the attic floor. Never again was Joan Smith to
enter Eunice's domain, and no final farewell was ever
to be spoken between them. Jacqueline's bedroom
door stood open. Joan went in and put the light on.

Eunice noticed that there was a patina of bedroom
dust, composed of talcum and fluff, on the polished
surfaces, and that the bed was less evenly made than
when she had made it. She set the tray down on one
of the bedside tables and gave the quilt a twitch.

Joan tiptoed around the room, lifting her high heels an inch above the carpet and giggling soundlessly on a series of small exhalations like a person imitating a steam engine. When she reached Jacqueline's side of the bed she picked up the photograph of George and laid it face downward.

"She'll know who did that," said Eunice.

"Doesn't matter. You said they can't do any more to you."

"No." After a small hesitation, Eunice laid the picture of Jacqueline face downward also. "Come on, we'd better have that tea."

Joan said, "I'll pour." She lifted the teapot and poured a steady stream into the center of the counterpane. Eunice retreated, one hand up to her mouth. The liquid lay in a lake, and then it began to seep through the covers.

"You've done it now," said Eunice.

Joan went out onto the landing and listened. She came back. She picked up a box of talcum, took off the lid, and hurled the box onto the bed. White clouds of powder rose, making Eunice cough. And now Joan had opened the wardrobe.

"What are you going to do?" Eunice whispered.

No answer from Joan. She was holding the red silk evening gown on its hanger. She set her fingers in the circle of the neckline and ripped the dress downward, so that she was holding the front in one hand and the back in the other. Eunice was frightened, she was appalled, but she was also excited. Joan's mounting frenzy had excited her. She too plunged her hands inside the wardrobe, where she found the green pleated dress she had so often ironed, and she ran into its bodice the points of Jacqueline's nail scissors. The scissors were snatched from her by Joan, who began indiscriminately slashing clothes, gasping with pleasure. Eunice trod heavily on the pile of torn cloth, she ground her heel into the glass of those framed photographs, she pulled out drawers, scattering jewelry and cosmetics and the letters, which fluttered from their ribbon binding. It made her laugh throatily while Joan laughed maniacally, and they were both confident that the music from below was loud enough to drown any noise.

It was, for the time being. While Eunice and Joan were making mayhem above their heads, the Coverdales were listening to one of the loudest solos in the whole opera, the Champagne Aria. Jacqueline heard it out, and then she left the drawing room to make coffee, choosing this opportunity because she disliked the Zerlina and feared she would make a hash of *Batti, batti.* In the kitchen she noticed that the kettle was still warm, so Eunice must have come back, and noticed too the shotgun on the table. But she supposed George had put it there for some purpose of his own before they had begun to watch television.

The sound of the drawing-room door opening, and footfalls across the hall floor, sobered Joan and Eunice. They sat down on the bed, looking at each other in a mock-rueful way, eyebrows up, lips caught under upper teeth. Joan switched off the light, and they sat in darkness until they heard Jacqueline cross the hall and reenter the drawing room.

Eunice kicked at a heap of mingled broken glass and nylon. She said, "That's torn it," quite seriously, not joining in Joan's laughter. "Maybe he'll get the police on us."

"He doesn't know we're here." Joan's eyes gleamed. "Got any wire cutters in the house, Eun?"

"I don't know. Could be in the gun room. What d'you want wire cutters for?"

"You'll see. I'm glad we did it, Eun. Oh, we have smitten him in his high places, in the bed of his lechery we have afflicted him. I am the instrument of the Lord's vengeance! I am the sword in His hand and the spear in His right hand!"

"If you go on like that they'll hear you," said Eunice. "I'm glad we did it too."

They left the tray on the table, the teapot in the middle of the bed. The light was on down in the hall. Joan went straight to the gun room and rooted about in George's toolbox.

"I'm going to cut the phone wire."

"Like they do on TV," said Eunice. She had ceased

to protest. She nodded approvingly. "It comes in over the front door," she said. "Stop them phoning the police, that will."

Joan came back, a silent smile glittering. "What shall we do now, dear?"

It hadn't occurred to Eunice that they would do anything more. Breaking things down here must necessarily be heard in the drawing room, and, police or not, she and this frail stick of a woman could easily be overpowered by four strong adults. "I don't know," she said, but this time her habitual response had a wistful note in it. She wanted the fun to go on.

"May as well be hanged for a sheep as a lamb," said Joan, picking up the shotgun and looking down one of its barrels. "Frighten them out of their wits, it would, if I fired this."

Eunice took the other gun off the wall. "Not like that," she said. "Like this."

"You're a dark horse, Eun. Since when've you been a lady gangster?"

"I've watched him. I can do it as well as he can."

"I'm going to try!"

"It's not loaded," said Eunice. "There's things called cartridges in that drawer. I've often watched him do it. They cost a fortune, those guns, couple of hundred each."

"We could break them."

"That's what you call it when you open them to load them. Breaking the gun's what you say."

They looked at each other, and Joan laughed with a sound like a peacock's shriek.

"The music's stopped," said Eunice.

It was twenty-five minutes to nine. Act One had come to an end, in the opera and in the kitchen.

20

In the lull between acts Jacqueline poured second cups of coffee for all of them. Melinda stretched and stood up.

"Marvelous," said George. "What do you think, darling?"

"Zerlina's awful. Too old and too tinkly. George, did you hear any sounds from upstairs during the minuet?"

"I don't think so. It was probably our *bête noire* slinking in."

"The last thing she does is slink, Daddy," said Melinda. "Sneaking, maybe. Oh, God, I've forgotten to stop the tape."

"It wasn't slinking or sneaking I heard, but breaking glass."

. Melinda switched off her recorder. "They were at a party," she said, referring to the opera. "I expect it was sound effects." The rest of what she was going to say was cut off by a thin shriek from somewhere outside the room.

"George!" Jacqueline almost shouted. "It's that Mrs. Smith!"

"I do believe it is," said George slowly and ominously.

"She's out in the kitchen with Miss Parchman."

"Very soon she'll be out in the cold with her marching orders." He got up.

"Oh, Daddy, you'll miss the beginning of Act Two.

148

Nasty old Parchment Face is probably just having a farewell party."

"I'll be two minutes," said George. He went to the door, where he paused and looked at his wife for the last time. Had he known it was the last time, that look would have been eloquent of six years' bliss and of gratitude, but he didn't know, so he merely cast up his eyes and pursed his mouth before walking across the hall and down the passage to the kitchen. Jacqueline considered going with him but thought better of it and settled back against the sofa cushions as Act Two began with the quarrel between Leporello and his master. The tape recorder was on. *Ma che ti ho fatto, che vuoi lasciarmi* (But what have I done to you that you wish to leave me)? *Oh, niente affatto; quasi ammazzarmi* (Oh, nothing at all, but almost killed me)! . . .

George opened the kitchen door, and there he stopped in amazement. His housekeeper stood on one side of the table, her stripy hair coming away from its pins, her pale face flushed maroon, facing the crane-chick figure of Joan Smith, befeathered in green and salmon pink. Each was holding one of his shotguns which she pointed at the other.

"This is monstrous," said George when he recovered his voice. "Put those guns down at once!"

Joan gave a babbling shriek. "Bang, bang!" she said. Some memory of war or war film came to her. *"Hande hoch!"* she shouted, and pointed the gun at his face.

"Fortunately for you, it isn't loaded." Calmly Major Coverdale of Alamein looked at his new watch. "I will give you and Miss Parchman thirty seconds to put those guns on the table. If you don't I shall take them from you by force, and then I shall call the police."

"You'll be lucky," said Eunice.

Neither woman moved. George stood stock-still for the full half-minute. He wasn't afraid. The guns weren't loaded. As the thirty seconds came to an end and Joan still pointed the gun at him, he heard faintly from the drawing room the beginning of Elvira's sweet and thrilling *O, taci, ingiusto core* (Be silent, treacherous heart)! His own was thudding steadily. He went up to Joan, grasped the gun, and gave a sharp grunt as Eunice shot him in the neck. He fell across the table, flinging out his arms to grasp its edge, blood shooting in a fountain from the severed jugular. Joan scuttered back against the wall. With an indrawn breath, Eunice fired the second barrel into his back.

At the sound of the two shots Jacqueline sprang to her feet with a cry of alarm. "For heaven's sake, what was that?"

"Mrs. Smith's van backfiring," said Melinda, and, dropping her voice because of the tape, "It always does that. There's something wrong with the exhaust."

"It sounded like a gun."

"Cars backfiring do sound like guns. Sit down, Jackie, or we'll miss this, and it's the loveliest song of all."

Be silent, treacherous heart. Beat not so in my breast. Elvira leaned from her window, Leporello and the Don appeared beneath it, and the great trio swelled on the two baritone voices and the soprano. Jacqueline sat down, glanced at the door. "Why doesn't your father come back?" she said nervously.

"He's shot the lunatic," said Giles, "and he doesn't know how to tell us."

"Oh, *Giles*. Darling, go and see, would you? I can't hear a sound."

"Of course you can't, Jackie, with this on," said Melinda with asperity. "You don't *want* to hear him bawling Parchman out, do you? All this rubbish is going to be on my tape, isn't it?"

Jacqueline put up her hands, fluttering them in a little gesture of apology, yet of anxiety too, and Giles, who had begun languidly to raise himself from his chair, slumped back into it. From the television came the softly plucked notes of Giovanni's mandolin. *Deh! vieni alla finestra* (Then come to the window) . . . Jacqueline, her hands clenched, obeyed his behest. She jumped up suddenly, went to the window on the left of the set, and parted the curtains. The tape forgotten, she cried out:

"Mrs. Smith's van is out there! It can't have been that we heard."

She turned back to face them, a disgruntled Menda, a bored, exasperated Giles. Her face was puckered with distress, and even Giles saw it, felt it, her tension and her rising fear. "I'll go," he sighed, beginning to shift himself very slowly like an old man with arthritis. He lounged toward the door as Joan Smith and Eunice Parchman passed from the kitchen into the passage.

"We'll have to kill the others now," said Eunice in the voice she used when speaking of some necessary measure not to be postponed, such as washing a floor.

Joan, who needed no encouragement, looked back at George. He was dead, but his watch lived on, and since his death the minute hand had passed from the ten nearly to the twelve. It was almost nine o'clock. She looked back once, and then up at Eunice with a great face-splitting smile. There was blood on her hands and face and on the jumper Eunice had knitted for her. They passed into the hall and the strengthening music, music which met them with a blast of baritone voice and plucked strings as Giles opened the drawing-room door. He saw the blood and shouted out.

He shouted, "Oh, Christ!" and turned back, a split second before Joan told him to.

"Get back in there. We've got guns."

Eunice was the first to follow him. A jumble of male voices singing roared in her head, and power, the chance at last to command and avenge, roared through her body. It strengthened her hands, which had failed her a little back there in the kitchen. They were hard and dexterous now as she leveled the reloaded gun. Jacqueline's face, blanched and terrified, was to her only the face which had sneered a little while handing over that valentine. Jacqueline's voice, screaming for her husband, was still the voice of a woman who read books and looked up from her letter-writing to murmur sarcastic courtesies. In those moments the words they cried and their pleas passed over her almost unheard, and by some strange metamorphosis, produced in Eunice's brain, they ceased to be people and became the printed word. They were those things in the bookcases, those patchy black blocks on white paper, eternally her enemies, hated and desired.

"You'd better sit down," she said. "You've got it coming to you."

Joan's laughter cut across her words. Joan shouted something from the Bible, and then Joan fired her gun. Eunice gasped. Not because she heard the screams or saw the blood but because Joan might do it first, Joan might beat her to it. She advanced, pointing her gun. She fired both barrels, reloaded while another shot rang in her ears, and then she emptied the two barrels into what lay on the Chinese carpet.

The music had stopped. Joan must have stopped it. The banging had stopped, and the screaming. A silence more profound, more soothing to the mind and the savage breast, filled the drawing room like a thick tangible balm. It held Eunice suspended. It petrified this stone-age woman into stone. Her eyelids dropped and she breathed evenly and steadily so that, had she had an observer, he would have supposed her fallen asleep where she stood.

A stone that breathed was Eunice, as she had always been.

21

The exalted calm of one who has performed a holy mission descended upon Joan Smith. She surveyed what she had done and saw that it was good. She had scattered the enemies of God, and thus purified herself. If the McNaughton Rules had been applied to her she would have passed the test, for though she had known what she was doing, she did not know it was wrong.

She was innocent in the true meaning of the word. And now she would drive down into Greeving and tell the village what she had done, proclaim it in the streets and shout it aloud in the Blue Boar. It was a pity she had cut the phone wire, for otherwise she could have lifted the phone and announced it to the operator. Calmly, majestically, she laid down the gun and picked up the tape recorder. It was still on. She pressed something and the little red light on it went out. Inside it was a record of her achievement, and it is a measure of Joan's madness that at that moment she saw herself, at some future time, playing the tape for the edification of the Epiphany breathren.

Of Eunice she took very little notice. Eunice stood immobile, still holding her gun, staring implacably at the bodies of Giles and Melinda, who lay side by side in death, closer to an embrace than they had ever been in life. But Joan had forgotten who Eunice was. She had forgotten her own name, and the past, and Shepherds Bush and Norman. She was alone, a titaness, an angel, and she feared nothing but that some malignant spirit, allied to the Coverdale interest, might yet intervene to prevent her from proclaiming the good news.

George's blood was on her jumper, on her hands and face. She let it dry there. Uncharacteristically, with a long slow stride, she walked toward the door and the hall, and Eunice was aroused from her contemplation.

"You'd better wash your face before you go," she said.

Joan ignored her. She opened the front door and looked for demons in the darkness. The drive and the garden were empty, and to Joan they seemed friendly. She got into the van.

"Suit yourself," said Eunice. "Have a good wash before you go to bed. And mind you don't say a word. Just keep quiet."

"I am the spear of the Lord of Hosts."

Eunice shrugged. That sort of thing didn't much matter, Joan always went on like that, and the village people would only think she was more crazy than ever. She went back into the house, where she had things to see to.

With only side lights on, Joan drove the van euphorically out of the grounds of Lowfield Hall. She drove with her head held high, looking to the right and the left, anywhere but ahead of her, and she smiled graciously as if to an admiring throng. It was a miracle she even reached the gates. But she did reach them and got about a quarter of a mile along the lane. There, where the lane bent rather sharply to avoid a high brick wall that enclosed the front garden of Mr. Meadows' farmhouse, she saw a white owl drop from one of the trees and flap heavily in front of her at windscreen level. Joan thought it was a demon sent by the Coverdales to get her. She stamped on the accelerator to smash through it and smashed instead into the wall. The front part of the van crumpled up like a concertina, and Joan's head crashed through glass into a twelve-inch-thick bastion of concrete faced with brick.

It was half-past nine. Mr. and Mrs. Meadows were visiting their married daughter in Sudbury, and there was no one else in the house to hear the crash. Norman Smith was in the Blue Boar, where they had had their own bit of excitement, although it wasn't until the following day that they realized how exciting it had been. He went home at ten-fifteen. His van wasn't parked between the village store and the triangle of grass, but he supposed Joan was still off somewhere with Eunice, it being Eunice's last night in Greeving, and a good thing too. No one passed down Greeving Lane (or, at least, no one reported the crash) until the Meadowses got home at twenty-five past ten. When they saw their ruined wall and the van with Joan lying unconscious half in and half out of it, they phoned first for an ambulance and then they phoned Norman Smith. Joan, who was alive though in a bad way, was taken to hospital, where they weren't going to worry about whether the blood on her was all hers or not, there was so much of it. So Joan Smith, who ought to have gone into a mental hospital months before, ended up in an intensive-care ward for the physically injured.

This was the second time that evening Norman had been afforded the sight of blood. Very nearly three hours before he was fetched to the scene of his wife's accident, two young men had walked into the saloon bar of the Blue Boar, and the smaller and younger of them had asked the licensee, Edwin Carter, where the men's room was. He wanted to wash his hands, for the left one appeared injured in some way, and blood had seeped through the handkerchief that bandaged it.

Mr. Carter directed him to the lavatory, and his wife asked if there was anything she could do in the way of first aid. Her offer was refused, no explanation of the injury given, and when the young man came back he had rebandaged his hand with a cleaner handkerchief. Neither of the Carters nor any of the patrons of the bar recalled actually having seen his hand, but only that there had been blood on the original bandage. The other witnesses were Jim Meadows of the garage, Alan and Pat Newstead, Geoff and Barbara Baalham and Geoff's brother Philip, and Norman Smith.

Mrs. Carter was to remember that the man with the injured hand drank a double brandy and his companion a half of bitter. They sat at a table, drank their drinks in less than five minutes, and left without speaking to anyone except to ask where they could get petrol at this hour, Meadows' garage being closed. Geoff Baalham told them there was a self-service petrol station on the main road past Gallows Corner and, describing how to find it, followed them out onto the Blue Boar's forecourt. There he noticed their car, an old Morris Minor Traveler, maroon bodywork in a wooden shooting brake frame. He didn't, however, notice the registration number.

They left the village by Greeving Lane, their route inevitably taking them past Lowfield Hall.

On the following day all those witnesses furnished the police with descriptions of these strangers. Jim Meadows said they both had long dark hair, were both dressed in blue denim, and the one whose hand was not injured was over six feet tall. The Carters agreed that the tall one had long dark hair, but their daughter, Barbara Baalham, said both had brown hair and brown eyes. According to Alan Newstead, the one with the injured hand had short fair hair and piercing blue eyes, but his wife said that, though piercing, the eyes were brown. Geoff Baalham said the short one had fair hair and gray corduroy jeans, while his brother insisted both wore denim jeans and the tall one had bitten nails. Norman Smith said the fair one had a scratch on his face and the dark one was no more than five-feet-nine.

All of them wished they had taken more notice at the time, but how were they to know they would need to?

Left alone, Eunice, who had wanted to "see to things," at first saw to nothing at all. She sat on the stairs. She had a curious feeling that if she did nothing but just went off in the morning with her cases, to the bus stop she had long ago located, to the station, and got to London, it would all be all right. They might not find the Coverdales for weeks, and when they did they wouldn't know where she was, would they?

A cup of tea would be nice, for she had never had that earlier one, Joan having poured the contents of the pot all over Jacqueline's bed. She made the tea, walking back and forth past George's body. The watch on his dead wrist told her it was twenty to ten. Now to pack. She had added very little to her personal property during those nine months, apart from what were truly consumer goods—sweets, chocolate, cake—and these she had consumed. Only a few hand-knitted garments swelled her stock of clothes. Everything was packed into Mrs. Samson's cases in much the same order as it had originally gone in.

Up here, in her room, it felt as if nothing had happened. Pity she had to go tomorrow really, for now there was no one to make her go, and she liked it here, she had always liked it. And it would be even better now that there was no one to interfere with her life.

It was rather early to go to bed, and she didn't think she would be able to sleep. This was exceptional for Eunice, who knew she could always sleep as soon as her head touched the pillow. On the other hand, the circumstances were exceptional too; never had she done anything like this before, and she understood this. She understood that all the excitement was bound to keep her awake, so she sat looking around the room, looking at her cases, not feeling in the mood for television and rather wishing she hadn't packed her knitting at the bottom of the big case.

She was still sitting there at a quarter to eleven, wondering what time the bus went in the morning and hoping it wouldn't be raining, when she heard the wail of a siren in Greeving Lane. The siren was on the ambulance that had come to fetch Joan Smith, but Eunice didn't know this. She thought it must be the police, and suddenly, for the first time, she was alarmed. Down to the first floor and Jacqueline's bedroom to see what was going on. She looked out of the window, but she could see nothing, and the wailing had died away. As she dropped the curtain the siren started up again, and after a few moments some vehicle she couldn't see but for its light howled up toward the Hall, passed the Hall, and charged off toward the main road.

Eunice didn't like it. It was very unusual in Greeving. What were they doing? Why were they out there? Her television viewing had taught her a little about police procedure. She put a bed light on and walked about the room, absently wiping every solid article Joan had touched, the broken glass and the ornaments and the teapot. Steve, in her serial, when he wasn't shooting people or chasing them in cars, was a great one for fingerprints. The police would be here in a minute, though she could no longer hear their siren. She went downstairs. She went into the drawing room and again put a light on. Now she could see she had been silly, thinking the police wouldn't find out. If they didn't come now, they would come tomorrow, for Geoff Baalham would bring the eggs in the morning, and if he couldn't get in he would look through the window and see George's body. To stop them suspecting her, there were quite a lot of things she must do. Wipe Joan's prints off the wire cutters, for one thing, wipe clean the guns.

She looked around the drawing room. On the sofa, splashed with blood, was an open copy of the *Radio Times*, and along with the bloodstains was some writing. Eunice hated that, far more than the stains. The first thing she should have done was destroy that copy of the *Radio Times*, have burned it in the sink with matches, or cut it up and buried it, or pushed it scrap by scrap down the waste-disposal unit. But she couldn't read. She closed it and, in an attempt to make things look tidier, put it with the Sunday papers in the stack on the coffee table. It bothered her to leave those dirty cups there, but she felt it would be a mistake to wash them up. Putting the television back in its proper place in the morning room would also add to the tidiness, and she lugged it across the hall, at last aware that she was quite tired.

There didn't seem anything else to be done, and the police car hadn't come back. Now, for the first time since she had wreaked this havoc, she looked long and steadily at George's body, and then, reentering the drawing room, at the bodies of his wife, his daughter, and his stepson. No pity stirred her, and no regret. She did not think of love, joy, peace, rest, hope, life, dust, ashes, waste, want, ruin, madness, and death, that she had murdered love and blighted life, ruined hope, wasted intellectual potential, ended joy, for she hardly knew what these things were. She did not see that she had left carrion men groaning for burial. She thought it a pity about that good carpet getting in such a mess, and she was glad none of the blood had splashed onto her.

Having spent so much time making things look all right, she was anxious that her good work should be seen. It had always brought her gratification, that the fruit of her labors was admired, though not by a smile or a word had she ever shown her pleasure. Why wait for the police to discover it when she herself was far away? They were about, she thought in her unclear way, they would come quite quickly. The best thing would be for her to tell them without delay. She picked up the phone and had started dialing before she remembered Joan had cut the wires. Never mind, a walk in the fresh air would wake her up.

Eunice Parchman put on her red coat and her woolly hat and scarf. She took a torch from the gun room and set off to walk to Greeving and the phone box outside the village store.

22

Detective Chief Superintendent William Vetch arrived in Greeving from Scotland Yard on Monday afternoon to take charge of the Coverdale Massacre Case, the St. Valentine's Day Massacre.

He came to a village few people in the great world had ever heard of but whose name was now on every front page, blazed from every television screen. He found a village where on this first day the inhabitants remained indoors, as if afraid of the open air, as if that open air had changed its quality overnight and become savage, inimical, and threatening. There were people in the village street, but those people were policemen. There were cars, police cars; all night and all day the drive to Lowfield Hall was jammed with the cars and vans of policemen and police photographers and forensic experts. But the people of Greeving were not to be seen, and on that day, February 15, only five men went to work and only seven children to school.

Vetch took over the Village Hall, and there he set up a "Murder Room." There, with his officers, he interrogated witnesses, examined evidence, received and made phone calls, spoke to the press—and had his first interview with Eunice Parchman.

He was an experienced officer. He had been a policeman for twenty-six years, and his career in the Murder Squad had been remarkable for displays of courage. He had personally arrested James Timson, the Manchester Bank Killer, and had led the group of officers who charged into the Brixton flat of Walter Eksteen, an armed man wanted for the murder of two security guards.

Among his juniors he had the reputation of fastening onto one particular witness in each case he handled, of relying on that person for support and even, according to those who did not like him, of befriending him or her. In the Eksteen case this had paid off, and he had been led to the killer by Eksteen's ex-mistress, whose trust he had won. The witness he chose for this role in the Coverdale case was Eunice Parchman.

No one had ever really liked Eunice. In their way, her parents had loved her, but that is a different thing. Mrs. Samson had pitied her, Annie Cole feared her, Joan Smith had used her. Bill Vetch actually liked her. From the time of that first interview he liked her. For Eunice didn't waste words or seem to prevaricate or show misplaced sentimentality, and she wasn't afraid to say when she didn't know.

He respected her for the way in which, having found four dead bodies in circumstances which had sickened the hearts of the police officers who first came, she had walked a mile in the dark to reach a call box. Suspicion of her hardly touched him, and a faint doubt, present before he saw her, vanished when she told him frankly that she had not liked the Coverdales and had been dismissed for insolence. This, anyway, was no middle-aged woman's crime, nor could it have been committed singlehanded. And already, before he saw Eunice, he had begun to mount the hunt for the man with the injured hand and his companion.

This is the statement which Eunice had made to the Suffolk officers on the previous night: "I went to Nunchester with my friend, Mrs. Joan Smith, at half-past five. We attended a religious service at the Epiphany Temple on North Hill. Mrs. Smith drove me back to Lowfield Hall and I got there at five to eight. I looked at the clock in the hall as I came in by the front door and it said five to eight. Mrs. Smith did not come in. She had not been feeling well and I told her to go straight home. There was a light on in the hall and in the drawing room. You could see the drawing-room light from outside. The drawing-room door was shut. I did not go into the drawing room. I never did after I had been out in the evening unless Mr. or Mrs. Coverdale called me. I did not go into the kitchen either, as I had had my tea in Nunchester after the service. I went upstairs to my own room. Mr. and Mrs. Coverdale's bedroom door was open but I did not look inside. I did some knitting and then I packed my cases.

"Mr. and Mrs. Coverdale usually went to bed at about eleven on a Sunday. Giles spent most evenings in his own room. I did not know if he was in his room, as the door was shut when I went upstairs. I did not think much about it. I was thinking about leaving on the next day, and I did not go out of my bedroom again until about eleven-thirty.

"It was not necessary for me to go downstairs to wash, as I had my own bathroom. I went to bed at eleven. The lights were always left on on the first-floor landing and on the stairs to the second floor. Mr. or Mrs. Coverdale turned them off when they came to bed. When I could see under my door that the lights were still on at eleven-thirty I got up and went to turn them off. I put on my dressing gown, as I had to go down to the first floor to turn that light off. Then I saw some clothes on the floor in Mr. and Mrs. Coverdale's bedroom, and some broken glass. I had not seen this when I came up, because then I had my back to the door. What I saw alarmed me and I went down to the drawing room. There I found the bodies of Mrs. Coverdale and Melinda Coverdale and Giles Mont. I found Mr. Coverdale dead in the kitchen. I tried to phone the police but could not get the dialing tone, and then I saw that the wire had been cut.

"I heard no unusual sounds between the time I came in and the time I found them. No one was leaving the Hall when I arrived. On my way home I may have passed cars, but I did not notice."

To this statement Eunice adhered, changing it not in a single particular. Sitting opposite Vetch, her eyes meeting his calmly, she insisted that she had arrived home at five to eight. The grandfather clock had stopped because George had not been there to wind it at ten on Sunday night. Did that clock keep good time? Eunice said it was sometimes slow, she had known it as much as ten minutes slow, and this was confirmed by Eva Baalham and later by Peter Coverdale. But in the days that followed, Vetch was often to wish that George's watch had been broken by shot, for of all elements in a murder case he most disliked confusion over time, and the difficulty of fitting the facts to the times was to cause him much frustration.

According to the medical experts, the Coverdales and Giles Mont had met their deaths after seven-thirty and before nine-thirty, rigor mortis having already begun when the bodies were first examined at a quarter past midnight. Its onset is accelerated by heat, and the drawing room and kitchen had been very warm, for the central heating remained on all night at Lowfield Hall in the depths of winter. Many other factors were taken into consideration—stomach contents, postmortem lividity, changes in cerebrospinal fluid—but Vetch could not persuade his experts to admit the possibility of death having occurred before half-past seven. Not when that heat, a temperature of nearly eighty, was borne in mind, not in the face of Eunice's evidence that the meal the Coverdales had eaten at six—tea and sandwiches and cake—had been completely digested. And Vetch himself thought it odd that a family who had eaten tea at six should start drinking coffee at, say, seven.

Nevertheless, it could just be made to work out. The two youths in denim had come into the Blue Boar at ten to eight. That gave them fifteen minutes in which to kill the Coverdales—for what motive? for kicks? for some revenge against the social class the Coverdales represented?—and five minutes in which to leave the Hall and drive to Greeving. By the time Eunice came in at five to (or five past) eight, they were a mile away, leaving death and silence behind them.

In that fifteen minutes they must also have ravaged the bedroom, though why they should have poured tea on the bed Vetch couldn't imagine. Wanton damage, he thought, for none of Jacqueline's jewelry had been taken. Or had they been looking for money and been surprised in their hasty plundering by one of the Coverdales? At some stage the man with the wounded hand must have removed one of the gloves he was wearing, for gloves had been worn, there were no prints, unless a glove had still been on the hand when shot grazed it. Fifteen minutes was enough, just enough in which to smash and tear and kill.

Vetch spent many hours questioning those patrons of the Blue Boar, among them Norman Smith, who had seen and spoken to the two young men in denim. And by Monday evening every police force in the country was searching for that car and its occupants.

Joan Smith lay in a coma in Stantwich General Hospital. But Vetch believed she had never entered the Hall that evening, and with her he concerned himself only to check that Eunice had been correct in stating that the two of them had left the Epiphany

Temple at seven-twenty. The brethren confirmed it, but not one of them told Vetch's officers that Joan Smith had threatened George Coverdale's life shortly before her departure. They hadn't known it was George she was raving about, and if they had, the conduct and desires of the Epiphany People must be kept from policemen who were not of the elect.

Eunice was allowed to remain at the Hall, for she had nowhere else to go and Vetch wanted her on the spot. The kitchen was open to her but the drawing room was sealed up, and that copy of the *Radio Times* sealed up inside it.

"I don't know," she said when Vetch asked her if George Coverdale had had enemies. "They had a lot of friends. I never heard of anyone threatening Mr. Coverdale." And she made him a cup of tea. While she told him about the Coverdales' life, their friendships, their habits, their tastes, their whims, the murderess and the investigating officer drank their tea at the table, well scrubbed by Eunice, on which George had fallen in death.

What had happened at Lowfield Hall struck the inhabitants of Greeving with incredulity, with horror, and some of them with sick sorrow. Necessarily, nothing else was talked about. Conversations that began on practical matters—what should they have for dinner, how was someone's flu, rain again and bitterly cold, isn't it?—turned inevitably to this massacre, this outrage. Who would do a thing like that? You still can't believe it, can you? Makes you wonder what the world's coming to. Jessica Royston wept and would not be comforted. Mary Cairne had Eleighs the builders to put up bars at her downstairs windows. The Jameson-Kerrs thought how they would never again go to Lowfield Hall, and the brigadier shuddered when he remembered pheasant shoots with George. Geoff Baalham, mourning Melinda, knew that it would be a long time before he could again bring himself to drive past Gallows Corner on a Friday or Saturday afternoon.

Peter Coverdale and Paula Caswall came to Greeving, and Paula, who was to stay with the Archers, collapsed from shock and grief within hours of her arrival. Peter stayed at the Angel in Cattingham. There, in the cold damp evenings, over the electric fire that inadequately heated his room, he sat drinking with Jeffrey Mont, who was staying at the Bull at Marleigh. He didn't like Jeffrey, whom he had never met before and who got through a bottle of whiskey a night, but he thought he would have gone mad without someone to talk to, and Jeffrey said that, without his company, he'd have killed himself. They went to the Archers' together to see Paula, but Dr. Crutchley had put her under sedation.

Jonathan Dexter, in Galwich, first learned of Melinda's death when he read of it in the paper. He did nothing. He did not check or get in touch with his parents or try to get in touch with Peter Coverdale. He shut himself up in his room and remained there, living on stale bread and milkless tea, for five days.

Norman Smith went dutifully to visit his wife every evening. He didn't want to go. More or less unconsciously, he would have liked Joan to die, because it was very pleasant on his own, but he would no more have said this to himself than he would have avoided going to see her. That was what a husband did when his wife was ill, so he did it. But because Joan couldn't move or speak or hear anything, he couldn't tell her the news. Instead he gossiped about it with other visiting husbands, and thrashed it over incessantly in the Blue Boar, where he was now able to spend as much time as he liked.

Nothing had been heard from Stantwich as to an inquiry into Joan's interference with the mails. Norman, who still retained some shreds of optimism in spite of what he had been through, supposed this was because the principal witness was dead. Or the postmaster had heard of Joan's accident and didn't like to harass him while his wife was ill.

His van had been towed to a garage in Nunchester. Norman went to Nunchester on the bus to find out

about it and was told by the garage proprietor that it
was a total write-off. A deal was done for the usable
parts of the van, and the garage man said, "By the
way, this was under the back seat," and gave him an
object which Norman thought was a transistor radio.

He took it home with him, put it on a shelf with a
pile of copies of *Follow My Star*, and forgot about it
for some days.

23

Identikit pictures of the two wanted men appeared
in every national newspaper on Wednesday, February 17, but Vetch hadn't much faith in them. If a
witness cannot remember whether a man's hair is fair
or brown, it is unlikely he will recall the shape of that
man's nose or forehead. The attendant at the self-
service petrol station a hundred yards from Gallows
Corner remembered the taller dark one of them. But
it was a self-service station, the dark youth had served
himself and had come into the glass-fronted office
only to pay. The attendant had not even seen the other man, could not say that there had been another
man, and remembered the car only because maroon is
a fairly unusual color for a Morris Minor Traveler.

It was from his recollection and that of Jim Meadows, Geoff Baalham, and the other Sunday-night
patrons of the Blue Boar that the pictures had been
made up. They evoked hundreds of phone calls to the
Murder Room in Greeving Village Hall from people
offering sightings of gray or green or black Minor
Travelers, or from those who possessed maron-col-

ored ones respectably locked up in garages. But each one of these calls had to be checked before they could be dismissed.

Appeals were made to every hotelkeeper and landlady in the country as to whether any of their guests or tenants possessed a car answering to the description given by Geoff Baalham and the garage attendant. Had it been missing from its usual parking place on Sunday? Where was it now? These appeals resulted in hundreds more phone calls and hundreds of fruitless interviews that continued through Wednesday and Thursday.

But on Thursday a woman who was neither a landlady nor a hotelkeeper phoned Vetch and gave him some information about a car answering the description of the wanted vehicle. She lived on a caravan site near Clacton on the coast of Essex, some forty miles from Greeving, and Vetch was talking to her in her own caravan not much more than an hour later.

Residents' cars were parked in a muddy and unsightly section of field adjacent to the entrance of the site, and Mrs. Burchall, though possessing no car of her own, had often noticed there a maroon-colored Traveler because it was the dirtiest vehicle in the park and, because of a flat rear tire, had sunk lopsidedly into the mud. This car had been in its usual place on the previous Friday, but she couldn't remember whether she had noticed it since. However, it was not there now.

The owner of the car turned out to be, or have been, a man called Dick Scales. Scales, a long-distance lorry driver, wasn't at home when they called at the caravan where he lived, and Vetch and his men talked to a middle-aged Italian woman who called herself Mrs. Scales but subsequently admitted she was not married. Vetch could get little out of her beyond cries of "*Mamma mia!*" and expostulations that she knew nothing about any car and it was all Dick's fault. She rocked about on a broken chair while she talked, clutching in her arms a fierce-looking little mongrel terrier. When would Dick be back? She didn't know. Tomorrow, next day. And the car? They were not to ask her about cars, she knew nothing of cars, couldn't drive. She had been in Milan with her parents since before Christmas, had returned only last week, and wished now she had never come back to this cold, horrible, godless country.

Police waited for Dick Scales on the M.1. Somehow or other they missed him, while Vetch in Clacton wondered uneasily about the setup. If Scales were guilty, how could the Carters, the Baalhams, the Meadowses, and the petrol-station attendant have mistaken a man of fifty for a tall dark youth?

At Lowfield Hall the drawing room remained sealed up, and several times a day, as Eunice came downstairs to the kitchen, she walked past that sealed door. She never thought of trying to get inside the room, although, had she wanted to, it would have been no very difficult task. The French windows were locked, but the keys to them hung on their hook in the gun room. To such small oversights as these the police are sometimes prone. But in this respect their lack of caution neither damaged their case nor benefited Eunice, for she had no idea that the one piece of evidence which could incriminate her lay behind that door, and they had already dismissed that evidence, or what they had seen of it, as so much wastepaper.

The one piece? Yes, for if she had secured it, been able to read what was written on it, it would have led her by now to that other. More precisely, she would have known what that other was and would not when the time came have rejected it with unthinking indifference.

She was calm, and she felt herself secure. She watched television and she plundered the deep freeze to make herself large satisfying meals. Between meals she ate chocolate, more than her usual quota, for though unconscious of any real nervous tension she found it a little disconcerting to encounter policemen daily. To maintain her stock of supplies, she walked down to the village store, where Norman

Smith presided alone, chewing gum from force of habit.

That morning he had had a phone call from Mrs. Elder Barnstaple to say that she would drop in and collect such copies of *Follow My Star* as Joan had not had time to distribute. Norman took them down from the shelf, and with them the object that had been found in the back of his van. But he didn't show it to Eunice. He mentioned it while selling her three Mars bars.

"Joan didn't loan a radio from you, did she?"

"I haven't got a radio," said Eunice, refusing the gift of her future and her liberty. She walked out of the shop without asking after Joan or sending her love. Mildly interested to note that there were fewer police about than usual, she observed the absence of Vetch's car from its usual place outside the Village Hall. Mrs. Barnstaple, arriving, put hers there instead, and Eunice favored her with a nod and one of her tight smiles.

Norman Smith took his second visitor into the parlor.

"That's a nice little tape recorder you've got there," said Mrs. Barnstaple.

"Is that what it is? I thought it was a radio."

Again Mrs. Barnstaple averred it was a tape recorder, and asked, if it wasn't Norman's, to whom it belonged. Norman said he didn't know, it had been found in the van after Joan's accident, and perhaps it belonged to one of the Epiphany brethren. In Mrs. Barnstaple's view, this was unlikely, but she would make inquiries.

Almost anyone with a spark of curiosity in his make-up would, after the object's function had been defined, have fiddled about with it and made it play. Not Norman. He was pretty sure he'd only get hymns or confessions out of it, so he put it back on the now empty shelf and went back to sell Barbara Baalham an air letter.

Some hours before, as a worried Dick Scales was beginning the drive from Hendon in northwest London to his home in Clacton, a young man with long dark hair walked into Hendon Police Station and, in a manner of speaking, gave himself up.

Friday, the day of the funeral.

It took place at two in the afternoon, and it was well-attended. The press came, and a few carefully chosen policemen. Brian Caswall came from London, and Audrey Coverdale from the Potteries. Jeffrey Mont, the worse (or perhaps the better) for drink, was there, and so was Eunice Parchman. The Jameson-Kerrs, the Roystons, Mary Cairne, Baalhams, Meadowses, Higgses, and Newsteads. Under a blue sky, as brilliant as on the day Giles Caswall was christened, the closest mourners followed the rector from the church door along a little winding path to the southeast corner of the churchyard. Rugged elms and yew trees' shade, and an east wind blowing. George Coverdale had bought a plot under those yews, and in this grave his body and the bodies of his wife and daughter were laid to rest.

Mr. Archer spoke these words from the Wisdom of Solomon: "For though they be punished in the sight of men, yet is their hope full of immortality. And having been a little chastised, they shall be greatly rewarded. . . ."

Giles, at his father's desire, was cremated at Stantwich, and there were no flowers at the brief service that was held for him. The wreaths that came for the Coverdales never reached the destination for which Peter intended them, Stantwich Hospital—to decorate Joan Smith's bedside?—but shriveled within an hour in the February frost. At the suggestion of Eva Baalham, Eunice sent a sheaf of chrysanthemums, but she never paid the bill the florist sent her a week later.

She was driven back to the Hall by Peter, who advised her to go upstairs and lie down, a suggestion which met with no opposition from Eunice, thinking of her television and her Mars bars. In her absence and that of the police, in the terrible silence and the harsh cold, he took away the kitchen table, chopped it to pieces, and burned it down by the blackthorn hedge while the frosty crimson sun went down.

Vetch did not attend the funeral. He was in London. There he heard from Keith Lovat the story which had been told to the Hendon police and, accompanied by Lovat, he went to the house in West Hendon where Michael Scales rented one furnished room and Lovat another. At the end of the garden were three lockup garages, surrounded by a high fence. On the concrete behind this fence and at the side of the garages, Vetch was shown what appeared to be a car concealed by a canvas cover. Lovat removed the cover to disclose a maroon-colored Morris Minor Traveler which, he told Vetch, he had bought from Michael's father, Dick Scales, on the previous Sunday.

The car, Lovat said, had been for sale for eighty pounds, and he and Michael had gone up to Clacton by train to take a look at it. They arrived there at three and had a meal in the caravan with Dick Scales and the Italian woman whom Lovat called Maria and referred to as Michael's stepmother.

"Maria had this little dog," Lovat went on. "She'd brought it back with her from Italy in a basket with a cover over it, and she'd got it through customs without them knowing. It was a snappy little devil, and I left it alone, but Mike kept playing with it, teasing it really." He looked at Vetch. "That was how it all happened, that was the cause of it."

The flat tire on the car having been changed for the spare one, he and Michael Scales decided to leave for home in it at seven, but not to take the A.12 from Colchester, a fast road which would have taken them into East London. Instead they intended to go westward to Sudbury and then south for Dunmow and Ongar, entering London by the A.11 and the North Circular Road to Hendon. But before they left Michael was again playing with the dog, offering it a piece of chocolate and snatching it away when the dog came to take it. The result of this was that the dog bit him on his left hand.

"We went just the same. Maria tied Mike's hand

up with a handkerchief, and I said he'd better have it
seen to when we got home. Dick and Maria got into a
bit of a panic on account of her bringing the dog in
like that, and Dick said they could get fined hundreds
and hundreds if they got caught. Well, Mike promised
he wouldn't go to a doctor or a hospital or anything,
though the blood was coming through the bandage by
then. We started off, and the fact is I lost my way. The
lanes were pitch-dark, and I thought I'd missed the
Sudbury road, though it turned out I was really on it.
Mike didn't know anything about people not being
allowed to bring animals into the country without
putting them in quarantine, so I told him a bit about
that, and when he said why not, I said it was on account of not spreading rabies. That really scared him,
that was the beginning of it."

They had turned into what was evidently Greeving
Lane. The time? About twenty to eight, Lovat said.
At the Blue Boar in Greeving Michael washed his
hand and had a double brandy. They were directed
to a self-service petrol station on the Sudbury road
which, Lovat realized, was the road they had mis-
takenly left half an hour before.

"Mike had got into a state by then. He was scared
he'd get rabies and scared to go to the hospital in case
he got his dad into trouble. We got home around elev-
en—I couldn't get more than forty out of the car—
and when we got home I parked it down there and
put that cover over it."

Lowfield Hall? said Vetch. They must twice have
passed Lowfield Hall on their way into and out of
Greeving.

For the first time Lovat's voice faltered. He hadn't
noticed a single house while driving along Greeving
Lane. Strange, thought Vetch, when you remembered
that Meadows' farmhouse on its raised ground
loomed over the only real bend in the road. But for
the time being he let it pass, and Lovat went on to
say that on the Tuesday he had realized it was he and
Michael Scales for whom the police were hunting. He
begged Michael to go with him to their local police
station, but Michael, who had been in touch with

Dick Scales by phone, refused. His hand had begun
to fester and swell, and he hadn't been to work since
Wednesday. On Thursday morning Dick Scales
phoned the Hendon house from a call box in the north
of England, and when he heard of his son's state he
said he would call in on his way south. He reached
Hendon at nine in the evening, and he and Michael
and Keith Lovat had sat up all night, discussing what
they should do. Dick wanted Michael to go to a doctor and say he had been bitten by a stray dog, mentioning nothing about the car or his visit to the caravan, and Michael was in favor of this. Lovat had been
unable to make them see his point of view, that all
the time they were getting themselves deeper into
trouble and could be charged with obstructing the police. Moreover, he was prevented from having repairs
done to the car and, as far as he could see, from using
it perhaps for months. At last he decided to act on
his own. When Dick had gone he walked out of the
house and went to Hendon Police Station.

It was a story not entirely consistent with this one
that Vetch finally elicited from Michael Scales. Scales
was lying in bed in a filthy room, his arm swollen up
to the elbow and streaked with long red lines, and at
the appearance of Vetch and his sergeant he began to
sob. When Vetch told him that he knew all about the
car, the possibly rabid dog, and the visit to the Blue
Boar at Greeving, he admitted everything—and admitted something about which Lovat had evidently
stalled. On their way into Greeving they had stopped
at the entrance to the drive of a large well-lighted
house, and Lovat had gone up the drive to ask for directions to Sudbury. However, before he reached the
door his courage had failed him, on account, Scales
said, of the clothes he was wearing and the dirt he
had got on himself from tinkering with the car.

After some prevarication, Lovat admitted this. "I
never knocked on the door," he said. "I didn't want to
scare the people, not at nighttime and in a lonely
place like that."

It could be true. Lovat and Scales struck Vetch as
being as pusillanimous and indecisive a pair as he

had ever come across. Describe the house, he said, and Lovat said it was a big place with two long windows on either side of the front door, adding that he had heard *music coming from the house* as he hesitated on the drive. The time? Twenty to eight, said Lovat, and Scales said nearer a quarter to.

Vetch had Maria Scales charged with contravening the quarantine laws, and Michael Scales was removed to hospital, where he was put into isolation. What to do with Lovat? There was as yet insufficient evidence to charge them with the murder, but by some string-pulling Vetch arranged with the resident medical officer to have Lovat taken into hospital also and kept in under observation. There, they were out of harm's way for the present, and Vetch, with a breathing space, considered what he had been told about the time and the music.

What music? The Coverdales' record player, radio, and television set were all in the morning room. Therefore it looked as if the music had been an invention of Lovat's, though there seemed no reason why he should have invented it. More probably he and Scales had arrived much earlier at Lowfield Hall and had killed the Coverdales—for what reason? It wasn't up to Vetch to find a reason. But they could have entered the Hall to wash, to cadge a drink, to use a phone, and had perhaps met with physical opposition from George Coverdale and his stepson. It fitted, and the time, if Lovat were lying, also fitted. But Vetch had to be sure of one thing to start with, or, as he told himself in the days that followed, face the music.

It was to the young Coverdales that he went for help, and at once Audrey Coverdale told him what had been perplexing her and yet what had seemed irrelevant to the discovery of the perpetrators of the crime.

"I've never been able to understand why they weren't watching *Don Giovanni*. Jacqueline wouldn't have missed that for the world. It's like saying an ardent football fan would miss the Cup Final."

But the television set was in the morning room,

and they couldn't have been in the morning room from seven onward, for they had taken coffee in the drawing room, and no amount of juggling with time could make that coffee-drinking take place before seven. On the other hand, guilty or not, Lovat had said he had heard music. On Sunday afternoon Vetch broke the seals on the drawing-room door and revisited the scene of the crime. He was looking for signs that the television set had been in this room but, finding none, it occurred to him to check on the time the opera had begun. Vetch could easily have secured himself a copy of the *Radio Times* for that week from any newsagent. He still does not know to this day what made him pick up the *Observer* from the coffee table on the chance a *Radio Times* might have been underneath it. But it was. He opened it at the relevant page and noticed that page was splashed with blood. If anyone had previously observed this, he had not been told of it. In the margin, between and beneath the blood splashes, were three scribbled notes:

Overture cut. Surely no ascending seventh in last bar of Là ci darem. *Check with M's recording.*

Vetch had seen enough examples of Jacqueline's handwriting to recognize that these notes had been made by her. And clearly they had been made by her while watching this particular broadcast. Therefore she had watched it or part of it. And, beyond a doubt, it had begun at seven. The only expert he had immediately to hand—and how much of an expert she was he couldn't tell, he knew nothing of music—was Audrey Coverdale. He had the door resealed, and lingered for ten minutes to drink the tea Eunice Parchman had made for him. While he chatted with her and Eunice told him she had heard no music when she came in at five to (or five past) eight, that the television set was always in the morning room and had been in the morning room at the time of her discovery of the bodies, the *Radio Times* was a few feet from her, shut up in his briefcase.

Audrey Coverdale was preparing to leave, for she had to be back at work in the morning. She confirmed that the notes were in Jacqueline's hand and quailed at the bloodstains, glad that her husband was not present to see them.

"What does it mean?" said Vetch.

"*Là ci darem* is a duet in the ninth scene of the first act." Audrey could have sung every aria from *Don Giovanni* and told Vetch, within minutes, the precise time at which each would occur. "If you want to know when it comes, it'd be—let me see—about forty minutes after the beginning."

Twenty to eight. Vetch simply didn't believe her. It was useless consulting amateurs. On Monday morning he sent his sergeant into Stantwich to buy a complete recording of the opera. It was played on a borrowed player in the Murder Room in the Village Hall, and to Vetch's astonishment and dismay *Là ci darem* occurred almost exactly where Audrey had said it would, forty-two minutes after the commencement of the overture. *Overture cut,* Jacqueline had written. Perhaps the whole opera had been cut. Vetch got on to the BBC, who let him have their own recording. The opera had been slightly cut, but only by three minutes in the first nine scenes of the first act, and *Là ci darem* occurred in the recording at seven thirty-nine. Therefore Jacqueline Coverdale had been alive at seven thirty-nine, had been tranquil, at ease, concentrating on a television program. It was impossibly farfetched to suppose that her killers had even entered the house by that time. Yet Lovat and Scales had been seen in the Blue Boar at ten to eight by nine independent witnesses. Someone else had entered Lowfield Hall after Lovat's departure and before five past—it now had to be five past eight.

Vetch studied Jacqueline's notes, almost the only piece of concrete evidence he had.

24

Looking through the Wanted column in the *East Anglian Daily Times*, Norman Smith found an insertion from a man who was seeking a secondhand tape recorder. He didn't hesitate for long before picking up the phone. Mrs. Barnstaple's inquiries had not found the tape recorder's owner, Joan still lay speechless, unable in any way to communicate, but it didn't cross Norman's mind to take the thing to police. Or, rather, it crossed his mind only to be dismissed as too trivial when the police were obviously occupied with matters of more moment. Besides, he might get fifty pounds for it, and this would be most welcome in his present penurious, carless state. Fifty pounds, added to the miserable sum for which the van had been insured, would just about buy him a replacement of much the same vintage as the wrecked one. He dialed the number. The advertiser was a free-lance journalist called John Plover who told Norman he would drive over to Greeving on the following day.

Which he did. Not only did he buy the tape recorder on the spot, but he also gave Norman a lift into Stantwich in time for the hospital visiting hour.

In the meantime, Vetch was extracting more information from the notes in the margin of the *Radio Times*. *Check with M's recording* didn't seem of much significance. He had already checked with two recordings—though not in pursuit of a spurious ascending seventh, whatever that might be—and nothing could shift that aria or put it ten minutes before the time it had actually occurred. Unless Jacqueline had made the note *before* she heard the aria on television, had been listening during the afternoon to a record of Melinda's, and wanted to check with the televised opera. But what she had written was the very reverse of that. Moreover, he was unable to find any record of *Don Giovanni* or any part of it in Lowfield Hall.

"I don't think my sister had any records of classical music," said Peter Coverdale, and then, "but my father gave her a tape recorder for Christmas."

Vetch stared at him. For the first time he realized that a recording need not necessarily mean a black disc. "There's no tape recorder in the house."

"I expect she took it back to university with her."

The possibility which this opened to Vetch was beyond any realistic policeman's dreams—that Melinda Coverdale had actually been recording when the killers came into the house, that the time might thus be precisely fixed, and the intruders' voices preserved. He refused to allow himself to speculate about that aspect of it. The first thing the killers would have done was remove the tapes and destroy them, then rid themselves of the recorder itself. The invaluable Eunice, the star witness, was called in.

She said, "I remember her dad giving it to her at Christmas. It was in her room in a leather case, and I used to dust it. She took it to college when she went back in January and she never brought it home after that." Eunice was speaking the truth. She hadn't seen the tape recorder since the morning she had listened in to Melinda's phone conversation. Joan had carried it out from the Hall, Joan who in her madness was a thousand times more sophisticated than Eunice would ever be, and Eunice had not even noticed she had anything in her hand.

While Vetch's men were scouring Galwich for that tape recorder, interrogating everyone Melinda had known, Eunice marched the two miles to Gallows Corner and caught the bus for Stantwich. In a side room off the Blanche Tomlin ward she found Norman Smith sitting by his wife's bedside. She hadn't bothered to tell him she was coming. She had come for the same reason that he came, because it was the thing to do. Just as you went to the weddings and the funerals of people you knew, so you went to the hospital to see them when they were ill. Joan was very ill. She lay on her back with her eyes closed, and but for the rise and fall of the bedclothes, you would have thought she was dead. Eunice looked at her face. She was interested to see what that stretched canvas looked like without paint on it. Stretched canvas was what it looked like, yellow-brown, striated. She didn't speak to it.

"Keep it nice, don't they?" she said to Norman after she had made sure there was no dust under the bed. Perhaps he thought she was speaking of his wife, who was also "kept nice," anchored to her drip feed, tucked up under a clean sheet, for he made no reply. They were both hoping, for different reasons, that Joan would go on like that forever and, going home together on the bus, each expressed the pious wish that such a vegetable existence would not be prolonged.

In forlorn hope, Vetch ordered a search of Lowfield Hall, including the long-disused cellar, and when that brought nothing to light, they began digging up the frostbound flowerbeds.

Eunice didn't know what they were looking for, and she was very little concerned. She made cups of tea and carried it out to them, the policemen's friend. Of much more moment to her were her wages or, rather, the lack of them. George Coverdale had always paid her her month's money on the last Friday in the month. That last Friday, February 26, would be tomorrow, but so far Peter Coverdale had given no sign that he intended to honor this obligation inherited from his father, which seemed to Eunice very remiss of him. She wasn't going to use the phone. She walked over to Cattingham and inquired for him at the Angel. But Peter was out. Peter, though Eunice didn't know this, was driving his sister back to London, to her husband and her children.

Vetch appeared at the Hall on the following morning, and Eunice resolved that he should be her go-between. And this Scotland Yard chief superintendent, Vetch of the Murder Squad, was only too happy to oblige. Of course he would get in touch with Peter Coverdale during the day, with pleasure he would apprise him of Miss Parchman's dilemma.

"I've baked a chocolate cake," said Eunice. "I'll bring you a bit with your tea, shall I?"

"Most kind of you, Miss Parchman."

As it happened, it wasn't a bit but the whole cake which Eunice was forced to sacrifice, for Vetch had chosen eleven o'clock to hold a conference in the morning room with three high-ranking officers of the Suffolk Constabulary. She left him with a quiet "Thank you, sir," and returned to the kitchen to think about getting her own lunch. And she was eating it at noon sharp, eating it off the counter in the absence of the table, when Vetch's sergeant walked in through the gun room with a young man Eunice had never seen before in tow.

The sergeant was carrying a large brown envelope with something bulky inside it. He gave Eunice a pleasant smile and asked her if Mr. Vetch was about.

"In the morning room," said Eunice, knowing full well whom you "sir"-ed and whom you didn't. "He's got a lot of folks with him."

"Thanks. We'll find our own way." The sergeant made for the door to the hall, but the young man stopped and stared at Eunice. All the color had gone out of his face. His eyes went wide and he flinched as if she'd sworn at him instead of speaking perfectly normally. He reminded her of Melinda in this same kitchen three weeks back, and she was quite relieved when the sergeant said, "This way, Mr. Plover," and hustled him out.

Eunice washed the dishes by hand and ate up her last bar of chocolate. Her last bar, indeed. She wondered if Vetch had yet done anything about Peter Coverdale and her wages. Outside they were still digging up the garden, in the east wind, under occasional flurries of snow. Her favorite serial tonight,

Lieutenant Steve in Hollywood or maybe Malibu
Beach, but she would enjoy it far more if she could be
sure her money was forthcoming. She went out into
the hall and heard music.

Music was coming from behind the morning-room
door. That meant they couldn't be doing anything
very important in there, nothing that wouldn't bear
a polite interruption. The music was familiar, she had
heard it before. Sung by her father? On the television?
Someone was singing. Foreign words, so it couldn't
have been one of Dad's.

Eunice raised her fist to knock on the door, let it fall
again as a voice from within the room shouted above
the music:

"Oh, Christ!"

She couldn't identify that voice, but she knew the
one that came next, a voice silenced now by massive
brain injury.

"Get back in there. We've got guns."

And the others. And her own. All blending with
the music, vying with it, drowning it in frenzy and
fear.

"Where's my husband?"

"He's in the kitchen. He's dead."

"You're mad, you're crazy! I want my husband, let
me go to my husband. Giles, the phone . . . ! No, no
. . . Giles!"

Eunice spoke to Eunice, across the days. "You'd
better sit down. You've got it coming to you."

A cackle from Joan. "I am the instrument of One
Above," and a shot. Another. Through the music and
the screams, the sound of something heavy falling.
"Please, please!" from the girl, and the reloaded guns
fired for the last time. Music, music. Silence.

Eunice thought she would go upstairs and repack
her things before retribution came from whatever it
was in there that acted out, in some way beyond her
understanding, the deaths of the Coverdales. But a
numbness stunned her mind, and she was less than
ever capable of reasoning. She began to walk toward
the stairs, relying on that strong body that had always
done so well by her. And then that body, which was

all she had, failed her. At the foot of the stairs, on the very spot where she had first stood on entering the Hall ten months before, where wonderingly she had seen herself reflected in a long mirror, her legs gave way and Eunice Parchman fainted.

The sound of her falling reached Vetch, who was nerving himself to play the tape once more to an audience of policemen, white-faced now and rigid in their chairs. He came out and found her where she lay, but he could not bring himself to lift her up or even touch her with his hands.

25

Joan Smith still lies speechless and immobile in Stantwich General Hospital. She is in a machine which keeps her heart and lungs functioning, and the medical powers that be are at present deciding whether it might not be a mercy to switch that machine off. Her husband is a clerk in a post office in Wales, and he still keeps the name of Smith. There are, after all, a lot of them about.

Peter Coverdale still lectures on political economy in the Potteries. His sister Paula has never recovered from the deaths of her father and Melinda, and she has had three sessions of electroconvulsive therapy in the past two years. Jeffrey Mont is drinking heavily and almost qualifies for the destination in which Joan Smith placed him at her second meeting with Eunice Parchman. These three are engaged in continuous litigation, for it has never been established whether Jacqueline predeceased her son or he her. If she died first, Giles briefly inherited Lowfield Hall, and thus it must now be his father's, the property of his next of kin. But if he died before his mother, the Hall should pass to George's natural heirs. Bleak House.

Jonathan Dexter, tipped for a First Class Honors degree, got a Third. But that was in the early days. He teaches French at a comprehensive school in Essex, has nearly forgotten Melinda, and is going steady with a member of the Science Department.

Barbara Baalham gave birth to a daughter whom they called Anne, because Melinda, which was Geoff's original choice, seemed a bit morbid. Eva cleans for Mrs. Jameson-Kerr and gets seventy-five pence an hour. They still talk about the St. Valentine's Day Massacre in Greeving, especially in the Blue Boar on summer evenings when the tourists come.

Eunice Parchman was tried at the Old Bailey, the Central Criminal Court, because they could not find an unbiased jury for the Assizes at Bury St. Edmund's. She was sentenced to life imprisonment, but in practice may not serve more than fifteen years. Some said it was an absurdly inadequate punishment. But Eunice was punished. The crushing blow came before verdict or sentence. It came when her counsel told the world, the judge, the prosecution, the policemen, the public gallery, the reporters scribbling away in the press box, that she could not read or write.

"Illiterate?" said Mr. Justice Manaton. "You cannot read?"

She answered when he pressed her. She answered, crimson-faced and shaking, and saw those who were not freaks or disabled as she was, write it down.

They have tried to reform Eunice by encouraging her to remedy her basic defect. Steadfastly, she refuses to have anything to do with it. It is too late. Too late to change her or avert what she did and what she caused.

Dust, Ashes, Waste, Want, Ruin, Despair, Madness, Death, Cunning, Folly, Words, Wigs, Rags, Sheepskin, Plunder, Precedent, Jargon, Gammon, and Spinach.

ABOUT THE AUTHOR

RUTH RENDELL is the author of numerous mystery novels, including, *A Sleeping Life, Make Death Love Me, The Face of Trespass, Some Lie and Some Die, Murder Being Once Done* and *No More Dying Then.* Her novel, *Shake Hands Forever,* won the annual silver cup presented by *Current Crime* for the Best British Crime Novel of 1975. The following year, *A Demon in My View* was awarded the Golden Dagger Award by the British Crime Writers Association. A former journalist, she lives with her husband and son in a home outside of London and in a seventeenth century cottage in Polstead, the Suffolk village best remembered as the site of a famous murder.

Ruth Rendell

"IS UNDOUBTEDLY ONE OF THE BEST WRITERS OF ENGLISH MYSTERY."

That's what Dorothy B. Hughes has said about this wonderfully talented writer. Mrs. Hughes added, "her characters are unusual but never bizarre, and she has a rhythm which bespeaks poetry in the background but never at the expense of chiller-killer plots."

However, it has taken some time for Mrs. Rendell to achieve this recognition. She began by writing short stories for the women's market, but received rejection after rejection. About seven years later, after the birth of her son, she tried again—this time writing a light sophisticated comedy. The English publisher agreed to take it only if Mrs. Rendell would rewrite. She refused and instead sent the publisher her first mystery story—which the company did publish (and Mrs. Rendell did rewrite it before publication).

Since then she has written sixteen other novels, every one of them receiving critical praise and three of them winning major awards: the Mystery Writers of America valued "Edgar" for THE FALLEN CURTAIN, the Crime Writers Association "Golden Dagger" for A DEMON IN

MY VIEW and *Current Crime* magazine's reader poll named SHAKE HANDS FOREVER as the best book of the year, over contenders such as Agatha Christie and Len Deighton.

Her novels are divided almost equally between detective stories and mystery stories. The detective novels feature Chief Inspector Wexford who appears in SOME LIE AND SOME DIE, MURDER BEING ONCE DONE, A SLEEPING LIFE and NO MORE DYING THEN. Her mysteries include: ONE ACROSS, TWO DOWN, SHAKE HANDS FOREVER, THE FALLEN CURTAIN, A DEMON IN MY VIEW, MAKE DEATH LOVE ME and A JUDGEMENT IN STONE. Her books have been translated into many languages including Danish, Swedish, Norwegian, French, Serbo-Croatian and Japanese.

Mrs. Rendell's audience continues to grow and so do the choruses of praise from her peers and critics. Here are just a few:

> She is one of the quiet English writers—avoiding blood and action, interested in relationships, willing to spend a good deal of time establishing background and mood . . . Rendell is awfully good. In any Rendell book you know that something unusual is going to happen.
> —*The New York Times Book Review*

> Each new book reinforces Mrs. Rendell's reputation as a powerful, literate writer with psychological insight who is not afraid to essay the new and different.
> —*Washington Post Book World*

> For the readers who have almost given up mysteries since the death of Josephine Tey, Rendell may be just the woman to get them started again.
> —*Ellery Queen's Mystery Magazine*

> Among the best mysteries published in recent years . . . Women, especially, take on a new dimension as she explores their various roles in modern society, using them first for similarities, then differences in a never ending counterpoint of personalities.
> —*The Armchair Detective*

PENGUIN BOOKS

THE HOWARDS OF CAXLEY

'Miss Read', or in real life Mrs Dora Saint, is a teacher by profession who started writing after the Second World War, beginning with light essays written under her own name mainly for *Punch*. She has written on educational and country matters for various journals, and worked as a script-writer for the B.B.C.

'Miss Read' is married, with one daughter, and lives in a tiny Berkshire hamlet. Her hobbies are theatre-going, listening to music and reading, and she is a local magistrate.

'Miss Read' has published numerous books, including *Village School* (1955), *Village Diary* (1957), *Thrush Green* (1959), *Fresh from the Country* (1960), *Winter in Thrush Green* (1961), *Miss Clare Remembers* (1962), an anthology, *Country Bunch* (1963), *Over the Gate* (1964), *The Market Square* (1966), *Village Christmas* (1966), *The Howards of Caxley* (1967), *The Fairacre Festival* (1968), *News from Thrush Green* (1970), *Farther Afield* (1974), *Battles at Thrush Green* (1975), *No Holly for Miss Quinn* (1976), *Village Affairs* (1977), *The White Robin* (1979), *Village Centenary* (1980), *Gossip from Thrush Green* (1981) and *Affairs at Thrush Green* (1983). Many of 'Miss Read's' books are published in Penguins together with two omnibus editions, *Chronicles of Fairacre* containing *Village School, Village Diary* and *Storm in the Village* and *Life at Thrush Green* containing *Thrush Green, Winter in Thrush Green* and *News from Thrush Green*. She has also written two books for children, *Hobby Horse Cottage* and *Hob and the Horse-bat*. The Red Bus Series for the very young, and a volume of autobiography, *A Fortunate Grandchild*.

The Howards of Caxley

PENGUIN BOOKS

Penguin Books Ltd, Harmondsworth, Middlesex, England
Viking Penguin Inc., 40 West 23rd Street, New York, New York 10010, U.S.A.
Penguin Books Australia Ltd, Ringwood, Victoria, Australia
Penguin Books Canada Limited, 2801 John Street, Markham, Ontario, Canada L3R 1B4
Penguin Books (N.Z.) Ltd, 182–190 Wairau Road, Auckland 10, New Zealand

—

First published by Michael Joseph 1967
Published in Penguin Books 1972
Reprinted 1976, 1985 (twice)

—

—

Printed and bound in Great Britain by
Cox & Wyman Ltd, Reading

—

Typeset in Garamond

To Pat and John with love

CONTENTS

1. Happy Independence

It was six o'clock on a fine May morning.

The market square was deserted. Long shadows lay across the cobblestones, reaching almost to the steps of St Peter's church. Pink sunlight trembled across its old grey stone, gilding the splendid spire and warming the hoary saints in their niches. A thin black cat, in a sheltered angle of the porch, washed one upthrust leg, its body as round and curved as an elegant shell. Not even the pigeons disturbed its solitude, for they still slept, roosting in scores on the ledges of the Corn Exchange and the Victorian Town Hall.

A hundred yards away, the river Cax, swollen with spring rains, swept in a shining arc through the buttercup fields. The haze of early hours lay over all the countryside which surrounded the little market town, veiling the motionless clumps of elm trees in the fields and the cottages still sleeping among their dewy gardens.

The minute hand of St. Peter's clock began its slow downhill journey from the gilded twelve, and Edward Howard, pyjama-clad at his bedroom window near by, watched it with mounting exhilaration. This was the life! How wonderful to be alive on such a morning, to be twenty-one and – best of all – to have a place of one's own!

He flung up the window and leaned out, snuffing the morning air like a young puppy. The sun touched his face with gentle warmth. It was going to be a real scorcher, he thought to himself happily. He laughed aloud and the thin cat, arrested in the midst of its toilet, gazed up at him, a tongue as pink as a rose petal still protruding from its mouth.

'Good morning!' called Edward civilly to the only other waking inhabitant of the market square. The cat stared at him disdainfully, shrugged, and then continued with its washing.

And Edward, turning towards the bathroom, followed its good example.

Lying in warm water, he ran an appraising eye round the bathroom and mused upon his good fortune. At this time last year he had been living at Rose Lodge, a mile away on the hill south of Caxley, with his mother and grandmother North. It had been his home for seven or eight years, and he had, he supposed, been reasonably happy there in the company of the two women. But these last few months of bachelor independence made him realize the restrictions which he had suffered earlier. Now there was no one to question his comings and goings. If he cared to stay out until two in the morning, there was no waiting tray, complete with hot chocolate in a vacuum flask, to reproach him. No parental note reminded him to bolt the door and switch off the landing light. It wasn't that he didn't love them, poor dear old things, thought Edward indulgently as he added more hot water to his bath, but simply that he had outgrown them.

'God bless Grandpa Howard!' said Edward aloud, as he sank back again.

It was good to be living in Caxley market square where his grandparents on both sides had built up their businesses. Here, in this house, of which he was now the proud owner, Bender North and his wife Hilda had lived for many years over their ironmongery shop. Edward could see his grandfather clearly now, in his mind's eye, a vast figure in a brown coat-overall striding among the coal scuttles and patty pans, the spades and milking pails, which jostled together beneath the pairs of hobnailed boots and hurricane lamps that swung from the ceiling above him. Soon afterwards, Bender and his wife had moved to Rose Lodge – a far more genteel address to Hilda's mind – and the glories of the great drawing room over the shop were no more. But Winnie, Edward's mother, and his Uncle Bertie North had described the red plush furniture, the plethora of ornaments and the floral arrangements of dried grasses and sea-lavender, with such vivid detail, that he felt quite familiar with the Edwardian splendour which had now vanished.

He knew, equally well, the sad story of the decline of Bender's business. It had been bought by a larger firm in the town and, later still, his grandfather Septimus Howard had taken it over. Sep still lived in the market square above his thriving bakery. The whole of the ground floor at North's he had transformed into a restaurant, almost ten years ago. It was, according to Caxley gossip, 'an absolute gold-mine', but there were few who grudged Sep Howard his success. Hardworking, modest, a pillar of the local chapel, and a councillor, the little baker's worth was appreciated by his fellow townsmen.

The business was to go to his son Robert, already a vigorous partner, when Sep could carry on no longer. Sep was now, in the early summer of 1939, a spry seventy-three, and there was no sign of his relinquishing his hold on family affairs. The acquisition of Bender's old home and the growth of the restaurant had given Sep an added interest in life. It was typical of his generosity, said his neighbours, that he had given Edward the house which had been Bender's when the boy attained the age of twenty-one. The restaurant, on the ground floor, would be Robert's in time, and the more shrewd of Caxley's citizens wondered why Sep could not foresee that there might be friction between Edward and his young uncle in the years to come.

But on this bright May morning all was well in Edward's world. It had needed courage to tell his two women-folk that he proposed to set up his own establishment, and even now, when he looked back on the scene at Rose Lodge, Edward winced.

15 The Market Square, still generally known in Caxley as 'North's', had fallen empty at Michaelmas 1938. The Parker family, who had been tenants for several years, had prospered, and bought a house in the village of Beech Green a few miles away. The property had become Edward's that same year on his twenty-first birthday. It was the most splendid present imaginable, for the boy had loved the house as long as he could remember. The idea of living there one day had been with him for

many years, a secret joyous hope which he fully intended to turn into reality.

'It's a big responsibility for a young man in your position,' Grandma North quavered, when the old home was first made over to him. 'I know your Grandpa Howard has arranged for a sum of money to keep the place in repair, but what happens when he's gone? You may have a wife and family to keep by then.'

'We'll all live there,' cried Edward cheerfully, 'and you shall come and tell us how badly we keep it, compared with your days.'

'Well, you may laugh about it now, my boy,' said the old lady, a little querulously, 'but I know what a big place that is to keep going. The stairs alone are a morning's work, and no one ever managed to keep that back attic free from damp. Your Grandpa Howard's never lived there as I have. He's no notion of what it means in upkeep.'

Hilda North had never liked Septimus Howard. She had watched him rise as her own husband had steadily declined. Old age did not mellow her feelings towards this neighbour of a life-time, and the marriage of her darling son Bertie to Kathy Howard and the earlier marriage of her daughter Winnie to Leslie, Edward's ne'er-do-well father, did nothing to allay the acrimony which she felt towards the Howard family.

'Thank God,' she said often to Edward, 'that you take after the North side of the family, despite your name. Your dear mother's been both father and mother to you. Really, I some-times think it was a blessing your father left her. She's better without him.'

Edward was wise enough to keep a silent tongue when the old lady ran on in this vein. He knew quite well that there was a strong streak of the Howards in his make-up. He hoped, in all humility, that he had something of Sep Howard's strength of character. He was beginning to guess, with some astonishment, that he might possess some of his erring father's attraction for the opposite sex.

He often wondered about his father. It was impossible to get a clear picture of him from either side of the family, and his own memories were hazy. Leslie Howard had decamped with an earlier love when Edward was four and the second child, Joan, only a few months old. As far as was known, he flourished, as the wicked so often do, in a Devonshire town. He had never been seen in Caxley again.

'Too ashamed, let's hope!' said Edward's grandmother North tartly, but Edward sometimes wondered. What was the result of that flight from the family? He had never heard his father's side of the affair. It was as tantalizing as a tale half-read. Would he ever know the end of the story?

Edward had dropped the bombshell on a mellow September evening, a week or two before Michaelmas Day, when the Parkers were to vacate his newly acquired property. The two women were sitting in the evening sunshine admiring the brave show of scarlet dahlias. Around them, the gnats hummed. Above them, on the telephone wires, were ranged two or three dozen swallows like notes on staves of music. Soon they would be off to find stronger sunshine.

It was too bad to shatter such tranquillity, thought Edward, pacing restlessly about the garden, but it had to be done. He spoke as gently as his taut nerves allowed.

'Mother! Grandma!' He stopped before the two placid figures. Sun-steeped, vague and sleepy, they gazed at him with mild expectancy. Edward's heart smote him, but he took the plunge.

'Don't let this be too much of a shock, but I'm thinking about living in the market square myself when the Parkers leave.'

His mother's pretty mouth dropped open. His grandmother did not appear to have heard him. He raised his voice slightly.

'At the old house, Grandma dear. I want to move in at Michaelmas.'

'I heard you,' said the old lady shortly.

'But why, Edward? Why?' quavered his mother. 'Aren't you happy here?'

To Edward's alarm he saw tears welling in his mother's blue eyes. Just as he thought, there was going to be the devil of a scene. No help for it then, but to soldier on. He sat down on the iron arm of the curly garden seat upon which the two were reclining, and put a reassuring arm about his mother's shoulders.

'Of course I'm happy here –' he began.

'Then say no more,' broke in his mother swiftly. 'What should we do without a man in the house? We're so nicely settled, Edward, don't go upsetting things.'

'What's put this in your head?' queried his grandmother. 'Getting married, are you?'

'You know I'm not,' muttered Edward, rising from his perch and resuming his prowlings. 'It's simply that the house is now mine, it's empty, and I want to live there.'

'But it will be far too big for you alone, Edward,' protested his mother. 'And far too expensive.'

'I've worked it all out and I can manage quite well. I don't intend to use all the house, simply the top floor. The rest can be let, and bring me in a regular income.'

'Well, I must say,' cried his mother reproachfully, 'you seem to have been planning this move for some time! I can't tell you what a shock it is.! I'd no idea you felt like this about things. What about poor Grandma? How do you think she is going to like it when there are only women left alone to cope with everything here?'

Winnie produced a handkerchief and mopped her eyes. Her mother, made of sterner stuff, sniffed militantly and Edward prepared to hear the old lady's vituperation in support of her daughter. What a hornet's nest he had disturbed, to be sure! But a surprise was in store.

'Let him go!' snapped old Mrs North testily. 'If he wants to go and ruin himself in that damp old shop by the river, then let him, silly young fool! I've lived alone before, and I won't be beholden to my grandchildren. He doesn't know when he's well off. Let him try managing that great place for a bit! He'll soon learn. And for pity's sake, Winnie, stop snivelling. Anyone'd think he was off to Australia the way you're carrying on!'

It had been too much to expect an ally at Rose Lodge, but the old lady's impatient dismissal of the affair greatly helped Edward. After a few uncomfortable days, whilst Edward tried to avoid his mother's martyred gaze and the sound of intermittent argument about the subject between the two women, he managed to make them see that he was adamant in his decision.

'Dash it all, I'm less than a mile away. I shall be in and out of Rose Lodge until you'll probably get fed up with me. I can do any odd jobs, and Tom comes twice a week for the garden. He's promised me to keep an eye on things. And you'll see Joan as regularly as you always do.'

Joan, Edward's sister, now eighteen, was in London, training to teach young children. Her vacations were lengthy and just occasionally she managed to get home on a Sunday during term-time. Edward had written to her telling of his plans and had received enthusiastic support. There was an unusually strong bond of affection between the brother and sister, forged in part by the absence of a father. Certainly, during the stormy period which preceded Edward's move, he was doubly grateful for Joan's encouragement.

As soon as the Parkers had gone to their new home, Edward put his plans into action. He decided to make the attic floor into his own domain, and the four rooms became a bedroom and sitting-room, both overlooking the market square and facing south, and a kitchen and bathroom at the back. He had papered and painted the rooms himself, and although the paper was askew in places and a suspicion of rust was already becoming apparent on the bathroom pipes, the whole effect was fresh and light.

Surveying his handiwork from the bath Edward felt a glow of pride. This was all his own. At times he could scarcely believe his good luck. The spacious rooms below were already occupied by a young bank clerk who had been at Caxley Grammar School with Edward some years before. He and his wife seemed careful tenants, likely to remain there for some time. Their first child was due in the autumn.

The future looked pretty bright, decided Edward, reviewing

the situation. He enjoyed his work as an agricultural engineer at the county town some fifteen miles away, and promotion seemed likely before long. The family appeared to have come round completely to the idea of his living apart and no one could possibly realise how exciting he found his newly-won independence.

And then there was his flying. He had joined the R.A.F.V.R. when he was eighteen and had first flown solo on a bright spring day over two years ago. It was the culmination of an ambition which had grown steadily in fervour since he was ten. Now most weekends were spent at the aerodrome west of Caxley and his yearly holiday was earmarked for annual training. He liked the men he met there, their cheerful company and their predictable jokes, but better still he liked the machines with their fascinatingly complicated engines and their breathtakingly flimsy superstructure.

In a few hours he would be in the air again, he thought joyfully, looking down on the patchwork of brown and green fields far below. For this was one of the blessed Sundays when he set off early in his two-seater Morris in his carefully casual new sports jacket and a silk scarf knotted about his neck in place of the workaday tie.

He stood up in the bath and began to towel himself vigorously. A pigeon cooed on the gutter above the steamy window. Edward could see the curve of its grey breast against the sky.

'Two rashers and two eggs,' called Edward to the bird, above the gurgle of the bath water swirling down the waste pipe, 'and then I'm off!'

A thought struck him. The car's spare tyre was at Uncle Bertie's garage. He must remember to pick it up on his way. The possibility of a puncture somewhere on Salisbury Plain, even on a fine May morning such as this, was not to be borne, especially on a day dedicated to flying.

He shrugged himself into his shabby camel-hair dressing-gown and went, whistling, in search of the frying pan.

2. The Shadow of War

EDWARD's Uncle Bertie was his mother's brother and now the head of the North family. He lived in a four-square red-brick house some yards from the busy High Street of Caxley where his motor business flourished.

One approached Bertie's house by way of a narrow lane. It started as a paved alley between two fine old Georgian buildings which fronted the pavements, but gradually widened into a gravelled track which led eventually to the towpath by the river Cax. Edward always enjoyed the sudden change from the noise of the street as he turned into this quiet backwater.

As he guessed, Bertie was already at work in the garden. Oil can in hand, he was bending over the mower when his nephew arrived. He straightened up and limped purposefully towards him, waving the oil can cheerfully. For a man who had lost one foot in the war, thought Edward, he moved with remarkable agility.

'You want your spare wheel,' said Bertie. 'I'll give you the garage key and you can help yourself.'

They moved towards the house, but Bertie checked suddenly to point out a thriving rose which was growing against the wall.

'Look at that, my boy! I planted it when your Aunt Kathy and I married. Just look at the growth it's made in these few years!'

Edward looked obediently, but he was already impatient to be off to his flying. Catching sight of the expression on his handsome nephew's dark young face, Bertie threw back his head and laughed.

'You're no gardener, Edward! I forgot. Too bad to hold you up. Come and say "Hello" to the family before you set off.'

His Aunt Kathy was beating eggs in a big yellow basin. Her dark hair was tucked into a band round her head so that she looked as if she were wearing a coronet. How pretty she was, thought Edward, as slim and brown as a gipsy! No wonder Uncle Bertie had waited patiently for her all those years. He remembered Grandma North's tart comments to his mother on the marriage.

'I should've thought Bertie would have had more sense than to marry into the Howard family. Look what it brought you – nothing but unhappiness! And a widow too. Those two children will never take to a stepfather – even one as doting as dear Bertie. I can see nothing but misery ahead for that poor boy!'

'"That poor boy"' is nearly forty,' his mother had replied with considerable vigour, 'and he's loved her all his life. Long faces and sharp tongues won't harm that marriage, you'll see.'

And all Caxley had seen. Bertie and Kathy, with her son and daughter by her first husband, were living proof of mature happiness, and when a son was born a year or so later, the little town rejoiced with them. Even Grandma North agreed grudgingly that it was all running along extraordinarily smoothly and put it down entirely to Bertie's exceptionally sweet North disposition.

'Where are the children?' asked Edward.

'Fishing,' replied Kathy, smiling. 'Unless you mean Andrew. He's asleep, I hope. He woke us at four this morning with train noises – shunting mostly. It makes an awful din.'

'That boy wants to look forward, not backwards,' observed Edward. 'He wants to get his mind on aeroplanes.'

'I think one air fanatic in the family is enough,' commented Bertie, handing over the key to the garage. 'Off you go. Have a good day.'

And Edward departed on the first stage of his journey westward.

'It would never surprise me,' said Bertie to his wife, when Edward had gone, 'to hear that Edward had decided to join the R.A.F. His heart's in aeroplanes, not tractors and binders.'

'But what about our business?' queried Kathy. 'I thought you'd planned for him to become a partner?'

'I shan't press the boy. We've two of our own to follow on if they want to.'

'But *flying*,' protested Kathy, sifting flour energetically into the beaten eggs. 'It's so dangerous, Bertie. Edward might be killed!'

'He might indeed,' observed Bertie soberly. And thousands more like him, he thought privately. He watched his pretty wife at her work, and thought, not for the first time, how much there was which he could not discuss with her. Did she ever, for one fleeting moment, face the fact that war was looming closer and closer? This uneasy peace which Chamberlain had procured at Munich could not last long. There was menace on every side. It must be met soon. Bertie knew in his bones that it was inevitable.

'What a long face!' laughed Kathy, suddenly looking up from her cooking. 'You look as though you'd lost a penny and found a halfpenny.'

She crossed the kitchen towards the oven, shooing him out of the way as if he were one of the children.

'It's time this sponge was in,' she cried. 'Don't forget Mum and Dad are coming to tea this afternoon. You'd better get on in the garden while the sun's out.'

She paused briefly by the window to gaze at the shining morning.

'Isn't it lovely, Bertie? When it's like this I can't believe it will ever be any different – just sunshine all the time. Do you feel that way too, Bertie?'

'I don't think I'm quite such an incurable optimist,' answered Bertie, lightly. 'More's the pity maybe.'

He made his way back to the mower, his thoughts still with him. The grass was still too wet to cut, he decided. He would take a stroll along the towpath and watch the river flowing gently eastward beneath the cloudless sky. There was something very comforting about flowing water when one's spirits were troubled.

He turned left outside his garden gate, his back to the town, and limped steadily towards the tunnel of green shade made by a dozen or so massive chestnut trees, now lit with hundreds of flower-candles, which lined the banks some quarter of a mile away. The sunshine was warm upon his back, and broke into a thousand fragments upon the surface of the running water, dazzling to the eye. Just before the dark cavern formed by the chestnut trees, the river was shallow, split by a long narrow island, the haven of moorhen and coot.

Here Bertie paused to rest his leg and to enjoy the sparkle of the fretted water and the rustling of the willow leaves on the islet. The shallows here were spangled with the white flowers of duckweed, their starry fragility all the more evident by contrast with a black dabchick who searched busily for food among them, undisturbed by Bertie's presence.

The mud at the side of the water glistened like brown satin and gave forth that peculiarly poignant river-smell which is never forgotten. A bee flew close to Bertie's ear and plopped down on the mud, edging its way to the brink of the water to drink. A water-vole, sunning itself nearby, took to the stream, and making for the safety of the island left an echelon of ripples behind its small furry head.

The change in temperature beneath the great chestnut trees was amazing. Here the air struck cold upon Bertie's damp forehead. The path was dark, the stones treacherously slimy and green with moss. There was something dark and secret about this part of the Cax. No wonder that the children loved to explore its banks at this spot! It was the perfect setting for adventure. To look back through the tunnel to the bright world which he had just traversed was an eerie experience. There it was all light, gaiety and warmth — a Kathy's world, he thought suddenly — where no terrors were permitted.

But here there was chill in the air, foreboding, and a sense of doom. He put a hand upon the rough bark of a massive trunk beside him and shuddered at its implacable coldness. Was this his world, at the moment, hostile, menacing, full of unaccountable fears?

He was getting fanciful, he told himself, retracing his steps.

It was good to get back into the sunshine, among the darting birds and the shimmering insects which played above the kindly Cax. He would put his morbid thoughts behind him and return to the pleasures of the moment. There was the lawn to be cut and the dead daffodils to be tied up. He quickened his pace, advancing into the sunshine.

In the market square the bells of St Peter's called the citizens of Caxley to Matins. Under the approving eyes of the bronze Queen Victoria whose statue dominated the market place, a trickle of men, women and children made their way from the dazzling heat into the cool nave of the old church. The children looked back reluctantly as they mounted the steps. A whole hour of inaction, clad in white socks, tight Sunday clothes, and only the hat elastic wearing a pink groove under one's chin to provide entertainment and furtive nourishment, loomed ahead. What a wicked waste of fresh air and sunshine !

Septimus Howard and his wife Edna crossed the square from his bakery as the bells clamoured above them, but they were making their way to the chapel in the High Street where Sep and his forbears had worshipped regularly for many years.

Automatically, he glanced across at Howard's Restaurant which occupied the entire ground floor beneath Edward's abode. The linen blinds were pulled down, the CLOSED card hung neatly in the door. His son Robert had done his work properly and left all ship-shape for the weekend. It was to be hoped, thought Sep, that he would be in chapel this morning. He was far too lax, in Sep's opinion, in his chapel-going. It set a poor example to the work people.

Edward's presence he could not hope to expect, for he and his sister Joan were church-goers, taking after the North side of the family. Not that they made many attendances, as Sep was well aware. He sympathized with Edward's passion for flying, but would have liked to see it indulged after he had done his duty to his Maker.

The congregation was sparse. No doubt many were gardening

or had taken advantage of the warmth to drive with their families for a day at the sea. It was understandable, Sep mused, but indicative of the general slackening of discipline. Or was it perhaps an unconscious desire to snatch at happiness while it was still there? After the grim aftermath of the war, and the grimmer times of the early thirties, the present conditions seemed sweet. Who could blame people for living for the present?

Beside him Edna stirred on the hard seat. Her dark hair, scarcely touched with grey, despite her seventy years, curled against her cheek beneath a yellow straw hat nodding with silk roses and a golden haze of veiling. To Sep's eye it was not really suitable headgear for the Sabbath, but it was impossible to curb Edna's exuberance when it came to clothes, and he readily admitted that it set off her undimmed beauty. He never ceased to wonder at the good fortune which had brought into his own quiet life this gay creature, whose presence gave him such comfort.

Now the minister was praying for peace in their time. Sep, remembering with infinite sadness the loss of his first-born Jim in the last war, prayed with fervent sincerity. What would happen to the Howards if war came again, as he feared it must? Robert, in his thirties, would go. Edward, no doubt, would be called up at once to the Royal Air Force. Leslie, his absent son whom he had not seen since he left Caxley and his wife Winnie years earlier, would be too old to be needed.

And he himself, at seventy-three? Thank God, he was still fit and active. He could continue to carry on his business and the restaurant too, and he would find time to work, as he had done earlier, for the Red Cross.

What dreadful thoughts for a bright May morning! Sep looked at the sunshine spilling lozenges of bright colour through the narrow windows across the floor of the chapel, and squared his shoulders.

He must trust in God. He was good and merciful. A way must surely be found for peace between nations. That man of wickedness, Adolf Hitler, would be put down in God's good time. He had reached the limit of his powers.

He followed Edna's nodding roses out into the sunny street. Someone passed with an armful of lilac, and its fragrance seemed the essence of early summer. Opposite, at the end of one of the roads leading to the Cax, he could see a magnificent copper beech tree, its young thin leaves making a haze of pink against the brilliant sky.

It was a wonderful day. It was a wonderful world. Surely, for men of faith, all would be well, thought Sep, retracing his steps to the market square.

But despite the warmth around him, there was a little chill in the old man's heart, as though the shadow of things to come had began to fall across a fine Sunday in May in the year 1939.

3. Evacuees in Caxley

As the summer advanced, so did the menacing shadow of war. It was plain that Germany intended to subdue Poland, and Caxley people, in common with the rest of Britain, welcomed the Prime Minister's guarantee that Britain would stand by the threatened country. The memory of Czechoslovakia's fate still aroused shame.

'Hitler's for it if he tries that game again with Poland,' said one worthy to another in the market square.

'If we gets the Russians on our side,' observed his crony, 'he don't stand a chance.'

There was a growing unity of purpose in the country. The ties with France, so vividly remembered by the older generation who had fought in the Great War, were being strengthened daily. If only the Government could come to favourable terms with Russia, then surely this tripartite alliance could settle Hitler's ambitions, and curb his alarming progress in Europe.

Meanwhile, plans went ahead for the evacuation of children, the issue of gas masks, the digging of shelters from air attacks, and all the civilian defence precautions which, if not particularly reassuring, kept people busy and certainly hardened their resolve to show Hitler that they meant business.

The three generations in the Howard and North families faced the threat of war typically. Septimus Howard, who had been in his fifties during the Great War of 1914–18, was sad but resolute.

'It's a relief,' he said, voicing the sentiments of all who heard him, 'to know where we stand, and to know that we are acting in the right way. That poor man Chamberlain has been sorely hoodwinked. He's not alone. There are mighty few people to-day who will believe that evil is still abroad and active. But now

26

his eyes are opened, and he can see Hitler for what he is – a liar, and worse still, a madman.'

Bertie North, who had fought in France as a young man and had lost a foot as a result, knew that the war ahead would involve his family in Caxley as completely as it would engage the armed men. This, to him, was the real horror, and the thought of a gas attack, which seemed highly probable, filled him with fury and nausea. Part of him longed to send Kathy and the three children overseas to comparative safety, but he could not ignore that inward voice which told him that this would be the coward's way. Not that Kathy would go anyway – she had made that plain from the start. Where Bertie was, there the family would be, she maintained stoutly, and nothing would shake her.

Only two things gave Bertie any comfort in this dark time. First, he would return to the army, despite his one foot.

'Must be masses of paper work to do,' he told Sep. 'I can do that if they won't let me do anything more martial, and free another chap.'

The second thing was the attitude of mind, in which the young men most involved faced the situation. Bertie remembered with bitter pain the heroic dedication with which his own generation had entered the war. High ideals, noble sacrifices, chivalry, honour and patriotism had been the words – and not only the words – which sent a gallant and gay generation into battle. The awful aftermath had been doubly poignant.

Today there was as much courage and as much resolution. But the young men were not blinded by shining ideals. This would be a grim battle, probably a long one. There was no insouciant cry of 'Over by Christmas', as there had been in 1914. They were of a generation which knew that it was fighting for survival, and one which knew too that in modern warfare there is no real victor. Whatever the outcome it would be a long road to recovery when the war itself was past.

Nevertheless, for Edward and his friends, hearts beat a little faster as action appeared imminent. What if Hitler had annexed an alarming amount of Europe? The Low Countries and

France would resist to a man, and the English Channel presented almost as great an obstacle to an invader today as it did to Napoleon. This year had given England time to get ahead with preparations. The uneasy peace, bought by Mr Chamberlain at Munich a year earlier, may have been a bad thing, but at least it had provided a breathing space.

'Thank God I'm trained for something!' cried Edward to his mother. 'Think of all those poor devils who will be shunted into the army and sent foot-slogging all over Europe! At least I shall have some idea of what I'm to do.'

He spent as much time training now as he could possibly manage. He had a purpose. It was a sober one, but it gave him inward courage. Whatever happened, he intended to be as ready and fit as youth, good health and steady application to his flying would allow.

Edward, most certainly, was the happiest man in the family despite the fact that he was the most vulnerable.

During the last week of August it became known that all hope of an alliance with Russia had gone. Triumphantly the Nazis announced a pact with the Soviet Union. Things looked black indeed for England and her allies, but assurances went out again. Whatever happened, Britain would stand by her obligations to Poland. After a period of anxiety over Russia's negotiations, it was good to know the truth.

On 24 August the Emergency Powers Bill was passed, together with various formalities for calling up the armed forces. Edward's spirits rose when he heard the news at six o'clock. How soon, he wondered, before he set off?

It was a few days later that the House of Commons met again. The question facing the country, said one speaker, was: 'Shall one man or one country be allowed to dominate Europe?' To that question there could be only one answer.

People in Caxley now prepared to receive evacuees from London and another nearby vulnerable town into their midst. No one could pretend that this move was wholeheartedly welcome. The genuine desire to help people in danger and to afford them a port in a storm, was tempered with doubts. Would strangers fit into the home? Would they be content? Would they be co-operative?

Sep and Edna had offered to take in six boys of school age. If they could have squeezed in more they would have done. Frankly, Edna welcomed the idea of children in the house again. The thought that they might be unruly, disobedient or difficult to handle, simply did not enter her head or Sep's.

'It is the least we can do,' said Sep gravely. 'How should we feel if we had ever had to send our children to strangers?'

Bertie and Kathy expected a mother and baby to be billeted with them in the house by the river. The fate of Edward's flat was undecided at the moment, and the future of Rose Lodge hung in the balance. There was talk of its being requisitioned as a nurses' hostel, in which case Winnie and her mother might move back to Edward's new domain in the market square.

'Proper ol' muddle, ennit?' observed the dustman to Edward. 'Still, we've got to show that Hitler.' He sighed gustily.

'Wicked ol' rat,' continued the dustman, 'getting 'is planes filled up with gas bombs, no doubt. You see, that's what'll 'appen first go off. You wants to keep your gas mask 'andy as soon as the balloon goes up. Can't think what them Germans were play-ing at ever to vote 'im in.'

He replaced the dustbin lid with a resounding clang.

'Ah, well,' he said indulgently, 'they're easy taken in – for-eigners!'

And with true British superiority he mounted the rear step of the dust lorry and rode away.

It was on Friday, 1 September that evacuation began and Caxley prepared for the invasion. Beds were aired, toys brought down from attics, welcoming nosegays lodged on bedroom man-telpieces and pies and cakes baked for the doubtless starving visitors.

'Isn't it odd,' remarked Joan Howard to her mother, as she staggered from the doorstep with a double supply of milk, 'how we expect evacuees to be extra cold and extra hungry? We've put twice as many blankets on their beds as ours, and we've got in enough food to feed an army.'

'I know,' agreed Winnie. 'It's on a par with woollies and shoes. Have you noticed how everyone is buying one or two stout pairs of walking shoes and knitting thick sweaters like mad? I suppose we subconsciously think we'll be marching away westward when war comes, with only a good thick sweater to keep out the cold when we're asleep under a hedge at night.'

'Very sensible,' approved old Mrs North, who was busy repairing a dilapidated golliwog which had once been Joan's. 'I can't think why you don't take my advice and stock up with Chilprufe underclothes. You'll regret it this time next year. Why I remember asking Grandpa North for five pounds when war broke out in 1914, and I laid it out on vests, combinations, stockings, tea towels and pillow slips – and never ceased to be thankful!'

Joan laughed. Despite the horrors which must surely lie ahead, life was very good at the moment. She had just obtained a teaching post at an infants' school in the town and was glad to be living at home to keep an eye on her mother and grandmother. As soon as things were more settled, however, she secretly hoped to join the W.A.A.F. or the A.T.S. Who knows? She might be posted somewhere near Edward.

It was not yet known if Rose Lodge would be wanted to house an influx of nurses. Meanwhile, the three women had prepared two bedrooms for their evacuees.

Winnie and Joan left the house in charge of old Mrs North and made their way towards the station. The local Reception Officer was in charge there, assisted by a dozen or so local teachers. Winnie and her daughter were bound for a school which stood nearby. Here the children would come with their teachers to collect their rations for forty-eight hours and to rest before setting off for their new homes. Winnie was attached to the Women's Voluntary Service Corps and as Joan's school was closed for the time being she had offered to go and help.

A train had just arrived at the station, and the children were being marshalled into some semblance of order by harassed teachers. The children looked pathetic, Joan thought, clutching bundles and cases, and each wearing a label. A gas mask, in a neat cardboard box, bounced on every back or front, and one's first impression was of a band of refugees, pale and shabby.

But, on looking more closely, Joan noticed the cheeks which bulged with sweets, the occasional smile which lightened a tired face and the efficient mothering by little girls of children smaller than themselves. Given a good night's rest, Joan decided, these young ones would turn out to be as cheerful and resilient a lot as she had ever met during her training in London.

Inside the school hall an army of helpers coped with earlier arrivals. To Joan's secret delight, and her mother's obvious consternation, she saw that Miss Mobbs was in charge. This formidable individual had once been a hospital sister in the Midlands but retired to Caxley to look after a bachelor brother some years before.

'Poor man,' Caxley said. 'Heaven knows what he's done to deserve it! There's no peace now for him.'

But running a home and cowing a brother were not enough for Miss Mobbs. Within a few weeks she was a driving force in several local organisations, and the scourge of those who preferred a quiet life.

At the moment she was in her element. Clad in nurse's costume, her fourteen-stone figure dominated the room as she swept from table to table and queue to queue, rallying her forces.

'That's the way, kiddies,' she boomed. 'Hurry along. Put your tins in your carrier bags and don't keep the ladies waiting!'

'Old boss-pot,' muttered one eight-year-old to her companion, much to Joan's joy. ''Ope 'Itler gets 'er.'

Miss Mobbs bore down upon Winnie.

'We've been looking for you, Mrs Howard. This way. A tin of meat for every child and your daughter can do the packets of sugar.'

Joan observed, with mingled annoyance and amusement, that

31

her mother looked as flustered and apologetic as any little pro-
bationer nurse and then remembered that, of course, years ago
her mother really had been one. Obviously the voice of authority
still twanged long-silent chords.

'Better late than never,' remarked Miss Mobbs with false
heartiness. But her strongly disapproving countenance made it
quite apparent that the Howards were in disgrace.

Glasses flashing, she sailed briskly across the room to chivvy
two exhausted teachers into line, leaving Joan wondering how
many more women were adding thus odiously to the horrors of
warfare.

She and her mother worked steadily from ten until four,
handing out rations to schoolchildren and their teachers and to
mothers with babies. A brief lull midday enabled them to sip a
cup of very unpleasant coffee and to eat a thinly spread fishpaste
sandwich. Joan, whose youthful appetite was lusty, thought wistfully of the toothsome little chicken casserole her mother had
left in the oven for Grandma North, and was unwise enough to
mention it in Miss Mobbs' hearing.

'It won't hurt some of us to tighten our belts,' claimed that
redoubtable lady, clapping a large hand over her own stiff leather
one. Joan noticed, uncharitably, that it was fastened at the last
hole already.

'We shan't beat Hitler without a few sacrifices,' she continued, putting three spoonsful of sugar into her coffee, 'and
we must be glad of this chance of doing our bit.'

Really, thought Joan, speechless with nausea, it was surprising
that Miss Mobbs had not been lynched, and could only suppose
that the preoccupation of those present, and perhaps a more
tolerant attitude towards this ghastly specimen than her own,
accounted for Miss Mobbs' preservation.

At four o'clock they returned to Rose Lodge to find that their
own evacuees had arrived and were already unpacking. Two
women teachers, one a middle-aged widow, and the other a girl
not much older than Joan, were sharing Edward's former room,
and a young mother with a toddler and a six-week-old baby

occupied the larger bedroom at the back of the house which had been Joan's until recently.

Grandmother North, trim and neat, her silver hair carefully waved and her gold locket pinned upon her dark silk blouse, was preparing tea. She looked as serene and competent as if she were entertaining one or two of her old Caxley friends. Only the flush upon her cheeks gave any hint of her excitement at this invasion.

'Where are we having it?' asked Joan, lifting the tray.

'In the drawing-room, of course,' responded her grandmother. 'Where else?'

'I thought – with so many of us,' faltered Joan, 'that we might have it here, or set it in the dining-room.'

'Just because we're about to go to war,' said Grandma North with hauteur, 'it doesn't follow that we have to lower our standards.'

She poured boiling water into the silver tea pot, and Joan could not help remembering the advertisement which she had read in *The Caxley Chronicle* that morning. Side by side with injunctions to do without, and to tackle one's own repairs in order to leave men free for war work, was the usual story from a local employment agency.

'Patronized by the Nobility and Gentry,' ran the heading, followed by :

'Titled lady requires reliable butler and housekeeper. 4 in family. 3 resident staff.'

There was a touch of this divine lunacy about her grandmother, thought Joan with amusement, and gave her a quick peck of appreciation.

'Mind my hair, dear,' said Mrs North automatically, and picking up the teapot she advanced to meet her guests.

'We're going to be a pretty rum household,' was Joan's private and unspoken comment as she surveyed the party when they were gathered together. Grandma North sat very upright behind the tea tray. Her mother, plump and kindly, carried food to the

33

visitors, while she herself did her best to put the young mother at her ease and to cope with Bobby's insatiable demands for attention. This fat two-year-old was going to cause more damage at Rose Lodge than the rest of them put together, Joan surmised.

Already he had wiped a wet chocolate biscuit along the cream chintz of the armchair, and tipped a generous dollop of milk into his mother's lap, his own shoes and Joan's. Now he was busy hammering bread and butter into the carpet with a small, greasy and powerful fist. His mother made pathetic and ineffectual attempts to control him.

'Oh, you are a naughty boy, Bobby! Look at the lady's floor! Give over now!'

'Please don't worry,' said Grandma North, a shade frostily. 'We can easily clean it up later.'

Joan felt sorry for the young mother. Exhausted with travelling, parted from a husband who had rejoined his ship the day before, and wholly overwhelmed by all that had befallen her, she seemed near to tears. As soon as was decently possible, she hurried Bobby upstairs to bed and made her escape.

Mrs Forbes, the older teacher, seemed a sensible pleasant person, though from the glint in her eye as she surveyed Bobby's tea-time activities, it was plain that she would have made use of a sharp slap or two to restrain that young gentleman. Her companion, Maisie Hunter, was a fresh-faced curly-haired individual whose appetite, Joan noticed, was as healthy as her own.

How would they all shake down together, she wondered, six women, and two babies — well, one baby and a two-year-old fiend might be a more precise definition — under the roof of Rose Lodge? Time alone would tell.

4. War Breaks Out

By Sunday morning, the visitors at Rose Lodge appeared to have settled down. This was by no means general in Caxley. Already, much to the billeting authorities' dismay, some mothers and children were making their way back to the danger zone in preference to the dullness of country living. Others were making plans to be fetched back to civilization during the week. Their hosts were torn between relief and the guilty feeling that they had failed in their allotted task of welcoming those in need.

The early news on the wireless said that the Prime Minister would speak at eleven-fifteen, and Mrs North invited the household to assemble in the drawing-room.

'I suppose this is it,' said Joan.

'And about time too,' rapped out the old lady. 'All this shilly-shallying!'

She, with Winnie and Joan were going to lunch at Bertie's. The parents of the young mother, Nora Baker, were coming to spend the day, and Mrs Forbes' son was paying a last visit before setting off to an army camp in the north.

'Let them have the house to themselves for the day,' Bertie said, 'and come and see us.'

And so it had been arranged.

Just before the broadcast, the inhabitants of Rose Lodge settled themselves in the drawing-room. Bobby, mercifully, had been put into his cot for his morning sleep, but the baby, freshly-bathed and fed, kicked happily on the floor enjoying the admiration of so many women.

By now it was known that an ultimatum had been handed to Germany to expire at 11 a.m. There was a feeling of awful solemnity when finally the Prime Minister's voice echoed through the room. There had been no reply to the ultimatum, he

35

told his anxious listeners, and in consequence we were already at war.

Joan felt a cold shiver run down her back. She shot a glance at the older women around her. Their faces were grave and intent. Only Nora Baker and her baby seemed unaffected by the terrible words. The baby gazed with blue, unfocused eyes at the ceiling, and its mother nodded and smiled gently.

'It is the evil things we shall be fighting against,' said Mr Chamberlain, 'brute force, bad faith, injustice, oppression and persecution.'

Old Mrs North nodded emphatically. A little nerve twitched at the corner of her mouth, but otherwise she looked calm and approving.

The speech ended and she turned off the set.

'Thank goodness, that poor man has done the right thing at last,' she said.

'Well, we know where we are,' agreed Mrs Forbes.

She had hardly finished speaking when the sound of wailing came from the distance, to be followed, seconds later, with a similar sound, five times as loud, as the air-raid siren at the Fire Station sent out its spine-chilling alarm.

'It *can't* be an air raid,' whispered Winnie. They all gazed at each other in incredulous perplexity.

'Trust the Germans,' said Mrs Norah brisky. 'Too efficient by half. And where did I leave my gas mask?'

'Gas!' gasped little Mrs Baker, snatching up the baby. She had become a greenish colour, and the child's pink face close to hers made her appear more terror-stricken than ever.

'I'll go and get the gas masks,' said Joan, and began methodically to shut the windows. How idiotic and unreal it all seemed, she thought, suddenly calm.

'I must get Bobby,' cried the young mother. 'Oh, my Gawd, who'd think we'd get gassed so soon?'

'I'll fetch him,' said Winnie. She and Joan ran upstairs to collect their gas masks, a bottle of brandy and – no one quite knew why – a rug and a box of barley sugar. Meanwhile the two teachers ran around the house closing windows and looking anxiously up into the sky for enemy invaders.

They were hardly back in the drawing-room before the sirens sounded again, but this time on one long sustained note which, they were to learn, heralded safety.

'That's the "All Clear",' cried Joan. 'What can have happened?'

'Very confusing,' said her grandmother severely. 'It was far better arranged in our war, with the Boy Scouts blowing bugles.'

'No doubt someone pressed the wrong button,' said Winnie. 'What a fright to give us all!'

Mrs Baker, her baby clutched to her bosom and a very disgruntled and sleepy Bobby clinging to her skirt, had tears running down her face. The others did their best to comfort her, and Joan insisted on administering a dose of brandy. It seemed a pity to have brought it all the way downstairs, she thought, and to take it back again unopened.

'D'you think it's safe to put them upstairs to sleep?' asked Mrs Baker pathetically.

'Perfectly,' said old Mrs North. 'Take my word for it, that stupid fellow Taggerty's at the bottom of this. Fancy putting him in charge at the A.R.P. place! If he's anything like that foolish cousin of his we had in the shop, he'll lose his head on every possible occasion. I hope he gets thoroughly reprimanded.'

'I don't think Taggerty has anything to do with it,' began Winnie. But her mother was already across the hall and beginning to mount the stairs.

'We must hurry,' she was saying. 'Bertie asked us there for twelve and we mustn't keep the dear boy waiting.'

If they had just ejected a troublesome wasp from the drawing-room she could not have been less concerned, thought Joan in admiration, following her small, upright figure aloft.

To Joan's and Winnie's delight, Edward was at Bertie's.

'We tried to ring you last night,' cried his mother, 'but there was no reply. How did you get on?'

'Don't talk about it,' said Edward, throwing up his hands

despairingly. 'I trotted along to report at the town centre and I'm on *indefinite leave*, if you please! *Indefinite leave*!'

'What exactly does that mean, dear?' asked Winnie anxiously.

'It means that I go back to work as usual, and sit on my bum waiting to be called up.'

'Language, Edward, language!' interjected his grandmother severely. 'There's no need to be vulgar just because you're disappointed.'

'No uniform?' said Joan.

'Only when I report each week,' said Edward. 'It seems the training units are bunged up at present. I suppose our turn'll come, but it's the hell of a nuisance, this hanging about.'

'At least you know what you will be doing when you do get started,' comforted Bertie. 'How are your evacuees, Mamma?'

'Very pleasant people,' said the old lady firmly. 'And yours?'

'Gone home,' said Kathy entering. 'Took one look at the bedroom and said it wasn't what they were used to.'

'Now, I wonder how you take that?' queried Joan.

'With a sigh of relief,' said Bertie, taking up the carving knife. 'She was quite the ugliest woman I've ever clapped eyes on, and the babies were something fearful. Enough to give us all night terrors.'

'Now, Bertie!' said his mother reprovingly. 'Don't exaggerate!'

'The trouble is,' said Edward, looking at his Aunt Kathy, 'your standards are too high. You don't know when you're well off.'

Bertie made no reply. But he smiled as he tackled the joint.

During the next few weeks, Caxley folk and their visitors did their best to shake down together, while the seasonal work went on in the mellow September sunshine. The harvest was gathered in, corn stacked, apples picked. In the kitchens frugal housewives made stores of jam and preserves, bottled their fruit and tomatoes and put eggs to keep in great buckets of isinglass.

Those who remembered the food shortages of the earlier war told gruesome tales to younger women.

'And I had to feed my family on puddings made of chicken maize on more than one occasion,' said one elderly evacuee. 'And not a spoonful of sugar to be had. You stock up with all you can. Rationing'll be tighter still this time.'

There was general dismay among farmers who had lost land to the defence departments. 'Where corn used to grow for hundreds of years,' *The Caxley Chronicle* reported one as saying, 'camps are now sprouting in profusion. Thousands of acres of good farmland have been sterilized for artillery ranges, exercise grounds for tanks, barracks and aerodromes.'

Edward, reading this at his solitary breakfast table snorted impatiently. They'd got to train *somewhere*, hadn't they? Oh, if only he could get started !

He flipped over the page.

'Petrol rationing hits delivery vans,' he read. 'Old cycles being brought out again.'

His eye caught a more bizarre morsel of wartime news.

'New Forest ponies may be painted with white stripes to make them more visible to motorists in the black-out.'

Edward laughed aloud.

'Good old *Caxley Chronicle* ! And what's on at the flicks this week?'

Will Hay in *Ask a Policeman* and Jessie Matthews in *Climbing High*, he read with approval. Below the announcement was a new wartime column headed 'Your Garden and Allotment in Wartime.'

'Thank God I'm spared that,' exclaimed Edward, throwing the paper into a chair. But the caption had reminded him that he had promised his Uncle Robert, who so lovingly tended the garden of their shared premises, that he would give him a lift this morning on his way to work.

Edward's Uncle Robert was the youngest of Sep Howard's children and only eleven years older than Edward. He felt towards this youthful uncle rather as he did towards the youngest child of Bender and Hilda North, his attractive aunt Mary, who was much the same age as Robert. They seemed more like an older brother and sister than members of an earlier generation.

Aunt Mary he saw seldom these days, which was a pity. She was a moderately successful actress, better endowed with dazzling good looks than brain, but hard working and with the good health and even temper which all three North children enjoyed.

'A messy sort of life,' Grandpa Sep Howard had commented once. 'I'm glad no child of mine wanted to take it up.' To Sep, staunch chapel-goer, there was still something of the scarlet woman about an actress.

Robert, of course, Edward saw almost daily. He did part of the supervision of Howard's bakery at the corner of the market square, but spent the major part of his time in running the restaurant on the ground floor below Edward's establishment.

Howard's Restaurant had flourished from the first and had now been in existence for about eight years. Sep's dream of little white tables and chairs set out on the lawn at the back of the property had come true. The garden, which had been Bender North's joy, remained as trim and gay as ever and added considerably to Caxley's attractions in the summer.

'I suppose you won't be running this little bus much longer,' observed Robert as they sped along.

'I've just enough petrol to keep her going for about a fortnight. With any luck I'll be posted by then.'

Robert was silent. Edward would dearly have liked to know Robert's feelings about the war, but he did not like to ask. No doubt Robert's job would be considered as a highly necessary one and he would be more advantageously employed there than in some humdrum post in one of the services. Nevertheless, Edward had not heard him mention volunteering or offering his services in any more martial capacity, despite the fact that he was only in his early thirties. In some ways, Edward mused, Robert was a rum fish.

Take this stupid business of his tenants, the couple who lived below his own flat and above Robert's restaurant, thought Edward. They were quiet people, taking care to be unobtrusive, but Robert had complained bitterly to Edward that the ceiling of the café was flaking and that this was due to the 'banging about upstairs.'

'And they had the cheek to say that the cooking smells from my restaurant went up into their sitting-room,' asserted Robert.

'Daresay they do, too,' said Edward equably. 'There's a pretty high stink of frying sometimes. I can even get a whiff on the floor above them.'

Robert's face had darkened.

'Well, you knew what to expect when you came to live over a restaurant,' he said shortly. 'The old man was a fool ever to think the property could be divided. The floors above my bit should have been kept for storing things.'

Edward had been amazed at the depth of feeling with which Robert spoke. For the first time in his carefree life, Edward realised that he was encountering jealousy, and a very unpleasant sight it was. Luckily, he had inherited a goodly portion of the Norths' equanimity and could reply evenly. But the barb stuck, nevertheless.

He dropped Robert now at his wholesaler's and drove on to the office. If only his posting would come through! There was no interest in his work during these tedious waiting days, and he was getting thoroughly tired of Caxley too, as it was at present. He was fed up with hearing petty tales about evacuees' head-lice and wet beds; and fed up too with the pomposity of some of the Caxleyites in positions of wartime authority. Somehow, in these last few weeks Caxley had become insupportable. He felt like a caged bird, frantic to try his wings, in more ways than one.

Ah well, sighed Edward philosophically as he turned into the yard at the side of the office, it couldn't be long now. Meanwhile, Will Hay and Jessie Matthews were on at the flicks. He would ask that nice little teacher, Maisie Something-or-other at Rose Lodge, to accompany him. At least it was a new face in dull old Caxley.

Edward was not alone in his frustration. This was the beginning of a period which later became known as 'the phoney war', when the Allied forces and those of the Germans faced each other in their fortresses and nothing seemed to happen.

The Caxley Chronicle echoed the general unease. 'Don't eat these berries!' said one heading. Foster parents should make sure that their charges knew what deadly nightshade looked like. Could they distinguish between mushrooms and toadstools?

The Post Office issued a tart announcement pointing out that it had a much depleted staff and far more work than usual.

Someone wrote to say that country people were being exploited. Why should a farm labourer, with about thirty shillings a week left after paying his insurance, feed the parents of his two evacuees when they spent Sundays with them? And who was expected to pay for the new mattress that was needed? There was no doubt about it – the heroic spirit in which the nation had faced the outbreak of war was fast evaporating, in this anticlimax of domestic chaos and interminable waiting.

'If anyone else tells me to Stand By or to Remain Alert,' said Bertie dangerously, 'I shall not answer for the consequences.'

'It's better than being told We're All In It Together,' consoled Kathy.

Joan, meanwhile, had started her new job, for the schools had reopened. A London school's nursery unit had been attached to the combined infants' school and this was housed in the Friends' Meeting House, a pleasant red-brick building perched on a little grassy knoll on the northern outskirts of Caxley. A Viennese teacher, who had escaped a few months before Austria was overrun by the Nazis, was in charge, and Joan was her willing assistant.

She loved the chattering children in their blue and white checked overalls. The day seemed one mad rush from crisis to crisis. There was milk to be administered, potties to empty, dozens of small hands and faces to wash, tears to be quenched, passions to be calmed and a hundred activities to take part in.

She loved, too, the atmosphere of the old premises. It was an agreeably proportioned building with high arched windows along each side. Round the walls were dozens of large wooden hat pegs used by Quakers of past generations. The floor was of scrubbed boards, charming to look at but dangerously splintery for young hands and knees.

Outside was a grassy plot. In one half stood a dozen or so small headstones over the graves of good men and women now departed. There was something very engaging, Joan thought, to see the babies tumbling about on the grass, and supporting themselves by the little headstones. Here the living and the dead met companionably in the autumn sunlight, and the war seemed very far away indeed.

A steep flight of stone steps led from the road to the top of the grassy mound upon which the Meeting House stood. An old iron lamp, on an arched bracket, hung above the steps, and Joan often thought what a pleasant picture the children made as they swarmed up the steps beneath its graceful curve, clad in their blue and white.

Her mother came on two afternoons a week to help with the children. Three afternoons were spent at the hospital, for Winnie did not want to tie herself to a regular full-time job, but preferred to do voluntary service when and where she could. There was her mother to consider and the evacuees. Winnie determined to keep Rose Lodge running as smoothly as she could, and only prayed that the proposal that it should be turned into a nurses' hostel would be quietly forgotten.

She found the small children amusing but thoroughly exhausting. The nursing afternoons were far less wearing.

She said as much to Joan as they walked home together one afternoon, scuffling the fallen leaves which were beginning to dapple the footpath with red and gold.

'I suppose it's because I was trained to nurse,' she remarked.

'Rather you than me,' responded Joan. 'It's bad enough mopping up a grazed knee. Anything worse would floor me completely.'

They turned into the drive of Rose Lodge and saw old Mrs North at the open front door. She was smiling.

'You've just missed Edward on the telephone. He's as pleased as a dog with two tails. He's posted at last to – now, what was it ? – a flying training school in Gloucestershire.'

'Well,' said Joan thankfully, 'there's one happy fellow in Caxley tonight !'

5. Grim News

EDWARD arrived at the flying training school on a dispiritingly bleak October afternoon. The aerodrome lay on a windswept upland, not unlike his own downland country. In the distance, against the pewter-grey sky, a line of woods appeared like a navy-blue smudge on the horizon; but for mile upon mile the broad fields spread on every side, some a faded green, some ashen with bleached stubble and some newly-furrowed with recent ploughing.

Edward surveyed the landscape from a window by his bed. His sleeping quarters were grimly austere. A long army hut, with about ten iron beds on each side, was now his bedroom. A locker stood by each bed, and the grey blankets which served as coverlets did nothing to enliven the general gloom.

But at any rate, thought Edward hopefully, he had a window by his allotted place and the hut was warm.

There was an old man working some twenty yards from the window where a shallow ditch skirted a corner of the aerodrome. A row of pollarded willows marked the line of the waterway, and the old man was engaged in slashing back the long straight boughs. His coat was grey and faded in patches, his face lined and thin. He wore no hat, and as he lunged with the bill-hook, his sparse grey hair rose and fell in the wind. It reminded Edward of the grey wool which catches on barbed wire, fluttering night and day throughout the changing seasons.

He seemed to be part of the bleached and colourless background – as gnarled and knotty as the willow boles among which he worked, as dry and wispy as the dead grass which rustled against his muddy rubber boots. But there was an intensity of purpose in his rhythmic slashing which reminded Edward, with a sudden pang, of his grandfather Sep Howard, so far away.

He turned abruptly from the window, straightened his tunic, and set off through the wind to the sergeants' mess.

He entered a large room furnished with plenty of small tables, armchairs, magazines and a bar. The aerodrome was one of the many built during the thirties, and still had, at the outbreak of war, its initial spruceness and comfort.

Edward fetched himself some tea, bought some cigarettes, and made his way towards a chair strategically placed by a bronze radiator. He intended to start the crossword puzzle in the newspaper which was tucked securely under his elbow. There were only five or six other men in the mess, none of whom he knew. But he had scarcely drunk half his tea and pencilled in three words of the puzzle before he was accosted by a newcomer.

'So you're here too?' cried his fellow sergeant pilot. Edward's heart sank.

There was nothing, he supposed, violently wrong with Dickie Bridges, but he was such a confoundedly noisy ass. He had met him first during voluntary training and found him pleasant enough company on his own, but unbearably boastful and excitable when a few of his contemporaries appeared. When parties began to get out of hand you could bet your boots that Dickie Bridges would be among the first to sling a glass across the room with a carefree whoop. He was, in peacetime, an articled clerk with a firm of solicitors in Edward's county town. Rumour had it that their office was dark and musty, the partners, who still wore wing collars and cravats, were approaching eighty, one was almost blind and the other deaf. However, as they saw their clients together, one was able to hear them and the other to see them, and the office continued to function in a delightfully Dickensian muddle. Edward could only suppose that with such a restricting background it was natural that Dickie should effervesce when he escaped.

Edward made welcoming noises and made room on the table for Dickie's tea cup. Typical of life, he commented to himself, that of all the chaps he knew in the Volunteer Reserve, it should be old Dickie who turned up! Nevertheless, it was good to see a familiar face in these strange surroundings and he settled back to hear the news.

'Know this part of the world?' asked Dickie, tapping one of Edward's cigarettes on the table top.

'No. First time here.'

'Couple of decent little pubs within three miles,' Dickie assured him. 'But twenty-odd miles to any bright lights — not that we'll see much of those with the blackout, and I hear we're kept down to it pretty well here.'

'Better than kicking about at home,' said Edward. 'I would have been round the bend in another fortnight.'

'Me too,' agreed Dickie.

Edward remembered the two old partners in Dickie's professional life and inquired after them.

'They've both offered their military services,' chuckled Dickie, 'but have been asked to stand by for a bit. If they can't get into the front line they have hopes of being able to man a barrage balloon in the local park. Even the blind one says he can see *that*!'

Edward, amused, suddenly felt a lift of spirits. Could Hitler ever hope to win against such delicious and lunatic determination? He found himself warming towards Dickie, and agreeing to try one of the two decent little pubs the next evening.

Back at Caxley the winter winds were beginning to whistle about the market square, and people were looking forward to their first wartime Christmas with some misgiving. The news was not good. A number of merchant ships had been sunk and it was clear that Hitler intended to try to cut the nation's lifelines with his U-boats.

Cruisers, battleships and destroyers had all been recent casualties, and there seemed to be no more encouraging news from the B.E.F. in France.

The evacuees were flocking back to their homes and the people of Caxley folded sheets and took down beds wondering the while how soon they would be needed again. Petrol rationing, food rationing and the vexatious blackout aggravated the misery of 'the phoney war'. In particular, men like Bertie, who had served in the First World War and were anxious to serve in the present conflict, could get no satisfaction about their future plans.

Sep Howard had added worries. His supplies were cut down drastically, and some of his finest ingredients, such as preserved fruit and nuts, were now impossible to obtain. It grieved Sep to use inferior material, but it was plain that there was no alternative. 'Quality', or 'carriage trade', as he still thought of it, had virtually gone, although basic fare such as bread and buns had increased in volume because of the evacuees in Caxley. His workers were reduced in numbers, and petrol rationing severely hampered deliveries.

But business worries were not all. His wife Edna was far from well and refused to see a doctor. Since the outbreak of war she had served in the shop, looked after the six evacuee boys, and run her home with practically no help. She attacked everything with gay gusto and made light of the giddiness which attacked her more and more frequently.

''Tis nothing,' she assured the anxious Sep. 'Indigestion probably. Nothing that a cup of herb tea won't cure.'

The very suggestion of a doctor's visit put her into a panic.

'He'll have me in hospital in two shakes, and I'd die there! Don't you dare fetch a doctor to me, Sep.'

It was as though, with advancing age, she was returning to the gipsy suspicions and distrust of her forbears. She had always loved to be outside, and now, even on the coldest night, would lie beneath a wide-open window with the wind blowing in upon her. Sep could do nothing with the wilful woman whom he adored, but watch over her with growing anxiety.

One Sunday evening they returned from chapel as the full moon rose. In the darkened town its silvery light was more welcome than ever, and Edna stopped to gaze at its beauty behind the pattern of interlaced branches. She was like a child still, thought Sep, watching her wide dark eyes.

'It makes me feel excited,' whispered Edna. 'It always has done, ever since I was little.'

She put her hand through Sep's arm and they paced homeward companionably, Edna's eyes upon the moon.

It was so bright that night that Sep was unable to sleep. Beside him Edna's dark hair stirred in the breeze from the window. Her breathing was light and even. A finger of moonlight glimmered on the brass handles of the oak chest of drawers which had stood in the same position for all their married life. Upon it stood their wedding photograph, Edna small and enchantingly gay, Sep pale and very solemn. The glass gleamed in the silvery light.

It was very quiet. Only the bare branches stirred outside the window, and very faintly, with an ear long attuned to its murmur, Sep could distinguish the distant rippling of the Cax.

An owl screeched and at that moment Edna awoke. She sat up, looking like a startled child in her little white nightgown, and began to cough. Sep raised himself.

'It hurts,' she gasped, turning towards him, her face puckered with astonishment. Sep put his arms round her thin shoulders. She seemed as light-boned as a bird.

She turned her head to look at the great glowing face of the moon shining full and strong at the open window. Sighing, she fell softly back against Sep's shoulder, her cloud of dark hair brushing his mouth. A shudder shook her body and her breath escaped with a queer bubbling sound.

In the cold moonlit silence of the bedroom, Sep knew with awful certainty that he held in his arms the dead body of his wife.

In the months that followed Sep drifted about his affairs like a small pale ghost. He attended to the shop, the restaurant, his chapel matters and council affairs with the same grave courtesy which was customary, but the spirit seemed to have gone from him, and people told each other that Sep had only half his mind on things these days. He was the object of sincere sympathy.

Edna Howard had not been universally liked – she was too wild a bird to be accepted in the Caxley hen-runs – but the marriage had been a happy one, and it was sad to see Sep so bereft.

Kathy was the one who gave him most comfort. If only Jim had been alive, Sep thought to himself! But Jim, his firstborn, lay somewhere in Ypres, and Leslie, his second son, was also lost to him. They had not met since Leslie left Winnie and went to live in the south-west with the woman of his choice.

Sep would have been desolate indeed without Kathy and Bertie's company. He spent most of his evenings there when the shop was closed, sitting quietly in a corner taking comfort from the children and the benison of a happy home. But he refused to sleep there, despite pressing invitations. Always he returned through the dark streets to the market square, passing the bronze statue of good Queen Victoria, before mounting the stairs to his lonely bedroom.

As the days grew longer the news became more and more sombre. The invasion of neutral Norway in April 1940 angered Caxley and the rest of the country. The costly attempts to re-capture Narvik from the enemy, in the weeks that followed, brought outspoken criticism of Mr Chamberlain's leadership. Events were moving with such savagery and speed that it was clear that the time had arrived for a coalition government, and on May 10 Mr Churchill became Prime Minister.

Earlier, on the same day, Hitler invaded Holland. The news was black indeed. Before long it was known that a large part of the British Army had retreated to Dunkirk. The question 'How long can France hold out?' was on everyone's lips.

'They'll never give in,' declared Bertie to Sep, one glorious June evening in his garden. 'I've seen the French in action. They'll fight like tigers.'

The roses were already looking lovely. It was going to be a long hot summer, said the weatherwise of Caxley, and they were to be proved right. It did not seem possible, as the two men paced the grass, that across a narrow strip of water a powerful enemy waited to invade their land.

'They'll never get here,' said Bertie robustly. 'Napoleon was beaten by the Channel and so will Hitler be. The Navy will see to that.'

'At times I half-hope they will get here,' said Sep with a flash of spirit. 'There will be a warm welcome! I've never known people so spoiling for an encounter.'

Bertie was enrolled as a Local Defence Volunteer, soon to be renamed the Home Guard, and enjoyed his activities. One day, he hoped, he would return to army duties, but meanwhile there was plenty to organize in the face of imminent invasion.

Edward, now commissioned, had been posted to a squadron of Bomber Command in the north of England and was engaged in night bombing. Dickie Bridges was one of his crew. His letters showed such elation of spirit that the family's fears for him were partly calmed. Edward, it was plain, was doing exactly what he wanted to do – he was flying, he was in the thick of things, he was at the peak of his powers and deeply happy. The mention of a girl called Angela became more frequent. She was a Waaf on the same station and Winnie surmised that much of Edward's happiness came from her propinquity.

On a glorious hot June day, while haymaking was in full spate in the fields around Caxley and children refreshed themselves by splashing in the river Cax, the black news came over the radio that France had fallen. Joan Howard heard it in a little paper shop near the nursery school at dinner time. The old man who kept the shop beckoned her to the other side of the counter, and she stood, holding aside a hideous bead curtain which screened the tiny living-room from the shop, listening to the unbelievable news. She grew colder and colder. What would happen now?

The old man switched off the set when the announcement was over and turned to face her. To Joan's amazement his expression was buoyant.

'Now we're on our own,' he exclaimed with intense satisfaction. 'Never trusted them froggies for all old Winston said. We're better off without 'em, my dear. What was you asking for? *The Caxley Chronicle?* Thank you, dear. That's threepence. And now I'm off to get me Dad's old shot-gun polished up!'

She returned up the steep hill to the nursery school with the dreadful news. Miss Schmidt, the Viennese warden, always so gay and elegant, seemed to crumple into a frail old lady when Joan told her what she had heard.

'He is unbeatable,' she cried, and covered her face with her hands. Joan remembered the man in the paper shop and felt courage welling up in her.

'Rubbish!' she said stoutly. 'He's got us to reckon with. We'll never give in!'

'That is what my people said,' Miss Schmidt murmured, 'and the Poles and the Dutch. All of us – and now the French. The devil himself is with that man. He will rule the world.'

'You must not think that!' cried Joan. 'You know what the Prime Minister has said: "We'll fight on for years, if necessary alone," and it's true! We've all the Empire behind us. We can't lose, we can't!'

A child came up at this moment clamouring urgently for attention, and Miss Schmidt wiped away her tears and returned to her duties. But Joan could see that she could not believe that there was any hope for this small island where she had found brief refuge.

As for Joan herself, in some strange way her spirits grew more buoyant as the day wore on. Walking home that afternoon, through the brilliant sunshine, the confident words of the old man echoed in her ears: 'Now we're on our own. Better off without 'em, my dear!' They were as exhilarating as a marching song.

All Caxley seemed to share her mood, she discovered during the next few days. There was a fierce joy in the air, the relish of a fight.

'I'm sharpening up my filleting knife,' said Bill Petty at the fish stall in the market. The son of fat Mrs Petty, now dead, who had served there for years, Bill was a cripple who could never hope to see active service. His gaiety was infectious.

'I'll crown that Hitler with a jerry!' cried his neighbour at the crockery stall. 'Very suitable, don't you think?'

The spirit of Caxley was typical of the whole nation, roused, alert and ready to fight. As Doctor Johnson said: 'When a man knows he is going to be hanged in a fortnight, it concentrates his mind wonderfully.' Caxley concentrated to the full. Feverishly, defence plans went forward, old weapons were unearthed from cupboards and attics, and everyone intended to make it a fight to the finish.

'The Pry Minister,' said the B.B.C. announcer, 'will speak to the nation at hah-past nine tonight.' And the nation, listening, rejoiced to hear that brave belligerent voice saying: 'What has happened in France makes no difference to our actions and purpose. We have become the sole champions now in arms to defend the world cause. We shall fight on unconquerable until the curse of Hitler is lifted from the brows of mankind. We are sure that in the end all will come right.'

And somehow, despite the disaster of Dunkirk, the shortage of weapons, and the acknowledged might of the enemy, the people felt sure that all would come right.

It was two days later that a letter arrived at Rose Lodge from Edward. It was short and to the point.

Angela and I have just got engaged. So happy. Will bring her down to see you next weekend.

Love to you all,
Edward.

6. Edward in Love

SHE would never do, thought Winnie, gazing at Angela. She would never do at all. And yet, what was to be done about it? There was Edward, his dark eyes — so like his father's — fixed upon the girl, and his face wearing the expression which her mother so aptly described as 'the-cat's-got-at-the-cream'.

The memory of her own disastrous infatuation rushed at her from across the years. Was Edward about to make such an error of judgement? Or was she herself over-sensitive to the circumstances?

She tried to rationalize her feelings as she poured tea in the drawing-room at Rose Lodge. After all, she did not really know the girl. She must have faith in Edward's judgement. He was twenty-three, quite old enough to know his own mind. He was certainly very much in love, by the look of things. But — was she?

It was impossible to tell from Angela's cool, polite demeanour. She was small and very fair, with the neat good looks which would remain unchanged for many years. Just so had Winnie's mother been, trim and upright, and only recently had come the grey hair and wrinkles of old age to mar the picture. Old Mrs North's sharp blue eyes were now assessing the girl before them and Winnie wondered what she would have to say when at last they were free to speak together.

She did not have long to wait. Edward took Angela to meet Bertie and Kathy and to show her something of Caxley. Winnie and her mother washed up the rarely-used fragile best china while their tongues wagged. Old Mrs North was surprisingly dispassionate. She loved Edward dearly and Winnie quite expected fierce criticism of his choice.

'Seems a ladylike sort of gal,' declared the old lady, dexterously exploring the inside of the teapot with the linen towel. 'And got her head screwed on, I don't doubt.'

'That's what worries me a bit,' confessed Winnie. 'Do you think she's in love with him? I think Edward's rather romantic, for all his shyness.'

'Hardly surprising,' commented her mother dryly. 'And I'd sooner see the girl level-headed about this business than getting foolishly infatuated. Let's face it, Winnie – we've seen what happens in that sort of situation in our own family.'

Winnie flushed. It was all so true, and yet, despite the wisdom of her mother's words, the nagging doubt remained. Was this girl the sort who could make Edward happy? She could only hope so.

They were married in August in a little grey church in the village by the aerodrome. Winnie and Joan had a nightmarish railway journey involving many changes and delays. They were the only representatives of Edward's family, for Bertie was now back in the army, blissfully happy in charge of fleets of army lorries at a maintenance unit. Kathy could not leave her family, and Sep and Robert were inextricably tied up with their business commitments.

Angela's mother was there. Her husband had left her some years before, but she was in the company of a prosperous-looking sixty-year-old who was introduced as 'a very dear friend'. Winnie disliked both on sight. Angela's mother was an older edition of the daughter, taut of figure, well dressed, with curls of unnaturally bright gold escaping from the smart forward-tilting hat. Her fashionable shoes, with their thick cork soles and heels, made Winnie's plain court shoes look very provincial. She sported a marcasite brooch in the shape of a basket of flowers on the lapel of her grey flannel suit, and spoke to Joan and Winnie in a faintly patronizing way which they both found intolerable.

She had travelled from Pinner in the friend's car, and Winnie would dearly have loved to inquire about the source of the petrol for this journey, but common decency forbade it.

The service was simple, the wedding breakfast at the local public house was informal, and the pair left for a two-day honeymoon somewhere in the Yorkshire dales. On their return the bridegroom would continue his bombing of Wilhelmshaven, Kiel or Bremen. How idiotic and unreal it all seemed, thought Winnie, making her way back to the station. The only real crumb of comfort was the memory of Edward's face, alight with happiness.

The golden summer wore on, and the blue skies above Caxley and the southern counties were criss-crossed with trails and spirals of silver vapour as the Battle of Britain raged in the air above the island. This was truly a battle for life and freedom as opposed to death and slavery at the hands of the Nazis. Across the channel the enemy amassed his armies of invasion, and by night and day sent waves of bombers to attack London and the southeast. The achievements of the R.A.F. gave the nation unparalleled hope of ultimate victory – long though it might be in coming.

The raids now began in earnest. The phoney war was at an end and the evacuees again began to stream from the stricken towns. Many of them spent the rest of the war away from their own homes. Many had no homes to return to. Many adopted the town of their refuge, grew up, married and became happy countrymen for the rest of their lives.

Sep's six boys had been found new billets when Edna died. Now he was anxious to have at least two back with him, despite the fact that his household help was sketchy. It was old Mrs North who thought of Miss Taggerty as housekeeper.

Miss Taggerty, almost as old as Sep, had once been in charge of Bender North's kitchenware department. She retired to look after an exasperating old father who was bed-ridden when being watched and remarkably spry on his pins when not, and who lived until the age of ninety-seven in a state of ever-growing demand. On his death, his cottage was due for demolition and poor, plain Miss Taggerty was to be made homeless.

The family had been anxious about Sep for some time. Joan very often called in to see her grandfather on the way home from school. He was touchingly grateful for her visits and Joan grew to love him, during this summer, more deeply than ever before. Bit by bit she began to realize how much Edna had meant to this lonely old man.

They sat together one hot afternoon in the little yard by the bakehouse, and Sep spoke of his lost wife. On the grey cobbles, near their outstretched legs, a beautiful peacock butterfly settled, opening and closing its bright powdery wings in the sunshine.

'Edna was like that,' said Sep in a low voice, almost as if he spoke to himself. 'As bright and lovely. I never cease to wonder that she settled with me – someone as humdrum and grey as that old cobblestone there. She could have had anyone in the world, she was so gay and pretty. I'd nothing to give her.'

'Perhaps,' said Joan, 'she liked to be near something solid and enduring, just as that butterfly does. If you are fragile and volatile then you are attracted to something stable. Surely that's why you and Grandma were so happy. You gave each other what the other lacked.'

'Maybe, maybe!' agreed Sep absently. There was a little pause and then he turned to look at his grandchild.

'You're a wise girl,' he said. 'Stay wise. Particularly when you fall in love, Joan. You need to consult your head as well as your heart when you start to think of marrying – and so many people will give you advice. Listen to them, but let your own heart and head give you the final answer.'

'I will,' promised Joan.

Later she was to remember this conversation. And Sep, with infinite sadness, was to remember it too.

Meanwhile, it was arranged for Miss Taggerty to take up her abode at Sep's house. The family was relieved to think that Sep would be properly looked after at last. With winter approaching, such things as well-aired sheets, good fires and a hot steak and kidney pudding made from rationed meat now and again, were matters of some domestic importance. With Miss Taggerty in the market square house the two evacuee boys could return, and Sep would be glad to feel that he was doing his war-time bit as well as having the pleasure of young company. As for Miss Taggerty, her cup of happiness was full. Used to a life of service, a gentle master such as Sep was a god indeed after the Moloch of her late father.

The winter of 1940 was indeed a bitter one. The war grew fiercer. Britain stood alone, at bay, the hope of the conquered nations and the inspiration of those who would later join in the struggle. The weather was unduly cold, fuel was short and food too. In Caxley, as elsewhere, this Christmas promised to be a bleak one.

But December brought one great glow of hope. The Lend-Lease Bill was prepared for submission to the United States' Congress. It meant that Britain could shape long-term plans of defence and attack with all the mighty resources of America behind her. It was a heart-warming thought in a chilly world.

Rose Lodge was to be the rendezvous for as many members of the Howard and North families as could manage it that Christmas. It looked as though it might be the last time that they would meet there, for, with the renewal of fighting, the question of turning the house into a nurses' hostel once again cropped up. This time it seemed most probable that it would be needed early in the New Year, and Winnie and her mother planned to move into the top floor of their old home, now Edward's, in the market square, for the duration of the war. At the moment, Robert was being allowed to use the flat as storage space. The thought of moving out his supplies was something of a headache but, as Sep pointed out rather sternly, it must be done.

Edward and Angela arrived late on Christmas Eve. He had three days' leave and they had been lucky enough to get a lift down in a brother officer's car, three jammed in the back and three in the front. They were to return in the same fashion on Boxing Night.

They were in great good spirits when they burst in at the door. It was almost midnight but old Mrs North insisted on waiting up and the two women had a tray of food ready by the fire.

'If only I had a lemon,' cried Winnie, pouring out gin and tonic for the pair, 'I think I miss lemons and oranges more than anything else. And Edward always says gin and tonic without lemon is like a currant bun with no currants!'

'Not these days, mum,' said Edward stoutly. 'Gin alone, tonic alone would be marvellous. To have the two together in one glass in war-time is absolutely perfect.'

'And how do you find domestic life?' Winnie asked her daughter-in-law.

'Wonderful, after those awful days in the W.A.A.F.,' said Angela. 'I potter about in my own time, and it's lovely to compare notes with the other girls who pop in sometimes when they're off-duty.'

She went on to describe the two rooms in which she and Edward now lived in the village near the aerodrome. Life in the services had obviously never appealed to Angela and her present circumstances, though cramped and somewhat lonely, were infinitely preferable.

'If only Edward hadn't to go on those ghastly raids,' claimed his wife: 'I stay up all night sometimes, too worried to go to bed. Luckily, there's a phone in the house, and I ring up the mess every so often to see if he's back.'

'You'd do better to go straight to bed with some hot milk,' observed Winnie. 'It would be better for you and far better for Edward too, to know that you were being sensible. It only adds to his worries if he thinks you are miserable.'

'I'm surprised you are allowed to ring up,' said Mrs North.

'Oh, they don't exactly *like* it,' said Angela, 'but what do they expect?'

Edward changed the subject abruptly. He had tried to argue with Angela before on much the same lines, and with as little effect.

'Shall we see all the family tomorrow?'

'Bertie and Kathy and the children are coming to tea. They're bringing your grandfather too. He misses Grandma, particularly at Christmas, and they will all be together for Christmas dinner at Bertie's.'

'And there's just a chance,' added his grandmother North, 'that Aunt Mary may look in. She starts in pantomime one day this week, and may be able to come over for the day.'

Edward stretched himself luxuriously.

'It's wonderful to be back,' he said contentedly. 'Nowhere like Caxley. I can't wait for this bloody war to be over to get back again.'

'Language, dear!' rebuked his grandmother automatically, rising to go up to bed.

Before one o'clock on Christmas morning all the inhabitants of Rose Lodge were asleep.

All but one.

Edward lay on his back, his hands clasped behind his head, staring at the ceiling. Beside him Angela slept peacefully. He was having one of his 'black half-hours' as he secretly called them. What hopes had he of survival? What slender chances of returning to Caxley to live? Losses in Bomber Command were pretty hair-raising, and likely to become worse. He could view the thing fairly dispassionately for himself, although the thought of death at twenty-four was not what he looked for. But for Angela? How would she fare if anything happened to him? Thank God there were no babies on the way at the moment. He'd seen too many widows with young children recently to embark lightly on a family of his own.

The memory of his last raid on Kiel came back to him with sickening clarity. They had encountered heavy anti-aircraft fire as they approached their target and the Wellington had been hit. Luckily not much damage was done. They dropped their load and Edward wheeled for home. But several jagged pieces of metal, razor-sharp, had flown across the aircraft from one side to the other, and Dickie Bridges was appallingly cut across the face and neck.

One of the crew had been a first-year medical student when he joined up, and tied swabs across a spouting artery and staunched the blood as best he could. Nevertheless, Dickie grew greyer and greyer as the Wellington sped back to base and it was obvious that something was hideously wrong with his breathing. Some obstruction in the throat caused him to gasp with a whistling sound which Edward felt he would remember until his dying day.

As they circled the aerodrome he was relieved to see the ambulance – known, grimly, as 'the blood cart' – waiting by the runway. Sick and scared, Edward touched down as gently as he could and watched Dickie carried into the ambulance. He knew, with awful certainty, that he would never see him alive again.

Dickie Bridges died as they were getting him ready for a blood transfusion, and next day Edward sat down with a heavy heart and wrote to his crippled mother. He had been her only child.

Damn all wars! thought Edward turning over violently in bed. If only he could be living in the market square, sharing his flat with Angela, starting a family, flying when he wanted to, pottering about with his friends and family in Caxley – what a blissful existence it would be!

And here he was, on Christmas morning too, full of rebellion when he should be thinking of peace and goodwill to all men. Somehow it hardly fitted in with total war, Edward decided sardonically.

He thought of all the other Christmas mornings he had spent under this roof, a pillowcase waiting at the end of the bed, fat with knobbly parcels and all the joy of Christmas Day spread out before him. They had been grand times.

Would this be the last Christmas for him? He put the cold thought from him absolutely. His luck had held so far. It would continue. It was best to live from day to day, 'soldiering on',

as they said. Enough that it was Christmas time, he was in Caxley, and with Angela!

He pitched suddenly into sleep as if he were a pebble thrown
into a deep pond. Outside, in the silent night, a thousand stars
twinkled above the frost-rimed roofs of the little town of Caxley.

7. The Market Square Again

THE New Year of 1941 arrived, and the people of Caxley, in company with the rest of the beleaguered British, took stock and found some comfort. The year which had passed gave reason for hope. Britain had held her own. Across the Atlantic the United States was arming fast and sending weapons in a steady stream to the Allied forces.

Even more cheering was the immediate news from Bardia in North Africa where the Australians were collecting twenty thousand Italian prisoners after one of the decisive battles in the heartening campaign which was to become known as the Desert Victory.

'The longer we hangs on the more chance we has of licking 'em!' pronounced an old farmer, knocking out his cherrywood pipe on the plinth of Queen Victoria's statue in the market square. He bent painfully and retrieved the small ball of spent tobacco which lay on the cobbles, picked one or two minute strands from it and replaced them carefully in his pipe.

'Not that we've got cause to get *careless,* mark you,' he added severely to his companion, who was watching the stubby finger ramming home the treasure trove. 'We've got to harbour our resources like Winston said – like what I'm doin' now – and then be ready to give them Germans what for whenever we gets the chance.'

And this, in essence, was echoed by the whole nation. 'Hanging on,' was the main thing, people told each other, and putting up with short commons as cheerfully as possible. It was not easy. As the months went by, 'making-do-and-mending' became more and more depressing, and sometimes well-night impossible. Another irritating feature of war-time life was the unbearable attitude of some of those in posts of officialdom.

It was Edward who noticed this particularly on one of his

63

rare leaves in Caxley. It occurred one Saturday afternoon when the banks were closed and he needed some ready money. Luckily he had his Post Office savings book with him and thrust his way boisterously through the swing doors, book in hand. Behind the counter stood a red-haired girl whose protruding teeth rivalled Miss Taggerty's.

Edward remembered her perfectly. They had attended the same school as small children and he had played a golliwog to her fairy doll in the Christmas concert one year. On this occasion, however, she ignored his gay greeting, and thrust a withdrawal form disdainfully below the grille, her face impassive. Edward scribbled diligently and pushed it back with his book, whereupon the girl turned back the pages importantly in order to scrutinize the signature in the front and compare it with that on the form. For Edward, impatient to be away, it was too much.

'Come off it, Foof-teeth!' he burst out in exasperation, using the nickname of their schooldays. And only then did she melt enough to give him a still-frosty smile with the three pound notes.

There were equally trying people in Caxley, and elsewhere, who attained positions of petty importance and drove their neighbours to distraction: air raid wardens who seemed to relish every inadvertent chink of light in the black-out curtains, shop assistants rejoicing in the shortage of custard-powder, bus conductors harrying sodden queues, all added their pinpricks to the difficulties of everyday living, and these people little knew that such irritating officiousness would be remembered by their fellow-citizens for many years to come, just as the many little kindnesses, also occurring daily, held their place as indelibly in their neighbours' memories. Friends, and enemies, were made for life during war-time.

Howard's Restaurant continued to flourish despite shortages of good quality food stuffs which wrung Sep's heart. Robert failed his medical examination when his call-up occurred. Defective eyesight and some chest weakness sent him back to running the restaurant. Secretly, he was relieved. He had dreaded the discipline and the regulations almost more than the dangers of active service. He was content to plough along his familiar furrow, fraught though it was with snags and pitfalls, and asked only to be left in peace. He said little to his father about his feelings, but Sep was too wise not to know what went on in his son's head.

The boy was a disappointment to him, Sep admitted to himself. Sometimes he wondered why his three sons had brought so much unhappiness in their wake. Jim's death in the First World War had taken his favourite from him. Leslie, the gay lady-killer, had betrayed his trust and vanished westward to live with someone whom Sep still thought of as 'a wanton woman', despite her subsequent marriage to his son.

And now, Robert. Without wife or child, curiously secretive and timid, lacking all forms of courage, it seemed, he appeared to Sep a purely negative character. He ran the restaurant ably, to be sure, but he lacked friends and had no other interests in the town. Perhaps, if marriage claimed him one day, he would come to life. As it was he continued his way, primly and circumspectly, a spinsterish sort of fellow, with a streak of petty spite to which Sep was not blind.

His greatest comfort now was Kathy. He saw more of her now than ever, for Bertie was away in the army, and she and the children were almost daily visitors to the house in the market square. She grew more like her dear mother, thought Sep, with every year that passed. She had the same imperishable beauty, the flashing dark eyes, the grace of movement and dazzling smile which would remain with her throughout her life.

Yes, he was lucky to have such a daughter – and such wonderful grandchildren! He loved them all, but knew in his secret heart that it was Edward who held pride of place. There was something of Leslie – the *best* of Leslie, he liked to think – something of the Norths, and a strong dash of himself in this beloved grandson. He longed to see children of Edward's before he grew too old to enjoy their company. Did his wife, that beautiful but rather distant Angela, really know what a fine man she had picked? Sometimes Sep had his doubts, but times were difficult for everyone, and for newly-weds in particular. With the coming of peace would come the joy of a family, Sep felt sure.

And for Joan too, he hoped. She was a North, despite her name, if ever there was one, and the Norths were made for domesticity. There flashed into the old man's mind a picture of his dead friend Bender North, sitting at ease in his Edwardian drawing-room, above the shop which was now Howard's Restaurant. He saw him now, contented and prosperous, surveying the red-plush furniture, the gleaming sideboard decked with silver, smoking his Turk's-head pipe, at peace with the world. Just as contentedly had Bertie settled down with Kathy. He prayed that Joan, in her turn, might find as felicitous a future in a happy marriage. It was good, when one grew old, to see the younger generations arranging their affairs, and planning a world which surely would be better than that in which Sep had grown up.

Joan was indeed planning her future, unknown to her family. She was still absorbed in her work at the nursery school and as the months of war crept by it became apparent that the chances of joining the W.A.A.F. became slighter.

For one thing, the numbers at the school increased rapidly. As local factories stepped-up their output more young women were needed, and their children were left in the care of the school. And then the Viennese warden was asked to take over the job of organizing nursery work for the whole county, and Joan, trembling a little at such sudden responsibility, was put in charge.

She need not have worried. Despite her youth, she was well-trained, and had had varied experience. Allied to this, her equable North temperament and her genuine affection for the children, made her ideally suited to the post. Two women had been added to the staff, one of them being Maisie Hunter who had arrived at the beginning of the war as an evacuee at Rose Lodge and who had remained in the neighbourhood. She was a tower of strength to Joan. The second teacher was a wispy young girl straight from college, anxious to do the right thing, and still with the words of her child-psychology lecturer ringing in her ears. Joan could only hope that face-to-face encounters with healthy three-year-olds would in time bring her down to earth a little, and give her confidence.

All this made Joan realize that her duty really lay with these young children and the job with which she had been landed. In some ways she regretted it. Her dream of being posted somewhere near Edward, perhaps even learning to fly one day, was doomed to fade. Nevertheless, this job was one equally valuable, and one which she knew she could tackle. It meant too that she could keep an eye on her mother and grandmother. Winnie was more active than ever, it seemed, but there were times when old Mrs North looked suddenly frail, and her memory, until now so acute, was often at fault. The oven would be left on, telephone messages were forgotten, spectacles and bags mislaid a dozen times a day and, worse still, the autocratic old lady would never admit that any of these little mishaps was her own fault. Physically, she was as active as ever, mounting the steep stairs to the flat in the market square as lightly as she had done when she lived there as mistress of the house so many years before.

All three women found the quarters somewhat cramped after Rose Lodge, but they all enjoyed living again in the heart of Caxley, close to their neighbours, and with the weekly market to enliven the scene each Thursday. They were handy too for the shops and for Sep's restaurant down below where they frequently called for a meal.

They found too that they were admirably placed to receive visits from their family and friends. Buses were few and far between, but the market square was a main shopping point, and friends and relations from the villages could call easily. Old Mrs North's sister, Ethel Miller, whose husband farmed at Beech Green, frequently came to see them bearing farm eggs, butter, an occasional chicken or duck — treasures indeed in wartime.

It was her Aunt Ethel who first introduced Michael to Joan. He was one of three junior army officers billeted at the farm, and Joan had heard a little about them all. They seemed to be a cheerful high-spirited trio and her aunt was devoted to them – indeed, so fulsome was she in her praise, that Joan had tended to think that their charms must be considerably overrated.

'Michael is picking me up at six o'clock,' said Aunt Ethel, glancing at the timepiece on the mantelpiece. She had been ensconced on the sofa when Joan came in from school at tea-time. 'He's had to collect some equipment from the station in the truck,' she explained, 'and offered me a lift.'

At ten past six they heard the sound of footsteps pounding up the stairs and Joan opened the door to admit the young man. He was full of apologies for being late, but he did not look particularly downcast, Joan observed. Aunt Ethel, anxious to get back to the family and the farm, made hurried farewells, and the two vanished after a few brief civilities. Joan, in spite of herself, was most impressed with the stranger.

He was exceptionally tall, a few inches over six feet, slender and dark. He had grey bright eyes with thick black lashes, and his face was lantern-jawed and pale. He was an Irishman, Joan knew, and he looked it. In the few words which he had spoken, Joan had recognized the soft brogue and the intonation full of Irish charm. A heart-breaker, if ever there was one, commented Joan amusedly to herself!

They did not meet again for some time, but one Saturday early in October, Joan offered to take some wool to the farm for her aunt.

'It will do me good to get some exercise,' she said, trundling out her bicycle from the shed where Bender had once kept mangles and dustbins, buckets and baths, in the old days.

It was a still misty day. Cobwebs were slung along the hedges like miniature hammocks. Droplets hung on the ends of wet twigs. There was a smell of autumn in the air, a poignant mixture of dead leaves, damp earth and the whiff of a distant bonfire.

Halfway to Beech Green a sharp hill caused Joan to dismount. She stood still for a moment to get back her breath. Above her a massive oak tree spread gnarled wet arms. Looking up into its intricacies of pattern against the soft pale sky she noticed dozens of cobwebs draped like scraps of grey chiffon between the rough bark of the sturdy trunk and the branches. Far away, hidden in the mist, a train hooted. Near at hand, a blackbird scrabbled among papery brown leaves beneath the hedge. Otherwise silence enveloped the girl and she realized, with a shock, how seldom these days she enjoyed complete solitude.

What a long time it was too, she thought, since she had consciously observed such everyday natural miracles as the cobwebs and the blackbird's liquid eye! Engrossed with the children and their mothers, walking to and from the nursery school along the pavements of Caxley, restricted by war from much outside activity, she had quite forgotten the pleasure which flowers and trees, birds and animals had subconsciously supplied. She freewheeled down the long hill to the farm, exhilarated by her unaccustomed outing.

Her aunt was busy making a new chicken-run and, with a quickening of the heart, Joan saw that Michael was wielding the mallet which drove in the stakes.

'You dear girl,' exclaimed Aunt Ethel, proffering a cold damp cheek to be kissed, while her fingers ripped open the package. 'Four whole ounces! I can't believe it! Now I shall be able to knit Jesse a good thick pair of winter socks. How on earth did Hilda manage it?'

'Sheer favouritism,' replied Joan. 'It was under-the-counter stuff, and passed over with much secrecy, I understand. They only had two pounds of wool altogether, Grandma said, and you had to be a real old blue-blooded Caxleyite to nobble an ounce or two.'

Michael laughed at this, and Joan found him more attractive than ever.

'Now hold the end of this wire,' directed Aunt Ethel, returning to the business in hand, 'and we'll be done in no time. Then you must stop and have lunch. It's rabbit casserole with lots of carrots.'

'S'posed to keep off night-blindness, whatever that is,' said Michael jerkily, between powerful blows with the mallet.

When the job was done and the excellent rabbit demolished, Michael and Joan sat in the warm farm kitchen and talked. Uncle Jesse was in the yard attempting to repair a wiring fault in his ancient Ford, while Aunt Ethel had gone upstairs 'to sort the laundry', she explained, although Joan knew very well that she was having the nap which she refused to admit she took every afternoon.

Michael talked easily. He told her about his home in Dublin and his family there.

'My old man keeps a hotel. Nothing in the five-star range, you know. Just a little place where the commercials stay over-night – but we've a quiet decent little house there and a grand garden.'

He had two sisters and a brother, he told her. His mother was an invalid, and he wanted to get back soon to see her.

'And what do you do,' asked Joan, 'when you're not in the Army?'

'I'm not too sure,' answered Michael. 'You see, I'd just got my degree at Trinity College when war broke out. Maybe I'll teach. I read modern languages. Oh, there now, I can't tell you what I'll do, and that's the truth!'

Joan was intrigued with the way the last word came out as 'troot'. Despite his vagueness about the future, it was apparent that he intended to do something worthwhile. She told him a little about her own work and he seemed deeply interested.

'You're lucky,' he said. 'You know where you're going. Maybe I'll know too before long, but let's get the war over first, I think. Somehow, it's difficult to make plans when you may be blown to smithereens tomorrow.'

He spoke cheerfully, his wide smile making a joke of the grim words.

'I wish I could see you home,' he said when at last Joan rose to go. 'But I'm on duty in half an hour. Can I ring you one day soon? Are you ever free?'

'I'm completely free,' Joan said.

'Good!' replied the young man with evident satisfaction.

They walked together to the front door of the farmhouse. Joan's dilapidated bicycle stood propped against the massive door-scraper which had served generations of muddy-booted Millers.

Across the lawn a copper beech tree stood against the grey-fawn sky, like some old sepia photograph, framed in the oblong of the doorway.

'It's a grand country,' said Michael softly.

'Lovelier than Ireland?'

'Ah, I'm not saying that! Have you never been?'

'Never.'

'You must go one day when the war's over. I'll look forward to showing it to you.'

'That would be lovely,' said Joan, primly polite. She mounted the bicycle and smiled her farewells. He saluted very smartly, eyes twinkling, and watched her ride away.

She reported on her visit to her mother and grandmother as they sat by the fire that evening, saying little about Michael. She was more deeply attracted than she cared to admit, and felt that she could not face any family probings.

Old Mrs North's sharp eye, however, missed nothing.

'An attractive young man, that Michael,' she said, briskly tugging at her embroidery needle. 'Even if he is Irish.'

Joan smiled.

'Pity he's a Roman Catholic,' continued the old lady. 'Off to seven o'clock mass as regular as clockwork, Ethel says. But there,' she added indulgently, 'I expect it keeps him out of mischief.'

Joan nodded. But her smile had gone.

8. The Invasion

EDWARD had been posted yet again. This time it was to a station in Wales where he would be a staff pilot, instructing others in the art of flying bombers. This was a rest period, for six months or possibly longer, between operational tours.

Angela was more than usually disgruntled at the move. She insisted on accompanying her husband wherever he might be, and was beginning to get heartily sick of other people's houses and unending domestic problems. As the war dragged on, she became steadily more discontented with her lot, and Edward was sincerely sorry for her. He knew how long the days were, cooped in two rooms, in someone else's home. He realized, only too well, the anxiety she suffered when he was on operations. And he was beginning to see that Angela had very few inner resources to give her refreshment and strength to combat her tedium.

She seemed to spend most of her time in the company of other young wives as bored as she was herself. They met for innumerable coffee parties and games of bridge. Edward had suggested more fruitful ways of spending the time. There was plenty of voluntary work to be done, helping in hospitals, schools, A.R.P. centres and so on but Angela's answer had been disturbing and illuminating.

'I married you to get out of the W.A.A.F. Why the devil should I put my head into another noose?'

It was not very reassuring to a newly-married man, and as the months lengthened into years Edward began to realize that Angela had meant every word of that remark. Perhaps they should have started a family, foolhardy though it seemed. Would things have been more satisfactory? He doubted it. Edward was too wise to pin his hopes on motherhood as a panacea to all marital ills, and he had observed other young couples' problems with babies in wartime. It was difficult enough to obtain accommodation without children. Those who had them were definitely at a disadvantage.

No, thought Edward, they had been right to wait. But would the time ever come when they both looked forward to children? With a heavy heart, he began to face the fact that Angela might have waited too long.

It was at the end of May when Edward and Angela made their next visit to Caxley.

'No family yet then?' Mrs North greeted them, with devastating directness. 'Why's that?'

Angela pointedly ignored the question. Edward laughed, hugged his diminutive grandmother and pointed out of the window to the market square.

'That partly,' he replied.

A steady flow of army transport was travelling across the square heading south to the ports. Lorries, armoured cars and tanks had been pouring through Caxley for days now, and the thunder of their passage shook the old house and caused headaches among the inhabitants.

But there was no heart-ache. This, they knew, was the start of a great invasion – an invasion in reverse. The time had come when this mighty allied force could cross the Channel and begin the task of liberating oppressed Europe. Who would have thought it? they bellowed to each other, against the din. Four years ago it was the British Isles which awaited invasion! The tables were turned indeed.

Edward was now stationed within eighty miles of Caxley and was back on operational duty. He had no doubt that he would be busy bombing supply bases and cutting the communications of the retreating enemy. He should see plenty of activity, he told himself. It would be good to support an attacking army in Europe.

'Make no mistake,' he told his family, 'we're on the last lap now. Then back to Caxley and peace-time!'

That afternoon, while Angela was at the hairdresser's, he walked through the throbbing town to see Bertie who was also on brief leave. He found him pushing the lawn mower, his fair hair turning more and more ashen as the grey hairs increased, but still lissom in figure and with the same gentle good looks.

They greeted each other warmly.

'Kathy's out on some W.V.S. ploy,' said Bertie, 'and the children are still at school. Come and have a look at the river. It's quieter there than anywhere else in Caxley at the moment. But, by God, what a welcome sound, Edward, eh? Great days before us, my boy!'

It was indeed peaceful by the Cax. The shining water slipped along reflecting the blue and white sky. Here and there it was spangled with tiny white flowers which drifted gently to and fro with the current. On the towpath, across the river, a cyclist pedalled slowly by, and his reflection, upside down, kept pace with him swiftly and silently. The moment was timeless and unforgettable.

'Tell me,' said Bertie, 'has Joan said anything to you about Michael?'

'Not much,' replied Edward, startled from his reverie by something in his uncle's tone. 'Why, what's up?'

'They're very much in love,' said Bertie slowly. 'And to my mind would make a very good pair. He's a Catholic, of course, but it doesn't worry me. I wondered if it would complicate matters with the family.'

'Grandfather'd hate it,' admitted Edward bluntly. 'And probably Grandma North. I can't see anyone else losing much sleep over it. Surely, it's their affair.'

'I agree,' said Bertie. They paced the path slowly. Edward noticed that Bertie's limp was more accentuated these days and remembered, with a slight shock, that his uncle must now be over fifty.

'After all,' continued Edward ruminatively, 'you can't call the Norths a deeply religious family – and Joan and I, for all we're called Howard, take after the Norths in that way. I can't truthfully say I'm a believer, you know. There's too much to accept in church teaching – I boggle at a lot of it. But for those who

74

really are believers, well, it's probably better to go the whole hog and be a Catholic, You know where you are, don't you ?'

'Meaning what?' asked Bertie smiling at Edward's honest, if inelegant, reasoning.

'Well, if Joan is as luke-warm as I am, and yet she recognizes that Michael has something in his faith which means something to him, then she may be willing for the children to be brought up in the same way. I just don't know. I've never talked of such things with her.'

They turned in their tracks and made their way slowly back. A kingfisher, a vivid arrow of blue and green, streaked across the water and vanished into the tunnel made by the thick-growing chestnut trees.

'Lucky omen !' commented Bertie.

'In love or war?' asked Edward, gazing after it.

'Both, I predict,' said Bertie confidently, limping purposefully homeward.

It was at the end of that same week that Michael and Joan mounted the stairs to the flat and told Winnie and her mother that they were engaged.

Edward and Bertie were back on duty, Michael was moving to the coast the next day with his unit. The young couple did not blind themselves to the risks of the next few days. The casualties would be heavy, and it was likely that the army would bear the brunt of the attack. But nothing could dim their happiness, and Winnie and old Mrs North were glad to give them their blessing.

When at last Michael had gone and Joan returned, pink and a little damp-eyed from making her farewells, Mrs North spoke briskly the thoughts which were shared, but would have been left unuttered, by Winnie.

'Well, dear, I'm very happy for you. I've always liked Michael, as you know, and as long as you face the fact that there will be a new baby every twelve months or so I'm sure it will work out well. You'll stay C. of E. I suppose?'

'No, Grandma,' replied Joan composedly. 'I shall become a Roman Catholic, like all those babies-to-be.'

'Pity!' said the old lady. 'Well, you know your own business best, I suppose. Sleep well, and remember to take that ring off whenever you put your hands in water. Goodnight, dears.'

She put up her soft papery cheek to be kissed as usual, and went off to bed.

Winnie looked at her daughter. She looked tired out. Who wouldn't, thought Winnie, with all she had been through, and with Michael off to battle at first light? And yet there was a calmness about her which seemed unshakeable. Just so had she herself been when breaking the news of her engagement to Joan's father. Please, she prayed suddenly, let her marriage be happier than mine! And happier than Edward's! It was the first time, she realized suddenly, that she had admitted to herself that Edward's marriage was heading for the rocks. Were they all to be doomed to unhappiness with their partners?

She put the dark fear from her and kissed her daughter affectionately.

'Bed, my love,' she said.

It was Sep, of course, who felt it most. Joan told him the news herself the next day. She found him pottering about in his bakehouse, stacking tins and wiping the already spotless shelves.

She thought how little the place had changed since she was a child. The same great scrubbed table stood squarely in the middle of the red-tiled floor. The same comfortable warmth embraced one, and the same wholesome smell of flour and newly-baked bread pervaded the huge building. And Sep too, at first sight, seemed as little changed. Small, neat, quiet and deft in his movements, his grey hair was as thick as ever, his eyes as kindly as Joan always remembered them.

'Sit 'ee down, sit 'ee down,' cried Sep welcomingly, pulling forward a tall wooden stool. 'And what brings you here, my dear?'

Joan told him, twisting Michael's beautiful sapphire ring

about her finger as she spoke. Sep heard her in silence to the end.

'I know you can't approve wholeheartedly, Grandpa,' said Joan, looking up at his grave face, 'but don't let it come between us, please.'

Sep sighed.

'Nothing can,' he said gently. 'You are part of my family, and a very dear part, as you know. And you're a wise child, I've always said so. Do you remember how you comforted me when your dear grandmother died?'

'You asked me then to choose wisely when I got married,' nodded Joan. 'I remember it very well. Do you think that I've chosen unwisely after all?'

'You have chosen a good man; I have no doubt of that,' replied Sep. 'But I cannot be happy to see you embracing his faith. You know my feelings on the subject. It is a religion which I find absolutely abhorrent, battening on the poor and ignorant, and assuming in its arrogance that all other believers are heretics.'

'Michael would tell you that it is the one gleam of hope in the lives of many of those poor and ignorant people,' replied Joan.

'Naturally he would,' responded Sep shortly. 'He is a devout Catholic. He believes what he is told to believe.'

He turned away and stood, framed in the doorway, looking with unseeing eyes at the cobbled yard behind the bakehouse. The clock on the wall gave out its measured tick. Something in one of the ovens hissed quietly. To Joan the silence seemed ominous. Her grandfather wheeled round and came back to where she sat, perched high on the wooden stool.

'We'll say no more. There must be no quarrels between us two. You will do whatever you think is right, I know, without being swayed by people round you. But think, my dear, I beg of you. Think, and pray. There are your children to consider.'

'I have thought,' replied Joan soberly.

'And whatever your decision,' continued Sep, as though he had not heard her interjection, 'we shall remain as we've always

77

been. I want you to feel that you can come to me at any time. Don't let anything – ever – come between us, Joan.'

She rose from the stool and bent to kiss the little man's forehead.

'Nothing can,' she assured him. 'Nothing, Grandpa.'

But as she crossed the market square, and paused by Queen Victoria's statue to let the war-time traffic thunder by, her heart was torn by the remembrance of Sep's small kind face, suddenly shrivelled and old. That she, who loved him so dearly, could have wrought such a change, was almost more than she could bear.

On the night of 5 June in that summer of 1944 a great armada sailed from the English ports along the channels already swept clear of mines. By dawn the next day the ships stood ready off the Normandy coast for the biggest amphibious operation of the war – the invasion of Europe.

Edward was engaged in attacking enemy coast-defence guns, flying a heavy bomber. As the first light crept across the sky, the amazing scene was revealed to him as he flew back to base. The line upon line of ships, great and small, might have been drawn up ready for a review. A surge of pride swept him as he looked from above. The fleet in all its wartime strength was an exhilarating sight. Edward, for one, had not the faintest doubt in his mind that by the end of this vital day victory would be within sight.

Excitement ran high in the country. News had just been received of the liberation of Rome under General Alexander's command, but people were agog to know what was going on across the strip of water which had so long kept their island inviolate.

At midday the Prime Minister gave welcome news to the House of Commons. 'An immense armada of upwards of four thousand ships, together with several thousand smaller craft, crossed the Channel,' he told them and went on to say that reports coming in showed that everything was proceeding according to plan. 'And what a plan !' he added.

It was the success of this vast enterprise, on sea and land simultaneously, which gripped the imagination of the country. Napoleon had been daunted by the Channel. Hitler, for all his threats, had been unable to cross it. The success of the allied British and American armies in this colossal undertaking was therefore doubly exciting.

The inhabitants of Caxley kept their radio sets switched on, eager to hear every scrap of news which came through. Joan longed to know where Michael was and how he was faring. There must have been heavy casualties, she knew, and the suspense was agonizing.

The Norths and Howards knew where their other fighting men were. Bertie was stationed not far from Poole, and Edward was based in Kent. They did not expect to hear or see much of the pair of them in these exciting times, but the fortunes of Michael, now somewhere in the thick of things in Normandy were the focus of their thoughts.

As the days went by they grieved for Joan watching anxiously for the postman's visits. There was sobering news during the next week, about stubborn enemy resistance at the town of Caen. It was apparent that failure to capture this key-point would mean that a large force of allied troops would be needed there for some time. Could the enemy make a come-back?

One sunny morning the longed-for letter arrived and Joan tore it open in the privacy of her bedroom. She read it swiftly.

My Darling Joan,

All's well here. Tough going, but not a scratch, and a grand set of chaps. We are constantly on the move – but in the right direction, Berlin-wards. The people here are being wonderful to us.

I can't wait to get home again. Look after yourself. I'll write again as soon as I get a chance.

All my love,
Michael

Joan sat down hard on the side of the bed and began to cry. There was a tap at the door and her grandmother looked in. Tears were rolling steadily down the girl's cheeks, splashing upon the letter in her hands.

A chill foreboding gripped the old lady. In a flash she remembered the dreadful day during the First World War when she had heard the news that Bertie was seriously wounded in hospital. The memory of that nightmare drive to see him was as fresh in her mind as if it had happened yesterday.

She advanced towards her granddaughter, arms outstretched to comfort.

'Oh, Joan,' she whispered. 'Bad news then?'

The girl, sniffing in the most unladylike way, held out the letter.

'No, Grandma,' she quavered. 'It's good news. He's safe.'

And she wept afresh.

9. Edward and Angela

It was the beginning of the end of the war, and everyone knew it. Perhaps this was the most hopeful moment of the long conflict. The free world still survived. Within a year Europe would be liberated, and two or three months later, hostilities would cease in the Far East. Meanwhile, a world which knew nothing yet of Belsen and Hiroshima, rejoiced in the victory which was bound to come.

It was the beginning of the end too, Edward realized, of his marriage. Things had gone from bad to worse. No longer could he blind himself with excuses for Angela's estrangement. Indifference had led to recriminations, petty squabbles, and now to an implacable malice on his wife's part. Edward, shaken to the core, had no idea how to cope with the situation now that things had become so bleakly impossible.

Any gesture of affection, any attempt on his part to heal the breach, was savagely rebuffed. Anything sterner was greeted with hysterical scorn. If he was silent he was accused of sulking, if he spoke he was told he was a bore.

It was about this time that an old admirer of Angela's appeared. She and Edward had been invited to a party at a friend's house. There was very little social life in the small Kentish town where they were then living, and Angela accepted eagerly. Edward preferred to be at home on the rare occasions when that was possible. He dreaded too the eyes which watched them, and knew that the break-up of their marriage was becoming all too apparent. But he went with good grace and secretly hoped that they would be able to get away fairly early.

It was a decorous, almost stuffy, affair. About twenty people, the local doctor and his wife, a schoolmaster, a few elderly worthies as well as one or two service couples, stood about the poorly-heated drawing-room and made falsely animated conversation. Their hostess was a large kindhearted lady swathed in black crêpe caught on the hip with a black satin bow. She was afflicted with deafness but courageously carried on loud conversations with every guest in turn. As the rest of the company raised their voices in order to make themselves heard, the din was overwhelming. Edward, overwrought and touchy, suddenly had a vision of the leafy tunnel of chestnut trees which arched above the Cax, and longed with all his soul to be there with only the whisper of the water in his ears.

As it was, he stood holding his weak whisky and water, his eyes smarting with smoke and his face frozen in a stiff mask of polite enjoyment. The doctor's wife was telling him a long and involved story about a daughter in Nairobi, of which Edward heard about one word in ten. Across the room he could see Angela, unusually gay, talking to an army officer whom he had not seen before.

They certainly seemed to enjoy each other's company, thought Edward, with a pang of envy. How pretty Angela was tonight! If only she would look at him like that — so happily and easily! The tale of the Nairobi daughter wound on interminably, and just as Edward was wondering how on earth he could extricate himself, he saw Angela's companion look across, touch Angela's arm, and together they began to make their way towards him.

At the same moment the doctor's wife was claimed by a faded little woman in a droopy-hemmed stockinette frock. They pecked each other's cheeks and squawked ecstatically. Thankfully, Edward moved towards his wife.

'Can you believe it?' cried Angela, 'I've found Billy again, after all these years! Billy Sylvester, my husband.'

'How d'you do?' said the men together.

'Billy has digs at the doctor's,' Angela prattled on excitedly. Edward wondered if he had heard all about the daughter in Nairobi, and felt a wave of sympathy towards the newcomer.

'We used to belong to the same sports club years ago,' continued Angela, 'before Bill went into the army. Heavens, what a lot of news we've got to exchange!'

'Mine's pretty dull,' said Billy with a smile. He began to talk to Edward, as the daughter of the house moved across to replenish their glasses. He had been in the town now for about a month it transpired, and was in charge of stores at his camp.

'Any chance of going overseas?' asked Edward.

'Not very likely,' replied Billy, 'I'm getting a bit long in the tooth, and my next move will be either up north or west, as far as I can gather.'

Edward watched him with interest, as they sipped amidst the din. He was probably nearing forty, squarely built, with a large rather heavy face, and plenty of sleek black hair. He spoke with a pleasing Yorkshire accent, and gave the impression of being a sound business man, which was indeed the case. He did not appear to be the sort of man who would flutter female hearts, but Angela's blue eyes were fixed upon him in such a challenging manner, that Edward wondered what lay hidden from him in the past. Probably nothing more serious than a schoolgirl's crush on the star tennis player at the club, he decided. Or, even more likely, yet another gambit to annoy an unwanted husband. He was getting weary of such pinpricks, he had to admit.

Nevertheless, he liked the fellow. He liked his air of unpretentious solidity, the fact that his deep voice could be heard clearly amidst the clamour around them, and the way in which he seemed oblivious of Angela's advances.

After some time, Edward saw one of his friends across the room. He was newly-married and his young shy wife was looking well out of her depth.

'Let's go and have a word with Tommy,' said Edward to Angela.

'You go,' she responded. 'I'll stay with Bill.'

And stay she did, much to the interest of the company, for the rest of the evening.

Edward saw very little of Billy Sylvester after that. Occasionally, they came across each other in the town, and on one bitterly cold morning they collided in the doorway of 'The Goat and

Compasses'. Angela, Edward knew, had seen something of him, but he had no idea how often they met. Angela spoke less and less, but she had let out that Billy had parted from his wife before the war, and that he had two boys away at boarding school.

Air attacks in support of the Allied forces were being intensified and Edward was glad to have so much to occupy him. He had been promoted again, and was beginning to wonder if he would stay in the Air Force after the war. In some ways he wanted to. On the other hand the restrictions of service life, which he had endured cheerfully enough in war-time, he knew would prove irksome and certainly Angela would be against the idea. He was beginning to long for roots, a home, a family, something to see growing. In his more sanguine moments he saw Angela in the Caxley flat, refurbishing it with him, starting life afresh. Or perhaps buying a cottage near the town, on the hilly slopes towards Beech Green, say, or in the pleasant southern outskirts of Caxley near the village of Bent? And then the cold truth would press in upon him. In his heart of hearts he knew that there could never be a future with Angela. She had already left him. The outlook was desolate. Meanwhile, one must live from day to day, and let the future take care of itself.

He returned home one wet February afternoon to find the flat empty. This did not perturb him, as Angela was often out. He threw himself into an armchair and began to read the newspaper. Suddenly he was conscious of something unusual. There was no companionable ticking from Angela's little clock on the mantelpiece. It had vanished. No doubt it had gone to be repaired, thought Edward, turning a page. He looked at his watch. It had stopped. Throwing down the paper, he went into the bedroom to see the time by the bedside alarm clock. The door of the clothes cupboard stood open and there were gaps where Angela's frocks and coats had hung.

Propped against the table lamp was a letter. Edward felt suddenly sick. It had come at last. His hands trembled as he tore it open.

Dear Edward,

Billy and I have gone away together. Don't try to follow us. Nothing you can do or say will ever bring me back. I don't suppose you'll miss me anyway.

Angela

At least, thought Edward irrelevantly, she was honest enough not to add 'Love'. What was to be done? He thrust the letter into his pocket and paced up and down the bedroom. He must go after her, despite her message. She was his wife. She must be made to return.

He stopped short and gazed out into the dripping garden. The tree trunks glistened with rain. Drops patterned on the speckled leaves of a laurel bush, and a thrush shook its feathers below.

Why must she be made to return? He was thinking as Sep might think, he suddenly realized. Angela was not a chattel. And what sort of life could they hope to live if he insisted on it? It was best to face it. It was the end.

The thrush pounced suddenly and pulled out a worm from the soil. It struggled gamely, stretched into a taut pink rubbery line. The thrush tugged resolutely. Poor devil, thought Edward, watching the drama with heightened sensibilities. He knew how the worm felt – caught, and about to be finished. The bird gave a final heave. The worm thrashed for a moment on the surface and was systematically jabbed to death by the ruthless beak above. Just so, thought Edward, have I been wounded, and just so, watching the thrush gobble down its meal, have I been wiped out. He watched the thrush running delicately across the wet grass, its head cocked sideways, searching for another victim.

He threw himself upon the bed and buried his face in the coverlet. There was a faint scent of the perfume which Angela used and his stomach was twisted with sudden pain. One's body, it seemed, lagged behind one's mind when it came to parting. This was the betrayer – one's weak flesh. A drink was what he needed, but he felt unable to move, drained of all strength, a frail shell shaken with nausea.

Suddenly, as though he had been hit on the back of the head, he fell asleep. When he awoke, hours later, it was dark, and he was shivering with the cold. His head was curiously heavy, as though he were suffering from a hangover, but he knew, the moment that he awoke, what had caused this collapse. Angela had gone.

The world would never be quite as warm and fair, ever again.

Meanwhile, in Caxley, Joan was receiving instruction from the local Roman Catholic priest, much to her own satisfaction and to her grandfather's secret sorrow.

The wedding was planned for the end of April, when Michael expected leave, and would take place in the small shabby Catholic church at the northern end of Caxley.

Old Mrs North made no secret of her disappointment.

'I've always hoped for a family wedding at St Peter's,' she said regretfully to Joan. 'Your dear mother would have made a lovely bride. I so often planned it. The nave is particularly suitable for a wedding. I hoped Winnie would have a train. Nothing more dignified – in good lace, of course. And the flowers! They always look so beautiful at the entrance to the chancel. Lady Hurley's daughter looked a picture flanked by arum lilies and yellow roses! D'you remember, Winnie dear? It must have been in 1929. I suppose there's no hope of you changing your mind, dear, and having the wedding at dear old St Peter's?'

'None at all,' smiled Joan. 'Of course, if I'd met Michael four or five hundred years ago we should have been married in St Peter's. But thanks to Henry the Eighth I must make do with the present arrangements.'

'Now, that's a funny thing,' confessed her grandmother. 'It never occurred to me that St Peter's was once Roman Catholic! It really gives one quite a turn, doesn't it?'

Preparations went on steadily. Joan got together a sizeable

quantity of linen and household goods. Kind friends and relatives parted with precious clothing coupons and she was able to buy a modest trousseau. Sep made the most elegant wedding cake consistent with war-time restrictions and embellished it, touchingly, with the decorations from his own wedding cake which Edna had treasured.

He had given Joan a generous dowry.

'You will want a house of your own one day,' he told her. 'This will be a start. I hope it won't be far from Caxley, my dear, but I suppose it depends on Michael. But I hope it won't be in Ireland. Too far for an old man like me to visit you.'

Joan could not say. Somehow she thought that Ireland would be her home in the future. As Sep said, it all depended on Michael.

One thing grieved her, in the midst of her hopeful preparations. Sep would be present at the reception, but he could not face the ceremony in the Catholic church. His staunch chapel principles would not allow him to put a foot over the threshold.

In the midst of the bustle came Edward's catastrophic news. Joan, herself so happy, was shocked and bewildered. The bond between Edward and herself was a strong one, doubly so perhaps, because they had been brought up without a father. She had never shared her mother's and grandmother's misgivings about Angela, for somehow she had felt sure that anyone must be happy with Edward, so cheerful, so dependable as he was. This blow made her suddenly unsure of her judgement. Loyalty to her brother made her put the blame squarely on Angela's shoulders. On the other hand, a small doubting voice reminded her of the old saw that it takes two to make a marriage.

Had Edward been at fault? Or was this tragedy just another side-effect of war? She prayed that she and Michael would be more fortunate.

Her mother took the news soberly and philosophically. She had known from the first that Angela would never do. Much as she grieved for Edward, it was better that they should part now, and she thanked Heaven that no children were involved in the parting.

It was old Mrs North, strangely enough, who seemed most upset. Normally, her tart good sense strengthened the family in times of crisis. This time she seemed suddenly old – unable to bear any more blows. The truth was that the ancient wound caused by Winnie's unhappy marriage to Leslie Howard, was opened again. With the controversial marriage of Joan imminent, the old lady's spirits drooped at this fresh assault. Edward was very dear to her. He could do no wrong. In her eyes, Angela was a thoroughly wicked woman, and Edward was well rid of her. But would any of her family find married happiness? Would poor Joan? Sometimes she began to doubt it, and looked back upon her own long years with Bender as something rare and strange.

Edward was at the wedding to give the bride away. He looked thinner and older, and to Joan's way of thinking, handsomer than ever. He refused to speak of his own affairs, and set himself out to make Joan's wedding day the happiest one of her life.

With the exception of Sep and Robert the rest of Joan's relations were there with Kathy's auburn-haired daughter as bridesmaid, and Bertie and Kathy's small son as an inattentive page. Michael's mother was too ill to travel and his father too was absent, but a sister and brother, with the same devastating Irish good looks as the bridegroom, were present, and impressed old Mrs North very much by their piety in church.

'I must say,' she said to Winnie, in tones far too audible for her daughter's comfort, 'the Catholics do know how to behave in church. Not afraid to bend the knee when called for!'

Winnie was glad that something pleased the old lady, for she knew that she found the small church woefully lacking in amenities compared with Caxley's noble parish church built and made beautiful with the proceeds of the wool trade, so many centuries earlier.

There were few Roman Catholics in Caxley. One or two families from the marsh, descended from Irish labourers who had built the local railway line attended the church. Two ancient landed families came in each Sunday from the countryside south of the town, but there was little money to make the church beautiful. To old Mrs North the depressing green paint, the dingy pews and, above all, the crucified figure of Christ stretched bleeding high above the nave, were wholly distasteful. A church, she thought, should be a dignified and beautiful place, a true house of God, and a proper setting for the three great dramas of one's life, one's christening, one's marriage and one's funeral. This poor substitute was just not good enough, she decided firmly, as they waited for the bride.

Her eyes rested meditatively upon the bridegroom and his brother, and her heart, old but still susceptible, warmed suddenly. No doubt about it, they were a fine-looking family. One could quite see the attraction.

There was a flurry at the end of the church and the bride came slowly down the aisle on her brother's arm. Old Mrs North struggled to her feet, and looking at her granddaughter's radiant face, forgot her fears. If she knew anything about anything, this was one marriage in the Howard family which would turn out well!

10. Victory

THE honeymoon was spent at Burford and the sun shone for them. The old town had never looked lovelier, Joan thought, for she had visited it often before the war. This was Michael's first glimpse of the Cotswolds. He could not have seen Burford at a better time. The trees lining the steep High Street were in young leaf. The cottage gardens nodded with daffodils, and aubrietia and arabis hung their bright carpets over the grey stone walls.

As May broke, they returned to Caxley and to neglected news of the world of war. Much had happened. A photograph of the ghastly end of Mussolini and his mistress, Signorina Petacci, shocked them as it had shocked the world. And now, the suicide of Hitler was announced. On the last day of April, as Joan and Michael had wandered along the river bank at Burford, Hitler and his newly-married wife, Eva Braun had done themselves to death, with pistol and poison.

A week later came the unconditional surrender of the enemy. By that time, Michael was back with his regiment, and Joan watched the celebrations of victory with her family in the market square.

The cross of St George fluttered on the flag pole of St Peter's, close by the flapping Union Jack at the Town Hall. The Corn Exchange was draped with bunting and some irreverent reveller had propped a flag in Queen Victoria's hand. The public houses were busy, sounds of singing were abroad and everywhere people stopped to congratulate each other and share their relief.

But there was still the knowledge that the war was not completely finished, and Joan listened with her family to the voice of Churchill giving the nation grave thoughts in the midst of rejoicing.

'I wish,' he said, 'I could tell you tonight that all our toils and troubles were over. But, on the contrary, I must warn you that there is still a lot to do, and that you must be prepared for further efforts of mind and body.' He went on to point out that 'Beyond all lurks Japan, harassed and failing, but still a people of a hundred millions, for whose warriors death has few terrors.'

He was listened to with attention; but the moment was too happy to darken with sober warnings. For most of his hearers one splendid fact dazzled them. Victory in Europe was accomplished. Victory in the rest of the world must follow soon. And then, after six bloody years, they would have peace at last.

In the months that followed, old Mrs North spoke joyfully of returning to Rose Lodge. Winnie had her doubts about the wisdom of this step. Now that there were only the two of them to consider, the house seemed over-large, and they must face the problem of little or no help in running it. Mrs North refused to be persuaded.

'I absolutely set my face against finding another place,' she declared flatly. 'Rose Lodge is my home, bought for me by your dear father. The nurses are moving out in a month or two. There's no reason at all why we shouldn't get out the old furniture from store and move in right away. Besides, Edward will want this flat again the minute he's demobbed. We must leave everything ready for him.'

Winnie was wise enough to drop the subject for the time being, but returned to the attack whenever she had a chance. It was no use. The old lady was unshakeable in her determination.

'Go back,' Bertie advised his sister. 'Dash it all, she's getting on for eighty! She may as well enjoy her own for the rest of her time. Rose Lodge was all she ever wanted when she lived in the market place, and she's had to do without it for years.'

'I suppose we must,' sighed Winnie. 'But I shall shut off some of the rooms. It's a house that eats fuel, as you know, I really don't think I can cope with the cleaning single-handed.'

'We're all getting old,' agreed Bertie cheerfully. 'But I bet

Mamma will be in and out of the locked rooms smartly enough with a duster.'

Soon after this Edward had a few days' leave, and within twenty-four hours was thanking his stars that his stay would be a short one. If anyone had ever told him that Caxley would pall, he would have denied it stoutly. But it was so.

He knew that he was under strain. He knew that Angela's desertion was a greater shock than he cared to admit. He was torn with remorse, with guilt, with what he might have left undone. He had thrown himself, with even more concentration, into his flying duties and now lived on the station, hoping, in part, to forget his trouble. All this added to the tension.

Perhaps he had relied too much on the healing powers of his native town. Perhaps, after all, he had outgrown the childhood instinct to return home when hurt. Perhaps the people of Caxley, his own family included, were as spent as he was after six years of lean times and anxiety. Whatever the causes, the results for Edward were plain. He could not return to Caxley to live, as things were.

His womenfolk said very little to him, but there was a false brightness in their tones when they did, and a sad brooding look of inner pain when they watched him. Edward found both unendurable. Bertie was the only person he could talk to, and to him he unburdened his heart.

'I just can't face it,' he said savagely, kicking the gravel on Bertie's garden path. 'Anyone'd think I was suddenly an idiot. They talk to me as though I'm a child who is ill. And then I snap at them, and feel an utter heel. God, what's going to be the end of it?'

'It's the hardest thing in the world,' observed Bertie, 'to accept pity gracefully. It's easy enough to give it.'

'It isn't only pity,' retorted Edward. 'There were two old cats whispering behind their hands in the restaurant, and I've had one or two pretty unpleasant remarks chucked at me. The top and bottom of it is that Caxley's little and mean, and I never saw it before. I feel stifled here – as though everyone has known and watched the Howards for generations. We're simply actors to them – people to look at, people to feed their own cheap desire for a bit of drama.'

'If you haven't realized that until now,' said Bertie calmly, 'you're a good deal more naïve than I thought. We all have to take our turn at being a nine days' wonder. It's yours now, and damned unpleasant too – but you'll be forgotten by next week when someone else crops up for the place in the limelight.'

'You're right,' agreed Edward bitterly. 'But it makes no difference to me for good, even if other people forget in a day or two. In any case I shall get a job elsewhere for a year or two, and then see how I feel about Caxley. What is there to bring me back?'

'Nothing,' said Bertie. 'Except us. I'm not trying to wring your withers and all that – but when this has blown over, I hope you'll want to come back to the family again.'

'Maybe I will. Maybe I won't. All I need now is to thrash about a bit and see other places and find a useful job. One thing, I'm alone now, and I'll take good care I stay that way. I've had enough of women's ways to last me a lifetime.'

Bertie observed his nephew's devastating, if sulky, good looks with a quizzical eye, but forbore to comment on his last remark.

'There's a chap in the mess at the moment,' continued Edward, 'whose father runs a factory for making plastic things – a sort of progression from perspex and that type of thing. He says there should be a great future in plastic materials. Might even make them strong enough for use in building and ships and so on.'

'Would you want to go in for that sort of thing?'

'I'm interested,' nodded Edward. 'Jim took me to meet the old boy a few weeks ago. I liked him. He's got ideas and he works hard. I know he wants to build up the works as soon as he can. If he offered me a job, I think I'd take it.'

'Where would it be?'

'Near Ruislip. I'd rather like to be near London, too.'

'It sounds a good idea,' agreed Bertie, glad to see that his companion could still be kindled into life. 'I hope it comes off.'

They wandered through the garden gate to the towpath. The Cax reflected the blue and white sky above it. In the distance a fisherman sat immobile upon the opposite bank. Edward looked upon the tranquil scene with dislike, and skimmed a pebble viciously across the surface of the water towards the town.

'And at least I'd get away from here,' was his final comment.

The Cax flowed on placidly. It had seen centuries of men's tantrums. One more made very little difference.

That evening the occupants of the flat above Howard's Restaurant descended for their dinner. They did this occasionally when the restaurant was shut, and Robert was agreeable. He waited on them himself and joined the family party at coffee afterwards.

Sep came across and Bertie too was present. It was a cheerful gathering. Although the curtains were drawn across the windows looking on to the market place, those at the back of the building remained pulled back, and the sky still glowed with the remains of a fine July sunset. The little white tables and chairs, set out upon the grassy lawn sloping down gently to the Cax, glimmered in the twilight. It was comfortably familiar to Edward, and even his frayed nerves were soothed by the view which had remained the same now for years.

It was Joan who brought up the subject of Edward's return to the flat.

'How soon, do you think,' she asked, 'before you can come home again?'

Better now than later, decided Edward.

'I don't think that I shall come back to Caxley for a while,' he answered deliberately.

'Why ever not?' exclaimed old Mrs North. 'It's your home, isn't it?'

Edward drew a crescent very carefully on the white tablecloth with the edge of a spoon, and was silent.

94

'Edward's quite old enough to do as he pleases, Mamma,' said Bertie quietly.

'I hope you will come back, dear boy,' said Sep, putting a frail old hand on his grandson's sleeve.

'One day, perhaps,' said Edward, putting his own hand upon his grandfather's. 'But I want to have a spell elsewhere. You understand?'

'I understand,' said the old man gravely. 'You know what is best for you.'

'There's no need to feel that you are pushing us out,' began his mother, not quite understanding the situation. 'You know that we shall go back to Rose Lodge very soon.'

'Yes, dear, I do know that,' replied Edward, as patiently as he could. He drew a circle round the crescent, turning the whole into a plump face with a large mouth. He became conscious of Robert's eyes fixed upon him, and put down the spoon hastily, like a child caught out in some misdemeanour. But it was not the mutilation of the white starched surface which gave Robert that intent look, as Edward was soon to discover.

It was now almost dark and Sep rose to go, pleading a slight headache.

'I shall see you again before you leave,' he said to Edward, turning at the door. Edward watched him cross the market square, his heart full of affection for the small figure treading its familiar way homeward.

The ladies too had decided to retire. Good-nights were said, and Bertie, Edward and Robert were alone at the table. Robert carefully refilled the three coffee cups. His face was thoughtful.

'Have you any idea,' he asked 'when you'll come back to Caxley?'

'None,' said Edward shortly. 'At the moment I feel as though I want to turn my back on it for good.'

A sudden glint came into Robert's eyes. It was not unnoticed by the watchful Bertie.

'In that case,' said Robert swiftly, 'you won't want the rooms upstairs. Would you think of letting me have them? I would give you a good price to buy the whole of this property outright.'

Edward looked at Robert in astonishment. His Uncle Bertie's face had grown pink with concern.

'Thanks for the offer,' said Edward shortly, 'but I wouldn't do anything to upset Grandpa Howard. And in any case, I don't intend to part with the property.'

'You've no business to make such a suggestion,' exclaimed Bertie. His blue eyes flashed with unaccustomed fire. Edward had never seen his uncle so angry, and a very intimidating sight he found it.

'If he doesn't want it, why hang on to it?' demanded Robert. A little nerve twitched at the corner of his mouth, and he glared across the table at his brother-in-law.

'He may want it one day,' pointed out Bertie, 'as well you know. It is unfair to take advantage of the boy at a time like this. More than unfair – it's outrageous!'

'He's being nothing more nor less than a dog in the manger,' retorted Robert heatedly. 'He doesn't want it, but he'll dam' well see I don't have it! Why on earth the old man ever made such a barmy arrangement I shall never know! I'm his son, aren't I? How does he expect me to run this place with no storage rooms above it? The old fool gets nearer his dotage daily – and others profit by it!'

Edward, who had grown tired of listening to the two men arguing his affairs as though he were not present, felt that he could stand no more.

'Oh, shut up, both of you,' he cried. 'We'll keep Grandpa out of this, if you don't mind. And forget the whole thing. You can take it from me, Robert, the house remains mine as he intended, whether I live here or not, and you must like it or lump it.'

He rose from the table, looking suddenly intensely weary.

'I'm off to bed. See you in the morning. Goodnight!'

'I'm off too,' said Bertie grimly. He limped towards the door of the restaurant as Edward began to mount the stairs to his own apartment.

He heard the door crash behind his uncle, and then two sounds, like pistol shots, as Robert viciously slammed the bolts home.

The sooner I get out of this, the better, determined Edward, taking the last flight of stairs two at a time.

The next morning he made his round of farewells cheerfully. Robert seemed to have forgotten the previous evening's unpleasantness and wished him well. Sep's handshake was as loving as ever. He called last of all on Bertie.

'I'm sorry I lost my temper last night,' Bertie greeted him. 'I hate to say this, Edward, but you must be wary of Robert. He's a man with a grievance, and to my mind he gets odder as the years go by.'

'I'll watch out,' smiled Edward, making light of it.

'He's let this separation of the house and the restaurant become an obsession,' continued Bertie, 'and he's decidedly unbalanced when the subject crops up. Hang on to your own, my boy. It would break Sep's heart if he thought you'd broken with Caxley for good.'

'I know that,' said Edward quietly.

They parted amicably, glad to know each other's feelings, and Edward made his way up Caxley High Street noticing the placards on the buildings and in shop windows exhorting the good people of Caxley to support rival candidates in the coming election. Not that there would be much of a fight in this secure Conservative seat, thought Edward. The outcome was a foregone conclusion. And so, he felt sure, was the return of the Conservative party to power. The hero of the hour was Winston Churchill. It was unthinkable that he should not lead the nation in peacetime, and as bravely as he had in these last five years of grim warfare.

He was right about Caxley's decision. The Conservative candidate was returned, but by a majority so small that his supporters were considerably shaken. When at last the nation's wishes were made known, and the Socialists were returned with a large majority, Edward was flabbergasted and disgusted, and said so in the mess.

Back in Caxley old Mrs North summed up the feelings of many of her compatriots, as she studied the newspaper on the morning of 27 July.

'To think that dear Mr Churchill has got to go after all he's done for the nation! The ungrateful lot! I'm thoroughly ashamed of them. The poor man will take this very hard, and you can't wonder at it, can you? I shall sit straight down, Winnie dear, and write to him.'

And, with back straight as a ramrod and blue eyes afire, she did.

The end of the conflict was now very close. Millions of leaflets demanding surrender were showered on the inhabitants of Japan. The last warning of 'complete and utter destruction' was given on 5 August. On the following day the first atomic bomb was cast upon Hiroshima, and on 9 August a second one was dropped on the city of Nagasaki. Within a week the terms set out by the Allied governments were accepted, and the new Prime Minister, Mr Attlee, broadcast the news at midnight.

Overwhelming relief was, of course, the first reaction. There were still a few places in the Far East where fighting continued, but virtually this was the end of the war. Soon the men would be back, and life would return to normal.

Sep surveyed the happy crowds from his bedroom window, and thought of that other victory, nearly thirty years earlier, when the flags had fluttered and the people of Caxley had greeted peace with a frenzy of rejoicing. Today there was less madness, less hysteria. It had been a long bitter struggle, and there had been many casualties, but the numbers had been less than in that earlier cruel war.

He remembered how he had stood grieving for his dead son amidst his neighbours' cheers. Thank God that his family had been spared this time! He looked down upon the bronze crown of Queen Victoria below him, and wondered inconsequently what she would make of a victory finally won by an atomic bomb. The descriptions of its ghastly power had affected Sep deeply. Now that such forces were known to the world, what did the future hold for mankind? What if such a weapon fell into the hands of a maniac like Hitler? Would the world ever be safe again?

Four young men, aflame with bonhomie and beer, had caught each other by the coat tails and were stamping round Queen Victoria's plinth shouting rhythmically 'Victory for us! Victory for us! Victory for us!' to the delight of the crowd.

Sep turned sadly from the window. Victory indeed, but at what a price, mourned the old man, at what a price!

Part Two
1945-1950

11. Edward Starts Afresh

THE return to Rose Lodge was accompanied by the usual frustrations and set-backs. The decorators waited for the plasterers' work to be completed. The electricians waited for the plumbers to finish their part. A chimney was faulty. Damp patches had appeared mysteriously on the landing ceiling. The paintwork inside and out showed the neglect of six years of war and hard wear.

At times Winnie wished that she had stuck to her guns and refused point blank to return. But her mother's joy was not a whit dampened by the delays, and she threw herself with zest into the job of choosing wallpaper and curtaining from the meagre stocks available. Tirelessly she searched the shops for all the odds and ends needed to refurbish her home. One morning she would be matching fringe for the curtains, or gimp for a newly upholstered chair; on the next she would be comparing prices of coke and anthracite for the kitchen boiler. She was just as busy and excited as she had been years ago, Winnie recalled, when the family moved to Rose Lodge for the first time. Bertie had been quite right. Rose Lodge meant everything to their mother, and it was obviously best that she should spend the rest of her days there.

They moved from the market square on a blustery November day. Ragged low clouds raced across the sky. The Caxley folk, cowering beneath shuddering umbrellas, battled against the wind that buffeted them. Vicious showers of rain slanted across the streets, and the removal men dripped rivulets from their shiny macintoshes as they heaved the furniture down the stairs and into the van.

But, by the evening, Winnie and her mother sat exhausted but triumphant one on each side of the familiar drawing-room hearth.

'Home, at last,' sighed the old lady happily, looking about her. It was still far from perfect. The curtains hung stiffly, the carpet had some extraordinary billows in it, the removal men had scraped the paint by the door and chipped a corner of the china cabinet, but she was content.

'And to think,' she continued, 'that Edward will be demobilized in a few weeks' time, and dear Bertie, and perhaps Michael, and we can all have a proper family Christmas here together. The first peacetime Christmas!'

'I wonder how Joan's managing,' answered Winnie, still bemused from the day's happenings. 'I hope she won't feel lonely.'

'Lonely?' echoed her mother, 'In the market place? Take my word for it, she's as right as ninepence with the flat to play with and her own nice new things to arrange. She'll thoroughly enjoy having a place of her own.'

'You're probably right, Mamma,' said Winnie. 'Early bed for us tonight. There are muscles aching in my back and arms which I never knew I had before.'

By ten o'clock Rose Lodge was in darkness and its two occupants slept the sleep of the happy and exhausted.

It was Joan who had written to Edward to ask if she and Michael might have the flat temporarily, and he was delighted to think of it being of use to the young couple. He had been offered a good post in the plastics firm, as he had hoped, and was already looking forward to finding a flat or a house somewhere near London and the job.

This suited Joan and Michael admirably. It was plain that the nursery school would close now that the war was over, despite the recommendations of the Education Act of 1944. Joan grieved at the thought, but numbers were dwindling steadily, as the men came back, and the evacuees moved away from Caxley. By Easter the school would be no more, and the Quaker meeting house which had echoed to the cries and mirth of the babies, tumbling about the scrubbed floor in their blue-checked overalls, would once more be silent and empty, but for the decorous meetings of the children's war-time hosts, the Friends.

She was glad, though, that she had a job to do, for it transpired that Michael's demobilization would be deferred. He was now in Berlin, and his fluency in German was of great use. He had been given further promotion and been asked to stay on until the spring, but he had Christmas leave and the two spent a wonderful week arranging their wedding presents and buying furniture for the future.

'None of this blasted utility stuff,' declared Michael flatly. 'I'm sick of that sign anyway. We'll pick up second-hand pieces as we go – things we shall always like.' And so they went to two sales, and haunted the furniture shops in Caxley High Street which offered the old with the new.

Christmas Day was spent at Rose Lodge to please Mrs North. Edward and Bertie, recently demobilized, were in high spirits. All the conversation was of the future and Winnie, surveying the Norths and Howards filling the great drawing-room, thought how right it was that it should be so. The immediate past was bleak and tragic; and, for her particularly, earlier years in this house held sad memories. She remembered arriving with Joan as a baby and Edward as a toddler to find her mother dressing the Christmas tree in just the same place as the present one. Leslie had left her, and the long lonely years had just begun. She often wondered what had become of him – the handsome charmer whose son was so shatteringly like him in looks – but hoped never to see him again. He had hurt her too cruelly.

One evening before Michael returned to Germany, Joan and he talked over their plans for the future. At one time he had thought of following up his Dublin degree with a year's training for his teacher's diploma, but now he had his doubts about this course.

'I don't think I could face sitting at a desk and poring over books again. The war's unsettled me – I want to start doing something more practical. I've talked to other fellows who broke their university course, or who had just finished, like me, and there are mighty few who have got the guts to return to the academic grind again. Somehow one's brain gets jerked out of the learning groove. I know for a fact mine has.'

He faced Joan with a smile.

'Besides,' he continued, 'I've a wife and a future family to support now. I must earn some money to keep the home together. We shan't want to stay in Caxley all our lives, you know, and we shall have to buy a house before long.'

'But what do you want to do?' asked his wife earnestly. 'I do understand about not wanting to go back to school, I couldn't face it myself. But what else have you thought of? It seems a pity not to use your languages.'

'I wouldn't mind doing the same sort of thing that my father does — hotel work. Here or abroad. I'm easy. And perhaps, one day, owning our own hotel. Or a chain of them.'

His eyes were sparkling. He spoke lightly, but Joan could see that there was an element of serious purpose behind the words.

'Or I could stay in the army. That's been put to me. What do you feel about that, my sweet?'

'Horrible,' said Joan flatly. 'I've had enough of the army; and the idea of moving from one army camp to another doesn't appeal to me one little bit. And you know how *backward* army children are, poor dears, shunted from pillar to post and just getting the hang of one reading method when they're faced with an entirely different one.'

Michael laughed at this practical teacher's approach.

'I can't say I'm keen to stay myself,' he agreed. 'Six years is enough for me. We'd be better off, of course, but is it worth it?'

'Never,' declared Joan stoutly. 'Let's be poor and lead our own lives.'

And with that brave dictum they shelved the future for the remainder of his leave.

Meanwhile, Edward had been finding out just how difficult it was to get somewhere to live near London. He tried two sets of digs whilst he was flat hunting and swore that he would never entertain the thought of lodgings again. The only possible hotel within striking distance of the factory was expensive, noisy, and decidedly seedy.

It was Jim, the son of his employer, who saved him at last.

'I've got a house,' he cried triumphantly one morning, bursting into the office which he shared with Edward. 'It's scruffy, it's jerry-built, but it's got three bedrooms and a garden. Eileen is off her head with delight. Now the boy can have a bedroom of his own, and the baby too when it arrives.'

Edward congratulated him warmly. Then a thought struck him.

'And what about the flat?'

'A queue for that as long as your arm,' began Jim. He stopped pacing the floor and looked suddenly at his colleague. 'Want it?' he asked, 'because if you do, it could be yours. The others can wait. I'll have a word with the old man.'

After a little negotiation, it was arranged, and Edward moved in one blue and white March day. A speculative builder, an old school friend of Edward's employer, had acquired the site a few years before the war, and had erected two pairs of presumably semi-detached houses, well placed in one large garden. Each house was divided into two self-contained flats, so that there were eight households all told in about an acre of ground.

The plot was situated at the side of an old tree-lined lane and was not far from a golf course. A cluster of fir trees and a mature high hedge screened the flats from the view of passers-by. The ground-floor tenants agreed to keep the front part of the garden in order, the upstairs tenants the back.

The rent was pretty steep, Edward privately considered, by Caxley standards, but he liked the flat and its secluded position and would have paid even more for the chance of escaping from digs and hotels. He surveyed his new domain thankfully. He had a sitting-room, one bedroom, a kitchen, a bathroom and a gloriously large cupboard for trunks, tennis racquets, picnic baskets and all the other awkward objects which need to be housed. He was well content.

He saw little of his neighbours in the first few weeks, and learned more about them from Jim than from his own brief encounters. His own flat was on the ground-floor, and immediately beside him lived a middle-aged couple, distantly related to the owner, and now retired. Edward liked the look of them. The wife had wished him 'Good morning' in a brisk Scots brogue and her husband reminded him slightly of his grandfather, Bender North.

Above them lived a sensible-looking woman, a little older than Edward himself, who mounted a spruce bicycle each morning and pedalled energetically away. Edward had decided that she was an efficient secretary in one of the nearby factories, but Jim told him otherwise.

'Headmistress of an infants' school,' he informed him. 'Miss Hedges — a nice old bird. She was awfully kind to Eileen when she was having our first. And the two above you are secretaries, or so they say. I'd put them as shorthand-typists myself, but no doubt they'll rise in the scale before very long. Flighty, but harmless, you'll find.'

'And decorative,' added Edward. 'And much addicted to bathing. One at night and one in the morning, I've worked out. There's a cascade by my ear soon after eleven and another just after seven each morning, down the waste pipe.'

'Come to think of it,' said Jim, 'I believe you're right. Trust a countryman to find out all the details of his neighbours' affairs ! It had never occurred to me, I must admit.'

'It's a pity my grandmother can't spend an afternoon there,' replied Edward. 'She'd have the life history of every one of us at her finger tips before the sun set ! Now, Jim, let's get down to work.'

The first Caxley visitors to the flat were his Uncle Bertie and Aunt Kathy, on their way to meet friends in London.

'You look so happy !' exclaimed his aunt, kissing him. She stood back and surveyed him with her sparkling dark eyes. 'And so smart !' she added.

'My demob suit,' said Edward, with a grimace. 'And tie, too.'

'Well, at least the tie's wearable,' observed Bertie. 'At the end of my war, I was offered the choice of a hideous tie or "a very nice neckerchief". How d'you like that?'

Edward pressed them for all the Caxley news. Bertie noticed that he was eager for every detail of the family. How soon, he wondered, before he would return? Certainly, he had visited Rose Lodge on several occasions, and his present home was conveniently near Western Avenue for him to make his way to Caxley within a short time. At the moment, however, it looked as though Edward was comfortably settled. His decree nisi was already through; before the end of the year he should be free, but as things were, it seemed pretty plain that his nephew was happy to return to a bachelor's existence.

The greatest piece of news they had to offer was that Joan was expecting a child in the late summer, and that Michael, now demobilized, had decided to learn more about the catering trade by working for a time in Howard's Restaurant. Sep had suggested this move, and although Michael realized that there might be difficulties, he was glad to accept the work as a temporary measure, until the baby arrived.

'And how has Robert taken it?' asked Edward, after expressing his delight at the prospect of becoming an uncle.

'Fairly quietly, so far. I don't think it would be very satisfactory permanently though. His temper is getting more and more unpredictable. Two waitresses have left in the last month. It's my belief he's ill, but he flatly refuses to see the doctor.'

'He's a queer customer,' agreed Edward, 'but times are difficult. He must have a devil of a job getting supplies. Food seems to be shorter now than during the war – unless it's because I'm a stranger here and don't get anything tucked away under the counter for me. I'd starve if it weren't for the works' canteen midday, and some of the stuff they dish up there is enough to make you shudder.'

'Father says that people mind most about bread rationing,' said Kathy. '"Never had it in our lives before," they said, really shocked, you know. And poor dear, he *will* get all these wretched bits of paper, bread units, *absolutely* right. You know what a stickler he is. I was in the shop the other day helping him. People leave their pages with him and then have a regular order for a cake, using so many each week. It makes an enormous amount of book work for the poor old darling. Sometimes I try to persuade him to give up. He's practically eighty, after all.'

'He won't,' commented Bertie, 'he'll die in harness, and like it that way. And Robert's more of a liability than a help at the moment. He resents the fact that Sep didn't hand over the business to him outright, when he gave you the house. It's beginning to become more of an obsession than ever, I'm afraid.'

'He was always dam' awkward about that,' said Edward shortly. 'Good heavens! Surely Grandpa can do as he likes with his own? If there's anything I detest it's this waiting for other men's shoes – like a vulture.'

'Vultures don't wear shoes,' pointed out Kathy, surveying her own neat pair. 'And whatever it is that screws up our poor Robert it makes things downright unpleasant for us all, particularly Father.'

'And Michael and Joan?'

'Michael's such a good-tempered fellow,' said Bertie, 'that he'll stand a lot. And Joan's at the blissfully broody stage just now. I caught her winding wool with Maisie Hunter the other evening with a positively maudlin expression on her face.'

'Maisie Hunter?' echoed Edward. 'I thought she'd got married.'

'Her husband-to-be crashed on landing at Brize Norton, about six weeks before the war ended.'

'I never heard that,' Edward said slowly. 'Poor Maisie.'

Bertie glanced at his watch and rose to go.

'Come along, my dear,' he said, hauling Kathy to her feet. 'We shall meet all the homegoing traffic, if we don't look out.'

Edward accompanied them to the gate and waved good-bye as the car rounded the bend in the lane. It was strange, he thought, how little he envied them returning to Caxley. It was another world, and one which held no attraction for him. Much as he loved his family, he was glad that he was free of the tensions and squabbles in which they seemed now involved.

He bent down to pull a few weeds from the garden bed which

bordered the path, musing the while on his change of outlook. He revelled in his present anonymous role. It was wonderful to know that one's neighbours took so little interest in one's affairs. It was refreshing to be able to shut the door and be absolutely unmolested in the flat, to eat alone, to sleep alone, and to be happy or sad as the spirit moved one, without involving other people's feelings. It was purely selfish, of course, he knew that, but it was exactly what he needed.

He straightened his aching back and looked aloft. An aeroplane had taken off from nearby Northolt aerodrome and he felt the old rush of pleasure in its soaring power. And yet, here again, there was a difference. He felt not the slightest desire to fly now. Would the longing ever return? Or would this numb apathy which affected him remain always with him, dulling pleasure and nullifying pain?

It was useless to try to answer these questions. He must be thankful for the interest of the new job, and for this present quietness in which to lick his wounds. Perhaps happiness and warmth, ambition and purpose, would return to him one day. Meanwhile, he must try and believe all the tiresome people who kept reminding him that 'Time was the Great Healer'.

Perhaps, they might, just possibly, be right.

12. A Family Tragedy

As the summer advanced, affairs in the market place went from
bad to worse. The aftermath of the war – general fatigue – was
felt everywhere. Food was not the only thing in short supply.
Men returning from active service found it desperately hard to
find somewhere to live. Women, longing for new clothes, for
colour, for gaiety, still had to give coupons for garments and for
material for making them, as well as for all the soft furnishings
needed. 'Makes you wonder who won the war!' observed
someone bitterly, watching Sep clip out the precious snippets
of paper entitling her to three loaves, and the feeling was everywhere.

Sep, hard-pressed with work and smaller than ever in old age,
maintained his high standards of service steadily. But he was a
worried man. The shop was doing as well as ever, but the returns from the restaurant showed a slight decline as the weeks
went by, and Sep knew quite well that Robert was at fault. It was
becoming more and more difficult to keep staff. Robert was short
with the waitresses in front of customers, and impatient and
sarcastic with the kitchen staff. How long, wondered Sep, before
Michael, who was working so wonderfully well, found conditions unendurable?

He made up his mind to take Robert aside privately and have
a talk with him. The fellow was touchy and might sulk, as he
had so often done as a boy, but at the rate he was going on Howard's Restaurant would soon be in Queer Street. Sep did not
relish the task, but he had never shirked his duty in his life, and
it was plain that this unpleasant encounter must take place.

He crossed the square from the shop as the Town Hall clock
struck eight. The restaurant was closed, the staff had gone and
Robert was alone in the kitchen reading *The Caxley Chronicle*.
Sep sat down opposite him.

'My boy, I'll come straight to the point. Business is slipping, as you know. Any particular reason?'

'Only that I'm expected to run this place with a set of fools,' muttered Robert, scowling at his clenched hands on the table top.

'I'm worried more about you than the business,' said Sep gently. 'You've been over-doing it. Why not take a holiday? We could manage, you know, for a week, say.'

Robert jumped to his feet, his face flushing.

'And let Michael worm his way in? Is that what you want? It's to be Edward all over again, I can see. What's wrong with me – your own son – that you should slight me all the time?'

'My boy –' began Sep, protesting, but he was overwhelmed by Robert's passionate outburst.

'What chance have I ever had? Edward has the house given him at twenty-one. The house that should have been mine anyway. Do I get given anything? Oh no! I can wait – wait till I'm old and useless, with nothing to call my own.'

His face was dark and congested, the words spluttered from his mouth. To Sep's horror he saw tears welling in his son's eyes and trickling down his cheeks. The pent-up resentment of years was bursting forth and Sep could do nothing to quell the violence.

'I've never had a fair deal from the day I was born. Jim was a hero because he got himself killed. No one was ever allowed to mention Leslie, though he was the kindest of the lot to me, and I missed him more than any of you. Kath's been the spoilt baby all her life, and I've been general dog's body. Work's all I've ever had, with no time for anything else. The rest of the family have homes and children. I've been too busy for girls. Edward and Bertie and Michael came back from the war jingling with medals. What did I get for sticking here as a slave? I'm despised, I tell you! Despised! Laughed at – by all Caxley –'

By now he was sobbing with self-pity, beating his palms against his forehead in a childish gesture which wrung his father's heart. Who would have dreamt that such hidden fires had smouldered for so long beneath that timid exterior? And what could be done to comfort him and to give him back pride in himself?

Sep let the storm subside a little before he spoke. His voice was gentle.

'I'm sorry that you should feel this way, my boy. You've let your mind dwell on all sorts of imagined slights. You were always as dear to me and your mother as the other children – more so, perhaps, as the youngest. No one blames you for not going to the war. You were rejected through no fault of your own. Everyone here knows that you've done your part by sticking to your job here.'

Robert's sobbing had ceased, but he scowled across the table mutinously.

'It's a lie! Everyone here hates me. People watch me wherever I go. They talk about me behind my back. I know, I tell you, I know! They say I couldn't get a girl if I tried. They say no one wants me. They say I'm under my dad's thumb – afraid to stand on my own feet – afraid to answer back! I'm a failure. That's what they say, watching and whispering about me, day in and day out!'

Sep stood up, small, straight and stern.

'Robert, you are over-wrought, and don't know what you are saying. But I won't hear you accusing innocent people of malice. All this is in your own mind. You must see this, surely?'

Robert approached his father. There was a strange light in his glittering eyes. He thrust his face very close to the old man's.

'My mind?' he echoed. 'Are you trying to say I'm out of my mind? I know well enough what people are saying about me. I hear them. But I hear other voices too – *private* voices that tell me I'm right, that the whisperers in Caxley will be confounded, and that the time will come when they have to give in and admit that Robert Howard was right all the time. They'll see me one day, the owner of this business here, the owner of the shop, the biggest man in the market square, the head of the Howard family!'

His voice had risen with excitement, his eyes were wild. From weeping self-pity he had swung in the space of minutes to a state of manic euphoria. He began to pace the floor, head up, nostrils flaring, as he gulped for breath.

'You'll be gone by then,' he cried triumphantly, 'and I'll see that Edward goes too. There will be one Howard only in charge. Just one. One to give orders. One to be the boss!'

'Robert!' thundered Sep, in the voice which he had used but rarely in his life. There was no response. Robert was in another world, oblivious of his father and his surroundings.

'They'll see,' he continued, pacing even more swiftly. 'My time will come. My voices know. They tell me the truth. "The persecutors shall become the persecuted!" That's what my voices tell me.'

Sep walked round the table and confronted his son. He took hold of his elbows and looked steadily into that distorted face a little above his own.

'Robert,' he said clearly, as though to a distraught child. 'We are going home now, and you are going to bed.'

The young man's gaze began to soften. His eyes turned slowly towards his father's. He looked as though he were returning from a long, strange journey.

'Very well, father,' he said. The voice was exhausted, but held a certain odd pride, as though remnants of glimpsed grandeur still clung to him.

He watched his father lock up. Sep, white-faced and silent, walked beside his son across the market square, watching him anxiously.

Robert, head high, looked to the left and right as he strode proudly over the cobbles. He might have been a king acknowledging the homage of his people, except that, to Sep's relief, the square was empty. When they reached their door Robert entered first, as of right, and swept regally up the stairs to his room, without a word.

When faithful old Miss Taggerty brought in Sep's bed-time milk, she found her master sitting pale and motionless.

'You don't look yourself, sir,' she said with concern. 'Shall I bring you anything? An aspirin, perhaps?'

'I'm all right. Just a little tired.'

'Shall I fetch Mr Robert?'

'No, no! Don't worry about me. I'm off to bed immediately.'

They wished each other good night. Sep watched the door close quietly behind the good-hearted creature, and resumed his ponderings.

What was to be done? Tonight had made plain something which he had long suspected. Robert's mind was giving way under inner torment. He was obsessed with a wrongful sense of grievance against himself, and worse still, a gnawing jealousy, aimed chiefly against Edward. These two evils had become his masters. These were 'the voices' which he claimed to hear, and which were driving him beyond the brink of sanity.

To Sep's generation, insanity in the family was something to be kept from the knowledge of outsiders. One pitied the afflicted, but one kept the matter as quiet as possible. So often, he knew from experience, attacks passed and, within a few months, rest and perhaps a change of scene, brought mental health again. It might be so with Robert.

He disliked the idea of calling in a doctor to the boy. Suppose that Robert were sent to a mental home? Would he ever come out again? Did doctors really know what went on in the human brain, and could they cure 'a mind diseased'? Wouldn't the mere fact of consulting a doctor upset his poor son's condition even more?

And yet the boy was in need of help, and he was the last person to be able to give it. How terrible it had been to hear that awful indictment of himself as a father! Was he really to blame? Had he loved him less? In all humility he felt that he could truthfully claim to have loved all his children equally – even Leslie, who had betrayed him.

And those fearful indications of a deluded mind – the assumption of omnipotence, of grandeur, to what might they lead? Would he become violent if he were ridiculed in one of these moods? Sep remembered the menacing glitter in his son's eyes, and trembled for him. What did the future hold for Robert?

He took his milk with him to the bedroom. The blinds were drawn against the familiar view of the market square and the indomitable figure of Queen Victoria. Miss Taggerty had turned the bedclothes back into a neat white triangle. Sep knelt beside the bed and prayed for guidance.

When he arose his mind was clear. He would sleep on this problem and see how things fared in the morning. There was no need to rush for help to the rest of the family. This was something to be borne alone if possible, so that Robert should be spared further indignities. He had suffered enough, thought Sep, torn with pity.

For a few weeks things went more smoothly. Robert never referred to that dreadful outburst. It was as though it had been wiped completely from his memory. For Sep, the incident was unforgettable, but he said nothing.

Nevertheless, it was obvious that the young man was in a precarious state of mind. Sep did what he could to relieve the pressure of work at the restaurant, and Michael's efforts ensured the smooth running of the place. His cheerfulness and good looks soon made him popular, which was good for trade but not, as Sep realized, for Robert's esteem.

Kathy, knowing that staff were hard to get at the restaurant offered to help whenever possible. She and Bertie realized that Robert was under strain, although they had no idea of the seriousness of his malaise.

'You'd be more use, my dear, in the shop,' said Sep. 'It would leave me free to go across to Robert's more often, and you know exactly where everything is at home.'

'I was brought up to it,' laughed Kathy. 'I'd enjoy it, you know, and now that the children are off my hands, it will give me an interest.'

Her presence was a great comfort to Sep, and meant that he could keep a discreet, if anxious, eye on affairs across the square.

During these uneasy weeks Joan's baby was born. It was a girl, and the family were all delighted. She was born in the nursing home to the north of Caxley, on the road to Beech Green and Fairacre, where so many other Caxley citizens had first seen the light. Michael was enormously pleased and visited his wife and daughter every evening.

Joan remained there for a fortnight. It was decided that she should go for a week or two to Rose Lodge to regain her strength, and submit to the welcome cossetings of her mother and grandmother. The house was certainly more convenient than the flat, and the baby would have the benefit of the garden air as well as the doting care of three women. She was to be christened Sarah.

'No hope of the poor little darling being christened at St Peter's, I suppose?' sighed Mrs North.

'You know there isn't,' replied Joan, smiling at her grandmother's naughtiness.

'I never seem to have any luck with family ceremonies,' commented the old lady. She brightened as a thought crossed her mind. 'Perhaps Kathy's girl one day?'

Soon after Joan returned to the flat trouble began again. Robert's antagonism towards Michael was renewed in a hundred minor insults. Despite his easy-going disposition, Michael's Irish blood was roused.

'The fellow's off his rocker,' declared Michael roundly one evening in the privacy of the flat. 'He's beginning to talk as though he's the King of England. Sometimes I wonder if we should stay.'

Letters from his family in Dublin had also unsettled him. His father was in failing health and it was plain that he longed for his son to return to carry on the hotel, although he did not press the boy to come if his prospects were brighter in Caxley. Joan did not know how to advise her husband. She herself half-feared the uprooting and the break with the family, especially with a young child to consider. On the other hand it was right that Michael should obey his conscience, and she would do whatever he felt was best. Certainly, as things were, there was nothing but petty frustrations for Michael in his work, and he had obviously learned all that could be learned from the comparatively small Caxley restaurant. It was time he took on something bigger, giving him scope for his ability.

She told her problem to her old friend Maisie Hunter, who was to be godmother to Sarah. Her answer was straightforward.

'Michael's trying to spare you. Tell him you'll be happy to go to Dublin, and then watch his face. I'm sure he wants to go back home, and he's bound to do well.'

She was right, and the couple had almost decided to break the news to Sep and Robert and to write to Michael's father, when two things happened to clinch the matter.

Joan had put her daughter to sleep in the pram in the little garden sloping down to the Cax, when Robert burst from the restaurant in a state of fury.

'I won't have that thing out here,' he said, kicking at a wheel. 'This is part of my restaurant, as you well know. You can clear off!'

'Robert!' protested Joan, much shocked. 'I've always used the garden. What on earth has come over you?'

Two or three curious customers, taking morning coffee, gazed with interest upon the scene from the restaurant windows. Joan was horribly aware of their presence, and took Robert's arm to lead him further away. He flung her from him with such violence that she fell across the pram. The child broke into crying, and Joan, now thoroughly alarmed, lifted her from the pram.

'You'll use the garden no more,' shouted Robert. 'You're trespassing on my property. And if you leave that contraption here I shall throw it in the river!'

At this moment, Michael arrived, and took in the situation at a glance.

'Take the baby upstairs,' he said quietly. 'I'll deal with this.'

He propelled the struggling and protesting Robert into the little office at the end of the restaurant and slammed the door, much to the disappointment of the interested customers. He thrust Robert into an arm chair, and turned to get him a drink from the cupboard. He was white with fury, and his hand shook as he poured out a stiff tot, but he was in command of himself and the situation. He was facing an ill man, and a dangerous one, he realized.

Robert leapt from the chair, as Michael put the glass on the desk, and tried to make for the door. Michael administered a hard slap to each cheek, as one would to an hysterical patient, and Robert slumped again into the chair.

'Drink this slowly,' commanded Michael, 'and wait here until I get back.'

He left the office, turned the key in the lock, and told good old John Bush who had been in Sep's employ for forty years, to take charge while he saw to his wife and let Sep know what was happening.

Later that evening Sep, Bertie and Michael held counsel.

'We must get a doctor to see him,' said Bertie firmly. 'I'll ring Dr Rogers tonight.'

'I blame myself,' said Sep heavily. 'He has not been himself for months. We should have got help earlier. It must be done now. I fear for Joan and the child if he is going to get these attacks of violence.'

'I want them to go back to Rose Lodge, but Joan is very much against it,' said Michael. 'But it's going to be impossible to stay over the restaurant, if he doesn't change his ways.'

'Let's get the doctor's verdict before we do anything more,' said Bertie.

Dr Rogers said little when he had examined his patient, but his grave looks alarmed Sep.

'Will he get better?' he asked anxiously. 'He's such a young man – so many years before him. What do you think?'

Dr Rogers would not commit himself, but provided various bottles of pills and promised to visit frequently. Meanwhile, he asked the family to call him in immediately if the symptoms of excessive excitement occurred again.

A few days later a letter arrived from Ireland from Michael's invalid mother. His father was sinking. Could he return? And was there any hope of him taking over the hotel?

'This settles it,' said Joan, looking at Michael's worried face as he read the letter again.

'But what about Howard's Restaurant? How will Sep manage?'

'John Bush can run the place blindfold. And Aunt Kathy would help, I know. Go and tell Sep what has happened. Take the letter.'

She knew full well how Sep would react.

'Of course you must go, my boy. Your father comes first, and your mother needs your presence at a time like this. You've been of enormous help to us here, but it's right that you should start a life of your own.'

And so, within two days, Michael returned to Dublin, and Joan and the baby were to join him as soon as possible. It was Bertie who drove them to Holyhead to catch the boat to Dun Laoghaire. Saying farewell to the family had been ineffably sad.

'I'll be back soon for a holiday,' she told them all bravely. It was hardest to say good-bye to Sep and Grandma North. They looked so old, so shattered at the parting.

'You are doing the right thing,' Sep assured her firmly. 'I'm sure you have a wonderful future in Ireland.'

Her grandmother was less hopeful and inclined to be tearful.

'Such a *long* way off, and a very wild sort of people, I hear. The thought of all those poor babies of yours being brought up in such *strange* ways quite upsets me. Do boil all the water, dear, whatever you do.'

Joan promised, and kissed her, hardly knowing whether to laugh or cry. Funny, exasperating, old Grandma! How long before she saw her again?

Dr Rogers' treatment seemed to have only a small sedative effect on Robert, but Sep tried to assure himself that the cure was bound to take a long time, and that his son's youth and a lessening of his work would finally ensure his recovery.

Kathy insisted on taking over the financial affairs of the restaurant while John Bush coped with the practical side. She was as quick at figures as her mother, Edna Howard, had been, and soon proved a competent business woman.

It was quite apparent that Robert resented her intrusion into his affairs, and Kathy ignored the snubs and sarcastic comments which punctuated the day's work. Robert was sick. Soon he would be better, and he would be happy again, she thought.

She was totally unprepared, therefore, for a sudden attack of the mania which had so appalled Sep months before. It happened, luckily, soon after the restaurant had closed and Kathy was checking the money. Perhaps the clinking of the coins reminded him of the fact that the business was not his. Perhaps the sight of his sister, sitting in the chair which had always been his own, inflamed him. No one would ever know; but resentment flared again, his voice grew loud and strident as he screamed his hatred of his family and his intention to get rid of them.

'My voices told me,' he roared at the terrified Kathy. 'They told me I would triumph, and I shall! Michael and Joan have gone. Old Bush will go, and you will go! There will be no one left but me – the unbeatable – the true heir!'

His lips were flecked with saliva, his eyes demented, as he bore down upon her. Dropping the money on the floor, Kathy tore open the door, and fled across the square to find help, the jingle of the rolling coins ringing in her ears.

The next day an ambulance took Robert and his attendants to the county mental hospital some twenty miles away. Sep, shattered, sat trying to understand Dr Rogers' explanation of his son's illness. He heard but one phrase in four and many of those were inexplicable to him. 'A progressively worsening condition,' he understood painfully well, but such terms as 'manic depressive' and the seriousness of 'hearing voices', as symptoms, meant nothing to the desolate old man.

To Sep, who knew his Bible, 'the voices' were simply Robert's demons – the outcome of the twin evils of jealousy and self-pity. Robert had been weak. He had succumbed to the temptations of his demons. His madness was, in part, a punishment for flying in the face of Providence.

When the doctor had gone, Sep stood at the back window and looked upon the row of willows lining the bank of the Cax. Three sons had once been his, gay little boys who had tumbled about the yard and moulded pastry in the bakehouse in their small fat hands.

One was long dead, one long-estranged, and now the last of the three was mad. Sep's life had been long and hard, but that moment by the window was the most desolate and despairing he had ever known.

13. New Horizons

EDWARD heard the news about Robert in a letter from his mother. He was deeply shocked, and very anxious about the effect this blow might have on his grandfather. He was thankful to know that his Aunt Kathy and John Bush were coping so ably with the restaurant, and glad to give permission to the faithful old employee to use his flat on the top floor. It would be some relief for Sep to know that there was someone reliable living on the premises.

He telephoned to the mental hospital that morning to hear how Robert was, but learnt very little more than his mother's letter had told him. He had the chance, however, of talking to the doctor in charge of the case, and asked to be kept informed of his progress, explaining his own relationship and his desire to do anything to spare the patient's very old father.

As he replaced the receiver Edward noted, with a start of surprise, how anxious he was. Robert had never been very close to him. They were eleven years and a generation apart. By temperament they were opposed, and resentment, which had no place in Edward's life, ruled his young uncle's. But this was a blow at the whole family, and Edward's reaction had been swift and instinctive. It was all very well to decide to cut loose, he admitted somewhat wryly to himself, but the old tag about blood being thicker than water held good, as this shock had proved.

He resolved to go to Caxley at the weekend to see how things were for himself. Sep was pathetically delighted with the surprise visit, and Edward was glad to find that he was taking Robert's illness so bravely.

'I should have insisted on getting medical advice earlier,' he told Edward. 'Robert is certainly having proper treatment now, and perhaps a spell away from us will quicken his recovery.'

They talked of many things. Edward had never known him quite so forthcoming about the business. Perhaps he realized that Edward himself was now a keen and purposeful business-man. It certainly amazed the younger man to realize how profit-able the old-established shop and the newer restaurant were, and what a grasp his grandfather had of every small detail in running them. Since Robert's departure, trade had improved. There were now no staff troubles with Kathy and John Bush in charge, and after a long day visiting his mother and grand-mother, Bertie and Kathy, Edward drove back to London very much happier in mind.

His own business affairs he found engrossing. He was now a partner in the firm, responsible chiefly for production and de-sign. At his suggestion they had expanded their range of plastic kitchen equipment and were now experimenting with domestic refrigerators and larger deep-freeze receptacles for shops. This venture was proving amazingly successful and Edward found himself more and more absorbed and excited by the firm's de-velopment. Suddenly, after the apathy which had gripped him, he had found some purpose in life. He discovered a latent flair for design, an appreciation of line and form put to practical use, which gave him much inward satisfaction. The costing of a project had always interested him. He was, after all, the grand-son of Bender North and Sep Howard, both men of business. He enjoyed planning a new design and then juggling with its economic possibilities. It was a fusion of two ways of thought and a new challenge every time it was undertaken.

He paid one or two visits to the continent to compare methods of production. He visited firms in Brussels and Paris who were engaged in much the same work as his own, and returned full of ideas. Jim and his father recognized that Edward was the most able of the three for this part of the business. His gaiety and charm, fast returning under the stimulus of new work, helped him to easy friendship. He had the ability to select ideas which could be adapted to their own business, and the power to explain them on his return to his partners. With Edward's drive, the firm was advancing rapidly.

In the early summer of 1947 Edward set off for a fortnight's visit to two firms in Milan. There were plumes of lilac blowing in the suburban gardens as the train rumbled towards the coast, and the girls were out and about in their pretty summer frocks. Edward approved of this 'new look' which brought back full skirts, neat waists, and gave women back the attractive curves which had been lost in the square military styles of wartime fashion. It was good to see colour and life returning to war-scarred England, to watch new houses being built, and see fresh paint brightening the old ones. There was hope again in the air, and the breezy rollicking tunes of the new musical Oklahoma exactly caught the spirit of the times – the looking-ahead of a great people to a future full of promise.

From Milan he made the long train journey to Venice, there to spend the last few days meeting an Italian industrial designer who lived there, and sight-seeing. From the moment that he emerged from the station into the pellucid brilliance of Venetian sunlight, he fell under the city's spell. The quality of the light, which revealed the details of brickwork and carving, exhilarated him. To take a gondola to one's hotel, instead of a prosaic bus or taxi, was wholly delightful. If only he could stay four months instead of four days!

His hotel was an agreeable one just off St Mark's Square. He looked from his window upon a gondola station. There were twenty or more black high-prowed beauties jostling together upon the water. Their owners were busy mopping and polishing, shouting, laughing and gesticulating. Edward liked their energy, their raffish good looks and the torrents of words of which he only understood one in ten.

Picturesque though the scene was he was to find that its position had its drawbacks. The noise went on until one or two in the morning and began again about six. Luckily, Edward, healthily tired with walking about this enchanted place, did not lose much sleep.

126

On the last morning he awoke with a start. He was in the grip of some inexplicable fear. He found himself bathed in perspiration and his mind was perturbed with thoughts of Robert. He tossed back the bed clothes and lay watching the trembling reflections of the sun on water flickering across the ceiling. Against this undulating background he could see the face of Robert – a sad, haunted face, infinitely moving.

Outside, the gondoliers exchanged voluble jests in the bright Italian sunshine. The waters of Venice lapped against the walls and slapped the bottoms of the gondolas rhythmically. An Italian tenor poured forth a cascade of music from someone's wireless set.

But Edward was oblivious of his surroundings. In that instant he was hundreds of miles away in the cool early dawn of an English market square. What was happening at home?

After breakfast he felt calmer. He packed his bags and paid his bill, glad to be occupied with small everyday matters and telling himself that he had simply suffered from a nightmare. But the nagging horror stayed with him throughout the long journey to England, and as soon as he arrived he rang his Uncle Bertie for news.

'Bad, I'm afraid,' said Bertie's voice, 'as you'll see when my letter arrives. Robert was found dead in the hospital grounds. They think he had a heart attack. We'll know more later.'

'When was this?' asked Edward.

Bertie told him. He must have died, thought Edward, as he had suspected, at the moment when he himself awoke so tormentedly in the hotel bedroom.

This uncanny experience had a lasting effect upon Edward's outlook. Hitherto impatient of anything occult, he, the least psychic of men, had discovered that not all occurrences could be rationally explained. It was to make him more sympathetic in the years to come and more humble in his approach to matters unseen.

Robert's tragic death had another effect on Edward's future. Unknown to him, Sep, when his first grief had passed, crossed the market square to enter the offices of Lovejoy and Lovejoy, his solicitors. There, the will which he had drafted so long ago was drastically revised, and when Sep returned to the bakery he was well content.

It was about this time that Edward heard that his ex-wife Angela had had a son by Billy Sylvester, her second husband. Edward was glad to hear the news. It should make Angela a happier person. Despite the misery which she had inflicted upon him, Edward felt no resentment. He soberly faced the fact that he could not exempt himself from blame. They had never had much in common, and it was largely physical attraction which had drawn them together. Now, with the baby to think of, she would have some interest in the future. Nevertheless, Edward felt a pang when he thought about the child. He might have had a son of his own if things had worked out.

But domesticity did not play much part in his present affairs, although he enjoyed running the little flat. He took most of his meals out, and he grew increasingly fond of London. His life-long love of the theatre could now be indulged, and by a lucky chance he was able to meet a number of theatrical people.

His Aunt Mary, younger sister of Bertie and his mother Winnie, and the acknowledged beauty of the family, had a small part in a well-written light comedy which had already run for eight months and looked as though it were settled in the West End for another two years. It was one of those inexplicable successes. No great names glittered in the cast, the play itself was not outstanding; but it was gay, the dialogue crisp, the settings and the costumes ravishing. It was just what theatre-goers seemed to want, and Aunt Mary hoped that they would continue to do so.

Edward took her out on several occasions after the show. He had always enjoyed her company, and found something exhilarating in the mixture of North common-sense, typified by his good-humoured Uncle Bertie, and the racy sophistication which her mode of life had added to it.

Two husbands, little mourned, lay in Aunt Mary's past. Many good friends of both sexes enlivened her present. She often brought one or more to Edward's supper parties, and he grew very fond of this animated company of friends, admiring the outward nonchalance which masked the resilience and dedication necessary to survive the ruthless competition of the stage world. They had something in common with businessmen, Edward decided. They needed to be long-sighted, ambitious and capable of grasping opportunity when it came. And, when times were hard, they must show the world a brave face to inspire confidence.

He liked to take out one or two of the pretty girls occasionally. It was good to laugh again, to be amused and to amuse in turn. He began to realize how little feminine company he had enjoyed. The war, early marriage, and the restrictions put upon him whilst awaiting his divorce, had combined with his temporary inner weariness to make him solitary. But although he enjoyed their company, there was not one among them with whom he would like to spend the rest of his days. The fact that they were equally heart-whole rendered them the more attractive.

More disturbing were the attentions of one of the girls who shared the flat above his own. As time passed, they had become better acquainted. Edward had used their telephone one evening when his own was out of order. He had stayed to coffee. Some evenings later they came to have a drink. From these small beginnings, not greatly encouraged by Edward, who enjoyed his domestic privacy, came more frequent visits by the girls.

Susan was engaged to a monosyllabic mountain of muscle who played Rugby football regularly on Wednesdays and Saturdays, and squash or badminton in between to keep himself fit for his place in the front row of the forwards. It was Elizabeth who was the more persistent of the two. She was small and dark, with an engaging cackling laugh, and Edward enjoyed her occasional company.

It was Elizabeth who called from the window, when he was gardening, offering him a drink. It was she who took in the parcels and delivered them to Edward when he returned from the office. And when he took to his bed with a short sharp bout of influenza it was Elizabeth who offered to telephone for the doctor and brought aspirins and drinks.

Edward, engrossed in his expanding business and intrigued with Aunt Mary's friends, had little idea of Elizabeth's growing affection. She was ardently stage-struck, and when she knew that Edward sometimes met people connected with the theatre, she grew pink with excitement. Edward found her touchingly young and unsophisticated. He invited her to come with him one evening to Aunt Mary's play, and to meet her afterwards.

It was a warm spring evening with London at its most seductive. A lingering sunset turned the sky to amethyst and turquoise. The costers' barrows were bright with daffodils, tulips and the first mimosa. In the brilliant shop windows, Easter brides trailed satin and lace. Hats as frothy as whipped egg-white, or as colourful as a handful of spring flowers, attracted the bemused window-gazers.

The play seemed to improve as its run lengthened, Edward thought. Aunt Mary queened it as becomingly as ever in all three acts. She was at her most sparkling afterwards at supper and brought a famous couple with her to dazzle Edward's young friend.

Later, while Edward was dancing with the actress and her husband was at the other side of the room talking with a friend, she watched Elizabeth's fond gaze follow Edward's handsome figure round the floor. He certainly was a personable young man, thought Aunt Mary, with family pride. He would have had a fine stage presence if he had cared to take up the profession.

'How well Edward fits into this sort of life,' said Elizabeth sighing. 'You can see that he loves London, and people, and a gay time.'

Aunt Mary, whose bright blue eyes missed nothing, either around her or in the human heart, seized her opportunity.

'I don't think you know Edward very well. He seems happy enough in town at the moment, but his roots are elsewhere. He doesn't know it yet himself, but Caxley will pull him back again before long. Of that I'm positive.'

'How can you say that?' protested Elizabeth. She looked affronted and hurt. 'What would Edward find in a poky little country town?'

'Everything worthwhile,' replied Aunt Mary composedly. 'He's his two Caxley grandfathers rolled into one, with a strong dash of my darling brother Bertie thrown in. That mixture is going to make a Caxley patriarch one day out of our dashing young Edward!'

'I don't believe it,' replied Elizabeth.

'Wait another ten years or so and you'll see,' promised Aunt Mary. But she felt quite certain that the pretty young thing beside her would not be prepared to wait at all. The role of country mouse would never do for her.

And that, thought Aunt Mary in her wisdom, was exactly as it should be.

14. Interlude in Ireland

WHILE Edward enjoyed the spring in London, the good people of Caxley greeted the returning warmth just as heartily. At Rose Lodge, the clumps of daffodils and pheasant-eyed narcissi which Bender had planted, so long ago, were in splendid bloom. Bertie's garden, close by the Cax, was vivid with grape hyacinths and crocuses beneath the budding trees. Even Sep's small flagged yard, behind the bakehouse, sported a white-painted tub of early red tulips, put there by Kathy's hand.

Pale-pink sticks of rhubarb with yellow topknots, the first pullets' eggs and bunches of primroses graced the market stalls. People were buying bright packets of flower seeds and discussing the rival merits of early potatoes. Felt hats were brushed and put away on top shelves, and straw ones came forth refurbished with new ribbon and flowers.

In the wide fields around Caxley the farmers were busy drilling and planting. Dim lights shone from lonely shepherds' huts as lambing continued. Along the hedges the honeysuckle and hawthorn put out their rosettes and fans of green, among the tattered tassels of the hazel catkins, and hidden beneath, the blue and white violets gave out the exquisite scent of spring from among their heart-shaped leaves.

Bertie, driving his mother to Beech Green one spring afternoon to visit her sister Ethel Miller, noticed the encouraging sights and sounds with a great sense of comfort. He always enjoyed being in this familiar countryside and remembered the long bicycle rides which he and the Howard brothers took when these same lanes were white with chalky dust and most of the traffic was horse-drawn.

It grieved him to see the new estates going up on the slopes flanking Caxley. People must be housed, but the gracelessness of the straight roads, the box-like structures packed too closely together, the narrow raw strips of gardens and the complete lack of privacy, saddened him. He would hate to have to live in a house like that, he thought, passing one garishly-painted one with a board outside saying: SHOW HOUSE, and he guessed that many future occupants would feel the same way, but be forced by circumstances to make the best of a bad job. It seemed to Bertie that for so little extra cost and care something lovely might have been built upon the fields he remembered, to give pleasure and pride to the dwellers there as well as to the town as a whole. As it was, this new development, in Bertie's opinion, was nothing but an eyesore and, as a block of houses embellished with moulded concrete weatherboarding came into view, he put his foot heavily on the accelerator to reach the sanctuary of leafy lanes beyond, unaltered since his boyhood.

It was good to arrive at the old farmhouse. Nothing seemed to have changed in the square panelled room which the Millers still called 'the parlour', and through the windows the copper beech, pink with young leaf, lifted its arms against the background of the mighty downs. Only such an observant eye as Bertie's would notice significant details of a fast-changing way of farming. Sacks of chemical fertilizer were stacked in a nearby barn. Strange new machinery had its place beside the old harvest binder which Bertie remembered his Uncle Jesse buying at a distant sale. Jesse's sons, it seemed, were abreast of modern methods.

The two old ladies gossiped of family affairs. There had been a letter that morning from Joan in Dublin.

'She's invited Edward to visit them later in the summer. That's the best of having a hotel, isn't it?'

'It could work both ways,' Bertie pointed out, amused at his mother's matter-of-fact approach. 'Suppose all your relations wanted to come for the summer. You wouldn't make much profit, would you?'

'Don't be tiresome, dear,' said his mother automatically, in the tone she had used ever since he could remember. Bertie smiled, and sampled his aunt's gingerbread in contented silence.

'Will he go?' asked Ethel. 'Who knows? He might meet a nice Irish girl.'

'Heaven forbid, Ethel! We've had quite enough mixed marriages in our family as it is!'

'They're not *all* Catholics over there,' said her sister with asperity. 'I know very well that quite a few of them are Christians.'

'You mean *Protestants*, surely, Aunt Ethel,' put in Bertie mildly. The old lady looked at him frostily and then transferred her gaze to her sister.

'That boy of yours, Hilda,' she observed severely, 'interrupts his elders and betters even more than he used to.'

'I'm so sorry,' said Bertie with due humility, and sat back with his gingerbread to play the role of listener only.

But, driving home again through the thickening twilight, Mrs North said:

'You mustn't mind what Ethel says, dear.'

'I don't, mamma,' replied Bertie calmly.

'She's getting old, you know, and a little peculiar in her ways.'

Bertie was about to say that Ethel was some years younger than she was herself, but had the sense to hold his tongue.

'Fancy suggesting that Edward might marry an *Irish* girl!' There was an outraged air about this remark which amused Bertie. If Aunt Ethel had suggested that Edward was considering marriage with an aborigine, his mamma could not have sounded more affronted.

'Irish girls are quite famous for their charm and good looks,' said Bertie. 'But I don't think you need to worry about Edward. No doubt he can find a wife when he wants one.'

'If ever!' snapped old Mrs North shortly. Bridling, she turned to watch the hedges flying by, and spoke no more until Bertie deposited her again at Rose Lodge.

The invitation to Ireland pleased Edward mightily. He missed his sister Joan, for despite their promises to visit each other, various reasons had prevented them from meeting and it was now eighteen months since they had seen each other.

Business affairs would keep Edward ceaselessly engaged for the next two or three months, but he promised to cross to Ireland during the last week of August. It would be his first visit to a country which had always intrigued him. He hoped, if he could arrange matters satisfactorily at the factory, to go on from Dublin to see something of the west coast. He looked forward eagerly to the trip.

When the time came he set off in high spirits. He was to make the crossing from Holyhead to Dun Laoghaire, and as the train rattled across Wales, Edward thought how little he knew of the countries which marched with his own. The war had fettered him, and for the last few years London had claimed him, apart from the occasional business trips abroad. Catching glimpses of Welsh mountains, and tumbling rivers so different from the placid Cax of home, he made up his mind that he would explore Wales and Scotland before he grew much older.

He slept soundly during the night crossing, and awoke to find the mailboat rocking gently in the great harbour of Dun Laoghaire, or Kingstown, as the old people at home still called it. Beyond the massive curves of the granite breakwaters, the little town basked in the morning sunshine. Gulls screamed above the glittering water. A maid twirled a mop from a window of the Royal Marine Hotel. A train, with a plume of smoke, chugged along the coast to Dublin. Edward's first glimpse of Ireland did not disappoint him.

He breakfasted aboard before meeting Joan and Michael who had driven the seven miles from Dublin to meet him.

'You both look younger – and fatter!' cried Edward with delight.

'It's Irish air and Irish food,' replied Joan, 'You see! You'll be twice the man at the end of your holiday.'

There was so much news to exchange on the drive to Dublin that Edward scarcely noticed his surroundings; but the soft, warm Irish air on his cheeks was strange and delicious.

Michael's father had died recently but his mother still made her home with them. Edward found her a gentler edition of his grandmother North, with some deafness which rendered her endearingly vague. Sarah, not yet two years old, with red curls and a snub nose, flirted outrageously with her uncle from the instant they met. She was in the care of a good-looking young nursemaid whose broad Irish speech Edward found entirely incomprehensible. She was equally incapable of understanding Edward, and for the duration of his stay they relied on smiles, and occasional interpretation from the family, for communication.

The hotel was small, but well placed in one of the quiet streets near Stephen's Green. Joan and Michael worked hard here and the business was thriving. Edward explored Dublin, mainly on his own, browsing at the bookstalls along the quays by the River Liffey, and admiring the hump-backed bridges which crossed its broad waters. Michael took time off from his duties to show him Trinity College, not far from the hotel, and Edward thought that the vast eighteenth-century library, its sombre beauty lit by slanting rays of sunlight, was one of the most impressive places he had ever seen.

On the third morning Joan received a letter which she read at the breakfast table with evident satisfaction.

'She can come. Isn't that good?' she said to her husband.

'Maisie Hunter,' she told Edward. 'She's staying with an aunt in Belfast and said she would come down if she could manage it. She's arriving tomorrow by train.'

Although Edward liked Maisie, he felt a slight pang of regret. He was so much enjoying his present circumstances in this new place and among the friendly people who always seemed to have time to stop and talk with a curious stranger. At the moment he was content to forget Caxley and all its inmates. He chided himself for such selfishness and offered to meet Joan's friend at the station.

'Take the car,' said Michael. 'She's bound to have a mountain of luggage.'

But all Maisie carried were two neat matching cases when Edward first saw her, in the distance, stepping from the train. She was thinner than he remembered her, and her brown hair, which used to hang to her shoulders, was now short and softly curled. It suited her very well, thought Edward, hurrying to meet her. Her obvious surprise delighted him.

'I'd no idea you were here! What a nice surprise.'

Her smile was warm, lighting up her sun-tanned face and grey eyes. No one could call Maisie Hunter a beauty: her features were not regular enough for such a description, but her skin and hair were perfect, and she had a vivacity of expression, combined with a low and lovely voice, which made her most attractive. Edward was now wholeheartedly glad to see her again.

'I've had a standing invitation to visit Joan,' she explained, as they drove towards Stephen's Green, 'and this seemed the right time to come. My aunt has her son and daughter arriving for a week's stay. But I didn't realize that I was interrupting a family reunion.'

Edward assured her truthfully that they were all delighted that she had come, and constituted himself as guide on this her first visit to Dublin.

'A case of the blind leading the blind,' he added, drawing up outside the hotel. 'But it's amazing how ready people are to drop what they are doing and take you wherever you want to go. Time stands still over here. That's Ireland's attraction to me.'

'You know what they say? "God made all the time in the world, and left most of it in Ireland." Now, where's my god-daughter?'

The next two or three days passed pleasantly. Edward and Maisie discovered the varied delights of Phoenix Park, revelling in the long walks across the windy central plain, watching the fine racehorses exercise and the little boys flying their kites in the warm summer breezes.

It was Michael who suggested that they took his car and set off to explore the western part of Ireland.

'I've a good friend who has a little pub on the shores of Lough Corrib,' he told them. 'There's no such modern nonsenses as telephones there, but tell him I sent you. He'll find room for you, without doubt, and the views there will charm your hearts from your breasts.'

Michael, waxing lyrical in the Celtic fashion, always amused Edward. Ireland was the finest place in the world, Michael maintained, and it was a positive sin not to see as much of its glories as possible during Edward's short stay. Persuaded, the two set out in the borrowed car, promising to return in a few days.

Edward had envisaged hiring a car and making this journey on his own. He had secretly looked forward to this solitary trip, stopping when and where he liked, sight-seeing or not as the mood took him. But now that he had a companion he found that he was enjoying himself quite as much. They were easy together, sometimes talking animatedly, sharing memories of Caxley characters, or sometimes content to relax in silence and watch the rolling green fields of Ireland's central plain slide past.

The welcome at 'The Star' was as warm as Michael had promised. It was a small whitewashed pub, set on a little knoll above the dark waters which reflected it. The sun was setting when they arrived, and long shadows streaked the calm surface of the lake. Edward thought that he had never seen such tranquillity. His bedroom window looked across an expanse of grass, close-cropped by a dozen or so fine geese, to the lake. Here and there on the broad waters were islets, misty-blue against the darkening sky. Moored against the bank were three white skiffs, and Edward made up his mind to take one in the morning to explore those secret magical places fast slipping into the veils of twilight.

But now the welcome scent of fried bacon and eggs came drifting from below, and he hurried down, trying to dodge the low beams which threatened his head, to find Maisie and their waiting meal.

Their brief holiday passed blissfully. They explored Galway and made a trip to the Aran Islands in driving rain, and lost their hearts, just as Michael said they would, to the sad grey-green mountains and the silver beaches of Connemara. But it was the waters of Lough Corrib, lapping beneath their windows at night and supplying them with the most delicious trout and salmon of their lives, which had the strongest allure.

On their last day they took a picnic and set off in the boat to row across to one of the many islands. Maisie was taking a turn at the oars and Edward, eyes screwed up against the dazzling sunshine, watched her square brown hands tugging competently and thought how much he would miss her. He had been happier in her company than he would have thought possible. He tried to explain to himself why this should be. Of course they had known each other, off and on, for almost ten years, so that they had slipped into this unexpected companionship with perfect ease. And then there was no tiresome coquetry about the girl, no playing on her femininity. She had tackled the long walks, the stony mountain tracks, and the quagmires too, with enthusiasm and with no useless grieving over ruined shoes. He remembered an occasion when they descended a steep muddy lane beside a tiny farm, lured by the distant prospect far below of a shining beach. Out of the cottage had run a stout Irishwoman who threw up her hands in horror to see their struggles through the mud.

'Come away now,' she cried, 'and go down through our farm yard. You'll be destroyed that way!'

He laughed aloud at the memory.

'What now?' queried Maisie, resting on her oars. Bright drops slid down their length and plopped into the lake. He told her.

'Once when I was out with Philip,' she began animatedly, and then stopped. Edward watched her expression change swiftly from gaiety to sadness. This was the first time that she had mentioned her dead fiancé's name. They had not talked of their past at all during these few lovely days.

139

She looked away across the lake and spoke in a low but steady voice, as though she had made up her mind to speak without restraint.

'Once when I was out with Philip,' she repeated, and continued with the anecdote. But Edward did not hear it. He was too engrossed with his own thoughts. From his own experience, he guessed that this moment was one of great advance for Maisie's progress towards full recovery from her grief. If Ireland had been able to thaw the ice which held her heart, then that alone would make this holiday unforgettable.

He became conscious that she was silent, and smiling at him.

'You haven't heard a word, have you?' she asked. 'Don't fib. I don't mind. D'you know that something wonderful has just happened to me?'

'Yes,' said Edward gently. 'I can guess.'

'I've never spoken about him. I couldn't. But somehow, here, with nothing but lake and sky, it seems easy. My family mind so much for me, I don't dare to talk of it. I can't face the emotion it brings forth.'

'I've had my share of that,' replied Edward. 'Someone – I think it was Uncle Bertie – told me once that it's the hardest thing in the world to receive pity. The damnable thing is that it takes so many forms – and all of them hell for the victim.'

He found himself telling the girl about his own family's attitude to his broken marriage, and the comfort he had found in his solitary life.

'We've been lucky in having that,' agreed Maisie. 'My Caxley flat has been a haven. I should have gone mad if I had been living at home. There's a lot to be said for a single existence. Wasn't it Katherine Mansfield who said that living alone had its compensations? And that if you found a hair in your honey it was a comfort to know it was your own?'

An oar slipped from its rowlock and the boat rocked.

'Here, let me row for a bit,' said Edward, restored to the present. They crept gingerly past each other exchanging places, and Edward pulled steadily towards the nearest island.

They picnicked on salmon and cucumber sandwiches and hard-boiled eggs, afterwards lying replete in the sun. A moorhen piped from the reeds nearby. The sun was warm upon their closed eyes. A little breeze shivered upon the surface of the lake and ruffled their hair.

'Damn going back,' said Edward lazily. 'I could stay here for ever.'

'Me too,' said Maisie ungrammatically. 'I feel quite different. You've been a great help, letting me talk about Philip. It was a thousand pities we never married, in more ways than one. Somehow one tends to build up a sort of deity from the person one's lost, and I think that is wrong. If we'd had a few years of married ups and downs perhaps I should have been able to bear it more bravely.'

'In some ways,' said Edward, 'you miss them more.' He remembered, with sharp poignancy, the perfume which Angela had used and how terribly it had affected him after their parting.

He propped himself on one elbow and looked down upon his companion. She looked very young and vulnerable, a long grass clamped between her teeth, her eyes shut against the sunlight. She'd had a tough road to travel, just as he had. Fortunately, he was further along that stony track, and knew that, in the end, it grew easier. He tried to tell her this.

'It gets better, you know, as you go on. All that guff about Time, the Great Healer, which irritates one so when one's still raw – well, it's perfectly true. I've just got out of the let-me-lick-my-wound-in-solitude state, which you're still in, and all the things which wise old people like Sep told me are coming true. Hope comes back, and purpose, and a desire to do something worthwhile – and, best of all, the perfectly proper feeling that it is *right* to be happy, and not to feel guilty when cheerfulness breaks in.'

Maisie opened her grey eyes, threw aside the grass and smiled at him.

'Dear Edward,' she said, 'you are an enormous comfort.'

They returned reluctantly to Dublin. Edward was to go back the next day to England. Maisie was going to her aunt's for a little longer.

'When do you go back to Caxley?' asked Edward, through the car window as Michael prepared to drive him to the station.

'Term starts on September the twelfth,' said Maisie. 'A Thursday. I'll probably go back on Tuesday or Wednesday.'

'I shall be down on Friday evening for the weekend,' said Edward with decision. 'Keep it free. Promise?'

'Promise,' nodded Maisie, as the car drove away.

15. Edward and Maisie

DURING the golden autumn months that followed Edward's visit to Ireland, work at the factory quickened its pace. Edward was as enthusiastic and conscientious as ever, but it did not escape the eyes of his partners that all his weekends were now spent at Caxley.

Elizabeth, in the flat above, watched Edward's car roar away early on Saturday mornings, or sometimes on Friday evenings, when pressure of work allowed. Aunt Mary, it seemed, was right when she predicted that Caxley would pull her attractive nephew homeward. What was she like, Elizabeth wondered, this Caxley girl who had succeeded where she had failed?

Not that she cared very much, she told herself defiantly. There were just as good fish in the sea, and the thought of spending her life in a tin-pot little dump like Caxley appalled her.

If Edward wanted to bury himself alive in a place like that, then she was glad that nothing had come of their affair. It was only, she admitted wistfully, that he was so extraordinarily handsome, and made such a wonderful escort. Meanwhile, it was no good grieving over her losses. Sensibly, she turned her attention to the other young men in her life. They might not have quite the same high standard of good looks and general eligibility as dear, lost Edward, but they were certainly more attainable.

In Caxley, of course, the tongues wagged briskly. The Howards had provided gossip of one sort or another for generations. There was that deliciously spicy affair of Sep's wife Edna, the Caxley folk reminded each other, when Dan Crockford painted her portrait and the shameless hussy had sat for it *unchaperoned*. True, she was fully dressed, they added, with some disappointment in their tones, but Sep had been very upset about it at the time. It had happened years ago, in the reign of King

Edward the Seventh in fact, but was still fresh in the memories of many old stalwarts of the market square.

Sep's rise in fortune was remembered too, and the buying of Bender North's old property, but there were few who grudged Sep his success. He bore himself modestly and his high principles were respected. Besides, he had faced enough trouble in his life with the death of his first-born in the war, and the going's-on of his second son Leslie. It must be hard to banish one's child, as Sep had done. Did he ever regret it, they asked each other? And then this last tragedy of poor Robert's! What a burden Sep had carried to be sure!

But this latest tit-bit was a pleasant one. It was a pity, of course, that Maisie Hunter was not a true-bred Caxley girl, but only a war-time arrival. On the other hand, as one pointed out to her neighbour over the garden hedge, a bit of fresh blood worked wonders in these old inter-married families of Caxley. And say what you like, if Maisie Hunter had chosen to stay all these years in Caxley, it proved that she had good sense and that she was worthy to marry into their own circle. It was to be hoped, though, that the children would take after Edward for looks. Maisie Hunter was *healthy* enough, no doubt, but certainly no oil painting – too skinny by half.

Thus flowed the gossip, but one important point was overlooked by the interested bystanders. It was taken for granted that Maisie Hunter would accept such a fine suitor with alacrity. The truth was that Edward's ardent and straightforward wooing was meeting with severe set-backs. Maisie was beset with doubts and fears which were as surprising to Edward as they were painful to the girl herself.

Was he truly in love with her, or simply ready for domesticity? Was he prompted by pity for her circumstances? The questions beat round and round in her brain, and she could find no answer.

She wondered about her own response. In the solitude of the little flat which had become so dear to her, she weighed the pros and cons of the step before her, in a tumult of confusion. She was now twenty-nine, and Edward was two years older. There was a lot to give up if she married. She was at the peak of a career she enjoyed. The idea of financial dependence was a little daunting, and she would hate to leave Caxley. She was not at all sure that she wanted to embark on the troubled seas of motherhood as soon as she married, and yet it would be best for any children they might have to start a family before she and Edward were much older.

And then, to be a *second* wife was so much more difficult than to be a *first*. Marriage, for Edward, had been such an unhappy episode. Could she make him as happy as he deserved to be? Would he secretly compare her with his first wife? Would he find her equally disappointing and demanding? Wouldn't it be safer if they didn't marry after all, she wondered, in despair?

It had all been so much simpler when she had become engaged to Philip. They had both been very young. Love, marriage, and children had seemed so simple and straightforward then. Now everything was beset with doubts and complications. Philip's death had shaken her world so deeply, that any decision was difficult to make. Edward's patience with her vacillations made her feel doubly guilty. It was not fair to subject him to such suspense, but she could not commit herself while she was so tormented.

Thus the autumn passed for Maisie in a strange blur of intense happiness and horrid indecision. Edward came to see her each weekend, and often she travelled to London to meet him after school. In his company she was at peace, but as soon as she returned to Caxley the nagging questions began again. The Howards and Norths were dismayed at the delay in Edward's plans. It was quite apparent that he was in love. What on earth could Maisie be thinking of to shilly-shally in this way? Wasn't their Edward good enough for her?

November fogs shrouded the market square. The Cax flowed sluggishly, reflecting sullen skies as grey as pewter. People hurried home to their firesides, looked out hot-water bottles, took to mufflers, complained of rheumatic twinges, and faced the long

THE HOWARDS OF CAXLEY

winter months with resignation. The gloom was pierced on November 14 that year by the news of the birth of a son to the Princess Elizabeth. The church bells rang in the market square, and from village towers and steeples in the countryside around. Their joyous clamour was in Maisie's ears as she pushed a letter to Joan into the pillar box at the corner of the market place.

It had taken her a long time to write, but even longer to decide if it should be written at all. But it was done, and now relief flooded her. All the things which she had been unable to tell Edward, she had written to his sister, and she begged for advice as unbiased as possible in the circumstances. Maisie respected Joan's good sense. In these last few agitated weeks, she had longed to talk with her, to discuss her doubts with someone of her own sex, age and background.

She awaited the reply from Ireland with as much patience as she could muster. No doubt Joan would take as much time and trouble with her answer as she herself had taken in setting out her problems. As the days passed, she began to wonder if it had been kind to press Joan on the matter. After all, she was an exceptionally busy person, and young Sarah took much of her attention.

At last the letter came. Maisie sped to the door, her breakfast coffee untasted. It lay, a square white envelope with the Irish stamp, alone on the door mat. Trembling, Maisie bent to pick it up. It was thin and light. Obviously, whatever message Joan sent was going to prove terse and to the point. She tore it open. Joan's neat handwriting covered only one side of the paper.

You darling ass,

All your ifs and buts are on Edward's account, I notice. Let him shoulder his own worries, if he has any, which I doubt — and please say 'Yes.' Go ahead and just be happy, both of you.

All our love,
Joan

P.S. Dr Kelly has just confirmed our hopes. Prepare for a christening next April.

Suddenly, the bleak November morning seemed flooded with warmth and light. This was exactly the right sort of message to receive – straightforward, loving and wise. How terrible, Maisie realized, it would have been to receive a long screed putting points for and against the marriage – merely a prolongation of the dreary debate which had bedevilled her life lately. Joan had summed up the situation at once, had recognized the nervous tension which grew more intense as time passed and had made Maisie's decision impossible. In a few lines she had pointed out something simple and fundamental to which worry had blinded her friend. Edward knew what he was undertaking. Maisie recalled his saying one evening, with a wry smile: 'You might give me credit for some sense. I've thought about it too, you know.'

She folded the letter, put it in her handbag like a talisman, and set off, smiling, for school.

'No long engagement for us,' said Edward firmly next weekend. 'You might change your mind again, and that I couldn't face.'

They had spent the winter afternoon visiting the family to tell them of their engagement and their future plans.

At Rose Lodge it was Grandma North who received the news with the greatest display of excitement.

'At last, a wedding in St Peter's!' she exclaimed, clapping her thin papery old hands together. Edward shook his head.

'Afraid not. For one thing we neither of us want it. And I don't think our vicar would relish a divorced man at his altar.'

'Not a church wedding?' faltered the old lady. 'Oh, what a disappointment! Really, it does seem hard!'

She rallied a little, and her mouth took on the obstinate curve which Edward knew so well.

'I'll have a word with the vicar myself, dear boy. Bender and I worked for the church all our lives, and the least he can do is to put on a nice little wedding service for our grandson.' She spoke as if the vicar would be arranging a lantern lecture in the church hall – something innocuous and sociable – with coffee and Marie biscuits to follow.

Edward broke into laughter. His grandmother began to pout, and he crossed the room in three strides and kissed her heartily. Unwillingly, she began to smile, and Winnie, watching them both, thought how easily Edward managed the wilful old lady whose autocratic ways grew more pronounced and embarrassing as the years passed.

'No, no church this time, but a wonderful wedding party at Sep's. He's already planning the cake decorations, and we shall expect your prettiest bonnet on the day.'

Mrs North appeared mollified, and turned her attention to more practical matters concerning linen, silver and china. It was clear that she was going to be busily engaged in the wedding preparations from now on.

And this time, thought Winnie, her eyes upon Edward and Maisie, there is happiness ahead. For a fleeting moment she remembered her first encounter with Angela, and the dreadful premonition of disaster to come. Now, just as deeply, she felt that this time all would be well for them both.

Sep too, had shared the same feeling when he had held their hands that afternoon and congratulated them.

'Dear boy, dear boy!' he repeated, much moved. His welcome to Maisie was equally warm. He had known and liked her for many years now. She would make Edward a good wife.

He accompanied them down the stairs from his parlour above the shop and said good-bye to them in front of the bow windows which displayed the delicious products of his bakehouse at the back. When they were out of sight, he glanced across at the fine windows above his restaurant across the square. Would Edward ever return there, he wondered? Would his children gaze down one day upon the varied delights of market day, as Edward had done, and his friend Bender's children had done, so long ago, when horses had clip-clopped across the cobbles and Edward the Seventh was on the throne?

He turned to look with affection at that monarch's mother,

small and dignified, surveying the passing traffic from her plinth.

'No one like her,' exclaimed Sep involuntarily. 'No one to touch her, before or since.'

Two schoolgirls, chewing toffee, giggled together and nudged each other. What a silly old man, talking to himself! They passed on, unseen by Sep.

He entered the shop, glad to be greeted by its fragrant warmth after the raw cold outside. For four reigns now he had served in this his own small kingdom. Sometimes, lately, he had wondered if he could rule for much longer, but now, with Edward's good news ringing in his ears, he felt new strength to face the future.

'I'll take some crumpets for tea,' he said to the assistant behind the scrubbed counter.

He mounted the stairs slowly, bearing his paper bag to Miss Taggerty. This, after all, he told himself, was the right way for a baker to celebrate.

The wedding was to be in January, and meanwhile Edward searched for a house or a larger flat than the one in which he now lived. Maisie accompanied him as often as her school work would allow.

It was a dispiriting task. New houses had gone up in abundance near Edward's factory, but neither he nor Maisie could face their stark ugliness, the slabs of raw earth waiting to be transformed into tiny gardens and the complete lack of privacy. Older houses, in matured gardens, never seemed to be for sale.

Back in Edward's little flat after an exhausting foray, Maisie kicked off her shoes and gazed round the room.

'What's wrong with this?' she asked.

'Why, nothing,' said Edward, 'except that it's hardly big enough for one, let alone two.'

'We haven't seen anything as comfortable as this,' replied Maisie. 'I'll be happy here, if you will. Let's start here anyway. If it becomes impossible we'll think again — but I simply can't look at any more places just now. I can't think why we didn't settle for this in the first place.'

Edward agreed, with relief. It might not be ideal, but the flat was quiet with an outlook upon grass and trees, and it would be simple for Maisie to run. He would like to have found something more splendid for his new wife, but their recent expeditions had proved daunting, to say the least. Maybe, in time, they could move much further away, to the pleasant greenness of Buckinghamshire, perhaps, where property was attractive and the daily journey to work would not be too arduous. Meanwhile, Edward's tiny flat, refurbished a little by Maisie, would be their first home.

There was snow on the ground on their wedding day, but the sun shone from a pale-blue cloudless sky. Steps and window sills were edged with white, and the pigeon's coral feet made hieroglyphics on the snowy pavements. Edward and Maisie emerged from the registrar's office into the market place, dazzled with the sunshine, the snow and their own happiness.

'I suppose,' said Mrs North to Bertie, as they followed the pair, 'that it's *legal*. I mean they *really are* married?'

'Perfectly legal, mamma,' Bertie assured her.

'It seems so *quick*,' protested the old lady. 'I do so hope you're right, Bertie. It would be terrible for them to find they were living in sin.'

The registrar, coming upon the scene and overhearing this remark, gave a frosty bow and marched stiffly away.

'Now you've offended him,' said Bertie, smiling.

'Hm!' snorted the old lady, unrepentant. 'Marrying people without even a surplice! Small wonder he hurries away!'

It was a gay party that gathered in Sep's restaurant. The wedding cake stood on a table by the windows which overlooked the snowy garden. The dark waters of the Cax gleamed against the white banks, and a robin perching upon a twig peered curiously at the array of food inside the window.

Edward gazed contentedly about him. Sep and his grandmother were nodding sagely across the table. Her wedding hat was composed of velvet pansies in shades of blue and violet. She had certainly succeeded in finding a beauty, thought Edward affectionately.

His mother and Bertie were in animated conversation. Aunt Kathy, gorgeous in rose-pink, glowed at the corner of the table, her children nearby. If only Joan could have been here it would have been perfect, but he and Maisie were to see her before long as they returned from their honeymoon.

He turned to look at his new wife. She wore a soft yellow suit and looked unusually demure. He laughed and took her hand. Another Howard had joined the family in the market square.

Far away, the quiet waters of Lough Corrib reflected the bare winter trees growing at the lake side.

There was no snow here. A gentle wind rustled the dry reeds, and the three white skiffs lay upside down on the bank, covered by a tarpaulin for the winter. The grey and white geese converged upon the back door of the inn, necks outstretched, demanding food.

A plume of blue smoke curled lazily towards the winter sky. Timeless and tranquil, 'The Star' gazed at its reflection in the water, and awaited its guests.

16. Harvest Loaves

ONE bright Sunday morning in April, Sep awoke with curious constriction in his chest. He lay still, massaging it gently with a small bony hand. He was not greatly perturbed. A man in his eighties expects a few aches and pains, and Sep had always made light of his ailments.

It was fortunate, he thought, that it was Sunday. On weekdays he continued to rise betimes, despite his family's protests, but on Sunday he allowed himself some latitude and Miss Taggerty prepared breakfast for eight o'clock.

Always, when he awoke, his first thoughts were of Edna. He lay now, remembering just such a shining morning, when he and Edna had taken the two boys for a picnic in the woods at Beech Green. Robert and Kathy were not born then, and Jim and Leslie had frisked before them like young lambs, along the lane dappled with sunshine and shadow. They had picked bunches of primroses, and eaten their sandwiches in a little clearing. Sep could see the young birch trees now, fuzzy with green-gold leaf. A pair of blackbirds had flown back and forth to their nestlings, and a young rabbit had lolloped across the clearing, its fur silvered and its translucent ears pink, in the bright sunshine.

Perhaps he remembered it so clearly, thought Sep, because they so rarely had a day out together. The shop had always come first. Edna must have found it a great tie sometimes, but he could not recall her complaining. She had been a wonderful wife. He missed her more and more. It was hard to grow old alone.

He sat up, suddenly impatient with his own self-pity, and a spasm of pain shot through him. It was so sharp and unexpected that he gasped in dismay. When it had abated a little, he lay back gingerly against the pillow. The bells of St Peter's were ringing for early service. It would soon be seven-thirty.

'Indigestion,' Sep told himself aloud. He tried to remember if he had eaten anything unusual on the previous day, but failed. His appetite was small, and he had never been in the habit of eating a heavy meal in the evening. Perhaps he had put too much sugar in his Horlicks. As he grew older he found himself becoming increasingly fond of sweet things. He must not be so self-indulgent.

He sat up carefully. The pain was dwindling, and he crossed slowly to the window. A few church-goers were mounting the steps of St Peter's. A milkman's float clanged and jangled on the opposite side of the square. It was a typical Sunday morning in Caxley – a scene which he had looked upon hundreds of times and always taken for granted.

But today, suddenly, it had a poignant significance for Sep. Would he see many more Sundays? Death must come soon, and he was unafraid – but Caxley was very dear, and hard to leave behind.

He shaved and dressed carefully in his sober Sunday suit in readiness for chapel, and in his mind there beat a line of poetry which he had heard only that week.

> Look thy last on all things lovely,
> Every hour –

It was good sense, Sep decided, descending the stairs slowly, as well as good poetry.

In the weeks that followed, the pain recurred. Sep found that his head swam sometimes when he bent down, or if he lifted a heavy pan in the bakehouse. He told no one of the disability, dismissing it as a passing ailment, unworthy of serious attention. He brushed aside Miss Taggerty's anxious inquiries. There was little affecting her master which her keen old eyes missed, but natural timidity kept her from expressing her fears to the rest of the family. Sep would brook no tale-telling, she knew well.

But the secret could not be kept for long. One warm May evening Sep set off along the tow path to see Kathy and Bertie.

Half a dozen naked boys splashed and shouted by the further bank. Clouds of midges drifted above the river, and swallows swooped back and forth, like dark blue arrows. From the oak tree near Bertie's garden gate, minute green caterpillars jerked on their gossamer threads. It was sultry, with a mass of dark clouds building up menacingly on the horizon. Soon there would be thunder, and the boys would scramble for home, leaving the placid surface of the river to be pitted with thousands of drops.

Bertie was in his vegetable garden, spraying the blackfly from his broad beans. Sep heard the rhythmic squish-squish of the syringe. Bertie was hidden from sight by a hawthorn hedge which divided the lawn from the kitchen garden. A blackbird flew out, squawking frenziedly, as Sep brushed the hedge. There were probably a dozen or more nests secreted in its length, Sep surmised, looking at it with interest. He turned to watch his son-in-law, still unaware of his presence, intent on washing away the sticky black pest.

Bertie wore well, he thought affectionately. His figure had thickened slightly, and his hair, still plentiful, had turned to silver. But his complexion was fresh and his blue eyes as bright as ever. He was becoming more like Bender as he grew older, but would never have the girth, or the bluster, of his father. Bender's ebullience had made Sep nervous at times. There was nothing to fear in his son.

At last he straightened up, and started when he saw Sep's slight figure at the end of the row.

'Good heavens! I didn't hear you arrive! How are you? Let me put this thing away and we'll go indoors.'

'No, no, my boy. Finish the job. There's rain on the way and there's no hurry on my account.'

Obediently, Bertie refilled his syringe and set off along the last row, Sep following. A flourishing plant of groundsel caught the old man's eye and he bent to pull it up. Immediately, the pain in his chest had him in its grip with such intensity that his head thumped. The rosette of groundsel, the damp earth and the pale green stalks of the bean plants whirled round and round

154

together, growing darker and darker, as the blood pounded in his head.

Bertie ran to pick up the old man who was in a dead faint and gasping alarmingly. His cheek and the grey hair at one temple were muddied by the wet soil. With difficulty Bertie managed to lift him in his arms and limped towards the house, calling for Kathy. Sep was as light as a bird, Bertie noticed, despite his agitation – lighter by far than his own young son, Andrew.

They put him on the couch and Kathy ran for smelling salts, while Bertie chafed the frail hands and watched him anxiously.

'We must call the doctor,' he said. As he spoke, Sep opened his eyes and shook his head slowly and wearily.

'No. No doctor,' he whispered.

'Some brandy?' urged Bertie.

'No, thank you,' said Sep, with a touch of his old austerity. Bertie realized that he had blundered.

'Some tea then?'

Sep nodded and closed his eyes again. Kathy ran to the kitchen and Bertie followed her.

'Whatever he says, I'm ringing for the doctor. This is something serious, I feel sure.'

Within ten minutes the doctor had arrived. There was no demur from Sep who, with the tea untasted, lay frail and shrunken against Kathy's bright cushions, with a blanket tucked around him. The examination over, the doctor spoke with false heartiness.

'You'll see us all out, Mr Howard. Just a tired heart, but if you take care of yourself, you'll be as sound as a bell for years yet. I'll write you a prescription.'

Bertie accompanied him into the lane, well out of ear-shot.

'Tell me the truth, doctor. How is he?'

'As I said. If he takes his pills regularly and avoids excessive exercise, he can tick over for a few more years. Your job is to persuade him to take things easily.'

'That's one of the hardest things in the world to ask me to do, but I'll try. Should he spend the night here?'

'It would be best. Tell him to stay there until I call again in the morning.'

Sep submitted to the doctor's orders with unusual docility, and as soon as he was settled in Kathy's spare room Bertie hurried to the market square to tell the news to Miss Taggerty.

It grieved Sep, in the months that followed, to lead such a comparatively inactive life. True, he rose at the usual time and supervised the shop, the restaurant, and the bakehouse, as he had always done, but he walked from place to place more slowly now, and tried not to mount his steep stairs more than was necessary. The doctor had advised him to rest after his midday dinner, and now that the weather was warm, he took to sitting in the old arbour by the river at the rear of the restaurant. This had been his old friend Bender's favourite spot, and Sep had made sure that it was kept as spruce as Bender would have wished.

Jasmine starred and scented its rustic entrance, and an Albertine rose added its splendour. Kathy made the rough seat comfortable with cushions, and provided a footstool and rug. It was a perfect sun trap, and as she went about her affairs in the restaurant, she could watch Sep dozing in sheltered warmth, or gazing at his life-long companion, the river Cax.

The family called to see Sep more often than usual. Hilda North took to paying Sep an occasional afternoon visit. Winnie drove her down the hill from Rose Lodge and left her to keep the old man company while she shopped in the town

The two old people, who shared so many common memories, were closer now than ever they had been, and as they took tea together in the arbour they enjoyed reminiscing about their early days in the market square when their children had played together in this same garden, and floated their toy boats on the river before them.

Edward and Maisie spent as many weekends in Caxley as they could, but both were busy, for Maisie had taken a part-time teaching post. Miss Hedges, the middle-aged headmistress who lived in a neighbouring flat, had soon discovered that Maisie was a trained teacher, and had no difficulty in persuading her to accompany her three mornings a week to school. Here Maisie helped children who were backward in reading and thoroughly enjoyed the work.

'But we don't call them "backward" these days, my dear,' said Miss Hedges with a twinkle. '"Less able" is the most forthright term we are allowed to use in these namby-pamby times!'

Maisie was glad to be doing something worthwhile again. She and Edward were blissfully happy, but he was off to work before half-past eight, the tiny flat was set to rights soon after, and Maisie was beginning to find time hanging heavily on her hands when Miss Hedges had appeared. It was a happy arrangement for them all.

Maisie found her new life absorbing. She looked back now upon her doubts and fears with amusement and incredulity. How right Joan had been, and how lucky she was to have found Edward! They had much in common. As a Londoner, Maisie shared Edward's love of the theatre and they spent many evenings there. Aunt Mary, going from strength to strength as she became better known as a character actress, saw them frequently, and was loud in her approval of Edward's choice.

'And when are you going to Caxley?' she inquired one September evening, after the play. She was in her dressing-room removing make-up with rapid expert strokes.

'The weekend after next,' replied Edward.

'I meant for good,' said his aunt. She noted Edward's surprise.

'Hadn't really thought about it,' said Edward frankly. 'This job is growing daily, and the journey from Caxley would take too long. We're still hoping for a house in the country somewhere, but it will have to be nearer than Caxley.'

Aunt Mary did not pursue the subject. How it would come about she did not know, but in her bones she felt quite sure that Edward and his Maisie were destined for Caxley one day.

She rose from her seat before the dressing table and kissed them unexpectedly.

'Give the old place my love,' she said. 'And all the people who remember me there. Particularly Sep – yes, particularly Sep!'

The last Friday in September was as warm and golden as the harvest fields through which Edward and Maisie drove to Caxley. It had been a good crop this year and the weather had been favourable. Most of the fields were already cut, and the bright stubble bristled cleanly in the sunshine.

Winnie was staking Michaelmas daisies in the garden of Rose Lodge when they arrived. Edward thought how well she looked, and his grandmother too, as they sipped their sherry and exchanged news.

'And Sep?' asked Edward.

'Fairly well,' said his grandmother. 'I had tea with him yesterday afternoon and he's looking forward to seeing you.'

'I'll go and have a word with him now,' said Edward. 'Coming?' he asked Maisie.

'Tell him I'll look in tomorrow morning,' she answered. 'I'll unpack and help here.'

'Don't be long,' called Winnie as he made for the car. 'There's a chicken in the oven, and it will be ready by eight o'clock.'

'That's a date,' shouted Edward cheerfully, driving off.

The long shadow of St Peter's spire stretched across the market place, but the sun still gleamed warmly upon Sep's shop and the windows of his house above it. Edward parked the car and looked around him with satisfaction. Choir practice was in session and he could hear the singers running through the old familiar harvest hymns. Queen Victoria wore a pigeon on her crown and looked disapproving. At the window of his own flat he could see old John Bush, peering at a newspaper held up to he light. This was the time of day when Sep's house had the best of it, Edward thought, and remembered how, as a boy, he had explained to his grandfather why he preferred Bender's old home to Sep's.

'It gets the sun most of the day,' he had told the old man. 'You only get it in the evening.'

But how it glorified everything, to be sure! The western rays burnished Sep's side of the square, gilding steps and door-frames and turning the glass to sheets of fire. Edward ran up the stairs, at the side of the closed shop, and called to his grand-father. Miss Taggerty greeted him warmly.

'He's pottering about downstairs, Mr Edward, having a final look at the Harvest Festival loaves, no doubt. The chapel folk are fetching them tomorrow morning for the decorations. Lovely they are! He did them himself. You'll find him there, you'll see.'

Edward made his way to the bakehouse. There was no one about at this time of day and the yard was very quiet. He entered the bakehouse and was greeted by the clean fragrance of newly-baked bread which had been familiar to him all his life. Ranged against the white wall stood two splendid loaves in the shape of sheaves of corn, with smaller ones neatly lined up beside them. There were long plaited loaves, fat round ones, Coburg, cottage, split-top – a beautiful array of every pattern known to a master baker.

And sitting before them, at the great table white and ribbed with a lifetime's scrubbing, was their creator. He was leaning back in his wooden arm chair, his hands upon the table top and his gaze upon his handiwork. He looked well content.

But when Edward came to him he saw that the eyes were sightless and the small hands cold in death. There, in the centre of his world, his lovely work about him and his duty done, Sep rested at last.

Dazed and devastated, an arm about his grandfather's frail shoulders, Edward became conscious of the eerie silence of the room. Across the square the sound of singing drifted as the boys in St Peter's choir practised their final hymn.

'*All is safely gathered in,*' they shrilled triumphantly, as the long shadows reached towards Sep's home.

17. Problems for Edward

In the bewildered hours that followed Sep's death, the family began to realize just how deeply they would miss his presence. He had played a vital part in the life of each one. He had been the lynch-pin holding the Norths and Howards together, and his going moved them all profoundly.

After the first shock was over, Edward and Bertie spent the weekend making necessary arrangements for the funeral, writing to friends and relatives, drafting a notice for *The Caxley Chronicle* and coping with the many messages of sympathy from the townsfolk who had known Sep all his life.

As they sat at their task, one at each end of Bertie's dining-room table, Bertie looked across at Edward. The younger man was engrossed in his writing, head bent and eyes lowered. His expression was unusually solemn, and in that moment Bertie realized how very like Sep's was his cast of countenance. There was something in the slant of the cheekbone and the set of the ear which recalled the dead man clearly. Age would strengthen the likeness as Edward's hair lost its colour and his face grew thinner.

There was also, thought Bertie, the same concentration on the job in hand. Edward had assumed this sudden responsibility so naturally that, for the first time, he felt dependent upon the younger man. He had slipped into his position of authority unconsciously, and it was clear to Bertie that Edward henceforth would be the head of the family. It was a thought which flooded Bertie with rejoicing and relief. It was all that Sep had hoped for in his wisdom.

The chapel in the High Street was full on the occasion of Sep's funeral. Edward had not realized how many activities Sep had taken part in in the town. He was a councillor for many years. He had been a member of the hospital board, the Red Cross committee, the Boys' Brigade, and a trustee of several local charities. All these duties he had performed conscientiously and unobtrusively. It was plain, from the large congregation, that Sep's influence was widely felt and that he would be sorely missed in Caxley's public life.

The coffin bore the golden flowers of autumn. The chapel was still decorated with the corn and trailing berries of Harvest Festival. Edward, standing between Maisie and his mother, with Kathy beautiful in black nearby, was deeply moved, and when, later, Sep was lowered into the grave beside his adored wife, the dark cypress trees and bright flowers of Caxley's burial ground were blurred by unaccustomed tears. Sep had been a father as well as a grandfather to him. It was doubly hard to say farewell.

But, driving back to Bertie and Kathy's after the ceremony, he became conscious of a feeling of inner calm. This was death as it should be – rest after work well done, port after storm. Death, as Edward had met it first during the war, was violent and unnatural, the brutal and premature end of men still young. Sep had stayed his course, and the memory of that serene dead face gave his grandson comfort now, and hope for the future.

He and Maisie said little on the journey back to town, but later that evening Maisie spoke tentatively.

'Did you wish – did you feel – that your father should have been there, Edward?'

'Yes, I did,' replied Edward seriously. 'As a matter of fact, I wrote to him and told him.'

'Where is he then? I'd no idea you knew where he was!'

'I haven't. Mother would never speak of him – nor, of course, would Sep. But I found an address among his papers when Uncle Bertie and I were putting things straight. Somewhere in Devon. Heaven alone knows if he's still there, but it might be sent on to him, if he's moved. I felt he should know.'

It was the first time that his father had been mentioned, though Maisie knew well the story of Leslie Howard's flight with an earlier love when Edward was only four and Joan still a baby in arms.

'Do you remember him?'

'Hardly at all. I can remember that he used to swing me up high over his head, which I liked. The general impression is a happy one, strangely enough. He was full of high spirits – probably slightly drunk – but willing to have the sort of rough-and-tumble that little boys enjoy.'

'And you've never wanted to see him again?'

'Sometimes, yes. Particularly when I was about sixteen or so. Luckily, Uncle Bertie was at hand always, so he got landed with my problems then. And I knew mother would have hated to see him again, or to know that I'd been in touch. As for Grandma North, I think she would have strangled my father with her bare hands if she'd clapped eyes on him again! He certainly behaved very badly to his family. Sep minded more than anyone. That's why he never spoke of him. He was such a kind man that I always thought it was extraordinary how ruthlessly he dealt with my father.'

'Sep was a man with exceptionally high principles,' said Maisie. She crossed the room to switch on the wireless, and paused on her way back to her chair to look down upon Edward. He was so solemn that she ruffled his thick hair teasingly.

'And a Victorian,' added Edward, still far away, 'with a good Victorian's rigid mode of conduct. It must have made life very simple in some ways. You knew exactly where you were.'

'You're going grey,' said Maisie, peering at the crown of his head, and Edward laughed.

'It's marriage,' he said, pulling her down beside him.

One morning, a week or so later, a long envelope with a Caxley postmark arrived for Edward. It was the only letter for him, but Maisie had a long one from Joan, full of news about the baby and Sarah's recovery from measles. Sipping her breakfast coffee, and engrossed in the letter from Ireland, she was unaware of the effect that Edward's correspondence was making upon him, until he pushed away his half-eaten breakfast and got up hastily.

He looked white and bewildered, and rubbed his forehead as he always did when perplexed.

'Not more bad news?' cried Maisie.

'No. Not really. I suppose one should say quite the opposite – but the hell of a shock.'

He handed her the letter and paced the room while she read it.

'He's left you *everything*?' queried Maisie in a whisper. 'But what about Aunt Kathy and your father and the other grand-children? I don't understand it.'

'They're all provided for – except for my father, which one would expect – by incredibly large sums of money. But the two businesses are for me, evidently.'

'Didn't he ever mention this to you?'

'Never. It honestly never entered my head. It's amazingly generous, but a terrific responsibility. I thought everything would be Aunt Kathy's, with perhaps a few bequests to the others. He'd already given me the house above the restaurant. This is staggering.'

'But lovely,' exclaimed Maisie. 'Dear Sep! He always wanted you in the market square.'

Edward paused in his pacing and looked at her in astonishment.

'Do you seriously suggest that I should run the business my-self? I don't know the first thing about baking – or catering for that matter.'

'You could learn,' pointed out Maisie. 'And running one business must be very like running another. And just think – to live in Caxley!' Her eyes were bright.

Edward continued to look distracted. His eye caught sight of the time and he gave a cry of dismay.

'I must be off. This will need a lot of thought. Lovejoy wants to see me anyway to sign some papers. We'll talk this over this evening, and go down again this weekend.'

'Don't look so worried,' comforted Maisie. 'Anyone would

think you'd been sentenced to death! In fact, you've been sentenced to a new life.'

'Not so fast, please,' begged Edward, collecting his belongings frenziedly. 'There's a great deal to consider – Sep's wishes, the family's reactions, whether we can cope with the business ourselves or get people in to manage it properly – a hundred problems! And what about my job here? I can't let Jim down after all he's done for me.'

Maisie pushed her agitated husband through the front door.

'Tell Jim what's happened,' she said soothingly. 'And calm down. I'm going back to celebrate in a second cup of coffee.'

The day seemed to drag by very slowly for Maisie. There was no school for her that morning, and although she was glad to have some time to collect her thoughts, she longed for Edward to return so that they could discuss this miraculous news.

For her own part she welcomed a return to Caxley. To live in the market square, either in Edward's house or in Sep's, would give her enormous pleasure. Her friends were there, and the thought of living so near all her in-laws, which might daunt many young wives, did not worry Maisie who had known the Howards and Norths now for so many years. She longed too to have a sizeable house to furnish and decorate. Here, in the tiny flat, she had found small scope for her talents. It would be lovely to choose curtains and wallpaper and to bring either of the two fine old houses to life again.

And what better place to raise a Howard family than in the heart of Caxley where their roots ran so deeply? This would mean too the end of the fruitless house-hunting which depressed them both. As she went mechanically about her household tasks, Maisie hoped desperately that Edward would be able to wind up the job satisfactorily here, and return to Caxley with a clear conscience and zest for what lay ahead.

Edward returned, looking less agitated than when he had departed for the office that morning.

'Jim is as pleased as if it had happened to him,' said he. 'We've gone into things as thoroughly as we can at this stage. He's quite happy for me to go whenever I like, but we've all sorts of negotiations going on at the moment, started by me mainly, and I must see those wound up before I'd feel free.'

'And when would that be?'

'I can't say. Probably in a few months' time.'

'A few *months*!' echoed Maisie, trying to keep the disappointment from her voice.

Edward looked across at her and laughed.

'You want to go back very badly, don't you?'

Maisie nodded.

'I'm beginning to think that I do, too, but I must clear up things at this end first. We'll see what Lovejoy says at the weekend, and how the family feels. Who knows? We may be back in the market square by the New Year. That is if I've mastered the bakery business by that time!'

As they drove to Caxley that weekend, Edward had some private misgivings. How would Aunt Kathy feel about the will? She had taken an active part in the business, and it seemed hard that no share in it had been left to her. It was true that Sep's bequest to her and her children had been characteristically generous, and of a magnitude which staggered Edward, but it was not quite the same as having a part in a thriving concern. And how would the rest of the family view his amazing good fortune? Edward had seen many united families rent assunder by wills, and could only hope that the Howards and Norths would be spared this ignominy. He approached Caxley with some trepidation.

His mother and grandmother greeted them with unfeigned delight.

'Which house would you settle in, dear?' asked Mrs North with the shattering directness of old age. She refused to believe that Edward did not know yet if he would be able to return to Caxley at all.

'But you must have known, dear, that Sep intended you to have the business?'

'I hadn't a clue, grandma, and that's the plain truth.'

'Neither had I,' said his mother.

'Well, he spoke to me about it, towards the end,' maintained Mrs North trenchantly 'and I agreed that it was an excellent idea.'

'Grandma, you are incorrigible!' exclaimed Edward, amused.

'It's high time you came back anyway, to look after your mother and me. And what about your own family? Married for nearly a year and no baby on the way! It's deplorable! What you need is some invigorating Caxley air.'

Edward and Maisie exchanged delighted glances.

'Yes, grandma,' said Edward meekly.

He walked up the familiar path to Bertie and Kathy's house with a nervousness he had never felt before. Kathy opened the door to him, put her arms round his neck, and kissed him soundly. All Edward's worries fled in the face of this warm embrace.

'We're all very pleased about it,' Bertie assured him, when they were settled by the fire. 'Although Sep never said a word about his settlements we guessed that this would be the way he wanted it.'

'Would you come in with me as a partner?' asked Edward of his aunt. She smiled and shook her head.

'You're a dear to think of it, but I'm fifty-six next birthday and shall be quite glad to be away from it all. Father's left us money, as you know, and I'm glad the business is yours – still in the family, with "Howard" over the door – but not giving me any more worries.'

They talked of Edward's plans, and he explained the necessity of staying in town to clear up his affairs at the factory.

'And I'm still not absolutely sure if I ought to come back to run the shop and restaurant myself, or whether I should try and get someone to manage them.'

'John Bush and I can hold the fort until you decide,' offered Kathy. 'But *please* think about taking it on yourself. You could do it easily, and think how pleased Sep would have been.'

'And Maisie will be,' added Bertie. 'Off you go to your appointment with Lovejoy! See what he advises.'

Mr Lovejoy, pink and voluble, succeeded in confusing Edward even more, by presenting him with a host of incomprehensible documents to peruse, and a torrent of explanation.

From amidst the chaos one thing emerged clearly to Edward. He was going to be a man of some wealth. Death duties would amount to a considerable sum, but if the business continued at its present rate he could expect an income far in excess of that which he now earned. He had no doubt, in his own mind, that with some rebuilding and more modern equipment, the two businesses could become even more lucrative.

He thanked Mr Lovejoy for his help and emerged into the pale October sunlight. Hardly knowing what he was about, he passed Howard's Restaurant and crossed to Sep's old shop. It was strange to think that all this now belonged to him.

He stepped into the shop in a daze. A young new assistant, unknown to him, asked him what he would like. Edward tried to pull himself together.

'Oh, a loaf,' he said desperately. 'Just a loaf.'

She picked out a stout crusty cottage loaf from the window, shrouded it in a piece of white tissue paper, and thrust it into his arms like a warm baby.

Edward gave her a florin, and she slapped some coins into his palm in return. He studied them with interest. It was time he knew the price of bread.

Still bemused, and clutching his awkward burden, he made his way towards the Cax. What had possessed him to buy a loaf, he wondered, exasperation overcoming his numbness!

He strode now with more purpose towards the tow path. The families of mallards and moorhens paddled busily at the edge of the water, as they had always done. Today, thought Edward, they should celebrate his inheritance.

He broke pieces of the loaf and threw them joyfully upon the Cax. Squawking, quacking, piping, the birds rushed this way and that, wings flapping, streaking the water with their bright feet, as they fought for this largesse.

Exhilarated Edward tossed the pieces this way and that, laughing at the birds' antics and his own incredible good fortune. What was it that the Scriptures said about 'casting thy bread upon the waters'? He would ask Grandma North when he returned.

He thrust the last delicious morsel into his mouth, dusted his hands, and walked home, whistling.

18. Edward Meets His Father

THE first frosts of autumn blackened the bright dahlias in the suburban gardens and began to strip the golden trees. Children were scuffling through the carpet of dead leaves as Edward drove to the factory one morning.

In his pocket lay a letter from his father. It was the first communication he had ever received from him, and it provided food for thought.

He studied it again in the privacy of his office. It was written on cheap ruled paper, but the writing was clear and well-formed. It had come from an address in Lincolnshire, and said:

My dear Edward,

Thank you for writing to tell me of the death of your grandfather.

To be frank, I had already seen a notice of it in *The Caxley Chronicle* which has been sent to me ever since I left the town.

I could not have attended the funeral, even if I had wished to do so, as the expense of the fare to Caxley made the trip impossible. I live alone here, in very straitened circumstances, my second wife having died two years ago.

I should very much like to see your mother again and, of course, you too, but I shall understand if it is not convenient. The contents of your grandfather's will are unknown to me, but I take it that he was stubbornly against me to the end.

Affectionately,
Leslie Howard

It was pretty plain, thought Edward, from the letter before him, that his father was as bitter as ever against Sep. Not once did he speak of him as 'my father' — but as 'your grandfather', and the final reference to the will disclosed a disappointed man. Nevertheless, Edward experienced a strong feeling of mingled pity and curiosity. His father must be getting on in years. He was certainly older than Uncle Bertie, and must now be approaching sixty. He sounded lonely too, as well as hard up.

He began to wonder how he lived. There had been two children by the second marriage, as far as he remembered. Was he perhaps living with one of them in Lincolnshire? He felt fairly certain that his mother would not wish to meet his father again, but he himself was suddenly drawn to the idea of seeing him. He turned the notion over in his mind, deciding not to do anything precipitous which might upset the family.

At the weekend, when he went once more to Caxley, he showed his mother the letter when they were alone. The vehemence of her reaction astonished him.

'He wrote to me at much the same time,' she told Edward, her face working. 'I tore up the letter. He's hurt me too much in the past, Edward. If anything, the bitterness has grown with the years. I wouldn't lift a finger to help him. He treated us all abominably, and if it hadn't been for his own father we should have been very hard up indeed. And now he has the nerve to approach us and – more than that – to expect money from Sep! The whole thing is despicable.'

It was obviously not the moment to tell his mother that he felt like visiting his father; but before he and Maisie left for home he broached the subject tentatively. He had already told Kathy and Bertie about Leslie's letter, and about the possibility of travelling to Lincoln to see how his father fared. They had both been sympathetic towards Edward's project, but had no desire to meet Leslie themselves.

'He's a charmer – or was –' said Bertie plainly, 'and a sponger. So be warned, my boy. And if your mother objects, I advise you to chuck up the idea. No point in opening old wounds.'

'I see that well enough,' responded Edward. 'But I don't like to think of him in want, when Sep has left us all so comfortably off.'

'Your feelings do you credit,' replied Bertie, 'but don't let yourself in for embarrassment in the future. Leslie might well have developed into an old-man-of-the-sea, always demanding more and more.'

As his nephew vanished up the lane to the High Street, Kathy looked at Bertie.

'Will he really go, do you think?'

'He'll go,' said Bertie. 'He feels it's his duty. He's Sep all over again when it comes to it – and the sooner we all realize it, the better.'

Luckily, Winnie's reactions to Edward's proposal were less violent than he had imagined.

'I can understand that you want to see him,' she said, rather wearily. 'He is your father after all. But I absolutely refuse to have any more to do with him. And nothing of this is to be mentioned to Grandma. She is too old for this sort of shock.'

Edward promised to be discreet, kissed his mother good-bye and drove back to London well content.

The next few weeks were unusually busy for Edward, and it was early December before the trip northwards could be arranged.

The clearing-up process at the factory was going well, but Edward was to remain one of the directors and there were a number of legal matters to arrange. Every other weekend he spent at Caxley, studying the business, and going through the accounts and staff arrangements with Kathy and John Bush. It was clear that they longed to hand over the responsibilities of the shop and restaurant which they had so bravely borne, and Edward hoped to move back to his own house as soon as the tenants in the floors below could find alternative accommodation. John Bush had been offered the little cottage where Edward and Joan had been born. A daughter, recently widowed, was to share it with him, and the old man made no secret of looking forward now to complete retirement.

Maisie was in her element choosing papers for the walls and material for curtains and covers. She went with Winnie to one or two furniture sales and acquired some fine pieces. Old Mrs North gave her the tea service which had graced her own table at the house in the market square, and Maisie liked to think of it in its own home again.

At the end of November she was delighted to discover that she was to have a baby in the early summer.

'We *must* get in before long,' she implored Edward. 'I must get everything ready for it while I'm still mobile.'

The family was as pleased as they were themselves at the news, and Mrs North's comment amused them all.

'At last,' she cried, 'we'll have a *christening* at St Peter's. Don't tell me you've anything against that?'

She was reassured, and set to work to knit half a dozen first-size vests with enthusiasm.

Edward set out alone on his journey, starting very early, as he wanted to make the return trip in the day.

It was cold and overcast when he set out, and rain began to fall heavily after an hour or so on the road. He had looked forward to this visit, but now a certain depression invaded him, due in part to the dismal weather and to general fatigue. Although he had made up his mind to return to the market square and to take up the duties laid upon him by Sep, he still had moments of doubt.

True, as Maisie had said, running one business was very like running another, but he was going to miss his trips abroad and his growing skill in designing. Life in London had been pleasant. Would he find Caxley too parochial after wider horizons? He could only hope that he was doing the right thing. In any case the thought of the baby being born in Caxley gave him enormous pleasure, and he looked forward to introducing it to all the varied delights of the Cax running through the garden.

He reached the town where his father lived a little before noon. Rain slashed against the side windows, and passing vehicles sent up showers of water across the windscreen. Wet grey-slated roofs and drab houses stretched desolately in all directions. Bedraggled people, bent behind dripping umbrellas, looked as wretched as their surroundings. Edward drove through the centre of the town and followed the route which his father's last letter had given.

He found the road, the house, switched off the car's engine and sat looking about him. It was less gloomy than parts of the town he had just traversed, but pretty dispiriting, nevertheless. The houses were semi-detached, and built, Edward guessed, sometime in the thirties. They were brick below and pebble-dash above, each having an arched porch with a red-tiled floor to it. The front gardens, now leafless, were very small. Here and there a wispy ornamental cherry tree, or an etiolated rowan, struggled for existence in the teeth of the winds which came from the North Sea.

The sharp air took his breath away as he made his way to the door. It was opened so quickly that Edward felt sure that his arrival had been watched. A plump breathless woman of middle age greeted him with an air of excitement. She wore a flowered overall and carried a duster.

'Come to see your dad?' she greeted him. 'He's been waiting for you. Come in. You must be shrammed.'

Edward, who had never heard this attractive word, supposed, rightly, that it meant that he must be cold, and followed her into the small hall. An overpowering smell of floor polish pervaded the house and everything which could be burnished, from brass stair rods to the chain of the cuckoo clock on the wall, gleamed on every side.

The door on the right opened and there stood a slight figure, taller than Sep, but less tall than Edward, gazing at him with the bright dark eyes of the Howards.

'Your son's come,' announced the woman. The words dropped into the sudden silence like pebbles into a still pool.

'Come in, my boy,' said Leslie quietly, and they went into the sitting-room together.

The meeting had stirred Edward deeply, and for a moment or two he could find nothing to say. His father was fumbling at the catch of a cupboard.

'Like a drink?'

173

'Thank you.'

'Whisky, sherry or beer?'

'Sherry, please.'

Edward watched his father pouring the liquid. He was very like Aunt Kathy. His hair was still thick, but now more grey than black. He had the same dark, rather highly arched, eyebrows, and the pronounced lines from nose to the corner of the upper lip which all the Howards seemed to have inherited from Sep. He was dressed in a tweed suit, warm but shabby, and his shirt was so dazzlingly white that Edward felt sure that his landlady attended to his linen.

The room was over-filled with large furniture and numerous knick-knacks, but a good fire warmed all, and old-fashioned red wallpaper, overpowering in normal circumstances, gave some cheer on a morning as bleak as this.

'You seem very comfortable here,' ventured Edward, glass in hand.

'They're good people,' said Leslie. 'He's a railway man, due to retire soon. I have two rooms. I sold up when the wife died. Came up here from the west country, and took a job with a car firm.'

'Are you still with them?' asked Edward.

'No,' replied Leslie briefly. 'Tell me about the family.'

Edward told him all that he could. He appeared quite unaffected by Robert's tragic end and his father's recent death, but Edward noticed that mention of his mother brought a smile.

'But she won't see me, eh?'

'I'm afraid not. I hope you won't try.'

'Don't worry. I treated her badly. Can't blame her for giving me the cold shoulder now. I shan't come to Caxley. I thought of it when I read of the old man's death, but decided against it. If there were any pickings I reckoned Lovejoy would let me know.'

There was something so casually callous about this last utterance, that Edward stiffened.

'Did you imagine that there would be?' he inquired. There

must have been an edge to his tone, for the older man shot him a quick glance.

'Can't say I did, but hope springs eternal, you know.'

He placed his glass carefully on the table beside him, and turned to face Edward.

'This looks like the only time I'll be able to put my side of the story, so I may as well tell it now. You knew my father well enough, I know, but only as an older man when he'd mellowed a bit. When Jim and I were boys he was too dam' strict by half. Chapel three times on Sundays and Lord knows how many Bible meetings of one sort or another during the week. Jim stuck it all better than I did – and then, as we got older, he didn't have the same eye for the girls as I had. He was more like Dad – I was like Mum. I don't think I ever loved my father. He said "No" too often.'

'But I know he was fond of all his children,' broke in Edward.

'Had a funny way of showing it,' observed his father bitterly. 'He drove me to deceit, and that's the truth. He was a narrow-minded bigoted old fool bent on getting to heaven at any cost. I can't forgive him.' He was breathing heavily.

'He was also brave, honest and generous,' said Edward levelly. His father seemed not to hear.

'And he poisoned Winnie's mind against me later. There was no hope of reconciliation while Father was alive.'

'That's not true,' said Edward, anger rising in him. 'My mother's mind was made up from the moment you parted!'

'Maybe,' replied Leslie indifferently. 'She was a North – as obstinate as her old man.' He laughed suddenly, and his face was transformed. Now Edward could see why Leslie Howard was remembered in Caxley as a charmer.

'Don't let's squabble,' he pleaded. 'We've a lot to talk over. Let's come out to a pub I know for our grub. Mrs Jones here is a dab hand with house-cleaning but her cooking's of the baked-cod-and-flaked-rice variety. I told her we'd go out'.

Edward was secretly sorry to leave the good fire and

over-stuffed armchair, but dutifully drove through the relentless rain to a small public house situated two or three miles away on a windswept plain. Over an excellent mixed grill Edward learnt a little more of his father's life.

'My boy was killed in France,' said Leslie, 'and the girl is married and out in Australia.'

It was queer, thought Edward, to hear of this half-brother and sister whom he had never seen. His father spoke of them with affection. Naturally, they were closer to him than he and Joan could ever have been.

'And then Ellen was ill for so long – three or four years, before she died. I got to hate that place in Devon. We had a garage there, you know. Dam' hard work and mighty little return for it.'

'What happened to it?' asked Edward.

'Sold everything up when Ellen went. Paid my debts – and they were plenty – and found this place. I wanted a change, and besides, the doctor told me to live somewhere flat. I've got a dicky heart. Same thing that took off my poor mum, I daresay.'

Gradually, Edward began to see the kind of life which was now his father's lot. He had fallen out with the car firm. It was obvious that he disliked being an employee after running his own business. It was also plain to Edward that if he did not have some regular employment he would very soon drift into a pointless existence in which drink would play a major part. Nevertheless, it seemed that there were grounds for believing that he had some heart complaint. The woman behind the bar, who seemed to be an old friend, had inquired about 'his attacks' with some concern, and both his parents had suffered from heart trouble.

For the past week he had been without work for the first time. He had heard of two book-keeping jobs in local firms and proposed to apply for them. Edward thought it sounded hopeful. As far as he could gather, his father's financial resources consisted of fifty pounds or so in the bank. This amount would not last long even in such modest lodgings as Mrs Jones'. This urgency to earn was a spur in the right direction, Edward surmised.

He paid the bill and drove his father home. The matter which had been uppermost in his mind was more complicated than he had first thought. He was determined to see that his father was not in want. Now that he had met him he was equally sure that this was not the time to offer financial help. If he did, the chances of Leslie's helping himself grew considerably slighter. Prudently, Edward postponed a decision, but made his father promise to let him know the outcome of his job-hunting.

'I'll write to you in a week or so,' said Leslie as they parted. 'I don't suppose we'll meet again, my boy. Better to make this the last time, I think. It was good of you to make the journey. Tell those who are interested how I am. I've got a soft spot for old Bertie. I wonder if he ever regretted marrying a Howard?'

'Never,' said Edward stoutly, driving off, and left his father laughing.

Driving back along the wet roads Edward pondered on the day's encounter. He was satisfied now that he had seen his father. He was well looked after, in fairly good health, and obviously as happy as he would be anywhere.

As soon as he heard that he was in work again he would make adequate provision against the future. He wanted to feel that there was a sum in the bank which would be available if the old man fell on hard times. But he must have a job – no matter how small the return – which would keep him actively occupied. His father's worst enemy, Edward saw, was himself. Too much solitude would breed self-pity and self-indulgence. He could see why Sep had never had much time for him. There was a streak of weakness which Sep would never have been able to understand or forgive.

'A rum lot, the Howards!' said Edward aloud, and putting his foot down on the accelerator, sped home.

19. Return to the Market Square

EDWARD found a surprising lack of interest in Leslie's welfare among the family. Aunt Kathy was perfunctory in her inquiries. His mother refused to discuss the matter. Maisie, naturally enough, was only vaguely interested in someone she had never met. Uncle Bertie alone seemed concerned, and listened attentively to Edward's account of all that had happened. He approved of Edward's decision to wait and see if a job materialized.

In the week before Christmas the awaited letter arrived. Leslie wrote enthusiastically. The post was in a large baker's. 'Back where I began,' was how he put it. He not only looked after the accounts but also took the van out twice a week to relieve other roundsmen. His weekly wage was modest but enough for his needs, he wrote.

Edward replied congratulating him, and telling him that he was paying the sum of two hundred and fifty pounds into his bank account which he hoped he would accept as a nest-egg and a Christmas present. He posted the letter with some misgivings. Was he simply trying to salve his conscience by handing over this money? He hoped not. What would Sep have thought? Well, maybe Sep would not have approved, but Edward had his own decisions to make now, he told himself firmly. He felt sure that it was right to supply his father with a bulwark against future storms. He felt equally sure that it had been right to wait until he was established in a suitable job before providing that bulwark. Now it was up to his father.

Everything was now planned for their removal from the flat to the market square. After innumerable delays, the old house was free of workmen and, freshly decorated, awaited its owners.

Maisie had enjoyed refurbishing the fine old rooms. The great drawing-room, with its three windows looking out upon the market place, was painted in the palest green, a colour which would show up well the mahogany pieces which she had bought at the sales. It was a splendid room, high and airy. Bender North had always appreciated it, admiring its fine proportions and its red plush furnishings, after a day in the shop below. Now his grandson would find equal domestic pleasure in the same room.

On the same floor, at the back of the building, were the dining room and kitchen, overlooking the small garden and the river Cax. Above them were three bedrooms and a bathroom, while on the top floor, in the old attics, Edward's flat remained much as it was, except that his sitting-room had been converted into a nursery for the newcomer.

'You'll have to put the window bars back again,' said Uncle Bertie when he inspected the premises. 'There were three to each window when I slept there. You took them out too hastily, Edward my boy!'

Edward and Maisie spent the last weekend in January at Rose Lodge. She was to see the furniture in on the Monday, with Winnie's help, while Edward would return to the flat to arrange things at that end. It was bitterly cold, and as she and Winnie directed operations on Monday morning, and dodged rolls of carpet and bedsteads, Maisie was thankful that they had faced the expense of central heating for the house. With the open market square before, and the river Cax behind, it had always felt cold. Now, with new warmth, the house seemed to come to life.

She took a particular interest in the larger of the back bedrooms, for here she planned to have the baby. She was determined that it should be born in the old house in the market square, and had already engaged the monthly nurse who was to sleep in the bedroom adjoining her own.

The view from the windows on this bleak January day was grey and cheerless. The pollarded willows lining the Cax pointed gaunt fingers towards the leaden sky. The distant tunnel of horse chestnut trees made a dark smudge above the river mist, but Maisie could imagine it in May when the baby was due to arrive. Then the willows would be a golden green above the sparkling water. The chestnut leaves would be bursting from their sticky buds. The kingfisher – harbinger of good fortune – should be flashing over the water, and on the lawn below the window the crocuses, yellow, purple and white, would be giving way to daffodils and tulips.

It was past nine o'clock when Edward arrived. Both of them were excited but exhausted, and went early to bed in the bedroom overlooking the market square. Maisie fell asleep almost immediately, but Edward lay on his back watching the pattern on the ceiling, made by the lamps in the market place.

Now and again the old house creaked, as wood expanded gently in the unaccustomed heat. Someone crossed the cobbles, singing, pausing in his tune to call good night to a fellow wayfarer. There was a country burr in the tone which pleased Edward.

How often, he wondered, had Grandfather North lain in this same room listening to the sounds of the square by night? He thought of Uncle Bertie and his own mother, sleeping, as children, on the floor above, where soon his own child would be bedded. It gave him a queer feeling of wonder and pride.

Tomorrow, he told himself, he must wake early and go downstairs to the restaurant and then across to the bakery. He was a market square man now, with a reputation for diligence to keep up! Smiling at the thought, he turned his face into the pillow and fell asleep.

Caxley watched Edward's progress, in the ensuing weeks, with considerable interest. On the whole, his efforts met with approval. He was applying himself zealously to the new work, and people were glad to see a young man in charge.

The assistants in the shop and restaurant spoke well of him, and the grape-vine of the closely-knit little town hummed busily with day-to-day reports – mainly favourable. Young Edward was taking on two new counter-hands. He was going to enlarge the storage sheds at the back of the bakery. He was talking of keeping the restaurant open later at night. He was applying for a liquor licence. Think of that! The more sedate chapel-goers could imagine Sep turning in his grave at the thought, but the majority of Caxley's citizens approved.

Edward himself was beginning to enjoy it all enormously. The years of solitary living, which had been all that he desired after the break-up of his first marriage, were behind him. He began to flourish in this new gregarious life and found pleasure in joining some of the local activities and meeting boyhood friends again. The Crockfords, grandchildren of the famous Dan who had painted Edna Howard so long ago, lived within walking distance and were frequent visitors. William Crockford, the present owner of the family mill which supplied Edward with much of his flour, introduced him to the Rotary Club and Edward became an energetic member. He also took up cricket again. He sometimes went dutifully with Maisie to concerts at the Corn Exchange which she, who was musical, thoroughly enjoyed, while Edward, who was not, leant back and planned future business projects while local talent provided mingled harmony and discord.

For there was, indeed, a great deal to plan. Edward, the product of two business families, saw clearly the possibilities of the future. Times were becoming more prosperous after the lean forties. People were buying more, and demanding more luxurious goods. Caxley families were prepared to dine out in the evenings. Caxley businessmen took their lunches in the town much more frequently. What is more, they brought their clients, and talked over deals at Howard's Restaurant.

There were more cars on the road, more wayfarers travelling from London westward, and from the Midlands southward. Caxley was a convenient stopping-place, as it had been in the days of the stage-coach. The restaurant trade was booming. It could become even more thriving with judicious re-organization.

Edward was so engrossed with his present commitments and his plans for the future that a letter which arrived for him one April morning came as a bolt from the blue. He could hardly believe his eyes as he read the document.

It was from the managing director of a firm of departmental stores well known to Edward. They were proposing to set up several more branches in provincial towns. The two sites belonging to Edward would be suitable for their purpose. The larger site would be used for their drapery and furnishing departments. Their Food Hall would probably be accommodated on the present bakery site. Perhaps Mr Howard would consider taking up a position of responsibility in this department, the salary to be arranged by mutual agreement? Naturally, there was a great deal to consider on both sides, but his firm had in mind the sum of — (here followed a figure so large that Edward seriously wondered if a nought or two too many had been added) and their agents were Messrs Ginn, Hope & Toddy of Piccadilly who would be glad to hear from Mr Howard if he were interested.

Edward handed the letter to Maisie in silence.

'Well?' she said, looking up at last.

'Some hopes!' said Edward flatly, stuffing it in his pocket. 'This is ours. We stay.'

As a matter of interest he showed the letter to the family before replying to it. As he expected, Bertie wholeheartedly agreed with his decision, but Kathy and the two ladies at Rose Lodge had doubts. This surprised Edward. The two properties had been their homes and livelihoods for so long that he had felt sure that they would be as forthright in their rejection of the offer as he was himself. How strange women were!

'It's such a lot of money,' said old Mrs North. 'After all, with that amount you could start up another business anywhere, or go back to the plastics place, dear, couldn't you?'

'Or simply invest it, and have a nice little income and a long holiday somewhere,' said his mother. 'There's no need to feel tied to Caxley simply because the business has been left to you.'

'But I *want* to be tied to Caxley!' Edward almost shouted. 'This is *our* business — the *Howard* business! Dammit all, it's the work and worry of three generations we're considering! Doesn't that mean anything?'

'Really,' tutted Mrs North, in some exasperation, 'men are so romantic about everything – even currant buns, it seems!'

'All we're trying to say,' said Winnie, more patiently, 'is that we should quite understand if you felt like accepting the offer, and I'm sure the rest of the family would agree.'

'Well, I don't intend to, and that's flat,' retorted Edward. He had not felt so out of patience with his womenfolk for years, and took a childish pleasure in slamming the front door as he departed.

He walked back through a little park, and sat down on one of the seats to cool off. Beds of velvety wallflowers scented the evening air, and some small children screamed on the swings, or chased each other round and round the lime trees. A few middle-aged couples strolled about, admiring the flowers and taking a little gentle exercise. It was the sort of unremarkable scene being enacted a hundred-fold all over the country on this mild Spring evening, but to Edward, in his mood of tension, it had a poignant significance.

Here, years ago, he had swung and raced. Before long, his own children would know this pleasant plot. These people before him, old and young, were of Caxley as he was himself. They all played their parts in the same setting, and with their neighbours as fellow-actors. And the centre of that stage was Caxley's market square. How lucky he was to have his place so firmly there – his by birthright, and now by choice as well! Nothing should make him give up this inheritance.

A very old man shuffled up to Edward's bench and sat down gingerly. His pale blue eyes watered, and a shining drop trickled down his lined cheeks into the far from clean beard which hid his mouth and chin.

His clothes were shabby, his boots broken. Edward guessed that he was making his way to the workhouse on the hill. He held a paper bag, and thrusting a claw-like hand inside, he produced a meat pasty. He gazed unseeingly before him as he munched, the pastry flaking into a shower of light crumbs which sprinkled his deplorable beard and greasy coat.

But it was not so much the old man who engaged Edward's attention as the blue and white paper bag which he held. It was very familiar to him. He had seen such bags since his earliest days – bright and clean, with 'Howard's Bakery' printed diagonally across the checked surface. Tonight, the sight of it filled him with a surge of pride. Here, he was, face to face with one of his customers, watching his own product from his own paper bag being consumed with smackings of satisfaction! Who would give up such rewards? He felt a sudden love for this dirty unknown, and rising swiftly, fumbled in his pocket and pressed half a crown into the grimy paw.

'Have a drink with it,' he said.

'Ta, mate,' answered the tramp laconically. 'Needs summat to wash this muck down.'

Edward walked home, savouring the delicious incident to the full. It warmed the evening for him. It added to his growing zest for life in Caxley, and to the enjoyment he felt, later that evening, when he pulled a piece of writing paper towards him and wrote a short, polite, but absolute rejection of the store's offer.

It was dark as he crossed the square to post it. He balanced the white envelope on his hand before tipping it, with satisfaction, into the pillar box. Now it was done, he felt singularly light-hearted, and walked jauntily back across the cobbles, smiling at Queen Victoria's implacable bulk outlined against the night sky.

At his doorway he turned to take a last breath of fresh air. The moon slid out from behind a ragged cloud, and touched the market square with sudden beauty.

Edward gave the scene a conspiratorial wink, opened his own door, mounted his own stairs and made his way to bed.

20. John Septimus Howard

It was six o'clock on a fine May morning.

The market square was deserted. Long shadows lay across the cobblestones, reaching almost to the steps of St Peter's church. At the window of his bedroom, in a crumpled suit, and with tousled hair, stood Edward. It had been one of the longest nights that he had ever known, but now peace, and the dawn, had arrived.

The monthly nurse, Mrs Porter, had been in the house with them for eight days. That she was expert in her profession, Edward had no doubt, but as a member of the household he had found her sorely trying. Her shiny red face and crackling starched cuffs and apron dominated every meal. She ate very slowly, but needed a large amount of food to keep her well-corseted bulk going, so that Maisie and Edward seemed to spend three times as long at the table.

Maisie was worried because the baby was overdue. Nurse Porter added to her anxiety by consulting the calendar daily and talking gloomily of her timetable which might well be completely thrown out by Maisie's tardy offspring. Her next engagement was in a noble household in the shires, a fact which gave her considerable satisfaction.

'And the Duchess,' she told Maisie daily, 'is *never* late. The two little boys arrived on the dot, and the little girl was two days early. You'll have to hurry up, my dear, or the Duchess will beat you to it.'

But yesterday, when Edward returned from the shop after tea, Maisie and the nurse were in the bedroom, and all, according to Nurse Porter, was going well. Maisie's comments, in the midst of her pains, were less euphemistic.

'Shall I stay with you?' asked Edward solicitously.

'Good heavens, no!' exclaimed Maisie crossly. 'It's quite bad enough as it is, without having to put a good front on it. Go a long way away — to Rose Lodge or somewhere, so that I can have a good yell when I want to.'

Thus banished, Edward took himself to the restaurant below, and pottered aimlessly about. Thank God, he thought honestly, Maisie was not one of the modern brigade who wanted a husband's support at this time! Although he intended to stay with her had she so wished, he was frankly terrified of seeing her in pain, and squeamish at the sight of blood. Dear, oh dear, thought Edward, rubbing his forehead anxiously, what poor tools men were when it came to it!'

He had no intention of going to Rose Lodge or anywhere else for that matter, until the child was born. He would stay as close as he could while it all went on. He suffered the common terrifying qualms about his wife's safety, and to calm his agitation set himself to such mechanical tasks as sorting out the cutlery and inspecting the table linen for possible repairs.

He could settle to nothing for long, however, and walked into the little garden on the dew-wet grass beside the river, looking up at the lighted window where the drama was being enacted. Every so often he mounted the stairs quietly and listened, but there was nothing to hear. On one of these sorties he encountered the nurse, and she took pity on him.

'She's doing splendidly,' she said. 'Come and have a look.'

Maisie looked far from splendid to Edward's eyes. She looked white and exhausted, but seemed glad to see him.

'Not long now,' said Nurse Porter, with what, to Edward, seemed callous indifference to her patient's condition. 'It should be here by morning.'

'By *morning*?' echoed Edward, appalled. The hands of the clock stood at a little before two. Would Maisie live as long, he wondered desperately?

'Go and make us all a nice pot of tea,' suggested the nurse, and Edward obediently went to the kitchen to perform his task. How parents could have faced ten, fifteen and even twenty such ordeals in days gone by, he could not imagine! He decided to have a whisky and soda when he had delivered the tea-tray to his task-mistress.

Later, as the first light crept across the countryside, he dozed in the arm chair, dreaming uneasily of white boats floating upon dark water. Could they be the little boats he floated as a boy upon the Cax? Or were they the white boats 'that sailed like swans asleep' on the enchanted waters of Lough Corrib? And where was Maisie? She should be with him. Had she slipped beneath the black and shivering water? Would he see her again?

A little before five Nurse Porter woke him. Her red face glowed like the rising sun, broad and triumphant. She held a white bundle which she displayed proudly to Edward.

'Want to see your son?' she asked. 'Six and a half pounds, and a perfect beauty.'

Edward looked upon his firstborn. A pink mottled face, no bigger than one of his own buns, topped by wispy damp hair, was all that could be seen in the aperture of the snowy shawl. Nurse Porter's idea of beauty, Edward thought, differed from his own, but the child looked healthy and inordinately wise.

'How's Maisie?' said Edward, now wide awake. 'Can I see her?'

'Asleep. You shall go in later. She's fine, but needs her rest.'

At that moment the baby opened his mouth in a yawn. Edward gazed at it, fascinated. There was something wonderfully clever about such an achievement when one considered that the child was less than an hour old. Edward felt a pang of paternal pride for the first time.

'He seeme a very forward child to me,' said Edward.

'Naturally!' responded Nurse Porter with sardonic amusement, and took her bundle back to the bedroom.

That was an hour ago. Since then he had seen his Maisie, well, but drowsy, drunk a pot of coffee and tried to marshal his incoherent thoughts. As soon as possible, he would telephone to Rose Lodge, but six o'clock calls might alarm the household.

He must let Bertie and Kathy know too as soon as they were astir.

Meanwhile, he gazed upon the market place, pink in the growing sunlight. A thin black cat, in a sheltered angle of St Peter's porch, washed one upthrust leg, its body as round and curved as an elegant shell, and suddenly Edward was back in time, over ten long years ago, when he had stood thus, watching the same familiar scene.

What a lifetime ago it seemed! Since then he had experienced war, an unhappy marriage and personal desolation. He had watched Robert's tragic decline and death, and lost Sep, his guide and example. He had shared, with his fellows, the bitterness of war, and the numbing poverty of its aftermath.

But that was the darker side of the picture. There was a better and brighter one. He had found Maisie, he had refound Caxley, and in doing so he had found himself at last.

A wisp of blue smoke rose from Sep's old house. Miss Taggerty was making up the kitchen boiler, thought Edward affectionately. In the bakehouse, work would already have started. The little town was stirring, and he must prepare, too, for another Caxley day. It was good to look ahead. It was good too, to think that John Septimus Howard, his son, would be the fourth generation to know this old house as home.

What was it that Sep used to say? 'There's always tomorrow, my boy. Always tomorrow.'

And with that thought to cheer him, Edward went to look, once more, upon the new heir to the market square.

MORE ABOUT PENGUINS, PELICANS
AND PUFFINS

For further information about books available from Penguins please write to Dept EP, Penguin Books Ltd, Harmondsworth, Middlesex UB7 0DA.

In the U.S.A.: For a complete list of books available from Penguins in the United States write to Dept DG, Penguin Books, 299 Murray Hill Parkway, East Rutherford, New Jersey 07073.

In Canada: For a complete list of books available from Penguins in Canada write to Penguin Books Canada Limited, 2801 John Street, Markham, Ontario L3R 1B4.

In Australia: For a complete list of books available from Penguins in Australia write to the Marketing Department, Penguin Books Australia Ltd, P.O. Box 257, Ringwood, Victoria 3134.

In New Zealand: For a complete list of books available from Penguins in New Zealand write to the Marketing Department, Penguin Books (N.Z.) Ltd, Private Bag, Takapuna, Auckland 9.

In India: For a complete list of books available from Penguins in India write to Penguin Overseas Ltd, 706 Eros Apartments, 56 Nehru Place, New Delhi 110019.

PENGUIN OMNIBUSES

☐ **The Penguin Complete Sherlock Holmes**
   Sir Arthur Conan Doyle   £5.95

With all fifty-six classic short stories, plus *A Study in Scarlet*, *The Sign of Four*, *The Hound of the Baskervilles* and *The Valley of Fear*, this volume contains the remarkable career of Baker Street's most famous resident.

☐ **The Alexander Trilogy Mary Renault**   £4.95

Containing *Fire from Heaven*, *The Persian Boy* and *Funeral Games* – her re-creation of Ancient Greece acclaimed by Gore Vidal as 'one of this century's most unexpectedly original works of art'.

☐ **The Penguin Complete Novels of George Orwell**   £5.50

Containing the six novels: *Animal Farm*, *Burmese Days*, *A Clergyman's Daughter*, *Coming Up For Air*, *Keep the Aspidistra Flying* and *Nineteen Eighty-Four*.

☐ **The Penguin Essays of George Orwell**   £4.95

Famous pieces on 'The Decline of the English Murder', 'Shooting an Elephant', political issues and P. G. Wodehouse feature in this edition of forty-one essays, criticism and sketches – all classics of English prose.

☐ **The Penguin Collected Stories of**
   Isaac Bashevis Singer   £4.95

Forty-seven marvellous tales of Jewish magic, faith and exile. 'Never was the Nobel Prize more deserved . . . He belongs with the giants' – *Sunday Times*

☐ **Famous Trials Harry Hodge and James H. Hodge**   £3.50

From Madeleine Smith to Dr Crippen and Lord Haw-Haw, this volume contains the most sensational murder and treason trials, selected by John Mortimer from the classic Penguin Famous Trials series.

PENGUIN OMNIBUSES

☐ *The Penguin Complete Novels of Jane Austen*   £5.95

Containing the seven great novels: *Sense and Sensibility, Pride and Prejudice, Mansfield Park, Emma, Northanger Abbey, Persuasion* and *Lady Susan*.

☐ *The Penguin Kenneth Grahame*   £3.95

Containing his wonderful evocations of childhood – *The Golden Age* and *Dream Days* – plus his masterpiece, *The Wind in the Willows*, originally written for his son and since then loved by readers of all ages.

☐ *The Titus Books* **Mervyn Peake**   £5.95

Titus Groan, Gormenghast and *Titus Alone* form this century's masterpiece of Gothic fantasy. 'It is uniquely brilliant . . . a rich wine of fancy' – Anthony Burgess

☐ *Life at Thrush Green* 'Miss Read'   £3.50

Full of gossip, humour and charm, these three novels – *Thrush Green, Winter in Thrush Green* and *News from Thrush Green* – make up a delightful picture of life in a country village.

☐ *The Penguin Classic Crime Omnibus*   £4.95

Julian Symons's original anthology includes all the masters – Doyle, Poe, Highsmith, Graham Greene and P. D. James – represented by some of their less familiar but most surprising and ingenious crime stories.

☐ *The Penguin Great Novels of D. H. Lawrence*   £4.95

Containing *Sons and Lovers, The Rainbow* and *Women in Love*: the three famous novels in which Lawrence brought his story of human nature, love and sexuality to its fullest flowering.

PENGUIN OMNIBUSES

☐ *The Penguin Brontë Sisters*   £4.95

Containing Anne Brontë's *The Tenant of Wildfell Hall*, Charlotte
Brontë's *Jane Eyre* and Emily Brontë's *Wuthering Heights*.

☐ *The Penguin Thomas Hardy 1*   £4.95

His four early Wessex novels: *Under the Greenwood Tree, Far From
the Madding Crowd, The Return of the Native* and *The Mayor of
Casterbridge*.

☐ *The Penguin Thomas Hardy 2*   £5.50

Containing the four later masterpieces: *The Trumpet-Major, The
Woodlanders, Tess of the D'Urbervilles* and *Jude the Obscure*.

These books should be available at all good bookshops or news-
agents, but if you live in the UK or the Republic of Ireland and have
difficulty in getting to a bookshop, they can be ordered by post.
Please indicate the titles required and fill in the form below.

NAME _____ BLOCK CAPITALS

ADDRESS _____

_____

_____

Enclose a cheque or postal order payable to The Penguin Bookshop
to cover the total price of books ordered, plus 50p for postage.
Readers in the Republic of Ireland should send £IR equivalent to the
sterling prices, plus 67p for postage. Send to: The Penguin Bookshop, 54/56 Bridlesmith Gate, Nottingham, NG1 2GP.

You can also order by phoning (0602) 599295, and quoting your
Barclaycard or Access number.

Every effort is made to ensure the accuracy of the price and availability of
books at the time of going to press, but it is sometimes necessary to increase
prices and in these circumstances retail prices may be shown on the covers of
books which may differ from the prices shown in this list or elsewhere. This list
is not an offer to supply any book.

**This order service is only available to residents in the UK and the Republic of
Ireland.**